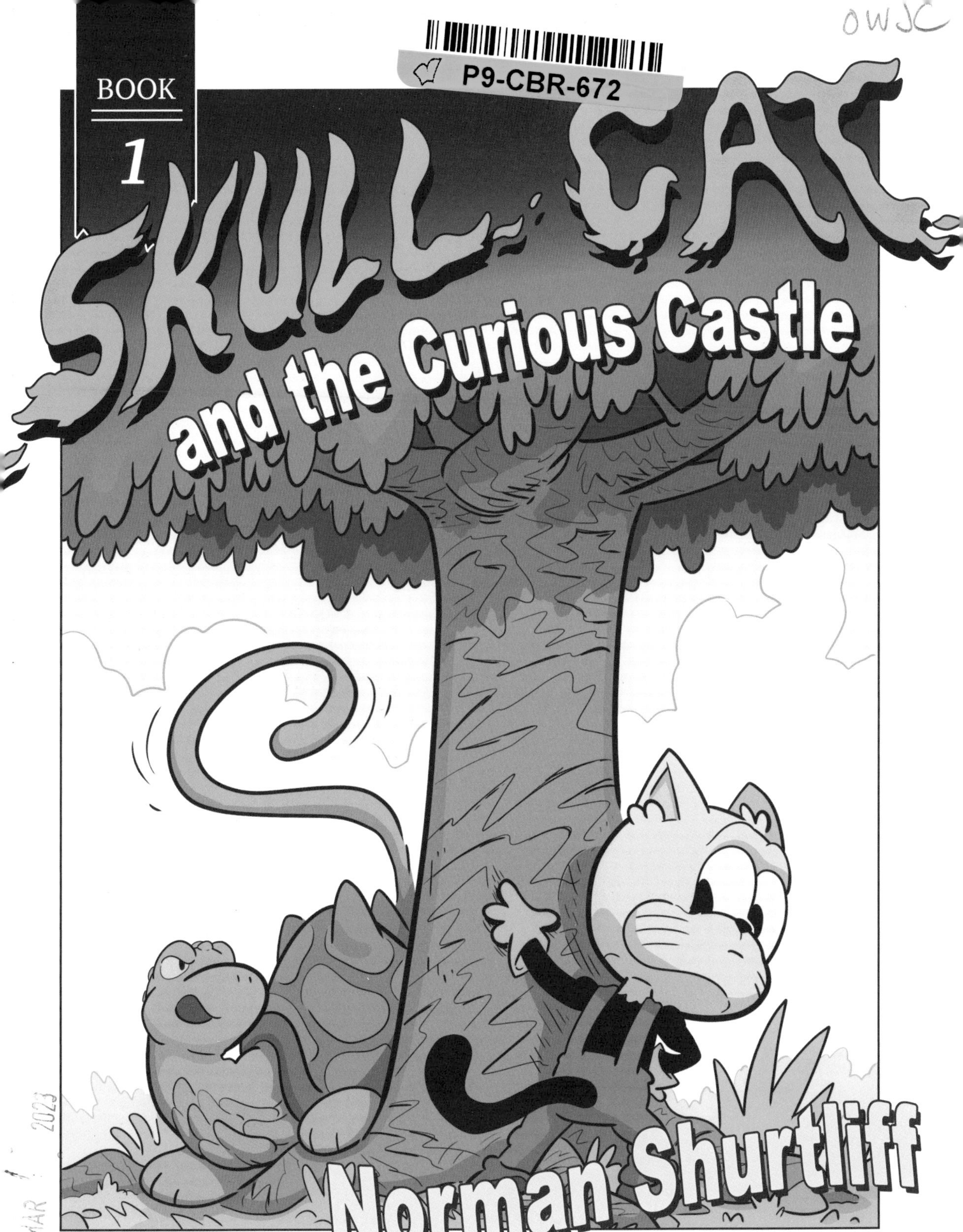
BOOK
1
SKULL CAT
and the Curious Castle
Norman Shurtliff

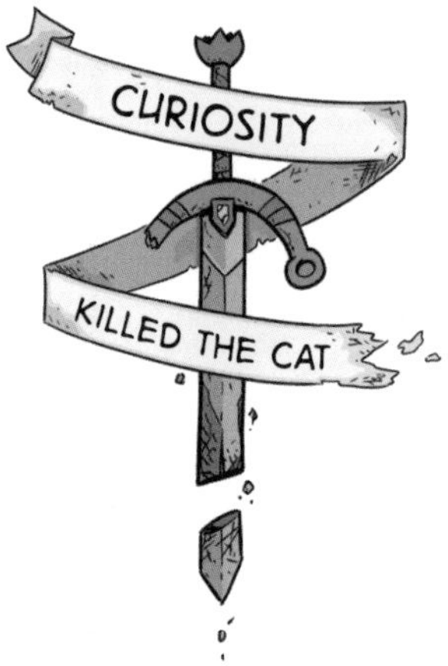
CURIOSITY
KILLED THE CAT

NORMAN SHURTLIFF
WWW.NORMANSHURTLIFF.COM
@SQUIDMANTIS

DEDICATED TO MY CHILDREN, WHO LIKE SPOOKY STORIES BUT NOT GETTING **_TOO_** SCARED.

THIS BOOK WAS YEARS IN THE MAKING, AND THROUGHOUT THAT TIME MANY PEOPLE OFFERED SUPPORT, ENCOURAGEMENT AND ADVICE. **_THANK YOU, EVERYONE!_** A SPECIAL THANK YOU TO MELANIE NICHOLS, WHOSE CRITIQUE BROUGHT ALL THE RIGHT CHANGES. TO MY WIFE, KICK, WHO KEPT OUR FAMILY FED AND ME MOTIVATED DURING THIS BOOK'S PRODUCTION. AND TO YOU, DEAR READER: YOUR INTEREST IN MY WORK MAKES A WORLD OF DIFFERENCE TO ME. THANK YOU!

EDITOR-IN-CHIEF: CHRIS STAROS

ISBN 978-1-60309-519-8 27 26 25 24 23 1 2 3 4 5

VISIT OUR ONLINE CATALOG AT WWW.TOPSHELFCOMIX.COM.

PRINTED IN KOREA.

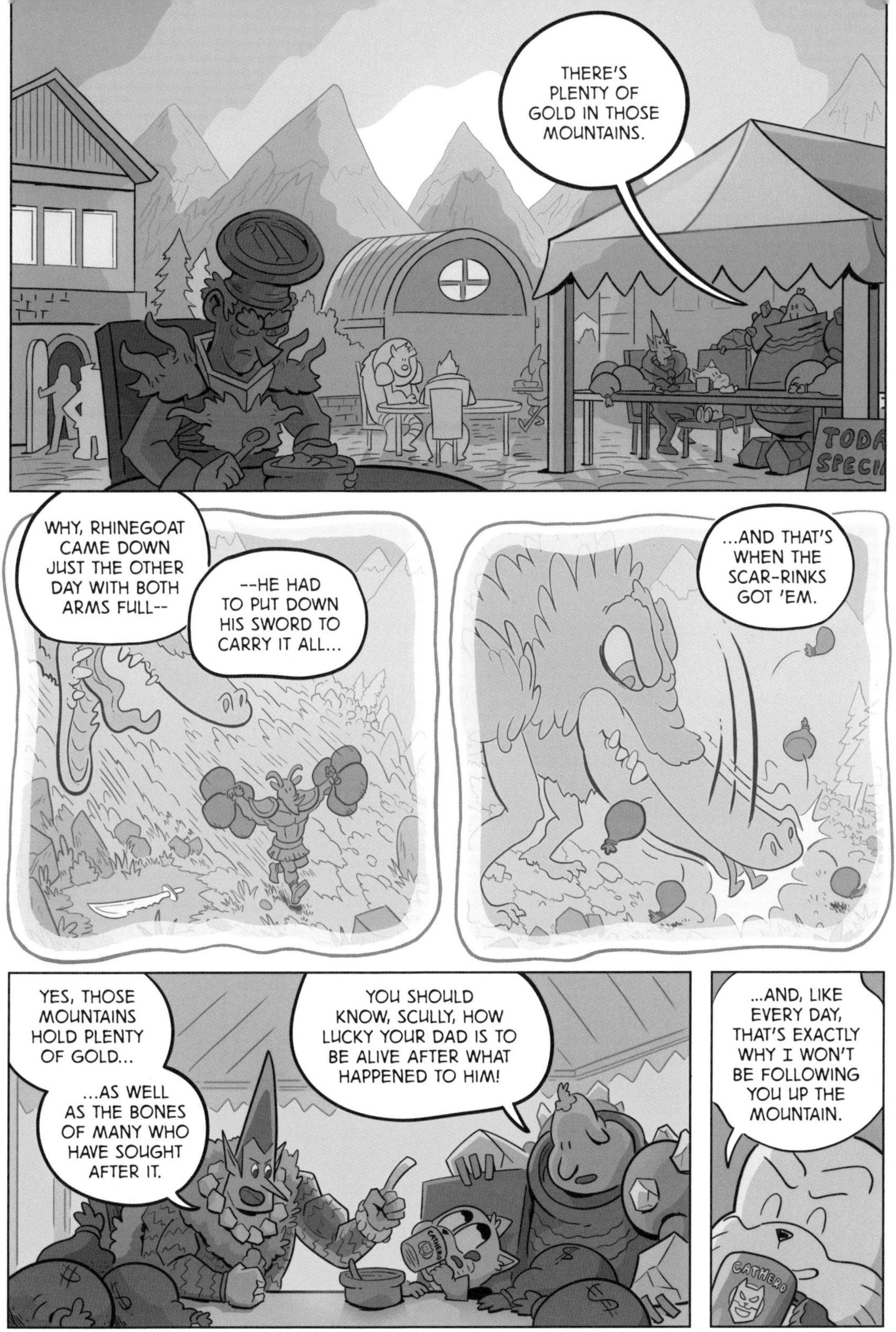
THERE'S PLENTY OF GOLD IN THOSE MOUNTAINS.
TODA SPECI
WHY, RHINEGOAT CAME DOWN JUST THE OTHER DAY WITH BOTH ARMS FULL--
--HE HAD TO PUT DOWN HIS SWORD TO CARRY IT ALL...
...AND THAT'S WHEN THE SCAR-RINKS GOT 'EM.
YES, THOSE MOUNTAINS HOLD PLENTY OF GOLD...
...AS WELL AS THE BONES OF MANY WHO HAVE SOUGHT AFTER IT.
YOU SHOULD KNOW, SCULLY, HOW LUCKY YOUR DAD IS TO BE ALIVE AFTER WHAT HAPPENED TO HIM!
CATHERO
...AND, LIKE EVERY DAY, THAT'S EXACTLY WHY I WON'T BE FOLLOWING YOU UP THE MOUNTAIN.
CATHERO

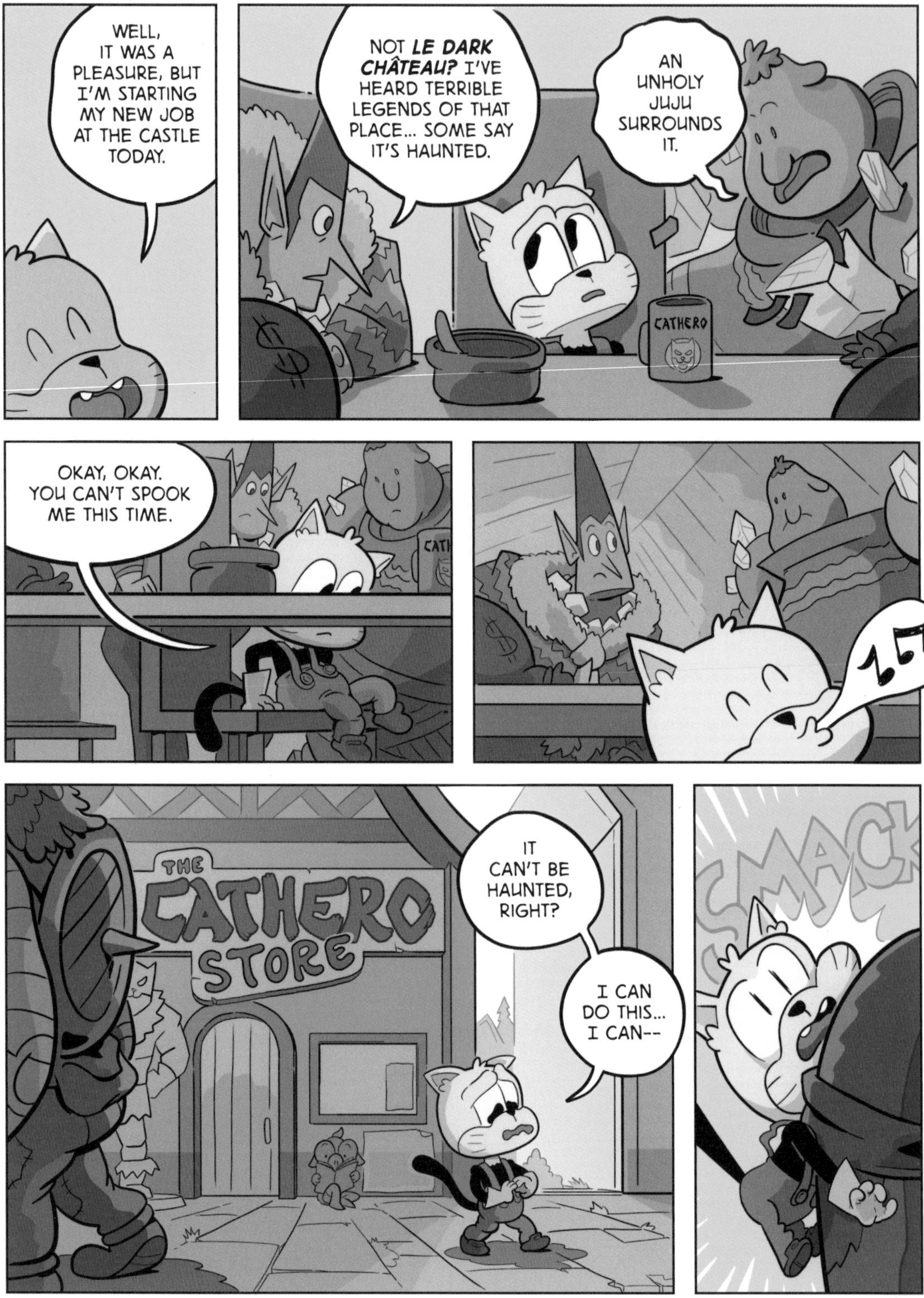

WELL, IT WAS A PLEASURE, BUT I'M STARTING MY NEW JOB AT THE CASTLE TODAY.
NOT ***LE DARK CHÂTEAU?*** I'VE HEARD TERRIBLE LEGENDS OF THAT PLACE... SOME SAY IT'S HAUNTED.
AN UNHOLY JUJU SURROUNDS IT.
CATHERO
OKAY, OKAY. YOU CAN'T SPOOK ME THIS TIME.
THE CATHERO STORE
IT CAN'T BE HAUNTED, RIGHT?
I CAN DO THIS... I CAN--
SMACK

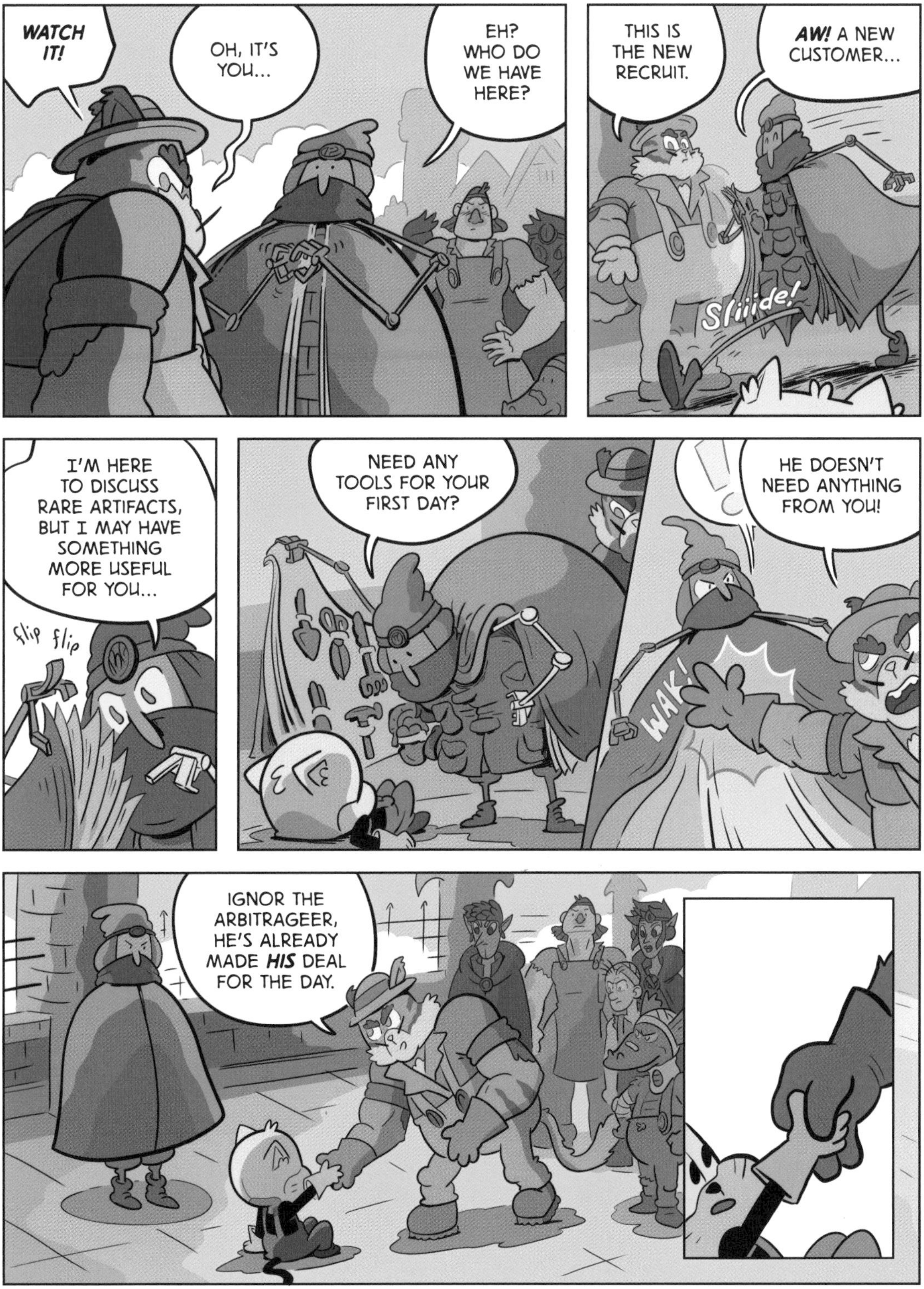
WATCH IT!
OH, IT'S YOU...
EH? WHO DO WE HAVE HERE?
THIS IS THE NEW RECRUIT.
AW! A NEW CUSTOMER...
Sliiide!
I'M HERE TO DISCUSS RARE ARTIFACTS, BUT I MAY HAVE SOMETHING MORE USEFUL FOR YOU...
flip flip
NEED ANY TOOLS FOR YOUR FIRST DAY?
!
HE DOESN'T NEED ANYTHING FROM YOU!
WAK!
IGNOR THE ARBITRAGEER, HE'S ALREADY MADE HIS DEAL FOR THE DAY.

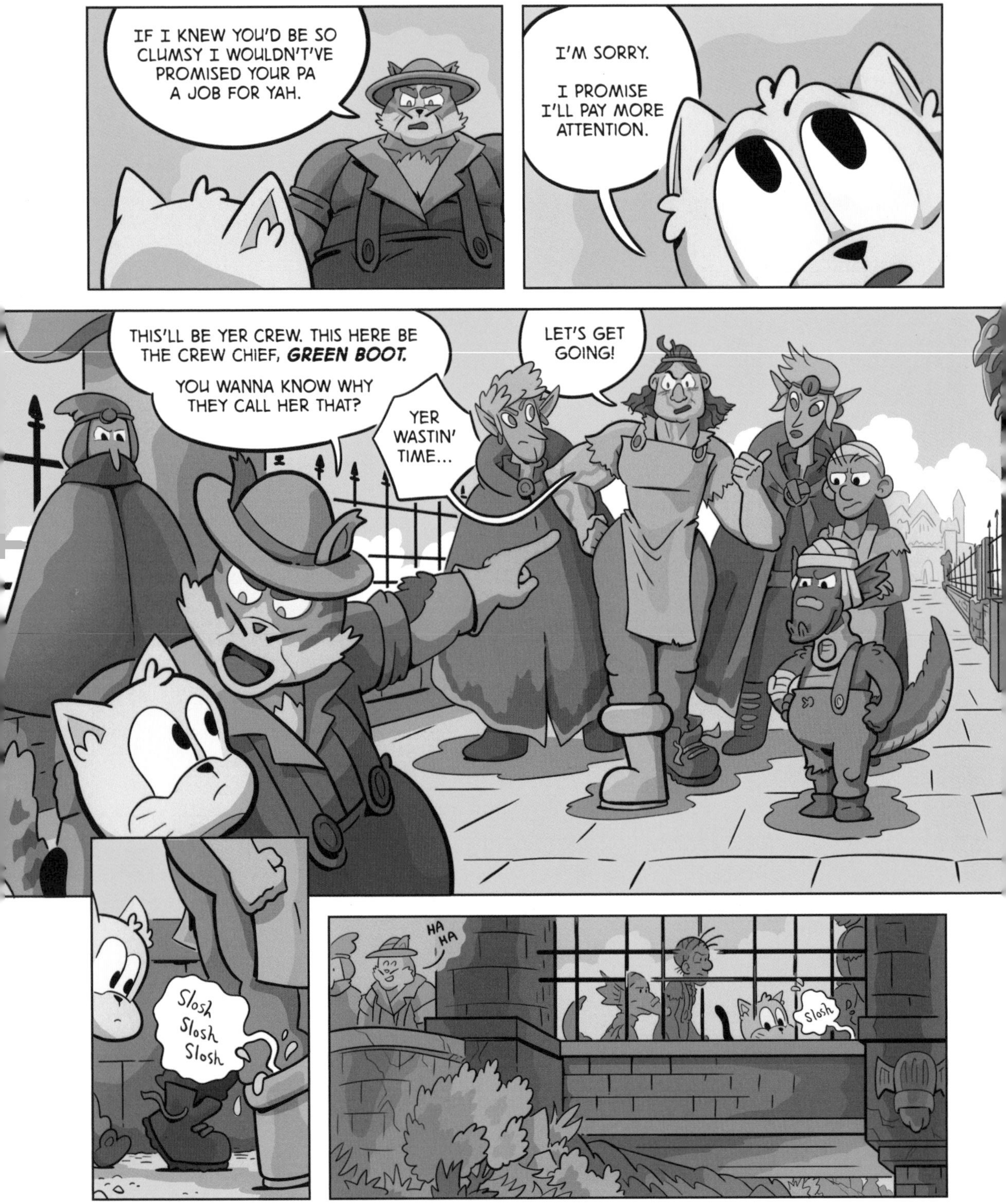
IF I KNEW YOU'D BE SO CLUMSY I WOULDN'T'VE PROMISED YOUR PA A JOB FOR YAH.
I'M SORRY.
I PROMISE I'LL PAY MORE ATTENTION.
THIS'LL BE YER CREW. THIS HERE BE THE CREW CHIEF, *GREEN BOOT.*
YOU WANNA KNOW WHY THEY CALL HER THAT?
LET'S GET GOING!
YER WASTIN' TIME...
Slosh Slosh Slosh
HA HA
Slosh

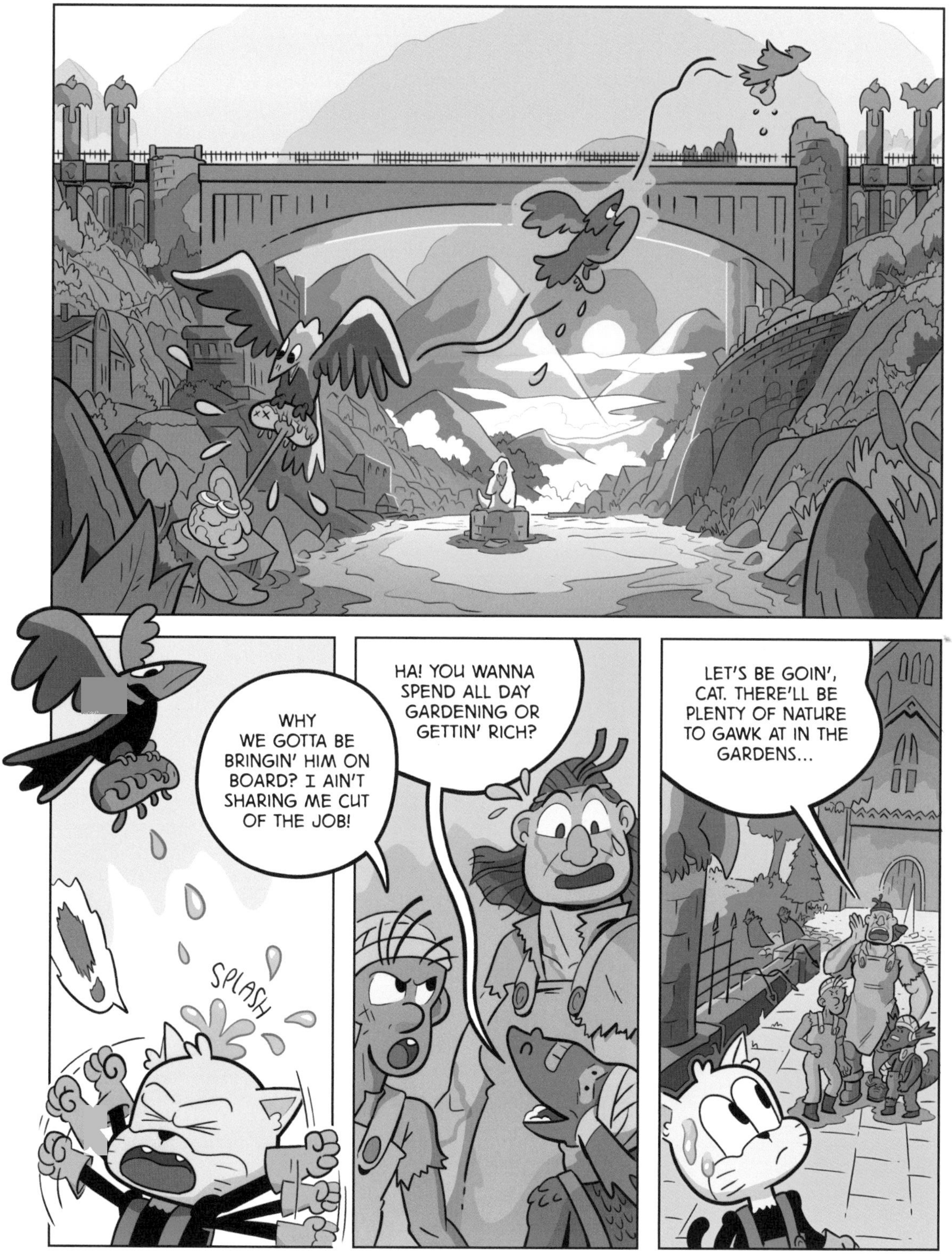
WHY WE GOTTA BE BRINGIN' HIM ON BOARD? I AIN'T SHARING ME CUT OF THE JOB!
SPLASH
HA! YOU WANNA SPEND ALL DAY GARDENING OR GETTIN' RICH?
LET'S BE GOIN', CAT. THERE'LL BE PLENTY OF NATURE TO GAWK AT IN THE GARDENS...

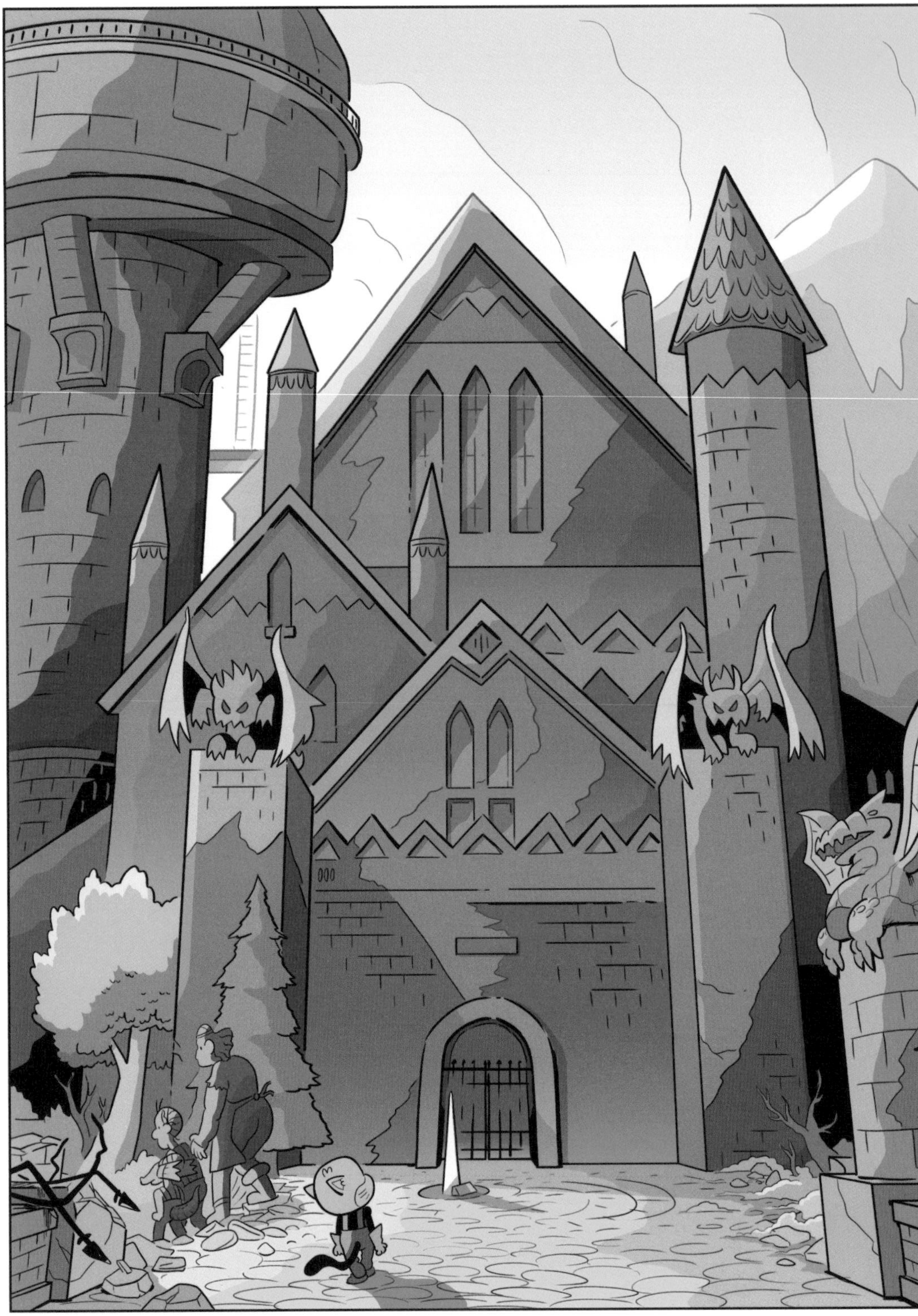

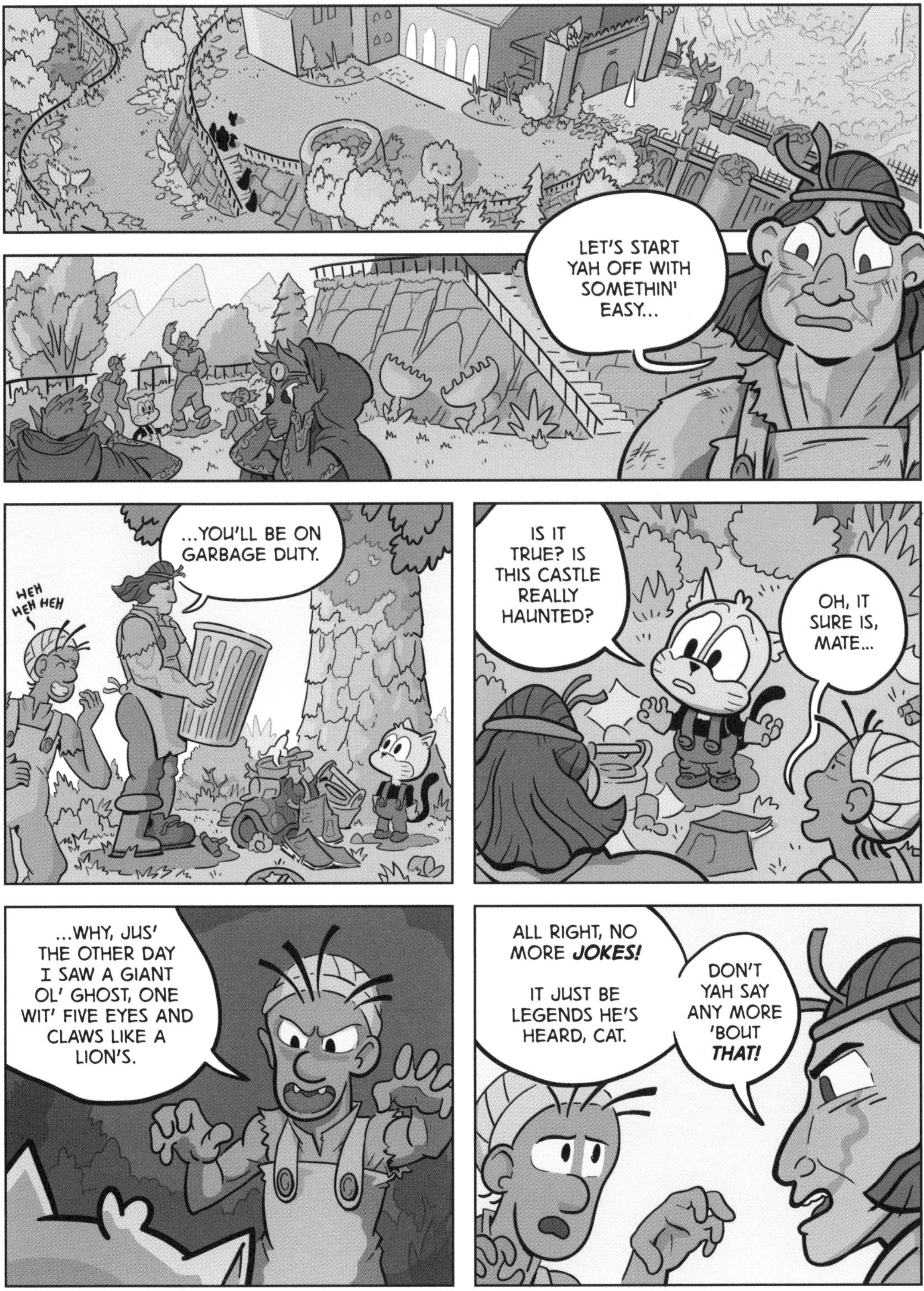
LET'S START YAH OFF WITH SOMETHIN' EASY...
...YOU'LL BE ON GARBAGE DUTY.
HEH HEH HEH
IS IT TRUE? IS THIS CASTLE REALLY HAUNTED?
OH, IT SURE IS, MATE...
...WHY, JUS' THE OTHER DAY I SAW A GIANT OL' GHOST, ONE WIT' FIVE EYES AND CLAWS LIKE A LION'S.
ALL RIGHT, NO MORE *JOKES!*
IT JUST BE LEGENDS HE'S HEARD, CAT.
DON'T YAH SAY ANY MORE 'BOUT *THAT!*

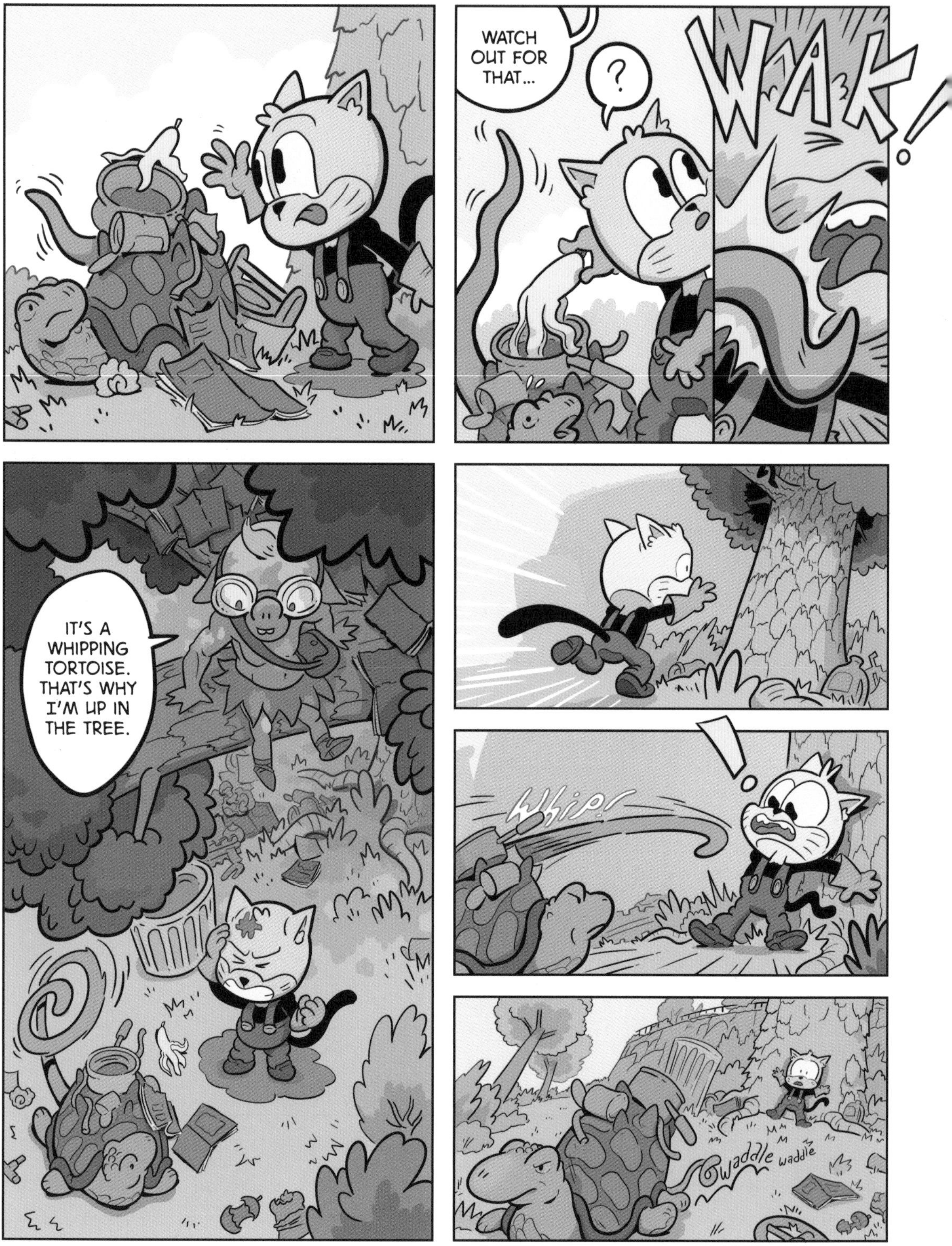
WATCH OUT FOR THAT...
?
WAK!
IT'S A WHIPPING TORTOISE. THAT'S WHY I'M UP IN THE TREE.
!
WHIP!
waddle waddle

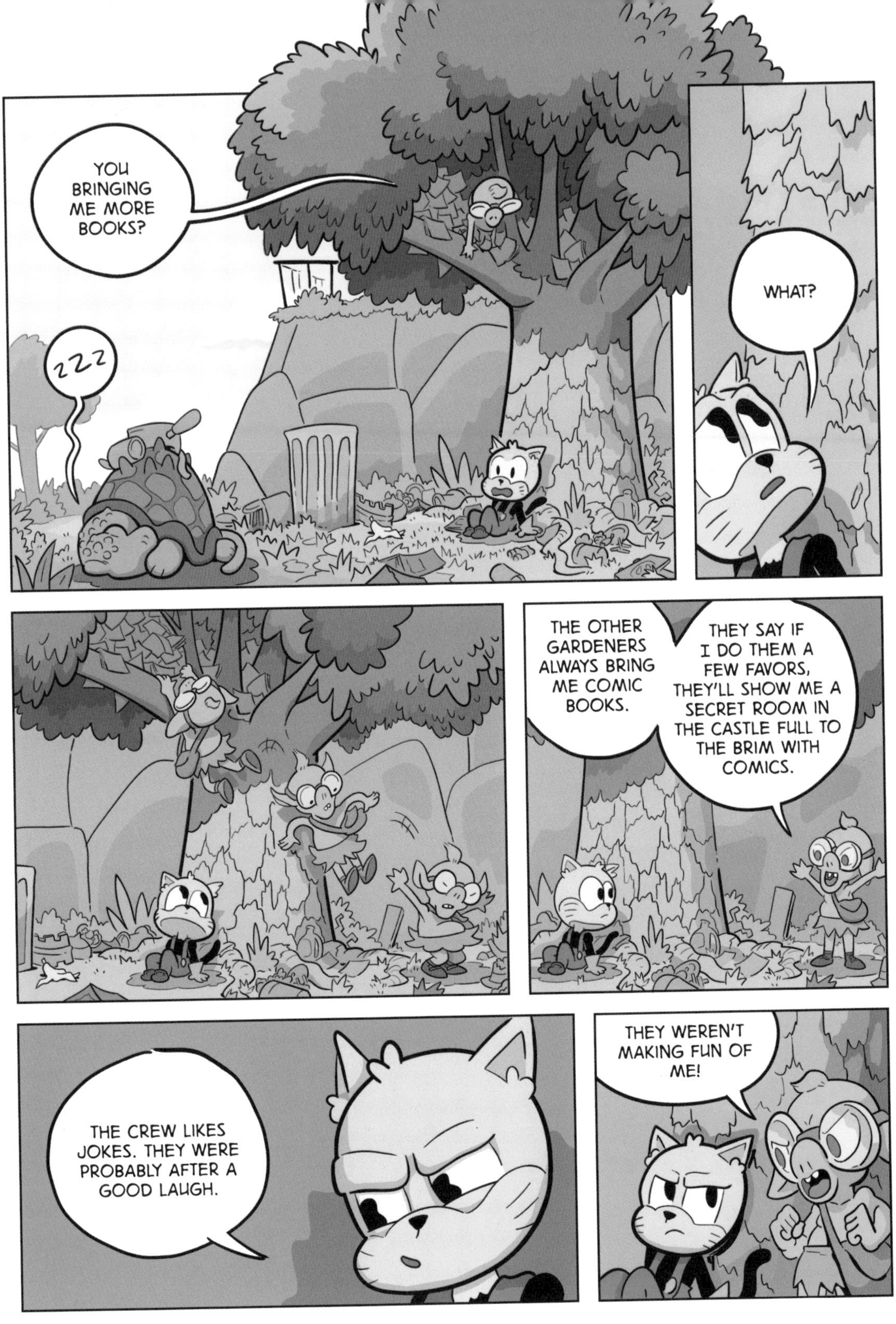
YOU BRINGING ME MORE BOOKS?
ZZZ
WHAT?
THE OTHER GARDENERS ALWAYS BRING ME COMIC BOOKS.
THEY SAY IF I DO THEM A FEW FAVORS, THEY'LL SHOW ME A SECRET ROOM IN THE CASTLE FULL TO THE BRIM WITH COMICS.
THE CREW LIKES JOKES. THEY WERE PROBABLY AFTER A GOOD LAUGH.
THEY WEREN'T MAKING FUN OF ME!

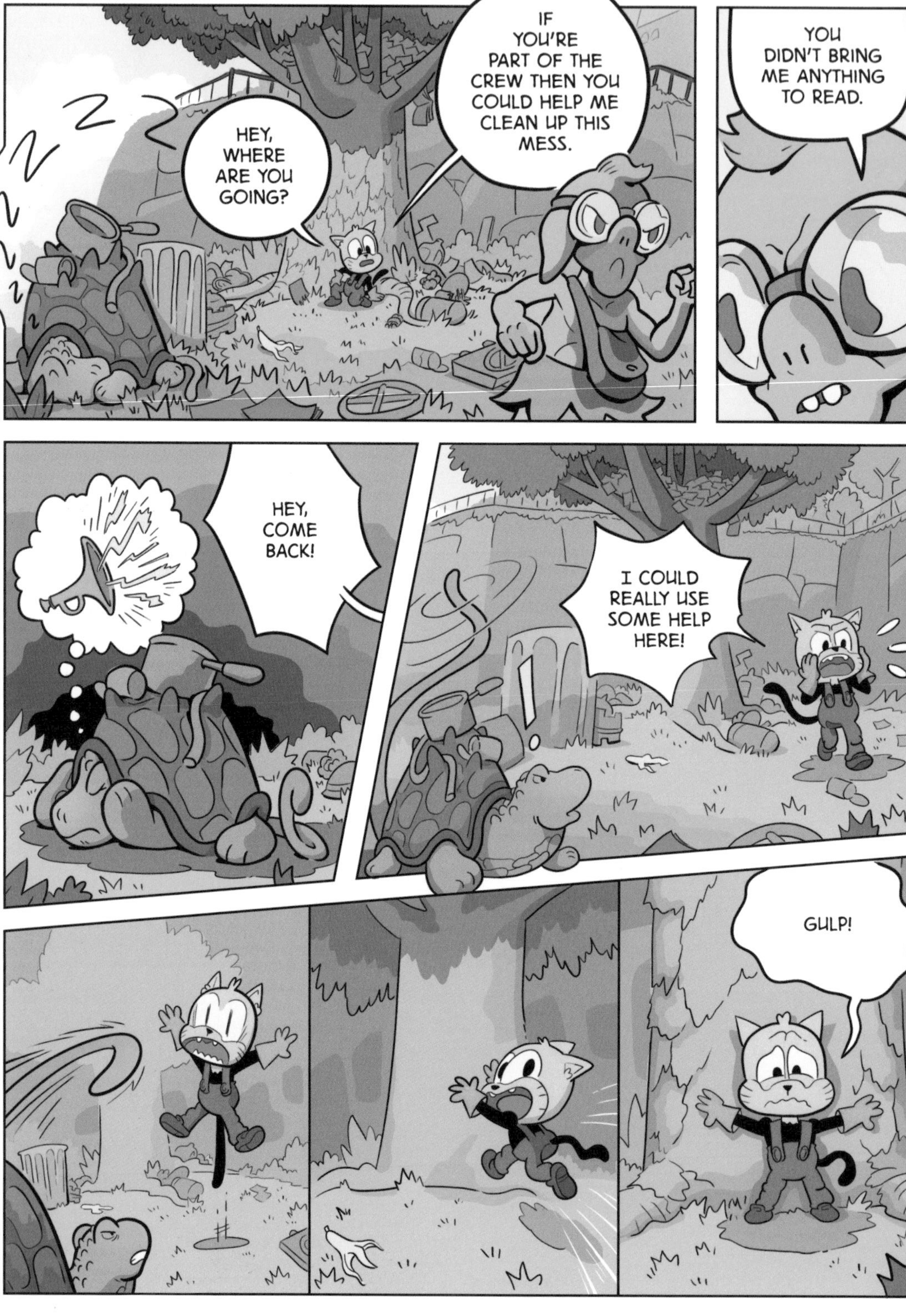
HEY, WHERE ARE YOU GOING?
IF YOU'RE PART OF THE CREW THEN YOU COULD HELP ME CLEAN UP THIS MESS.
YOU DIDN'T BRING ME ANYTHING TO READ.
HEY, COME BACK!
I COULD REALLY USE SOME HELP HERE!
GULP!

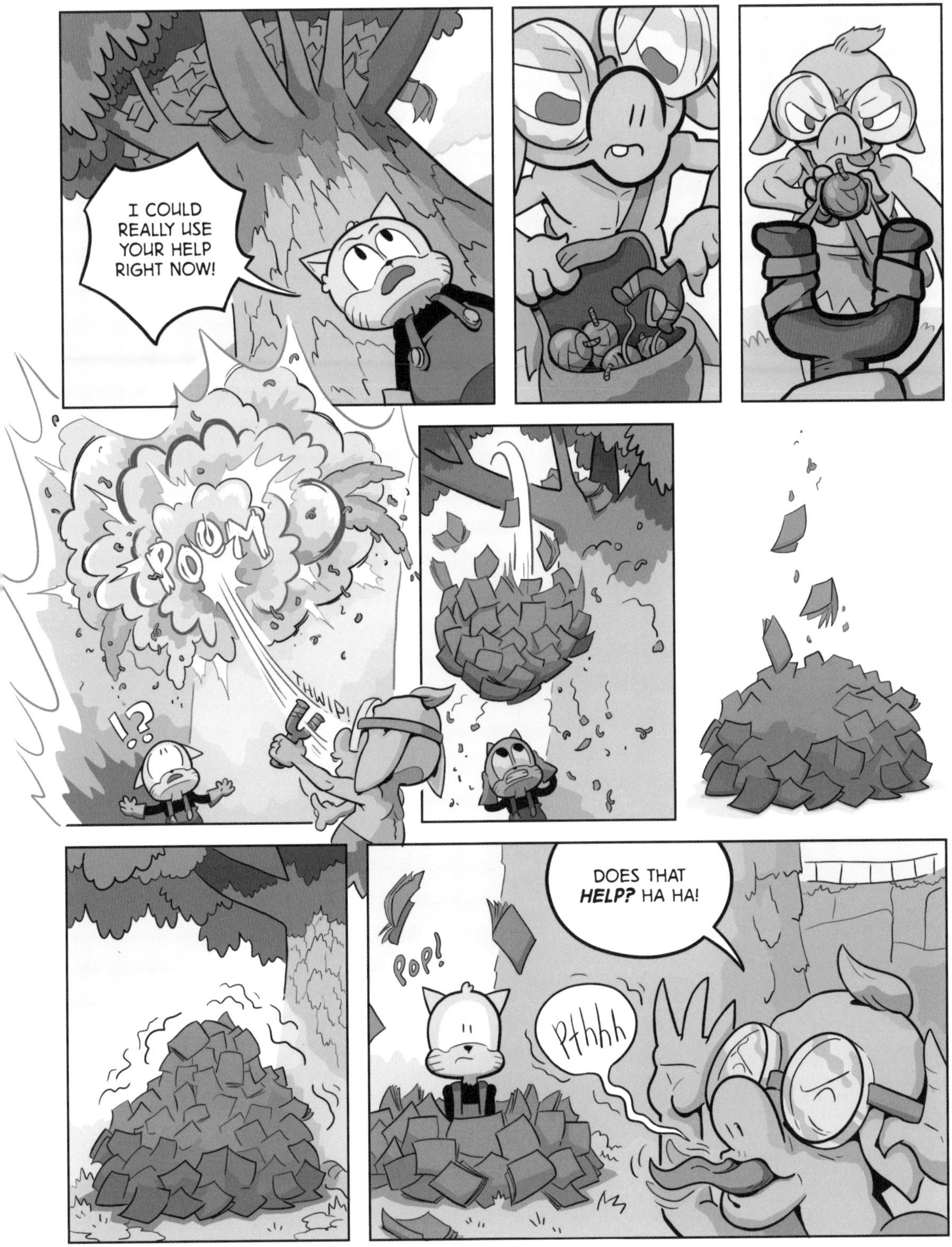
I COULD REALLY USE YOUR HELP RIGHT NOW!
!?
POOM
THWIP!
DOES THAT HELP? HA HA!
POP!
Pthhh

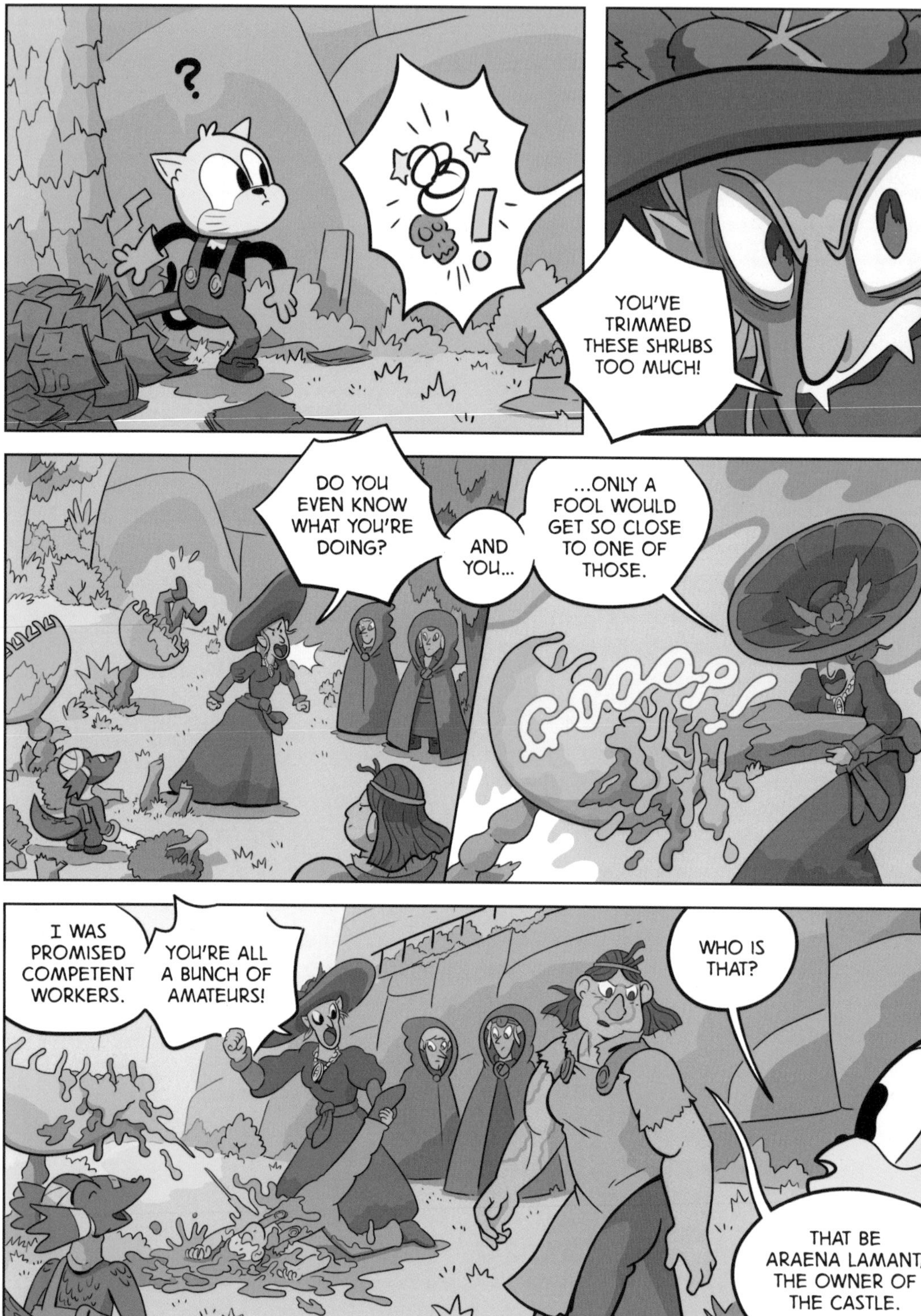
?
YOU'VE TRIMMED THESE SHRUBS TOO MUCH!
DO YOU EVEN KNOW WHAT YOU'RE DOING?
AND YOU...
...ONLY A FOOL WOULD GET SO CLOSE TO ONE OF THOSE.
GOOOP!
I WAS PROMISED COMPETENT WORKERS.
YOU'RE ALL A BUNCH OF AMATEURS!
WHO IS THAT?
THAT BE ARAENA LAMANT, THE OWNER OF THE CASTLE.

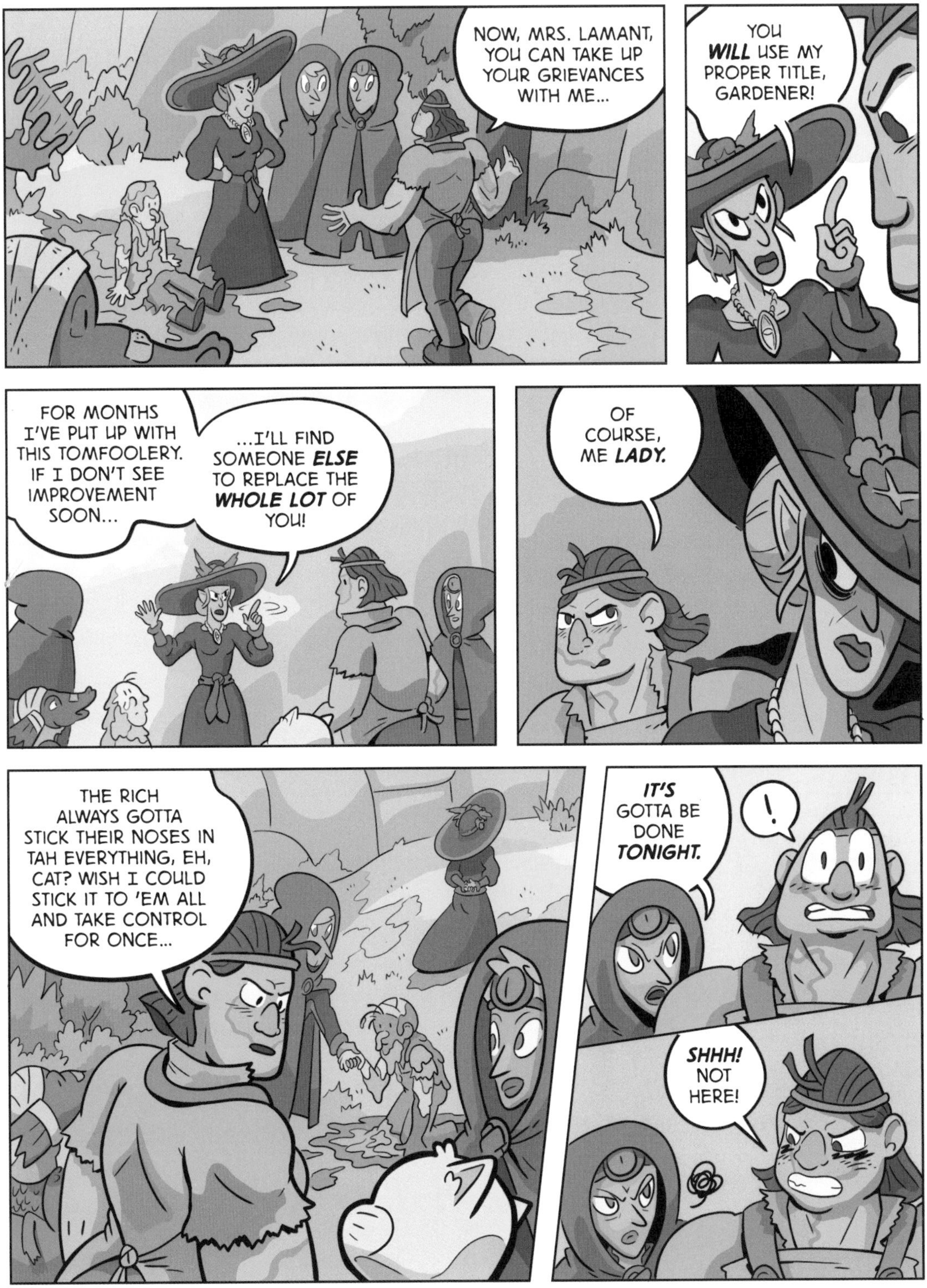
NOW, MRS. LAMANT, YOU CAN TAKE UP YOUR GRIEVANCES WITH ME...
YOU WILL USE MY PROPER TITLE, GARDENER!
FOR MONTHS I'VE PUT UP WITH THIS TOMFOOLERY. IF I DON'T SEE IMPROVEMENT SOON...
...I'LL FIND SOMEONE ELSE TO REPLACE THE WHOLE LOT OF YOU!
OF COURSE, ME LADY.
THE RICH ALWAYS GOTTA STICK THEIR NOSES IN TAH EVERYTHING, EH, CAT? WISH I COULD STICK IT TO 'EM ALL AND TAKE CONTROL FOR ONCE...
IT'S GOTTA BE DONE TONIGHT.
!
SHHH! NOT HERE!

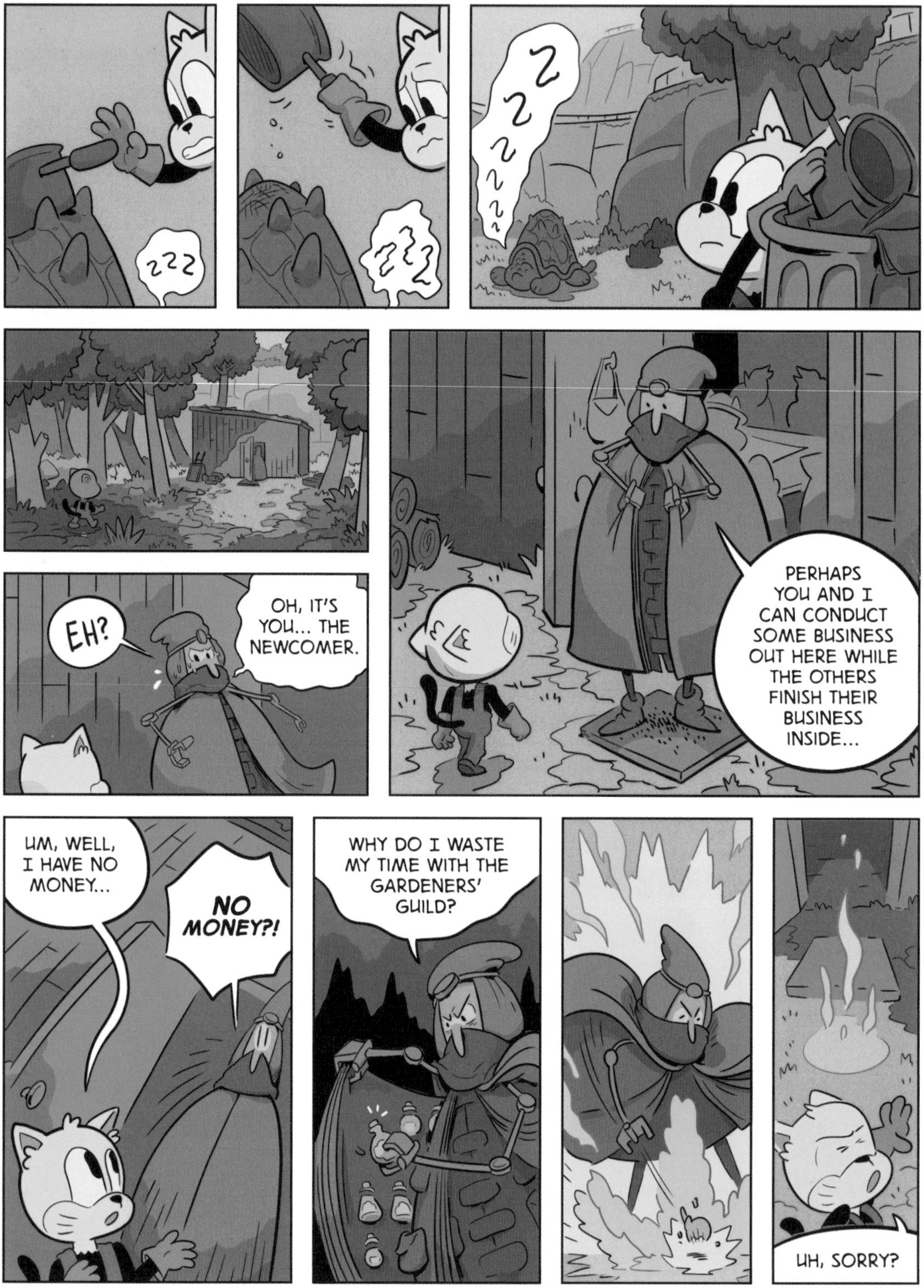
ZZZ
ZZZ
ZZZZZZ
EH?
OH, IT'S YOU... THE NEWCOMER.
PERHAPS YOU AND I CAN CONDUCT SOME BUSINESS OUT HERE WHILE THE OTHERS FINISH THEIR BUSINESS INSIDE...
UM, WELL, I HAVE NO MONEY...
NO MONEY?!
WHY DO I WASTE MY TIME WITH THE GARDENERS' GUILD?
UH, SORRY?

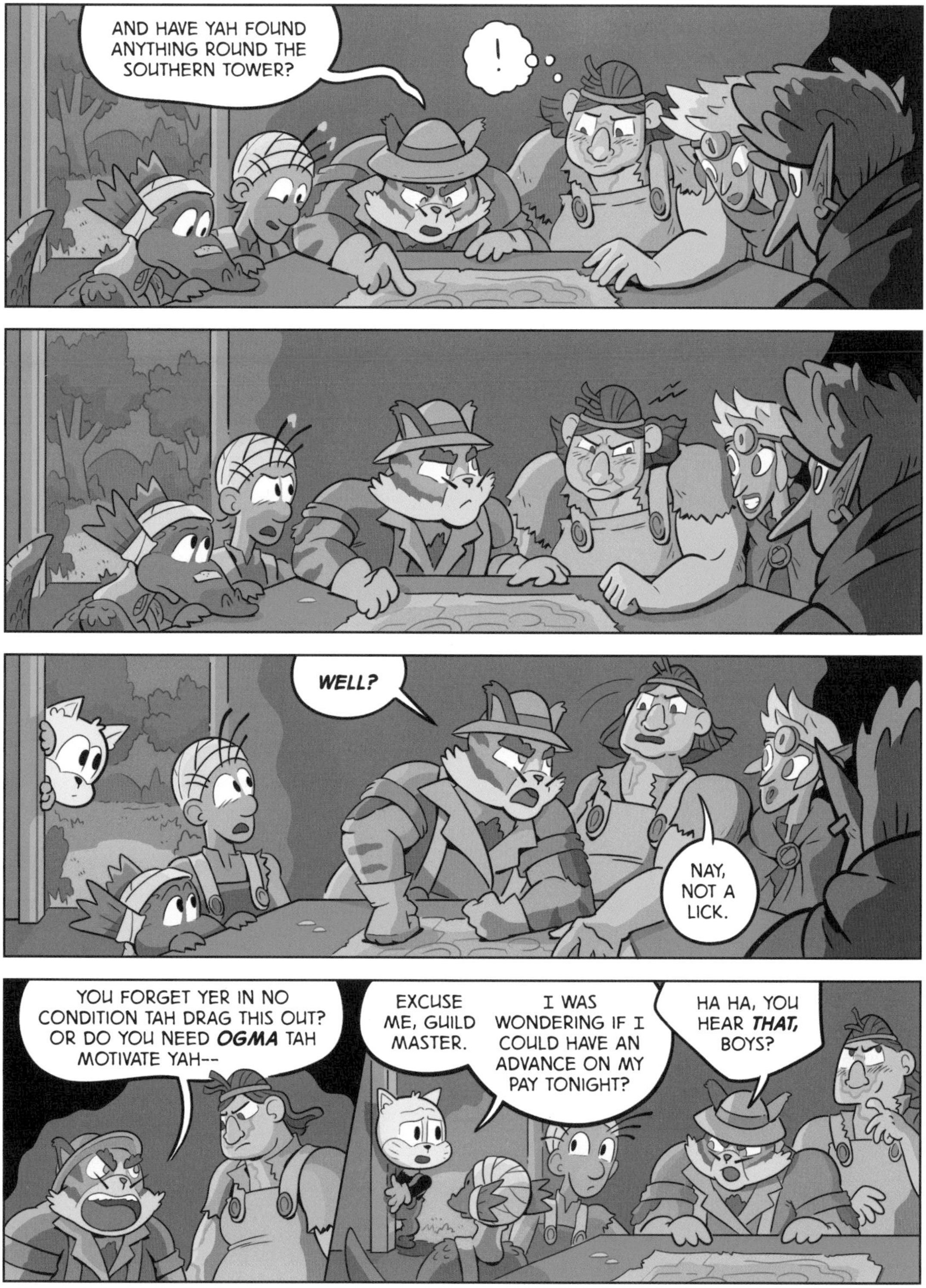
AND HAVE YAH FOUND ANYTHING ROUND THE SOUTHERN TOWER?
!
WELL?
NAY, NOT A LICK.
YOU FORGET YER IN NO CONDITION TAH DRAG THIS OUT? OR DO YOU NEED **OGMA** TAH MOTIVATE YAH--
EXCUSE ME, GUILD MASTER.
I WAS WONDERING IF I COULD HAVE AN ADVANCE ON MY PAY TONIGHT?
HA HA, YOU HEAR **THAT,** BOYS?

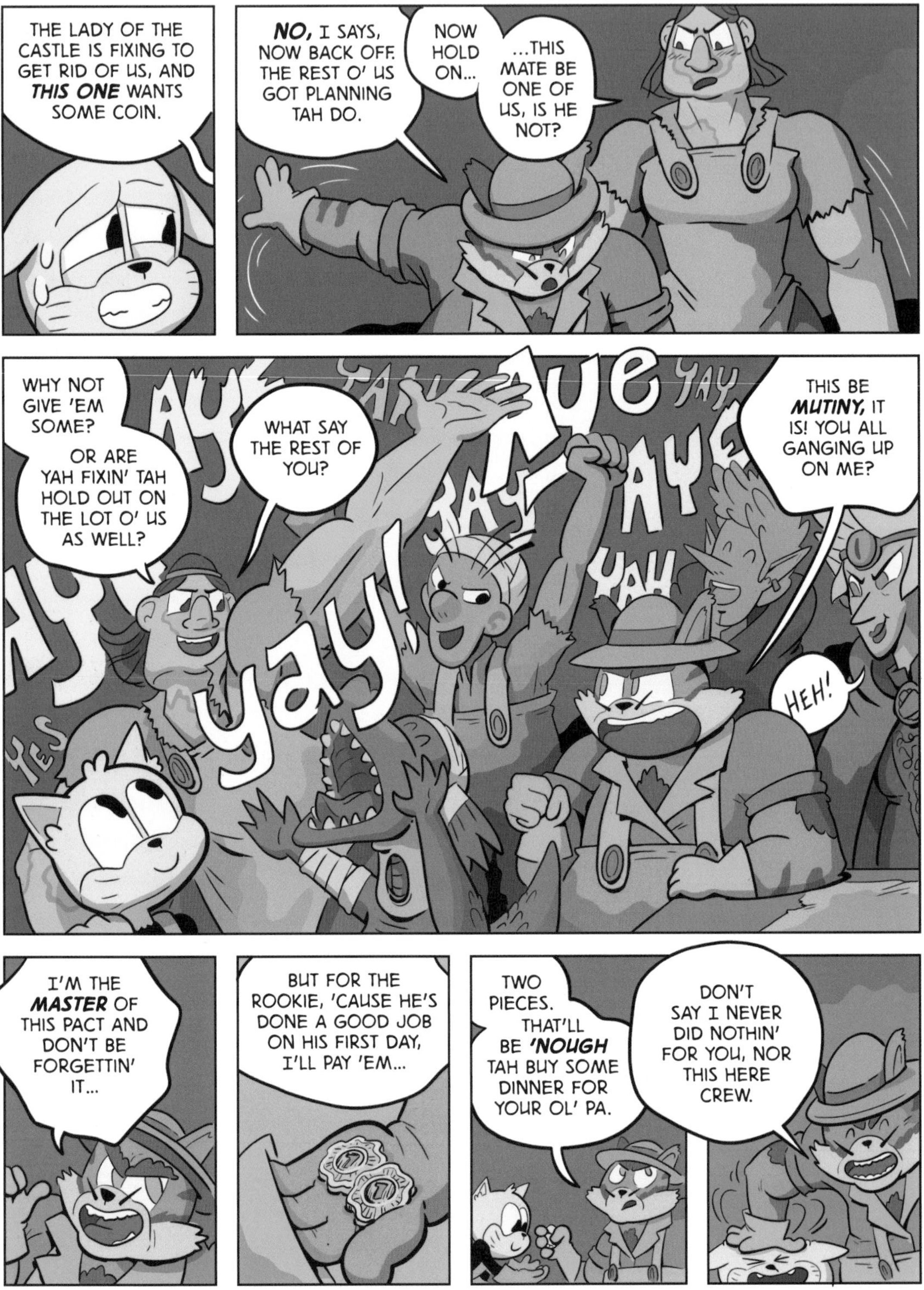
THE LADY OF THE CASTLE IS FIXING TO GET RID OF US, AND THIS ONE WANTS SOME COIN.
NO, I SAYS, NOW BACK OFF. THE REST O' US GOT PLANNING TAH DO.
NOW HOLD ON...
...THIS MATE BE ONE OF US, IS HE NOT?
WHY NOT GIVE 'EM SOME?
OR ARE YAH FIXIN' TAH HOLD OUT ON THE LOT O' US AS WELL?
WHAT SAY THE REST OF YOU?
AYE
YAY
AYE
YAY
AYE
YAH
YAY!
YES
THIS BE MUTINY, IT IS! YOU ALL GANGING UP ON ME?
HEH!
I'M THE MASTER OF THIS PACT AND DON'T BE FORGETTIN' IT...
BUT FOR THE ROOKIE, 'CAUSE HE'S DONE A GOOD JOB ON HIS FIRST DAY, I'LL PAY 'EM...
TWO PIECES.
THAT'LL BE 'NOUGH TAH BUY SOME DINNER FOR YOUR OL' PA.
DON'T SAY I NEVER DID NOTHIN' FOR YOU, NOR THIS HERE CREW.

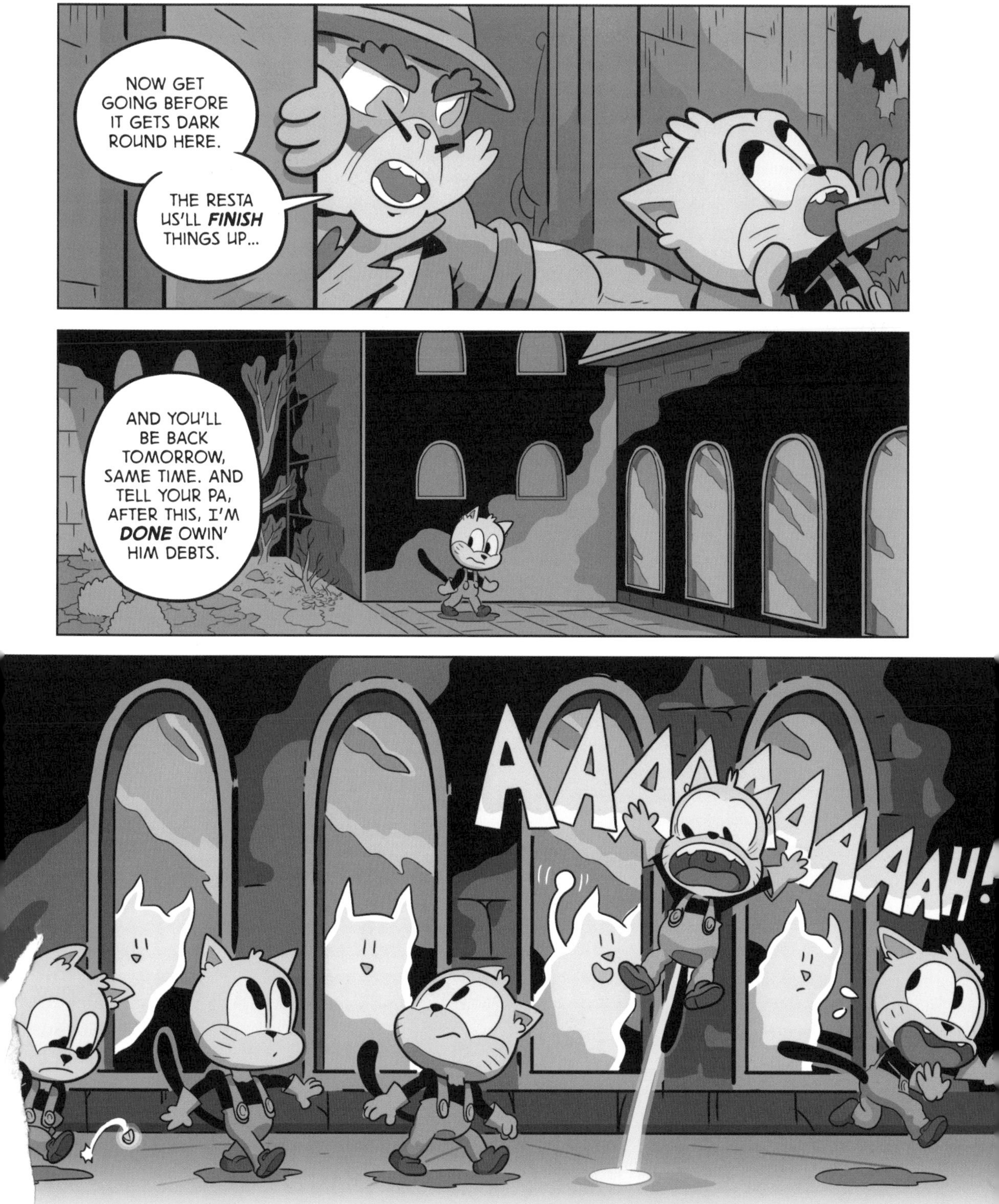
NOW GET GOING BEFORE IT GETS DARK ROUND HERE.
THE RESTA US'LL FINISH THINGS UP...
AND YOU'LL BE BACK TOMORROW, SAME TIME. AND TELL YOUR PA, AFTER THIS, I'M DONE OWIN' HIM DEBTS.
AAAAAAAAAAH!

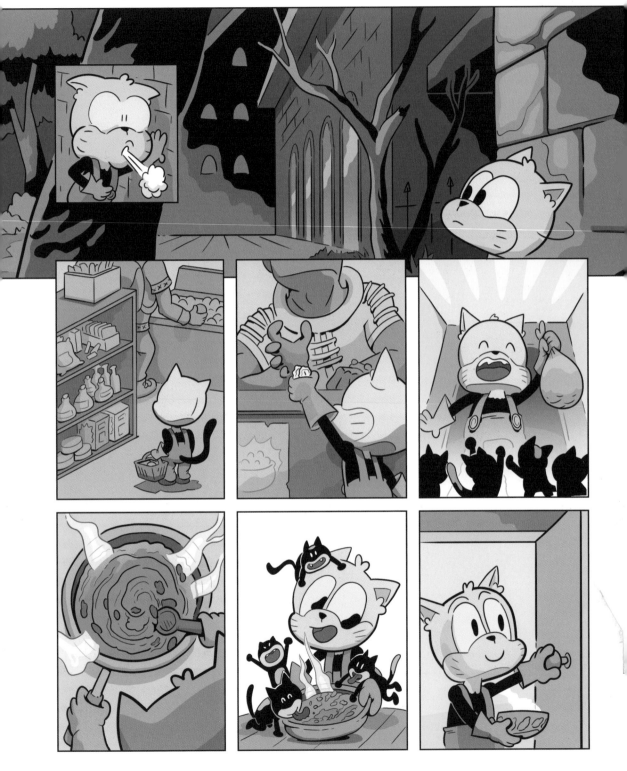

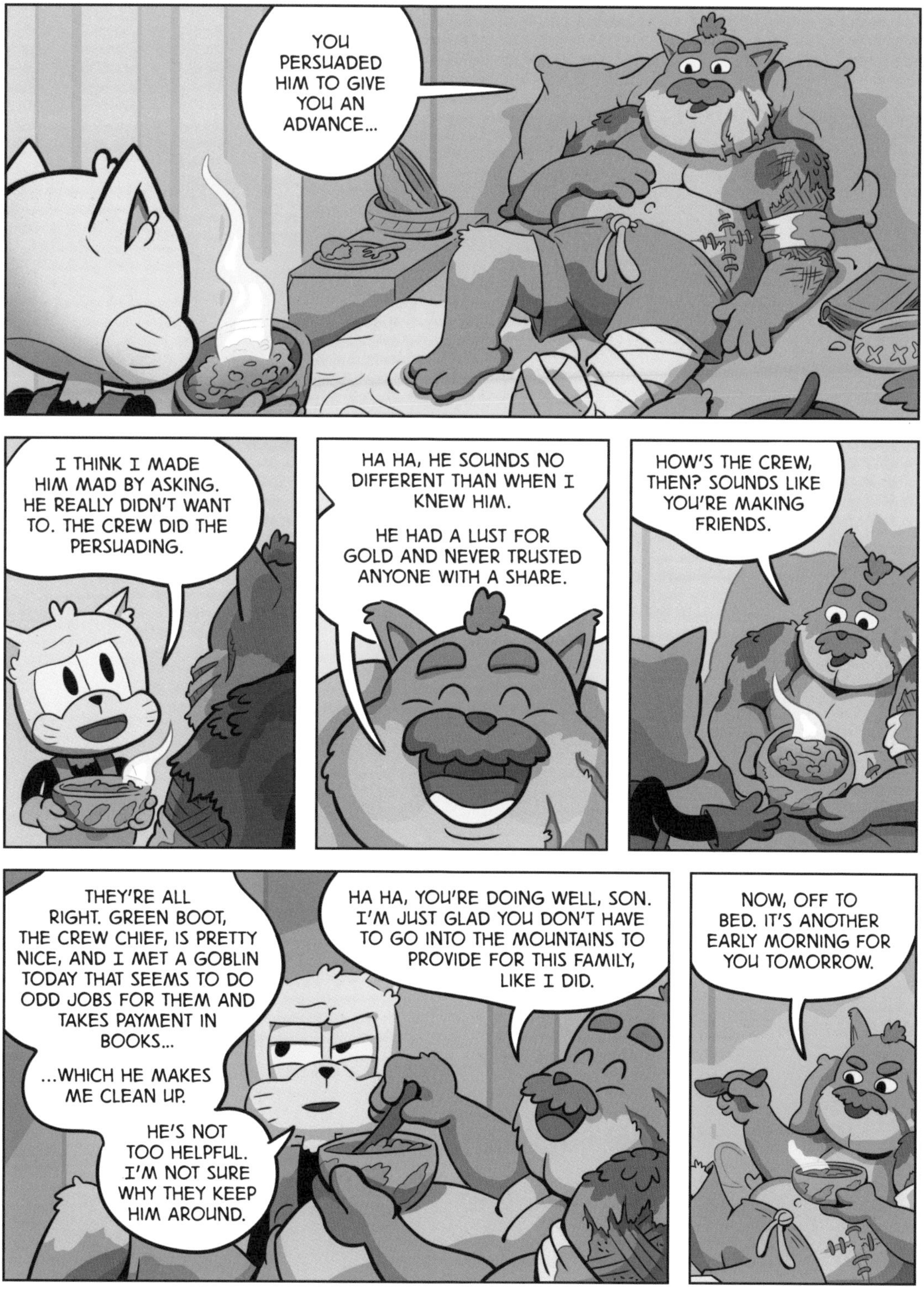
YOU PERSUADED HIM TO GIVE YOU AN ADVANCE...
I THINK I MADE HIM MAD BY ASKING. HE REALLY DIDN'T WANT TO. THE CREW DID THE PERSUADING.
HA HA, HE SOUNDS NO DIFFERENT THAN WHEN I KNEW HIM.
HE HAD A LUST FOR GOLD AND NEVER TRUSTED ANYONE WITH A SHARE.
HOW'S THE CREW, THEN? SOUNDS LIKE YOU'RE MAKING FRIENDS.
THEY'RE ALL RIGHT. GREEN BOOT, THE CREW CHIEF, IS PRETTY NICE, AND I MET A GOBLIN TODAY THAT SEEMS TO DO ODD JOBS FOR THEM AND TAKES PAYMENT IN BOOKS...
...WHICH HE MAKES ME CLEAN UP.
HE'S NOT TOO HELPFUL. I'M NOT SURE WHY THEY KEEP HIM AROUND.
HA HA, YOU'RE DOING WELL, SON. I'M JUST GLAD YOU DON'T HAVE TO GO INTO THE MOUNTAINS TO PROVIDE FOR THIS FAMILY, LIKE I DID.
NOW, OFF TO BED. IT'S ANOTHER EARLY MORNING FOR YOU TOMORROW.

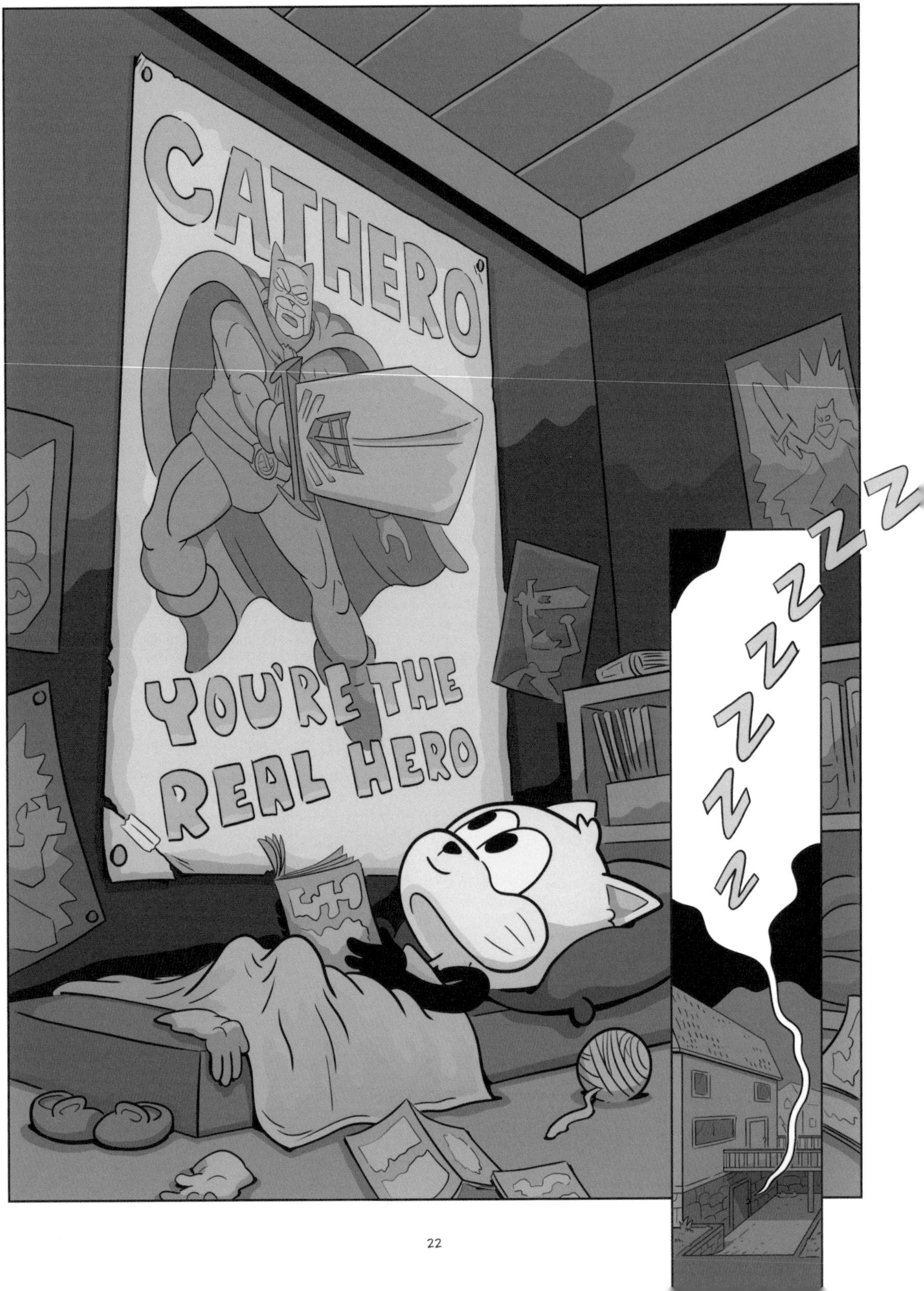
CATHERO
YOU'RE THE REAL HERO
ZZZZZZZZZ

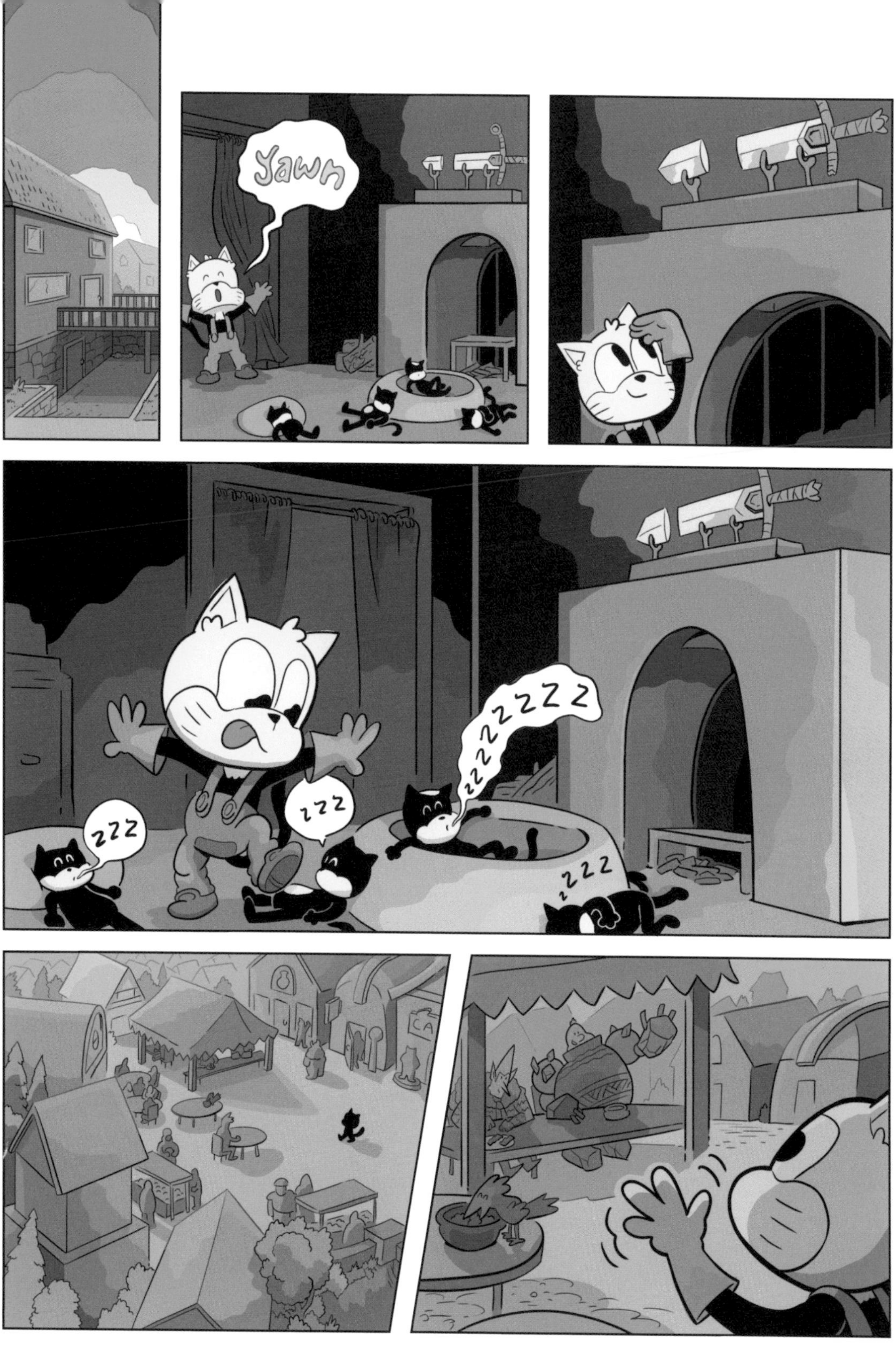
Yawn
ZZZ
ZZZ
zzzzzzzZZ
zZZZ
CA

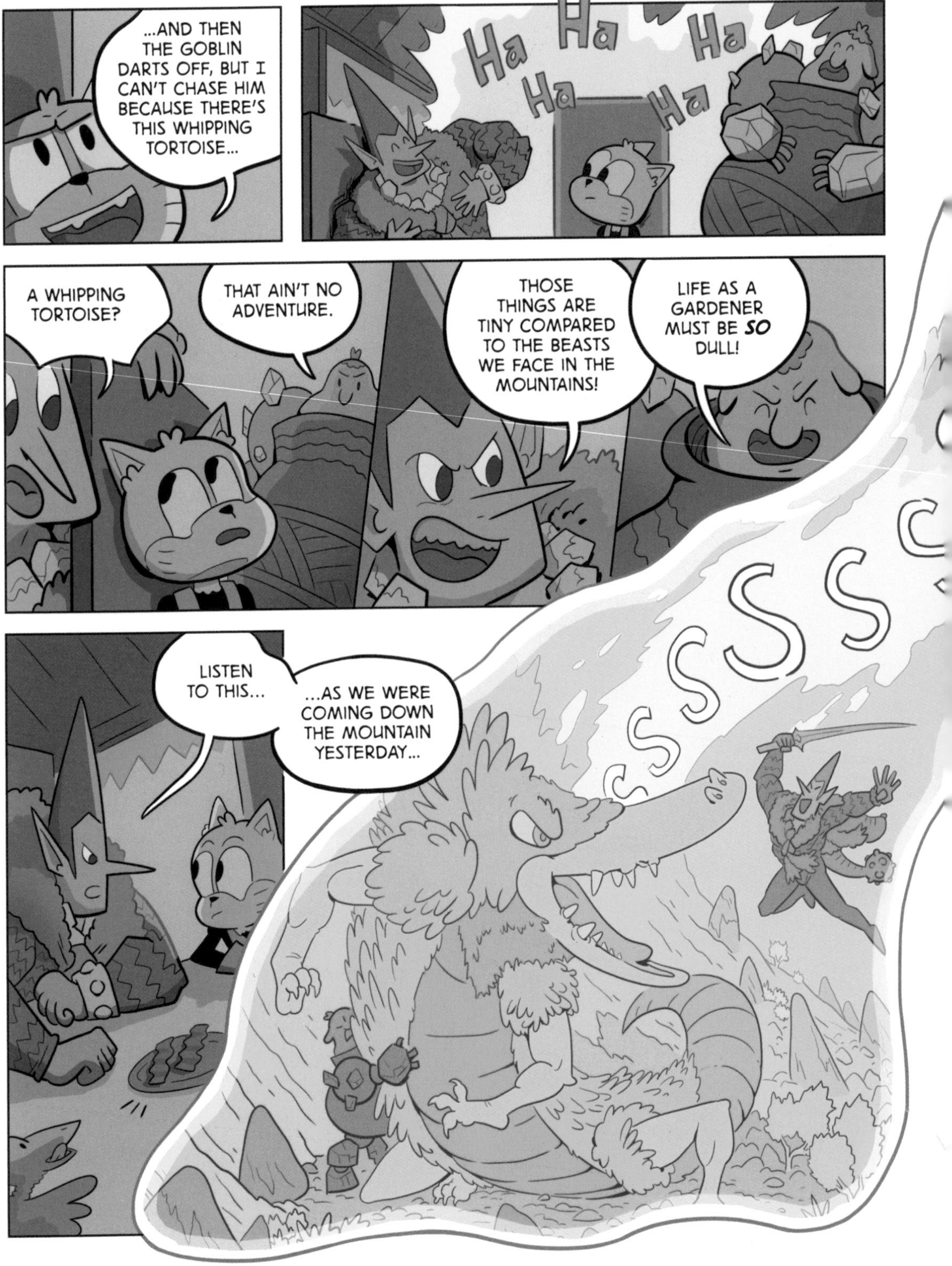
...AND THEN THE GOBLIN DARTS OFF, BUT I CAN'T CHASE HIM BECAUSE THERE'S THIS WHIPPING TORTOISE...
Ha Ha Ha Ha Ha
A WHIPPING TORTOISE?
THAT AIN'T NO ADVENTURE.
THOSE THINGS ARE TINY COMPARED TO THE BEASTS WE FACE IN THE MOUNTAINS!
LIFE AS A GARDENER MUST BE **SO** DULL!
LISTEN TO THIS...
...AS WE WERE COMING DOWN THE MOUNTAIN YESTERDAY...
SSSSSS

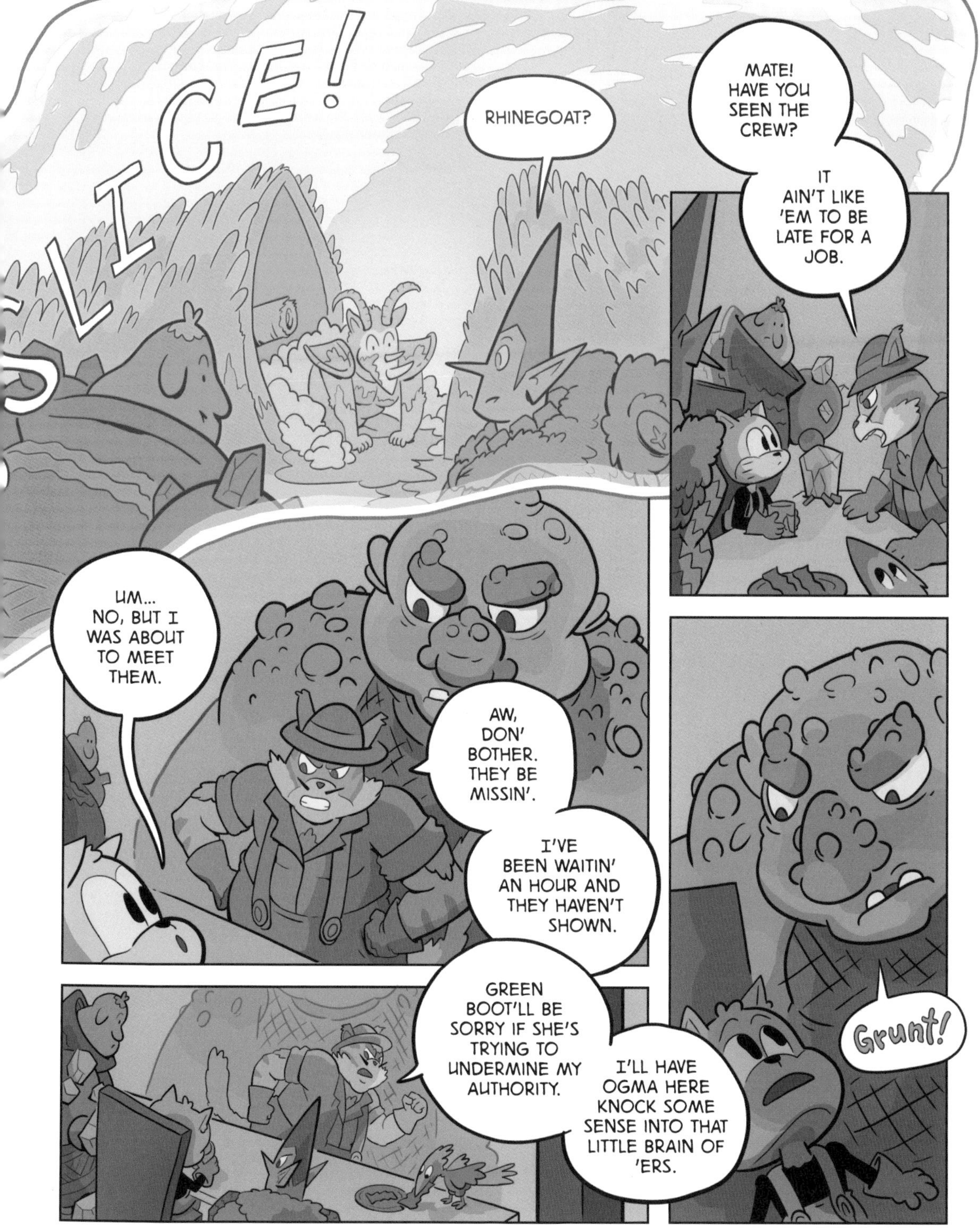
SLICE!
RHINEGOAT?
MATE! HAVE YOU SEEN THE CREW?
IT AIN'T LIKE 'EM TO BE LATE FOR A JOB.
UM... NO, BUT I WAS ABOUT TO MEET THEM.
AW, DON' BOTHER. THEY BE MISSIN'.
I'VE BEEN WAITIN' AN HOUR AND THEY HAVEN'T SHOWN.
GREEN BOOT'LL BE SORRY IF SHE'S TRYING TO UNDERMINE MY AUTHORITY.
I'LL HAVE OGMA HERE KNOCK SOME SENSE INTO THAT LITTLE BRAIN OF 'ERS.
Grunt!

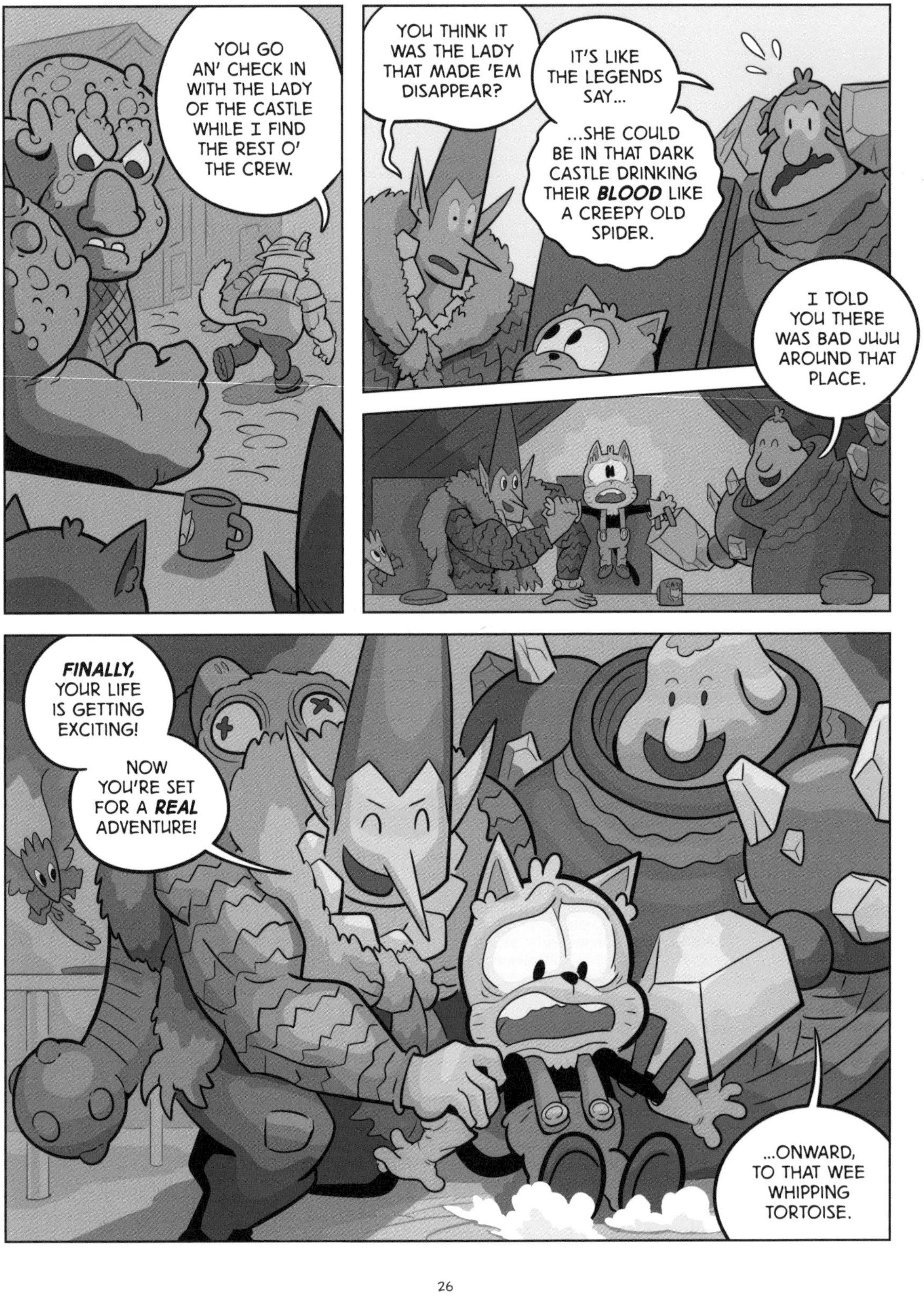
YOU GO AN' CHECK IN WITH THE LADY OF THE CASTLE WHILE I FIND THE REST O' THE CREW.
YOU THINK IT WAS THE LADY THAT MADE 'EM DISAPPEAR?
IT'S LIKE THE LEGENDS SAY...
...SHE COULD BE IN THAT DARK CASTLE DRINKING THEIR **BLOOD** LIKE A CREEPY OLD SPIDER.
I TOLD YOU THERE WAS BAD JUJU AROUND THAT PLACE.
FINALLY, YOUR LIFE IS GETTING EXCITING!
NOW YOU'RE SET FOR A ***REAL*** ADVENTURE!
...ONWARD, TO THAT WEE WHIPPING TORTOISE.

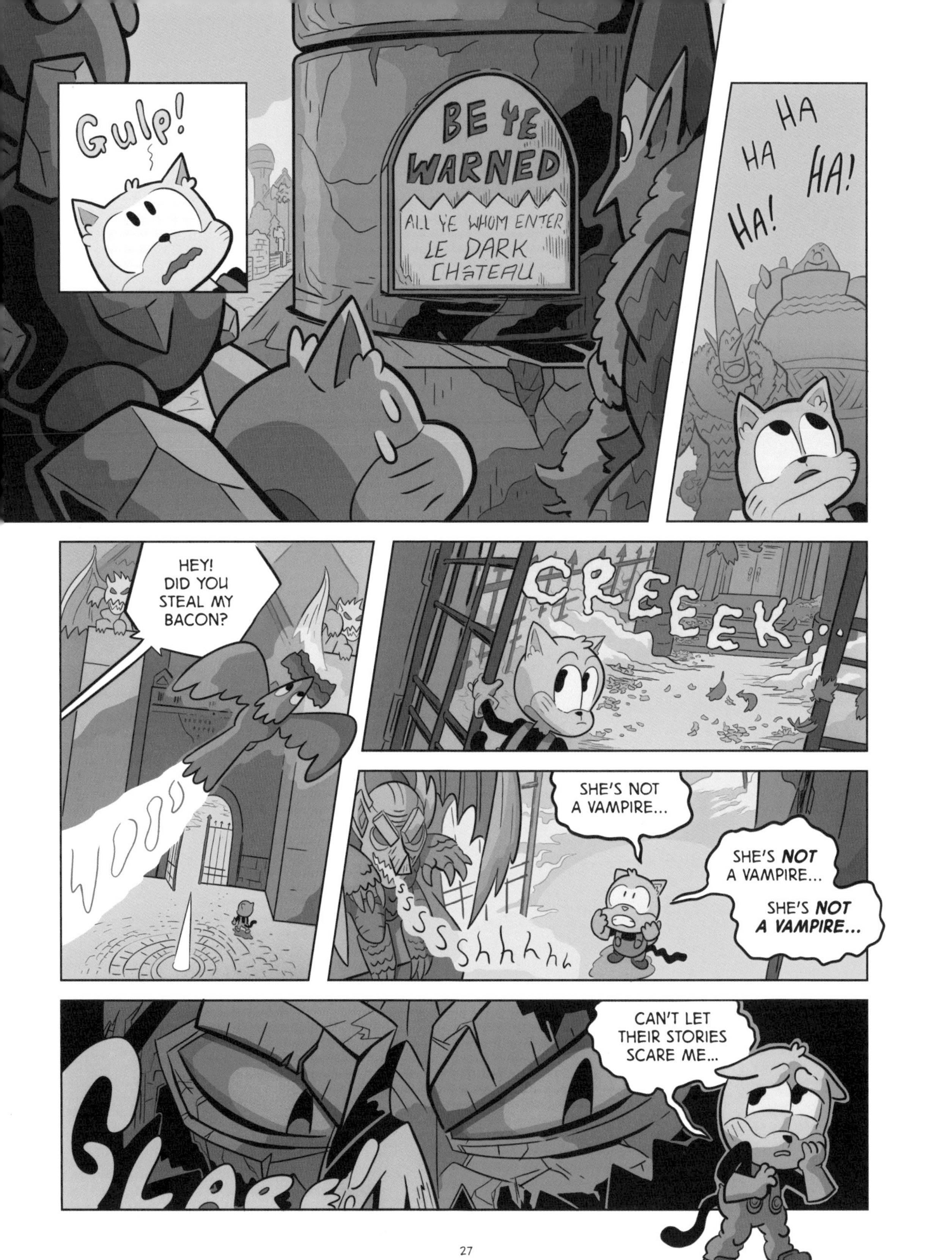
Gulp!
BE YE WARNED
ALL YE WHOM ENTER LE DARK CHÂTEAU
HA HA HA! HA HA!
HEY! DID YOU STEAL MY BACON?
CREEEK...
SHE'S NOT A VAMPIRE...
SHE'S **NOT** A VAMPIRE...
SHE'S **NOT** ***A VAMPIRE...***
Ssshhhhh
CAN'T LET THEIR STORIES SCARE ME...

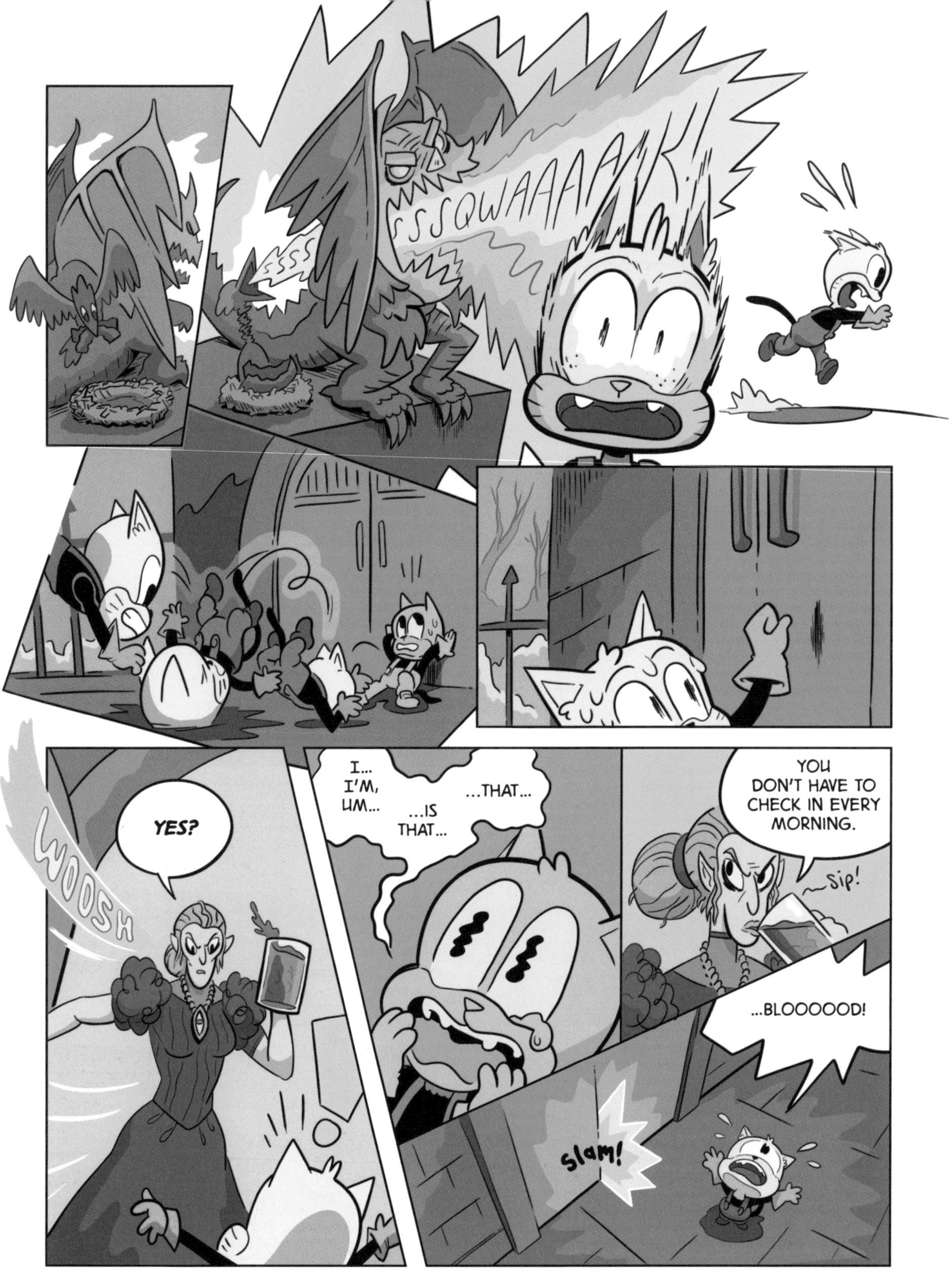
SSSS
SSSQWAAAAAK!
YES?
WOOSH
I... I'M, UM...
...IS THAT...
...THAT...
YOU DON'T HAVE TO CHECK IN EVERY MORNING.
SIP!
...BLOOOOOD!
SLAM!

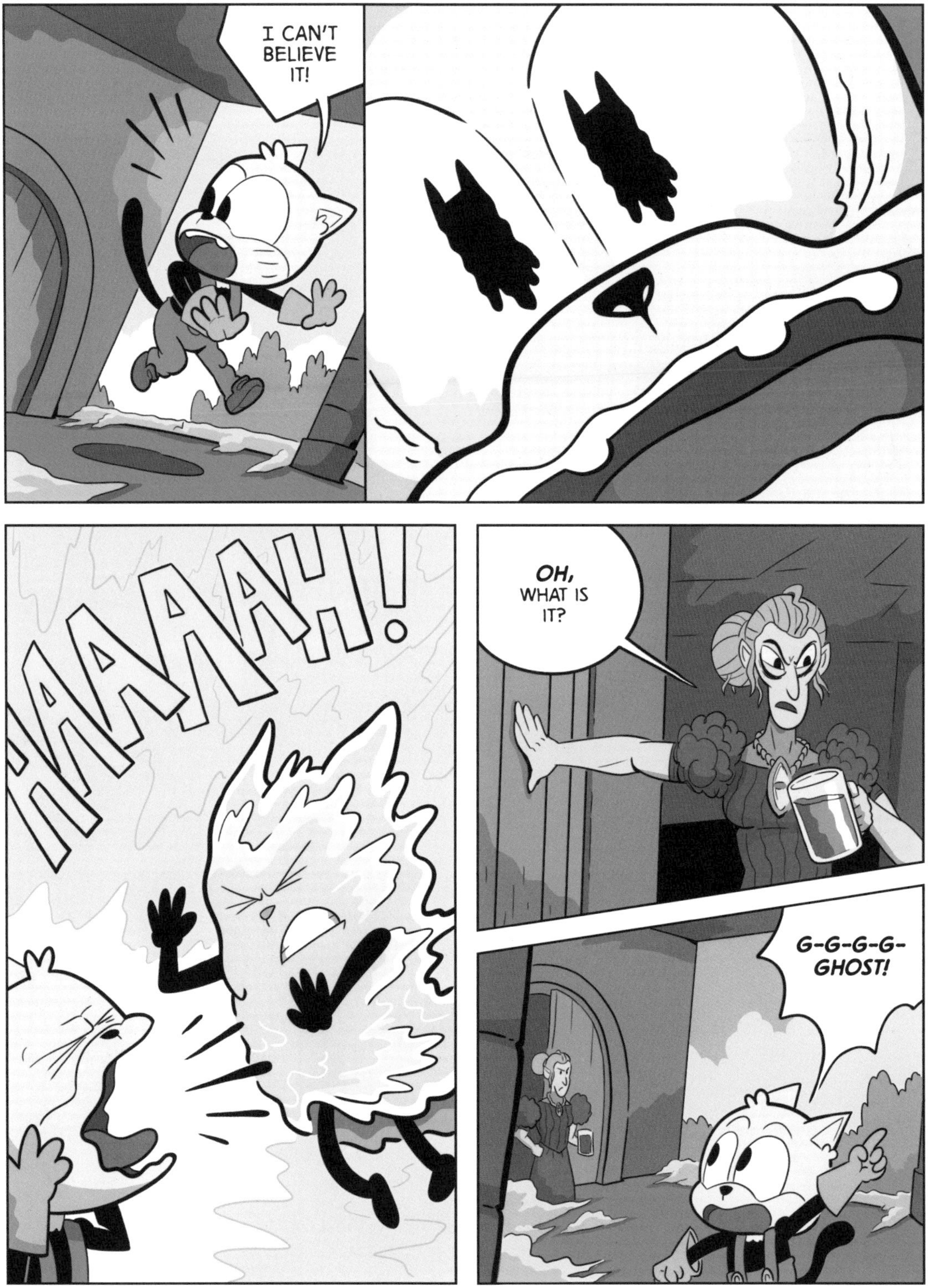

I CAN'T BELIEVE IT!
HAAAAH!
OH, WHAT IS IT?
G-G-G-G-GHOST!

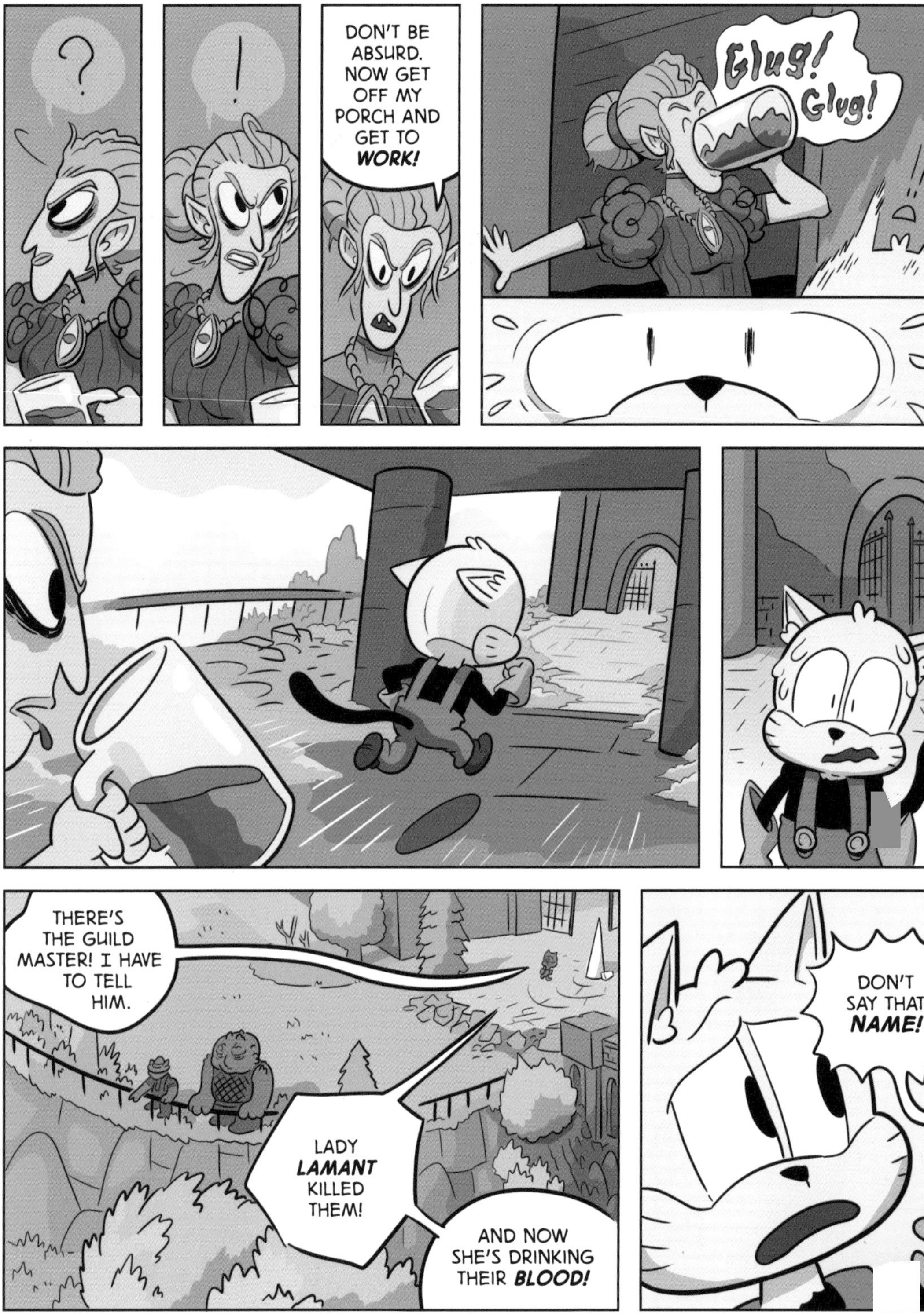
?
!
DON'T BE ABSURD. NOW GET OFF MY PORCH AND GET TO WORK!
Glug! Glug!
THERE'S THE GUILD MASTER! I HAVE TO TELL HIM.
LADY LAMANT KILLED THEM!
AND NOW SHE'S DRINKING THEIR BLOOD!
DON'T SAY THAT NAME!

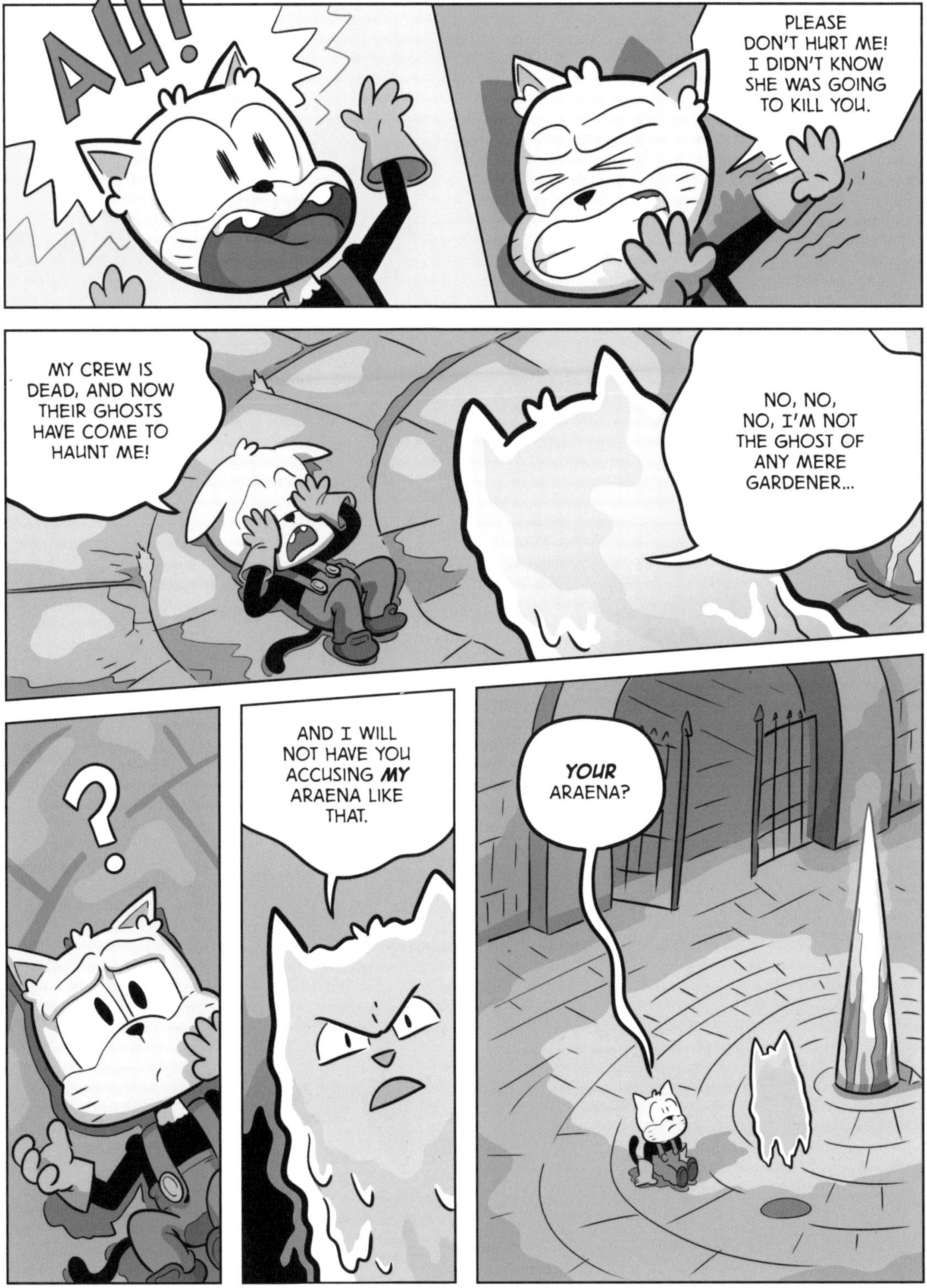
AH!
PLEASE DON'T HURT ME! I DIDN'T KNOW SHE WAS GOING TO KILL YOU.
MY CREW IS DEAD, AND NOW THEIR GHOSTS HAVE COME TO HAUNT ME!
NO, NO, NO, I'M NOT THE GHOST OF ANY MERE GARDENER...
?
AND I WILL NOT HAVE YOU ACCUSING ***MY*** ARAENA LIKE THAT.
YOUR ARAENA?

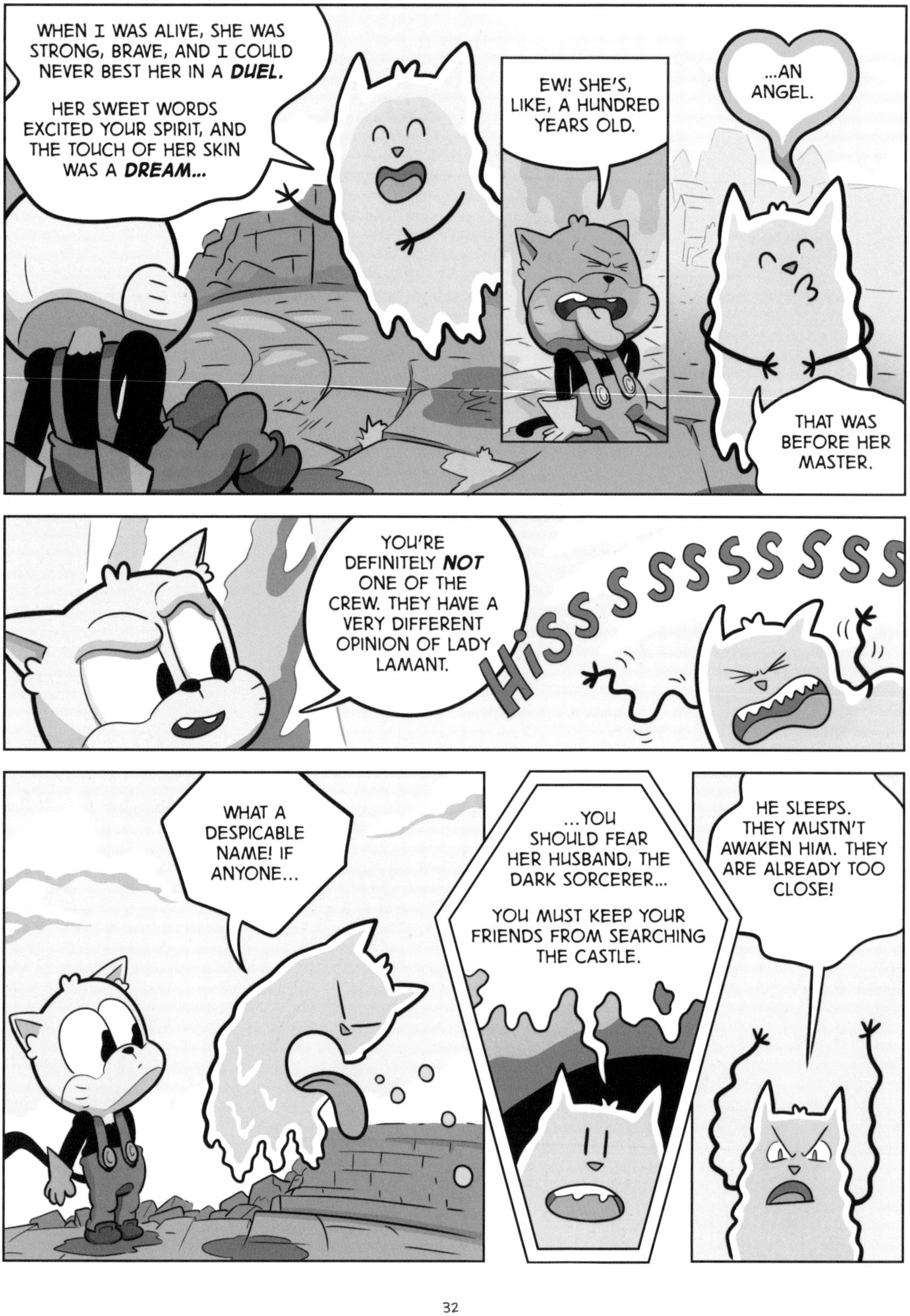
WHEN I WAS ALIVE, SHE WAS STRONG, BRAVE, AND I COULD NEVER BEST HER IN A DUEL.
HER SWEET WORDS EXCITED YOUR SPIRIT, AND THE TOUCH OF HER SKIN WAS A DREAM...
EW! SHE'S, LIKE, A HUNDRED YEARS OLD.
...AN ANGEL.
THAT WAS BEFORE HER MASTER.
YOU'RE DEFINITELY NOT ONE OF THE CREW. THEY HAVE A VERY DIFFERENT OPINION OF LADY LAMANT.
HISSSSSSSSSSS
WHAT A DESPICABLE NAME! IF ANYONE...
...YOU SHOULD FEAR HER HUSBAND, THE DARK SORCERER...
YOU MUST KEEP YOUR FRIENDS FROM SEARCHING THE CASTLE.
HE SLEEPS. THEY MUSTN'T AWAKEN HIM. THEY ARE ALREADY TOO CLOSE!

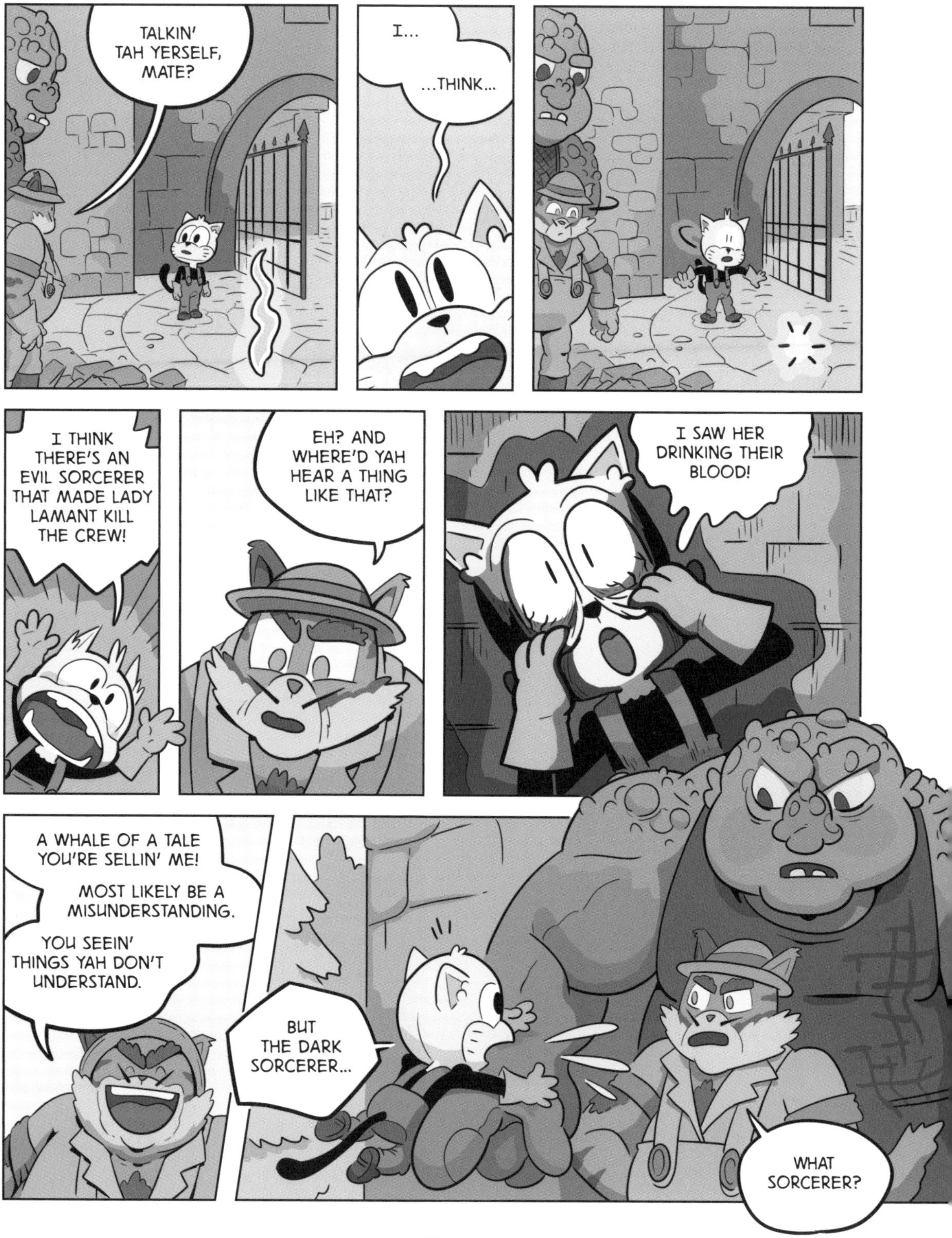
TALKIN' TAH YERSELF, MATE?
I...
...THINK...
I THINK THERE'S AN EVIL SORCERER THAT MADE LADY LAMANT KILL THE CREW!
EH? AND WHERE'D YAH HEAR A THING LIKE THAT?
I SAW HER DRINKING THEIR BLOOD!
A WHALE OF A TALE YOU'RE SELLIN' ME!
MOST LIKELY BE A MISUNDERSTANDING.
YOU SEEIN' THINGS YAH DON'T UNDERSTAND.
BUT THE DARK SORCERER...
WHAT SORCERER?

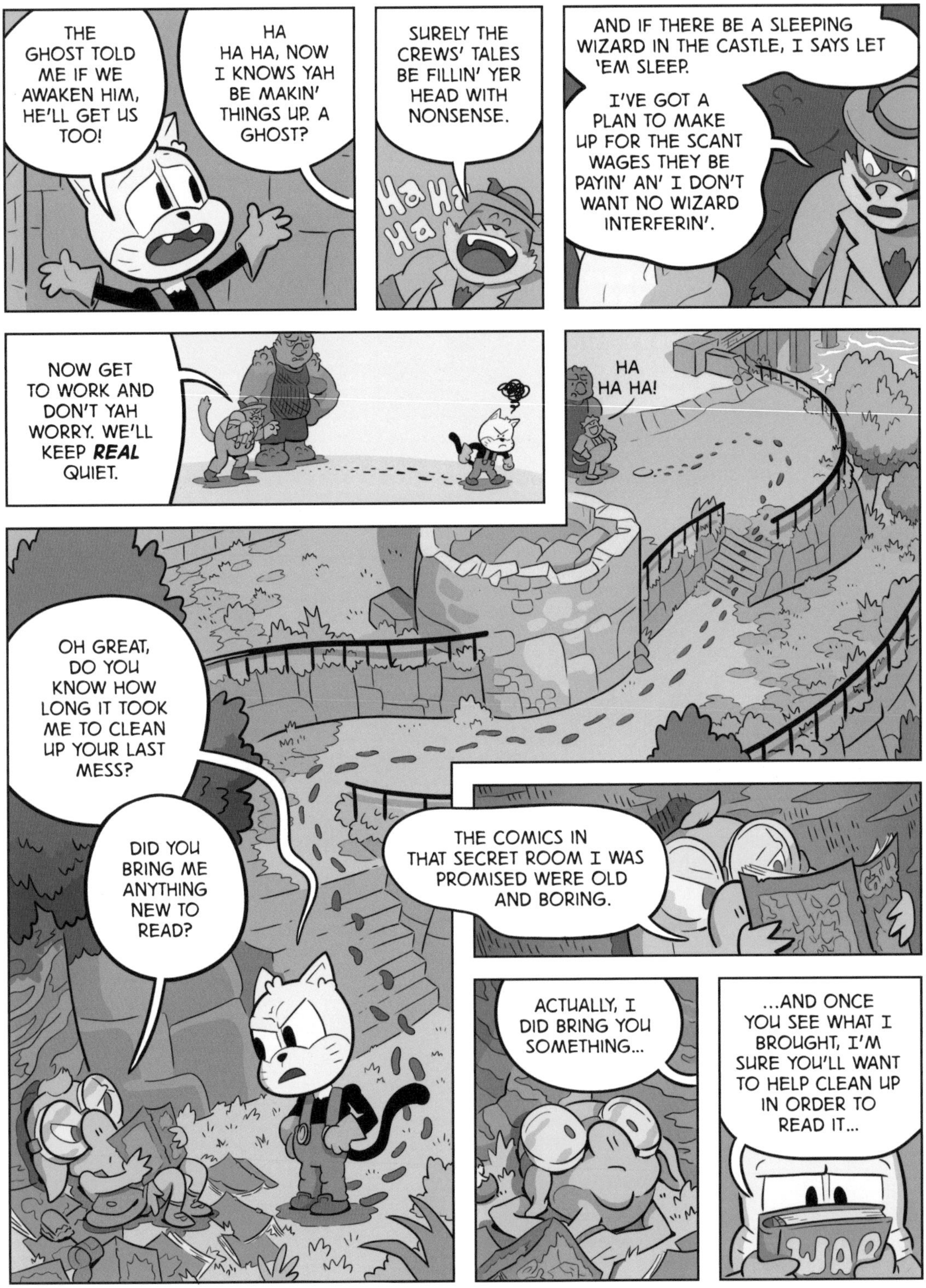
THE GHOST TOLD ME IF WE AWAKEN HIM, HE'LL GET US TOO!
HA HA HA, NOW I KNOWS YAH BE MAKIN' THINGS UP. A GHOST?
SURELY THE CREWS' TALES BE FILLIN' YER HEAD WITH NONSENSE.
Ha Ha Ha
AND IF THERE BE A SLEEPING WIZARD IN THE CASTLE, I SAYS LET 'EM SLEEP.
I'VE GOT A PLAN TO MAKE UP FOR THE SCANT WAGES THEY BE PAYIN' AN' I DON'T WANT NO WIZARD INTERFERIN'.
NOW GET TO WORK AND DON'T YAH WORRY. WE'LL KEEP ***REAL*** QUIET.
HA HA HA!
OH GREAT, DO YOU KNOW HOW LONG IT TOOK ME TO CLEAN UP YOUR LAST MESS?
DID YOU BRING ME ANYTHING NEW TO READ?
THE COMICS IN THAT SECRET ROOM I WAS PROMISED WERE OLD AND BORING.
ACTUALLY, I DID BRING YOU SOMETHING...
...AND ONCE YOU SEE WHAT I BROUGHT, I'M SURE YOU'LL WANT TO HELP CLEAN UP IN ORDER TO READ IT...
WAP

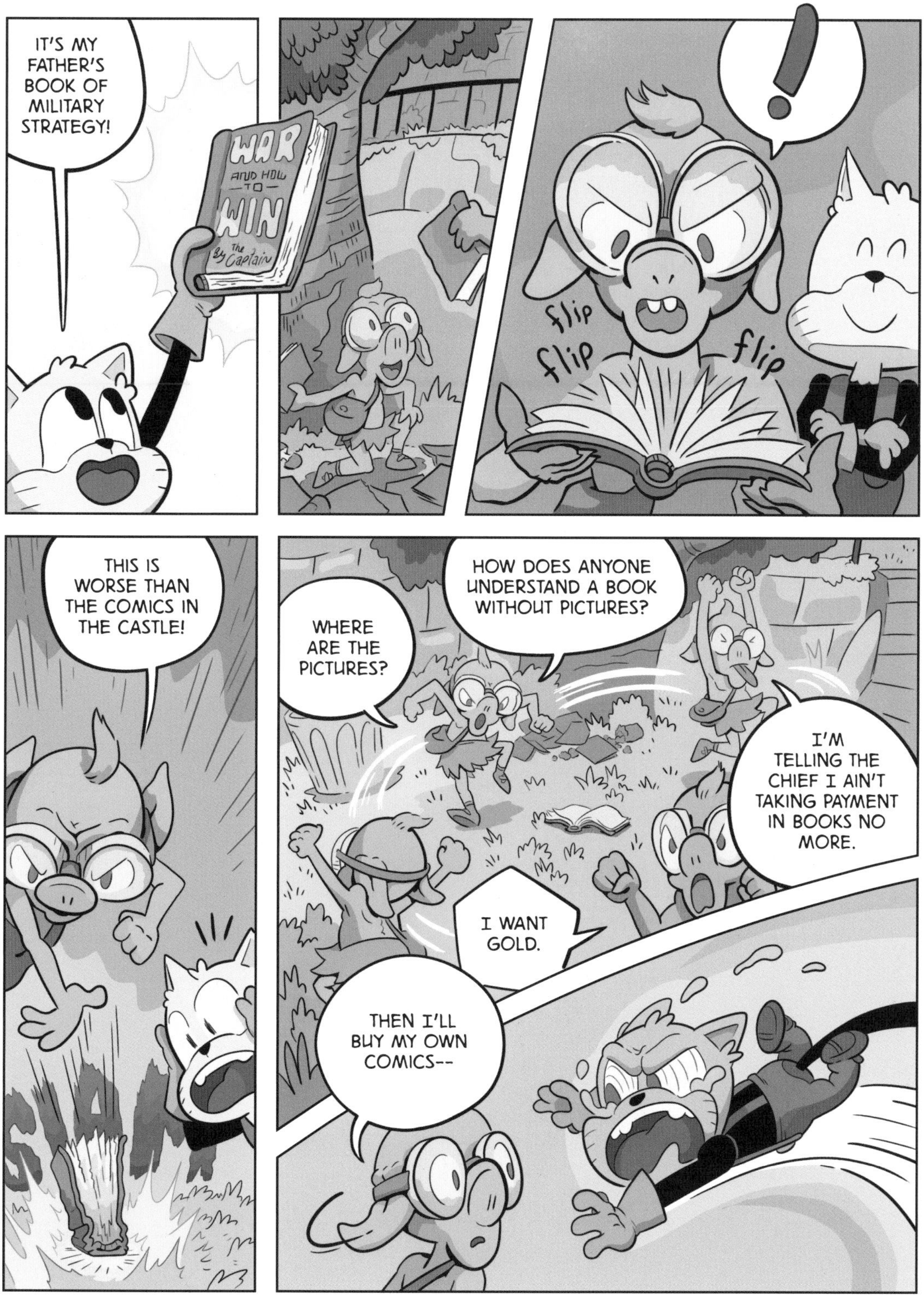
IT'S MY FATHER'S BOOK OF MILITARY STRATEGY!
WAR AND HOW TO WIN
The By Captain
!
flip flip flip
THIS IS WORSE THAN THE COMICS IN THE CASTLE!
HOW DOES ANYONE UNDERSTAND A BOOK WITHOUT PICTURES?
WHERE ARE THE PICTURES?
I'M TELLING THE CHIEF I AIN'T TAKING PAYMENT IN BOOKS NO MORE.
I WANT GOLD.
THEN I'LL BUY MY OWN COMICS--

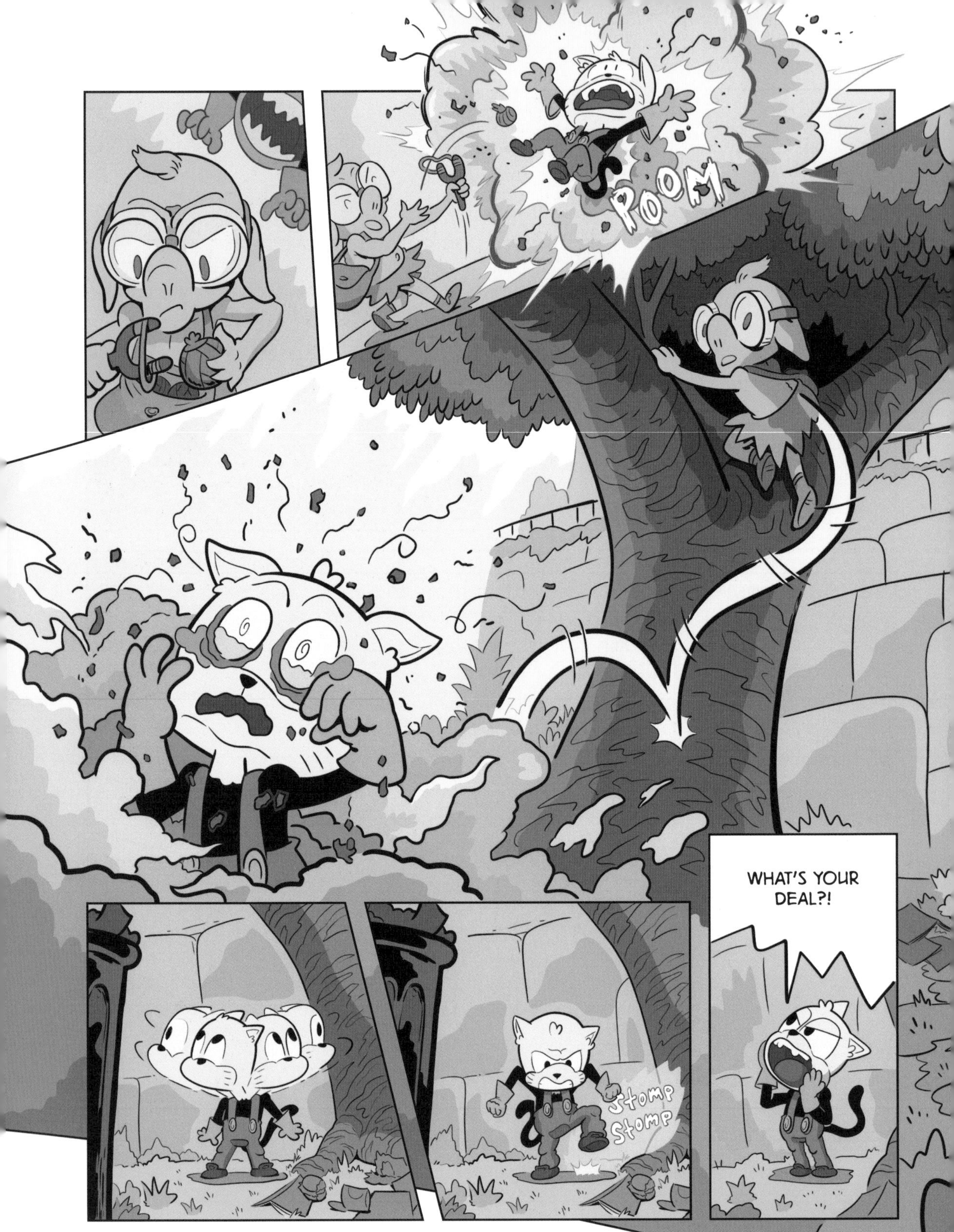
POOM
Stomp
Stomp
WHAT'S YOUR DEAL?!

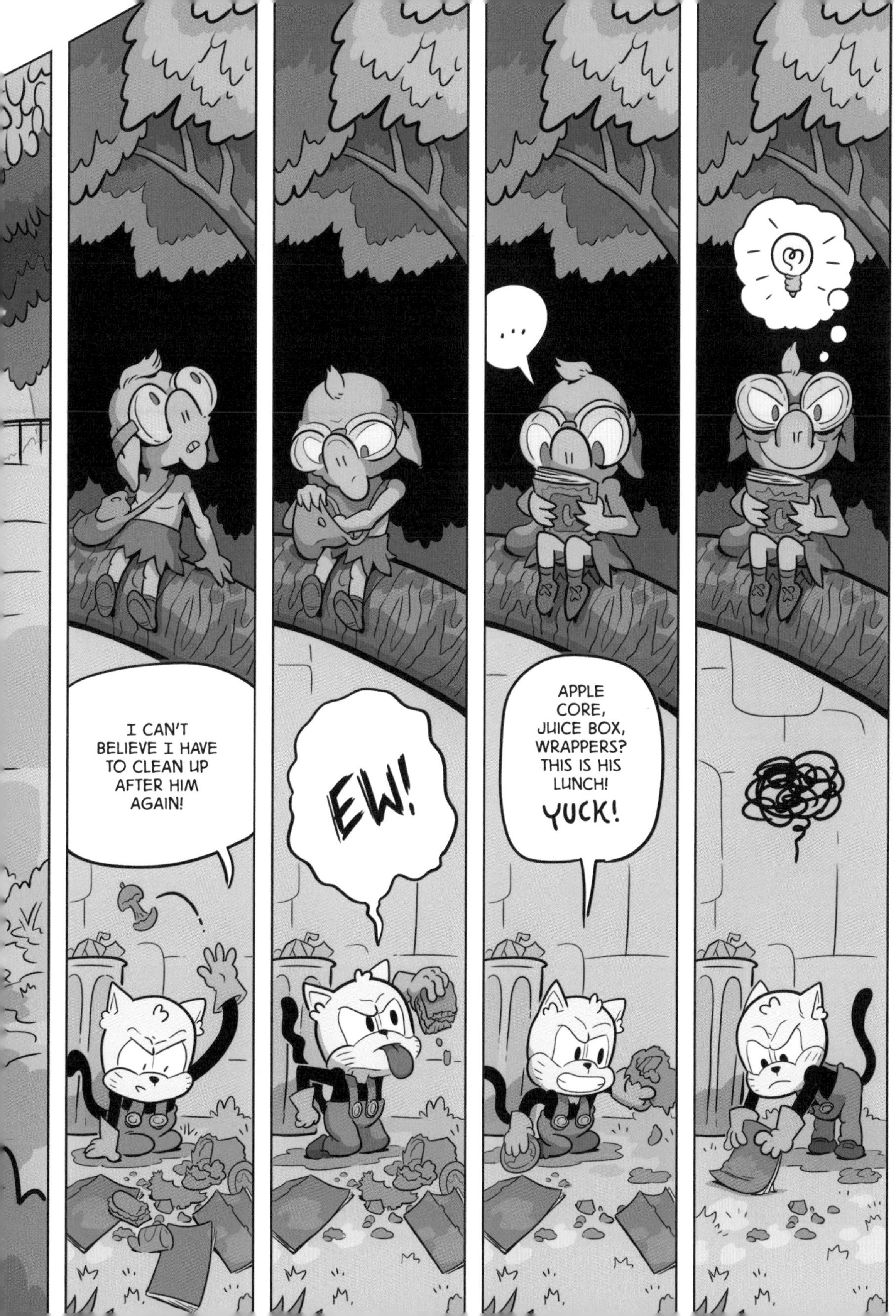
I CAN'T BELIEVE I HAVE TO CLEAN UP AFTER HIM AGAIN!
EW!
...
APPLE CORE, JUICE BOX, WRAPPERS? THIS IS HIS LUNCH!
YUCK!

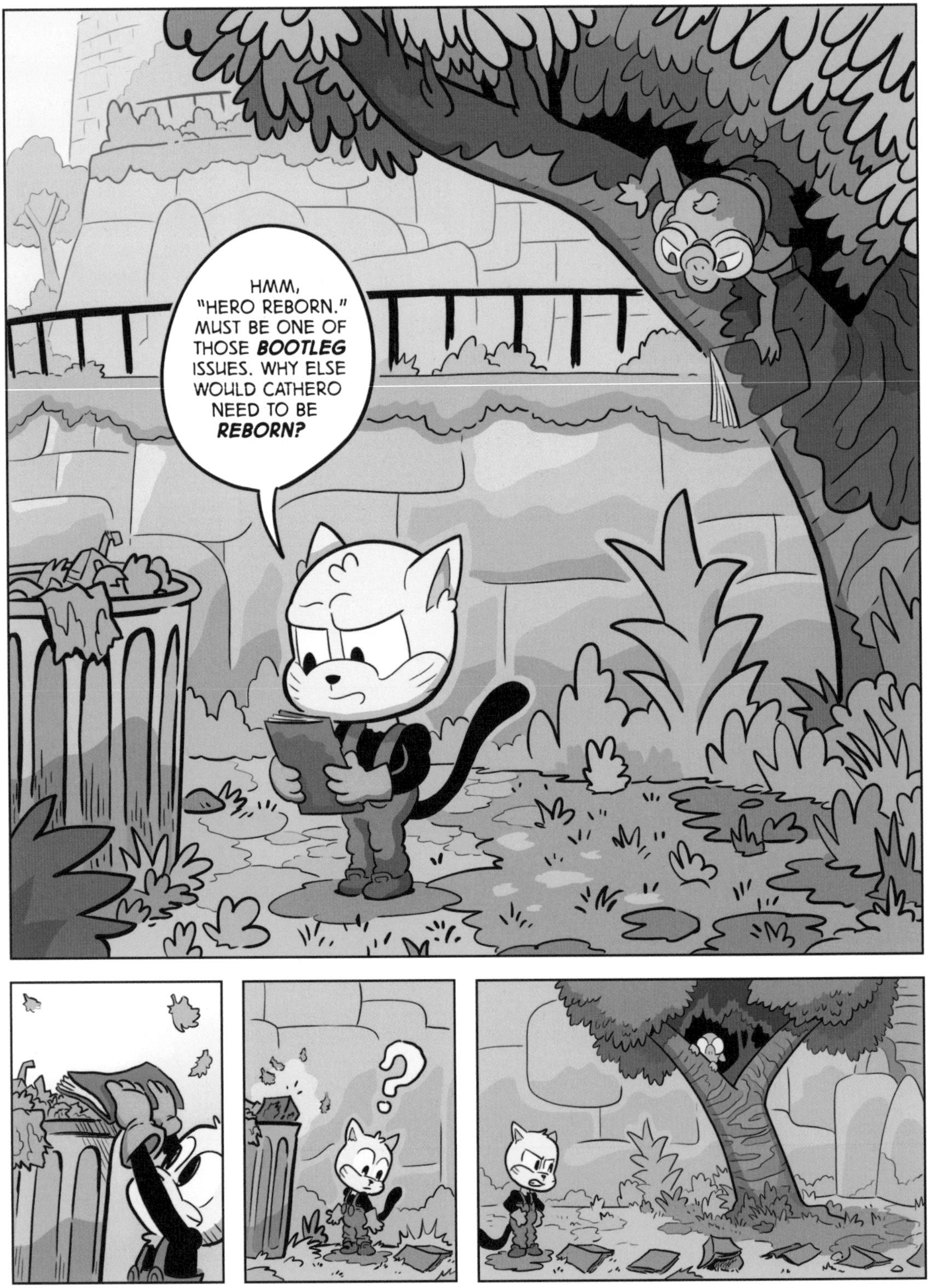
HMM, "HERO REBORN." MUST BE ONE OF THOSE **BOOTLEG** ISSUES. WHY ELSE WOULD CATHERO NEED TO BE **REBORN?**
?

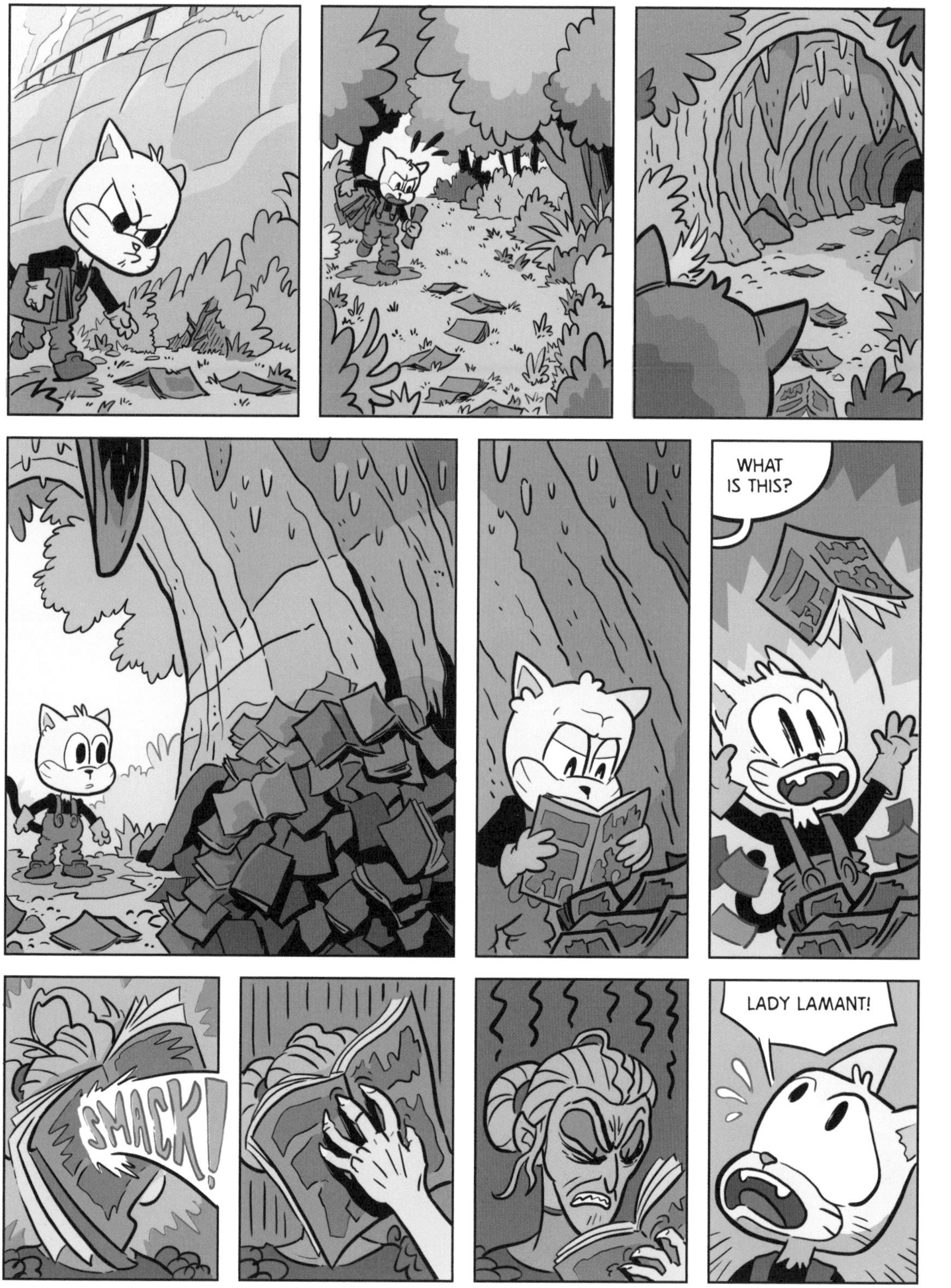
WHAT IS THIS?
SMACK!
LADY LAMANT!

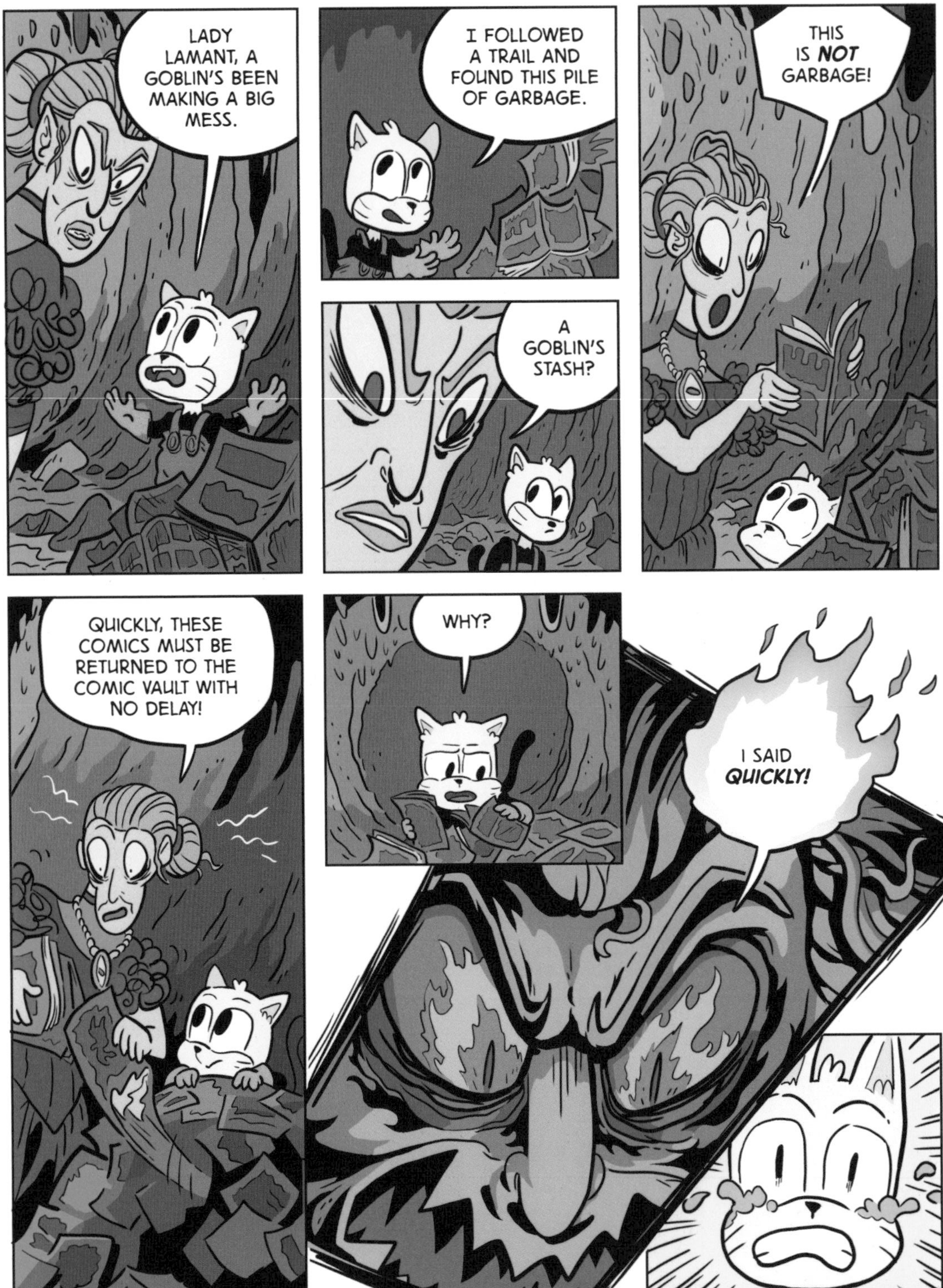
LADY LAMANT, A GOBLIN'S BEEN MAKING A BIG MESS.
I FOLLOWED A TRAIL AND FOUND THIS PILE OF GARBAGE.
A GOBLIN'S STASH?
THIS IS **NOT** GARBAGE!
QUICKLY, THESE COMICS MUST BE RETURNED TO THE COMIC VAULT WITH NO DELAY!
WHY?
I SAID ***QUICKLY!***

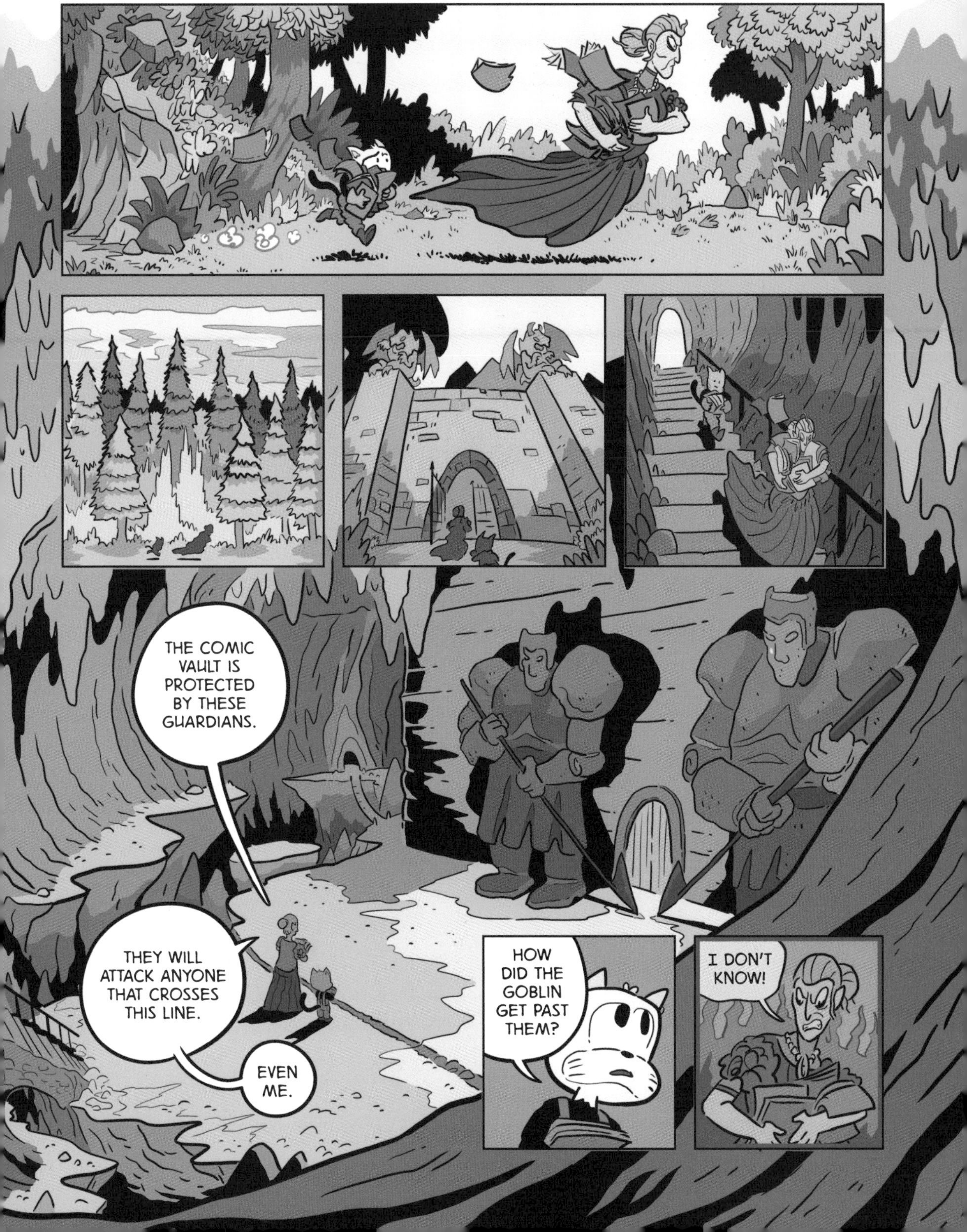
THE COMIC VAULT IS PROTECTED BY THESE GUARDIANS.
THEY WILL ATTACK ANYONE THAT CROSSES THIS LINE.
EVEN ME.
HOW DID THE GOBLIN GET PAST THEM?
I DON'T KNOW!

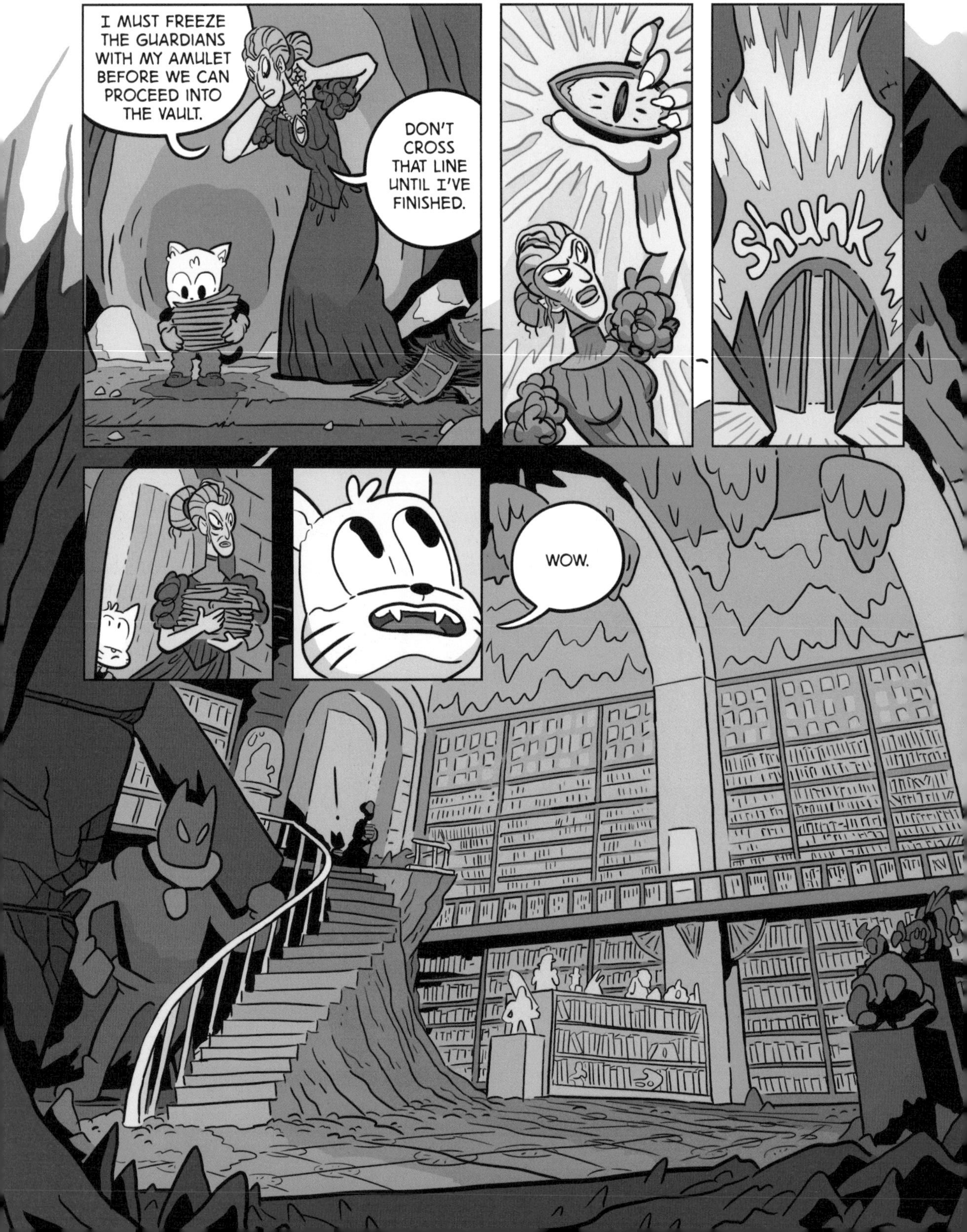
I MUST FREEZE THE GUARDIANS WITH MY AMULET BEFORE WE CAN PROCEED INTO THE VAULT.
DON'T CROSS THAT LINE UNTIL I'VE FINISHED.
SHUNK
WOW.

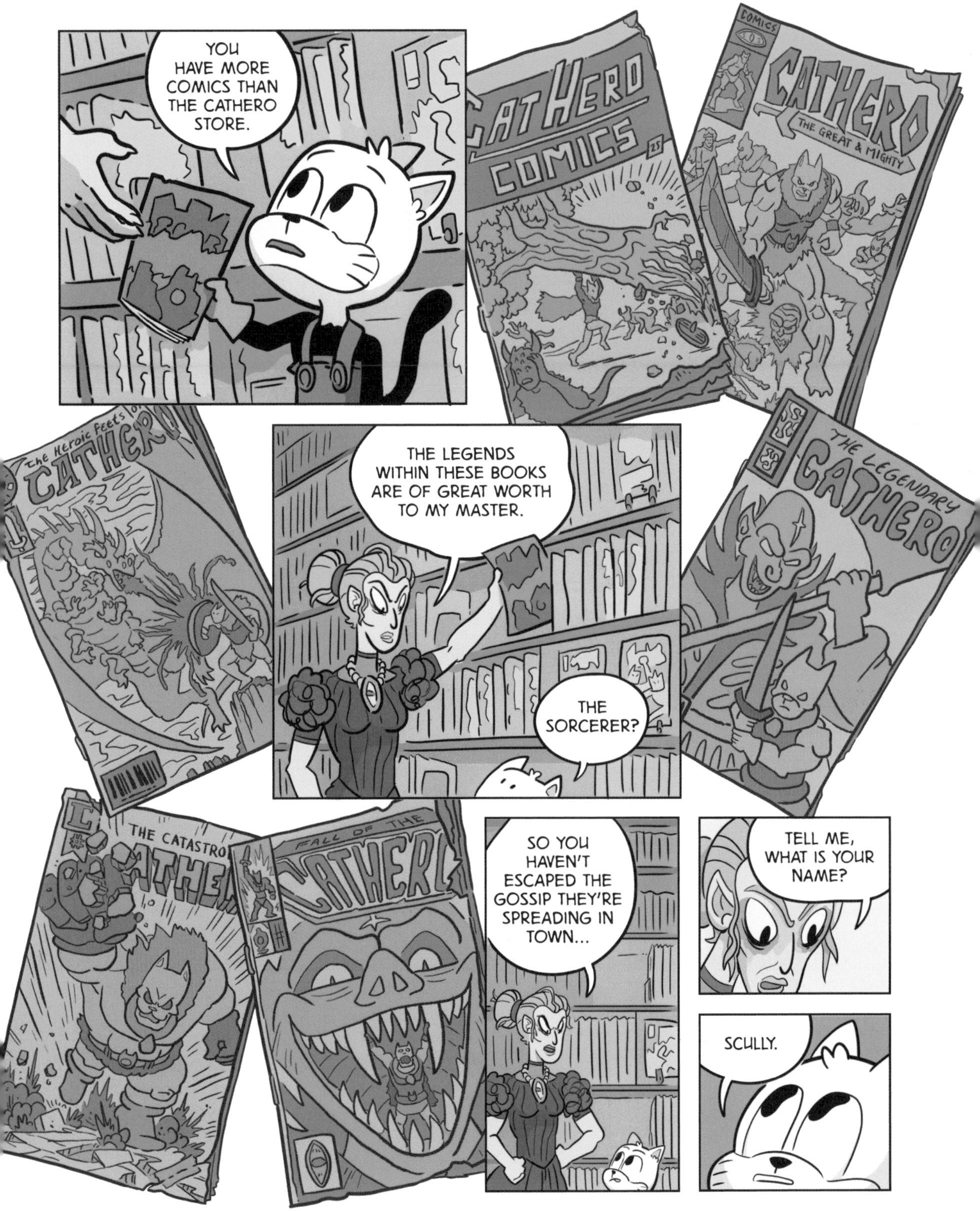
YOU HAVE MORE COMICS THAN THE CATHERO STORE.
CATHERO COMICS
CATHERO THE GREAT & MIGHTY
The Heroic Feets of CATHERO
THE LEGENDS WITHIN THESE BOOKS ARE OF GREAT WORTH TO MY MASTER.
THE SORCERER?
THE LEGENDARY CATHERO
FALL OF THE CATHERO
SO YOU HAVEN'T ESCAPED THE GOSSIP THEY'RE SPREADING IN TOWN...
TELL ME, WHAT IS YOUR NAME?
SCULLY.

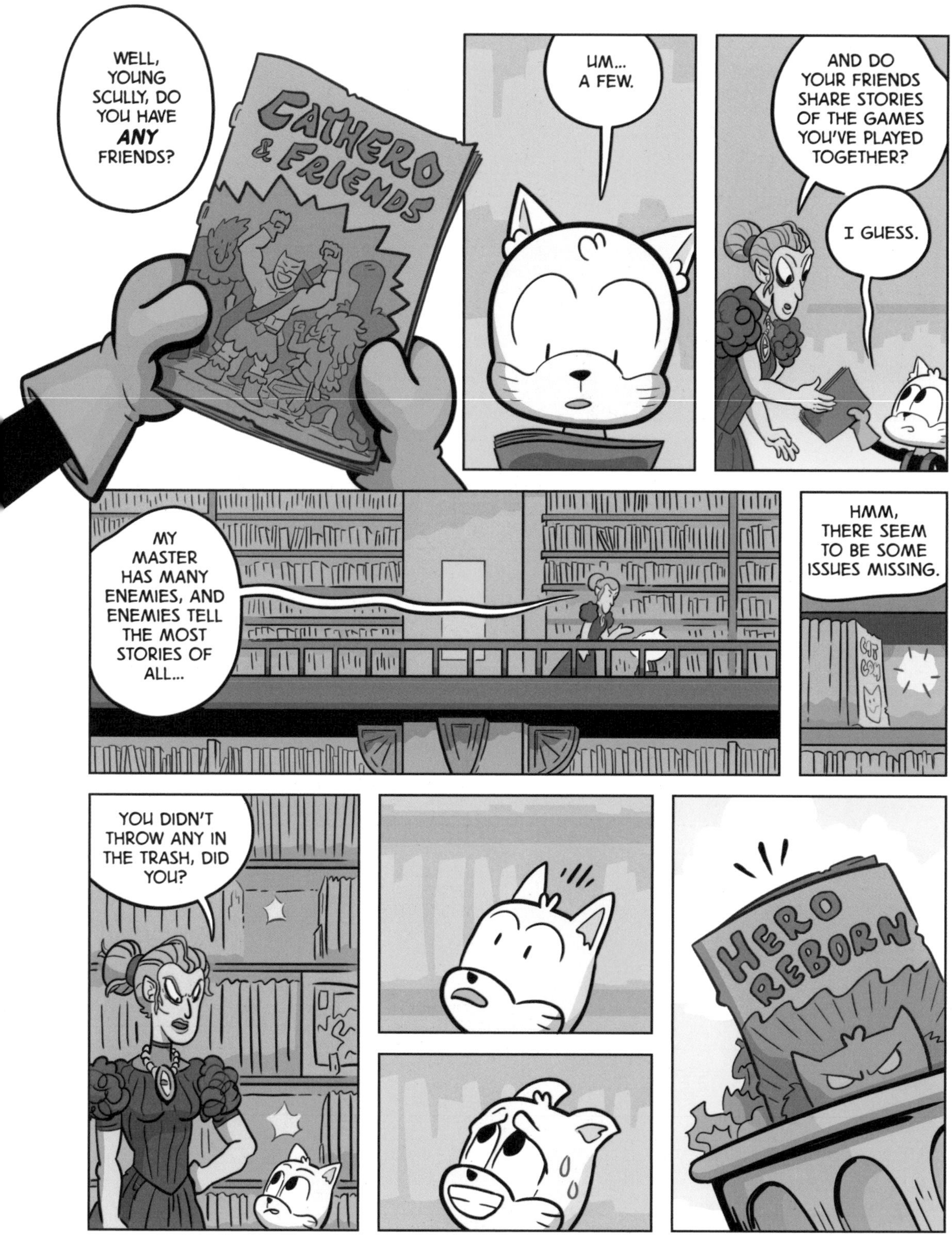
WELL, YOUNG SCULLY, DO YOU HAVE ANY FRIENDS?
CATHERO & FRIENDS
UM... A FEW.
AND DO YOUR FRIENDS SHARE STORIES OF THE GAMES YOU'VE PLAYED TOGETHER?
I GUESS.
MY MASTER HAS MANY ENEMIES, AND ENEMIES TELL THE MOST STORIES OF ALL...
HMM, THERE SEEM TO BE SOME ISSUES MISSING.
YOU DIDN'T THROW ANY IN THE TRASH, DID YOU?
HERO REBORN

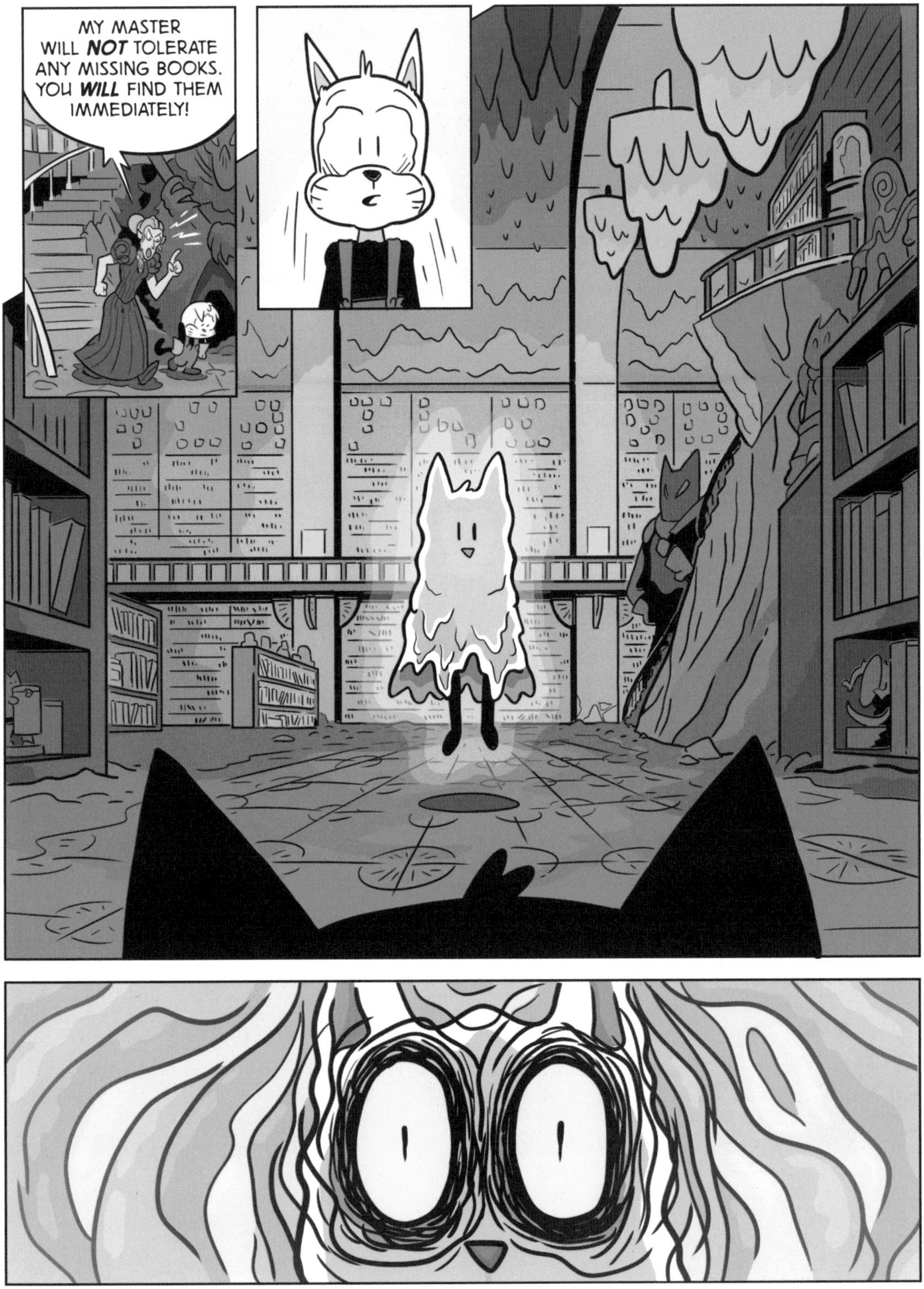
MY MASTER WILL NOT TOLERATE ANY MISSING BOOKS. YOU WILL FIND THEM IMMEDIATELY!

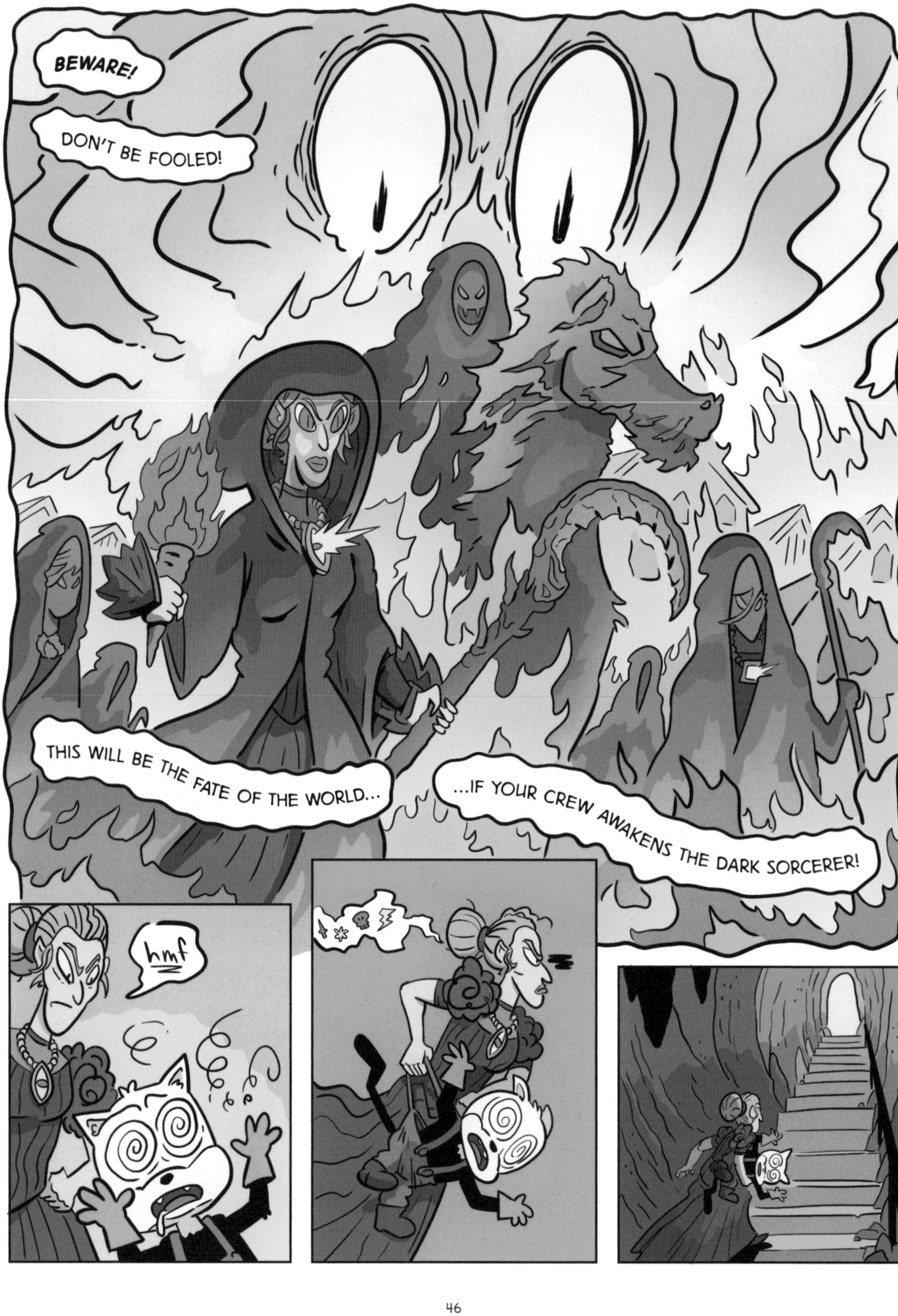
BEWARE!
DON'T BE FOOLED!
THIS WILL BE THE FATE OF THE WORLD...
...IF YOUR CREW AWAKENS THE DARK SORCERER!
hmf

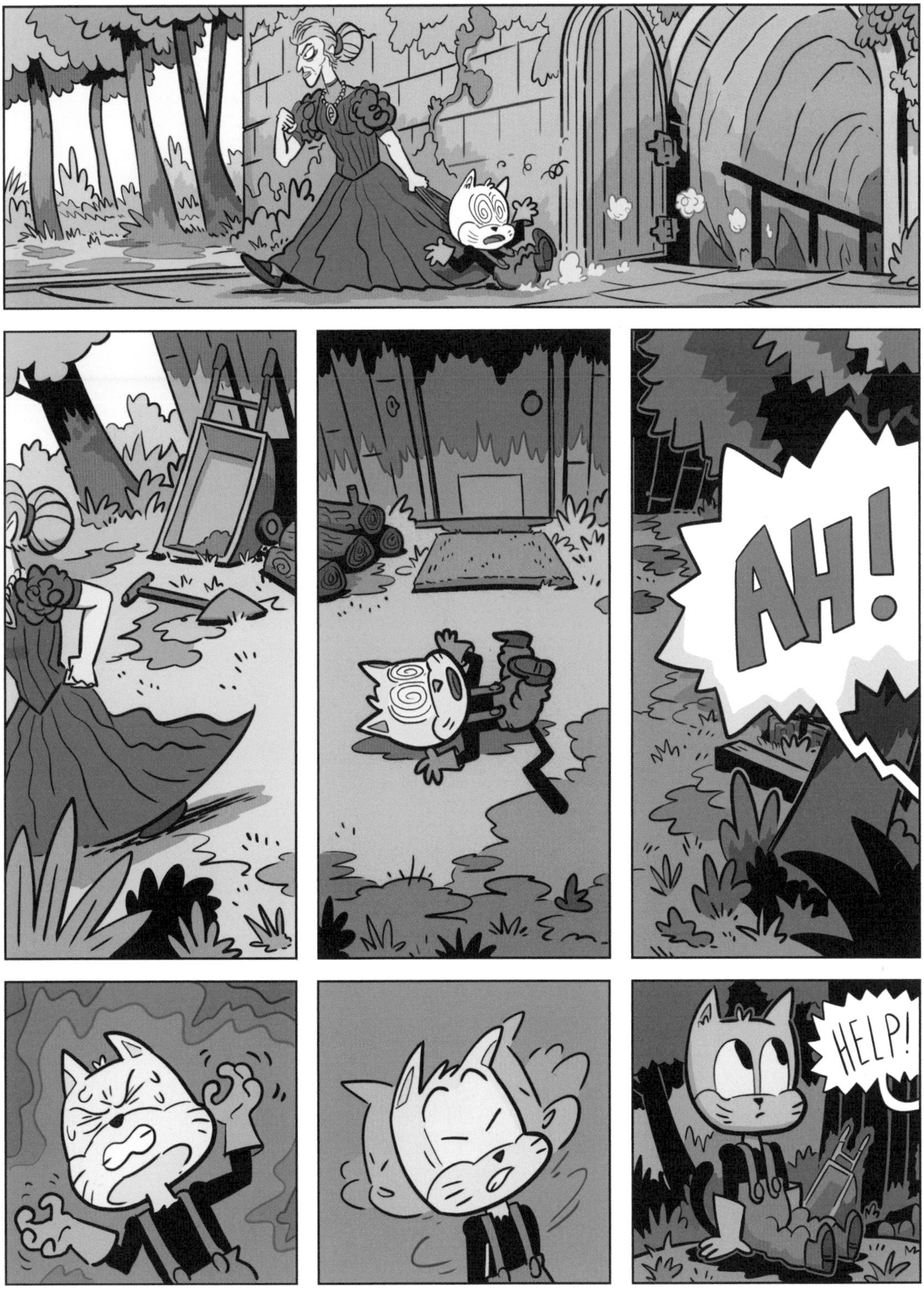
AH!
HELP!

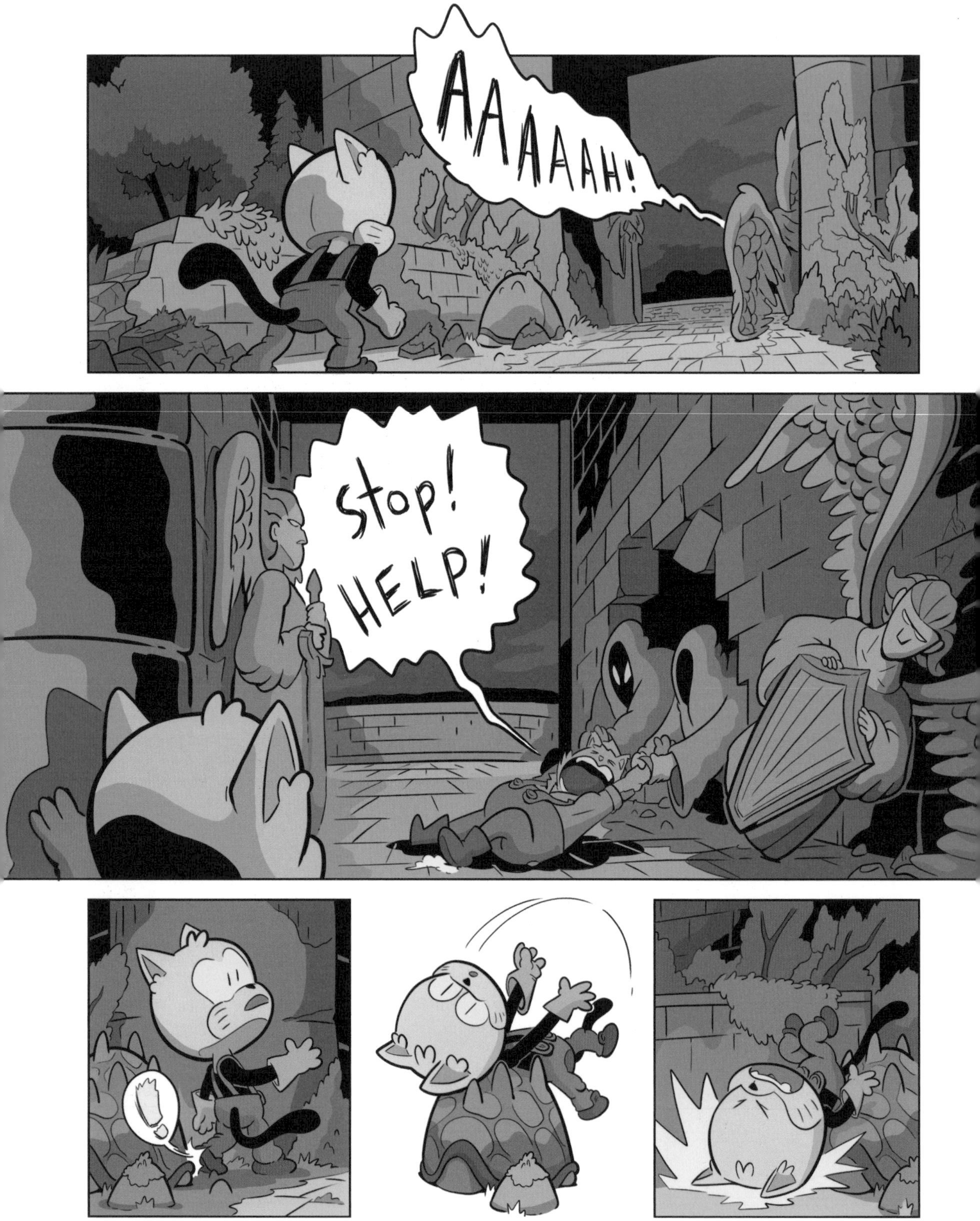
AAAAAAH!
Stop!
HELP!

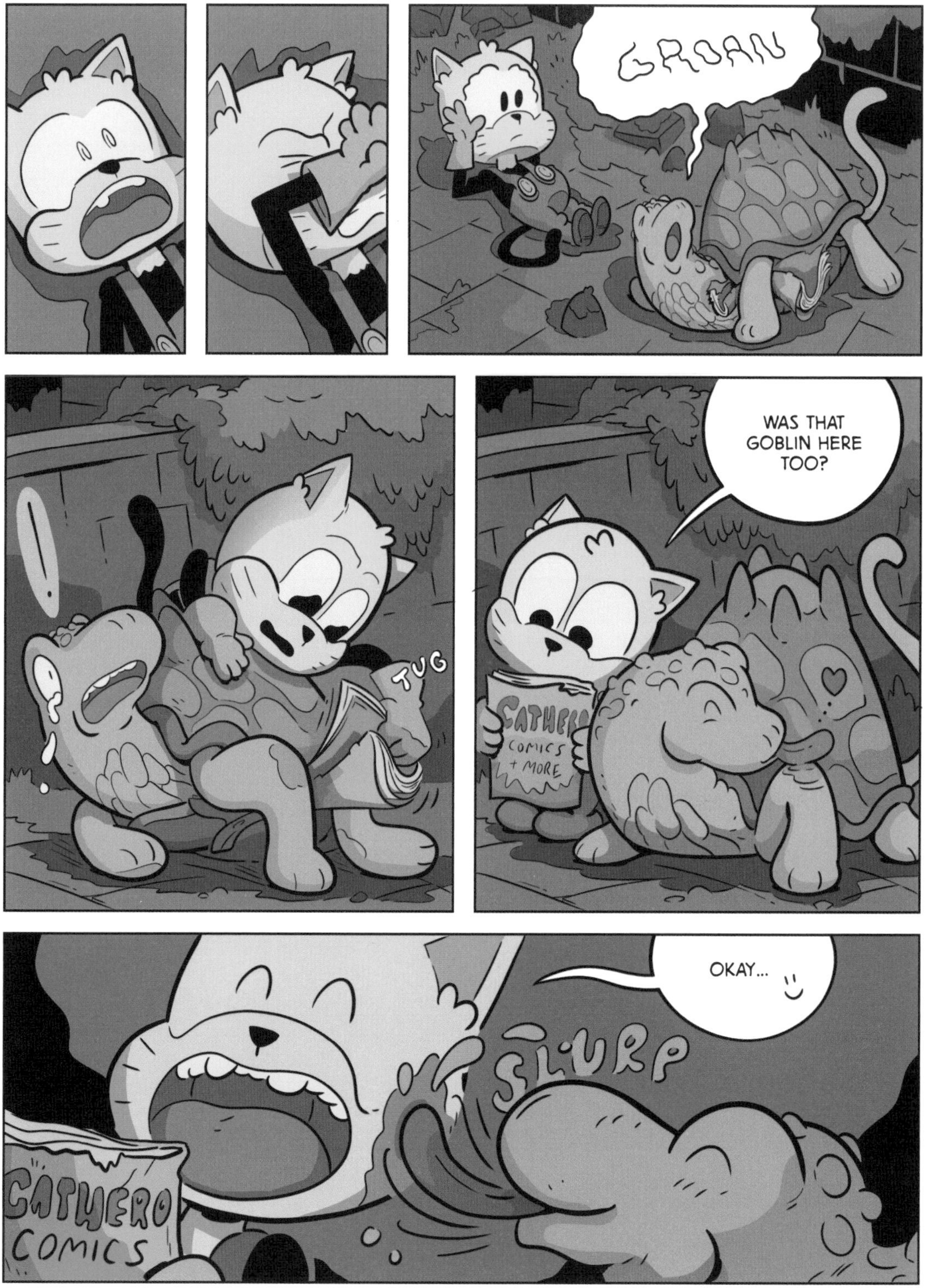
GROAN
!
TUG
WAS THAT GOBLIN HERE TOO?
CATHERO COMICS + MORE
OKAY...
SLURP
CATHERO COMICS

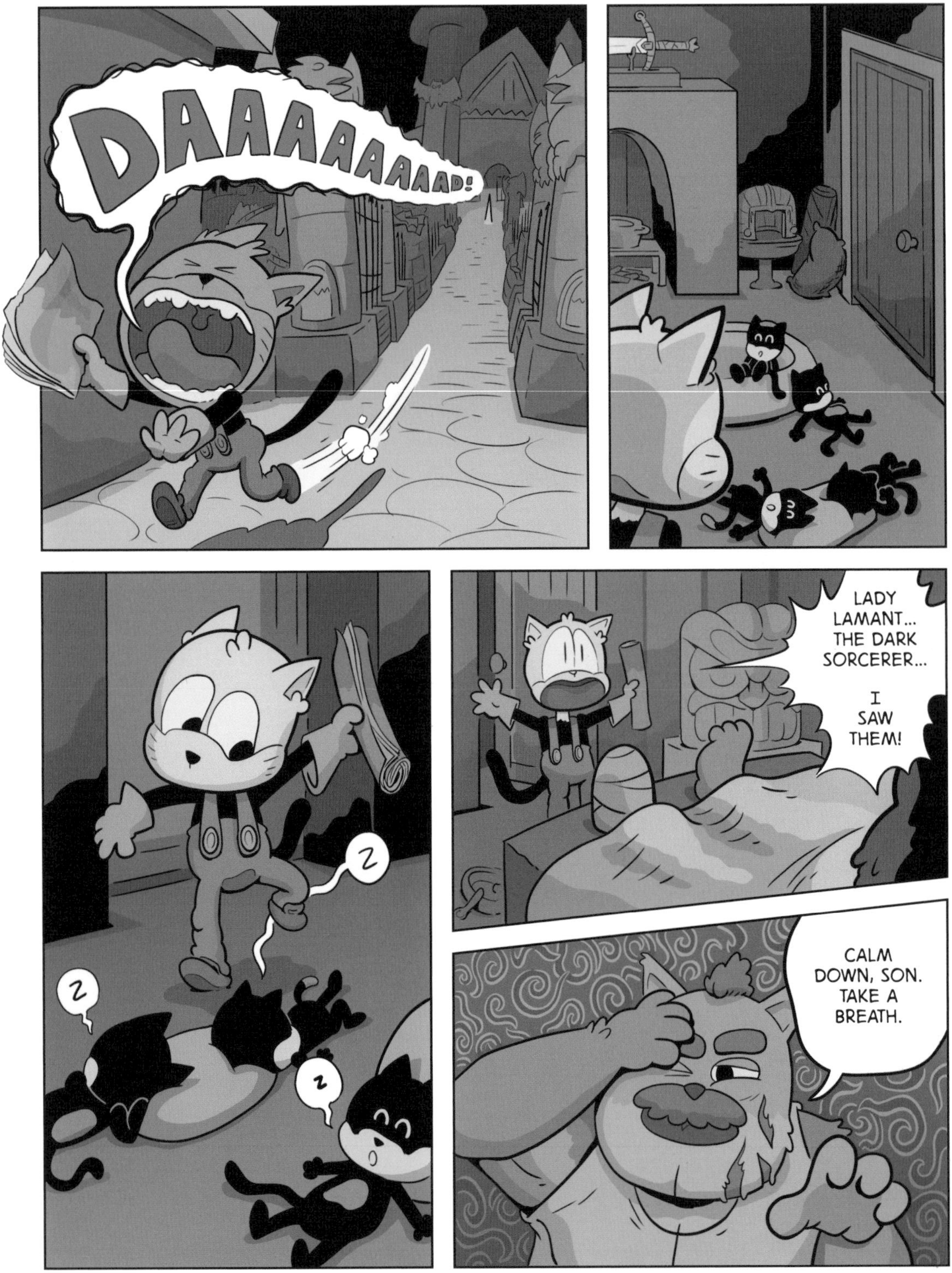
DAAAAAAAAAAD!
LADY LAMANT... THE DARK SORCERER...
I SAW THEM!
CALM DOWN, SON. TAKE A BREATH.

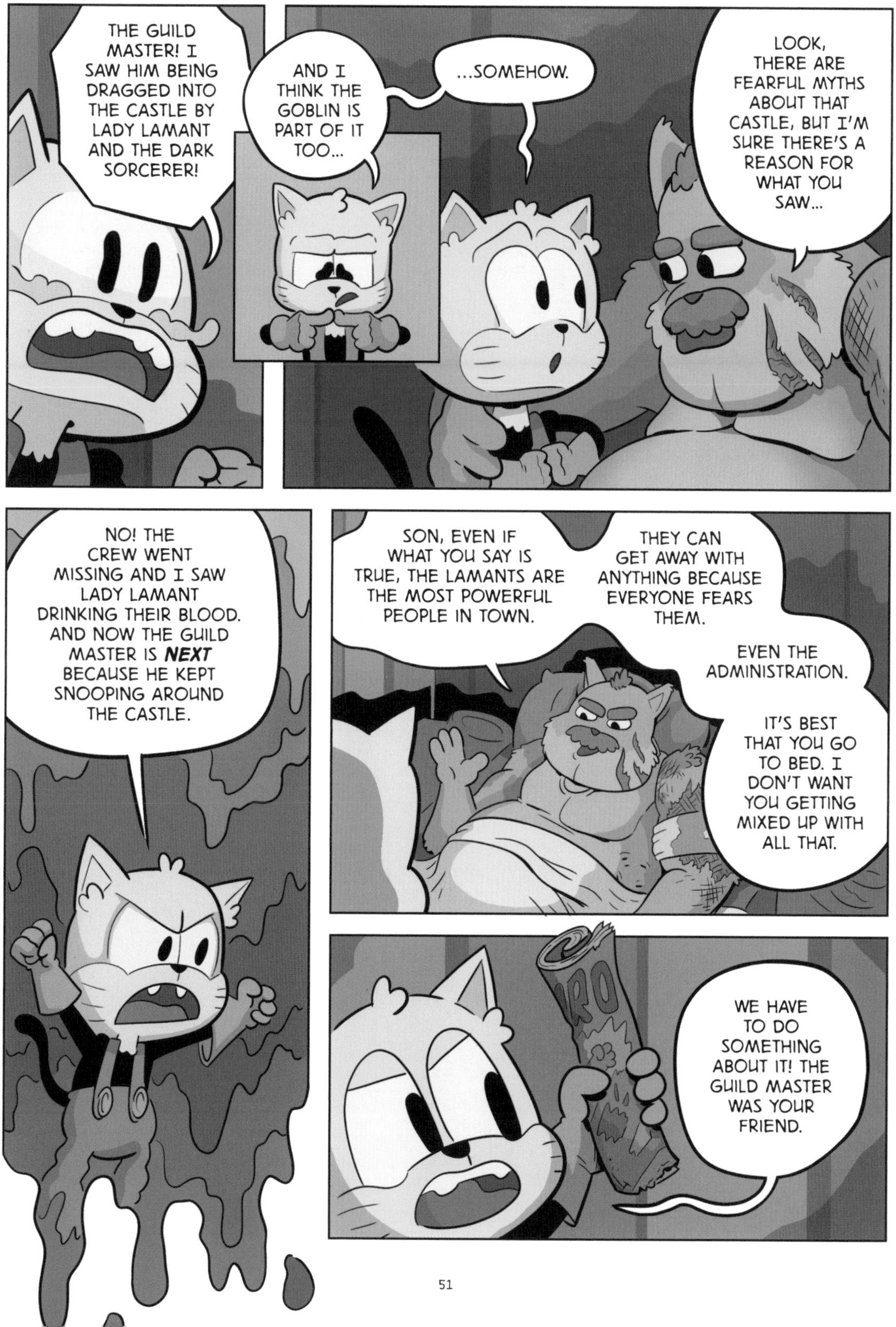
THE GUILD MASTER! I SAW HIM BEING DRAGGED INTO THE CASTLE BY LADY LAMANT AND THE DARK SORCERER!
AND I THINK THE GOBLIN IS PART OF IT TOO...
...SOMEHOW.
LOOK, THERE ARE FEARFUL MYTHS ABOUT THAT CASTLE, BUT I'M SURE THERE'S A REASON FOR WHAT YOU SAW...
NO! THE CREW WENT MISSING AND I SAW LADY LAMANT DRINKING THEIR BLOOD. AND NOW THE GUILD MASTER IS ***NEXT*** BECAUSE HE KEPT SNOOPING AROUND THE CASTLE.
SON, EVEN IF WHAT YOU SAY IS TRUE, THE LAMANTS ARE THE MOST POWERFUL PEOPLE IN TOWN.
THEY CAN GET AWAY WITH ANYTHING BECAUSE EVERYONE FEARS THEM.
EVEN THE ADMINISTRATION.
IT'S BEST THAT YOU GO TO BED. I DON'T WANT YOU GETTING MIXED UP WITH ALL THAT.
WE HAVE TO DO SOMETHING ABOUT IT! THE GUILD MASTER WAS YOUR FRIEND.

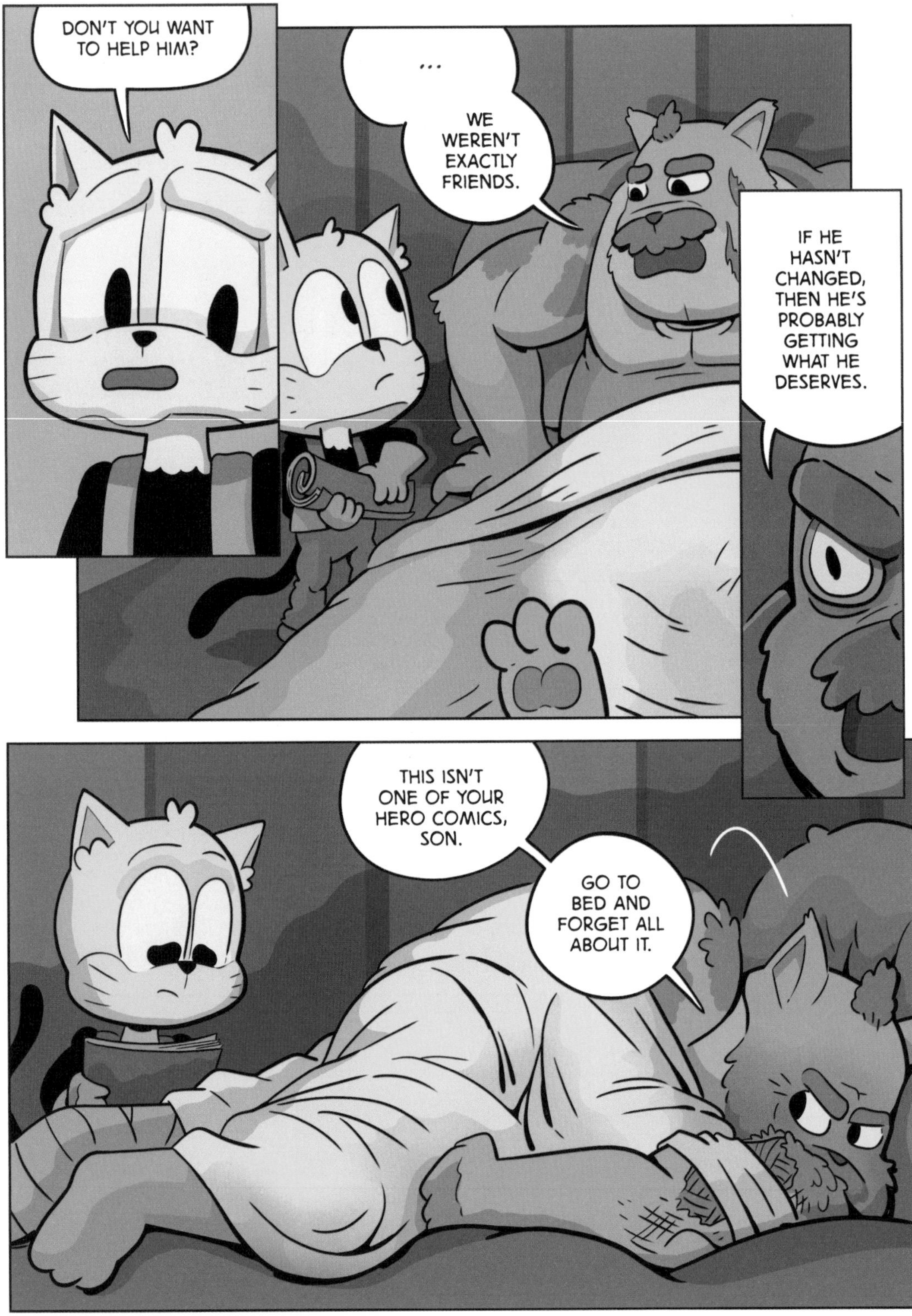
DON'T YOU WANT TO HELP HIM?
...
WE WEREN'T EXACTLY FRIENDS.
IF HE HASN'T CHANGED, THEN HE'S PROBABLY GETTING WHAT HE DESERVES.
THIS ISN'T ONE OF YOUR HERO COMICS, SON.
GO TO BED AND FORGET ALL ABOUT IT.

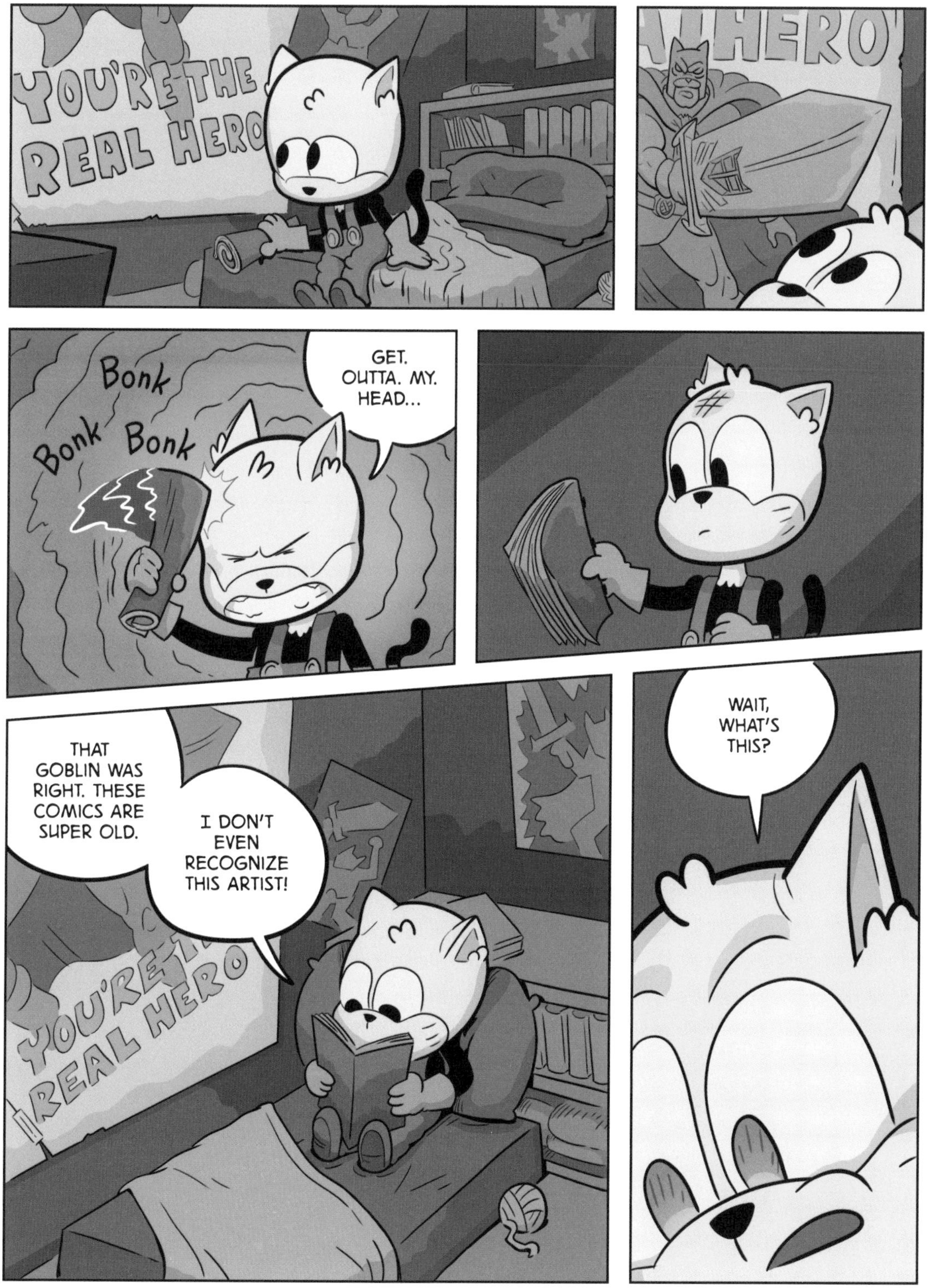
YOU'RE THE REAL HERO
HERO
Bonk
Bonk Bonk
GET. OUTTA. MY. HEAD...
THAT GOBLIN WAS RIGHT. THESE COMICS ARE SUPER OLD.
I DON'T EVEN RECOGNIZE THIS ARTIST!
YOU'RE THE REAL HERO
WAIT, WHAT'S THIS?

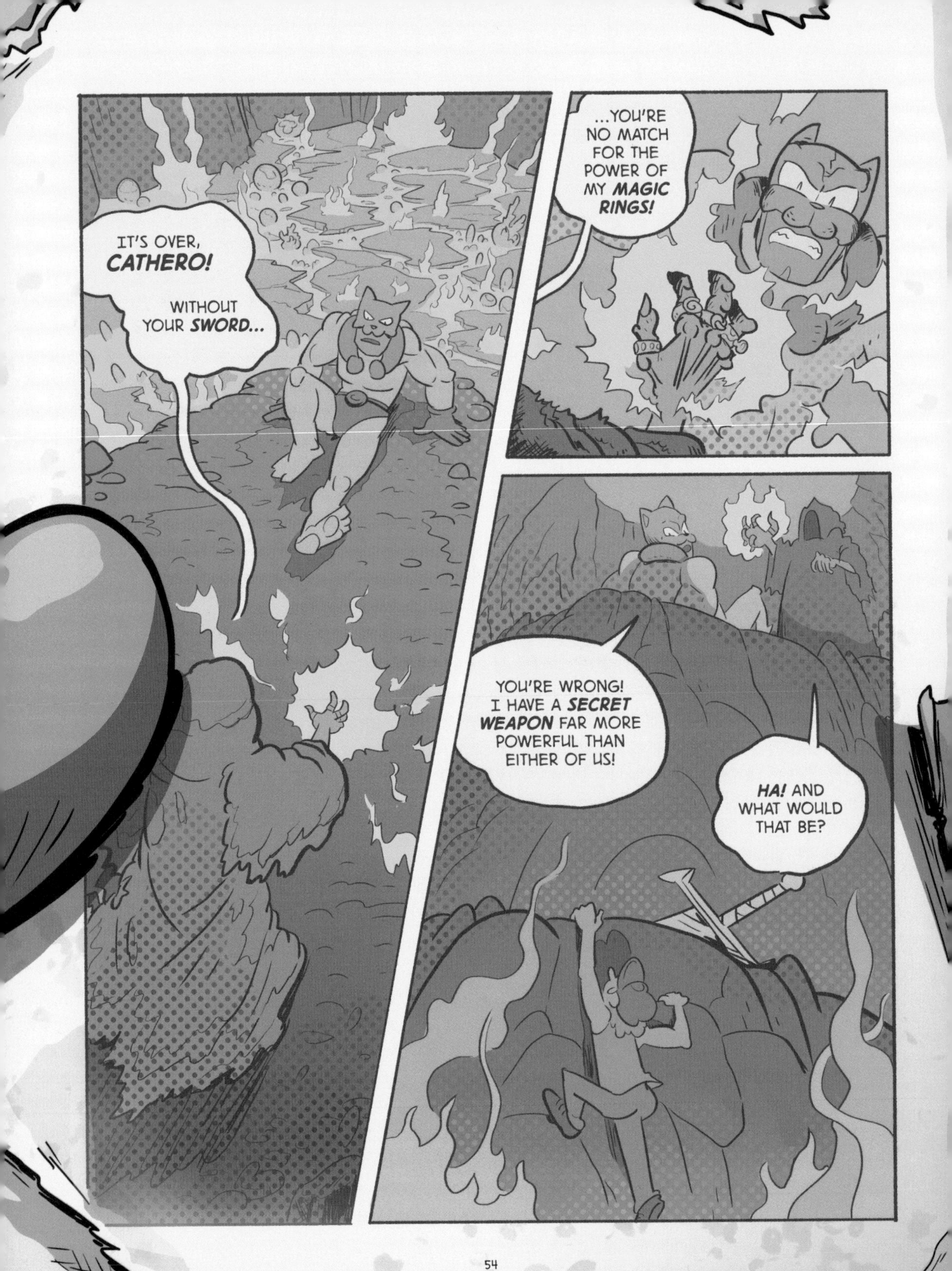
IT'S OVER, CATHERO!
WITHOUT YOUR SWORD...
...YOU'RE NO MATCH FOR THE POWER OF MY MAGIC RINGS!
YOU'RE WRONG! I HAVE A SECRET WEAPON FAR MORE POWERFUL THAN EITHER OF US!
HA! AND WHAT WOULD THAT BE?

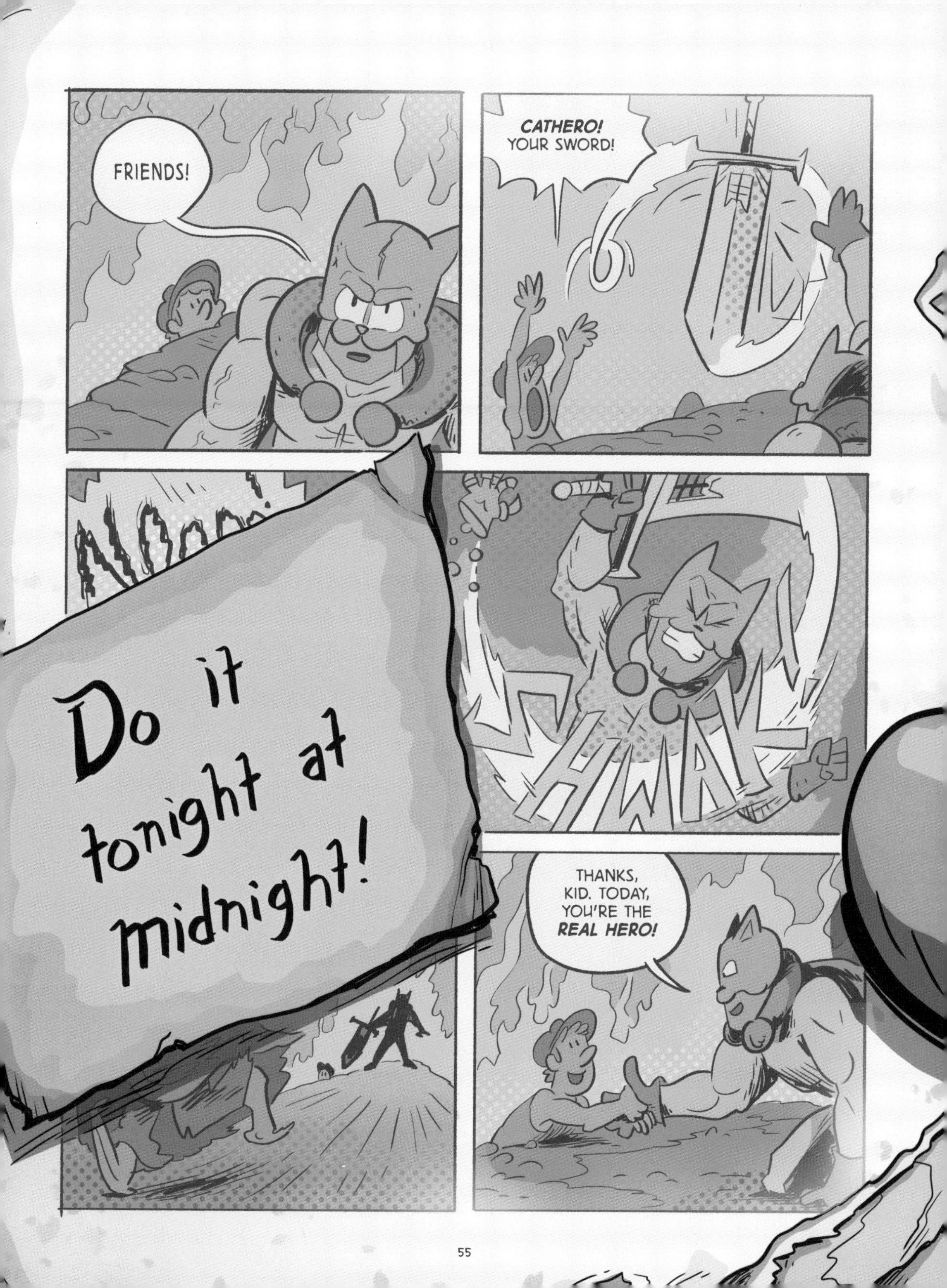
FRIENDS!
CATHERO! YOUR SWORD!
NOOO!
Do it tonight at midnight!
SHWAK!
THANKS, KID. TODAY, YOU'RE THE REAL HERO!

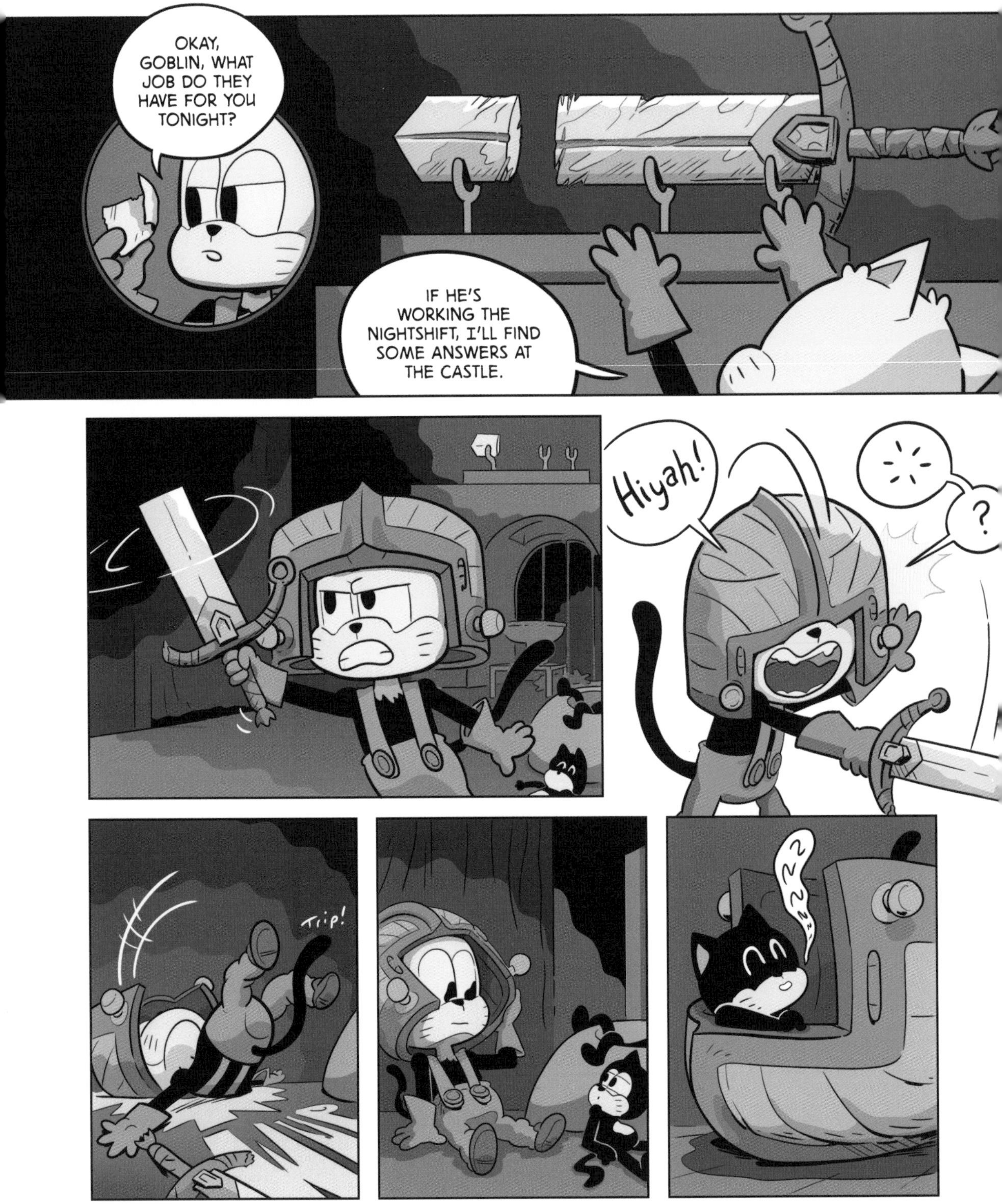

OKAY, GOBLIN, WHAT JOB DO THEY HAVE FOR YOU TONIGHT?
IF HE'S WORKING THE NIGHTSHIFT, I'LL FIND SOME ANSWERS AT THE CASTLE.
Hiyah!
?
Trip!

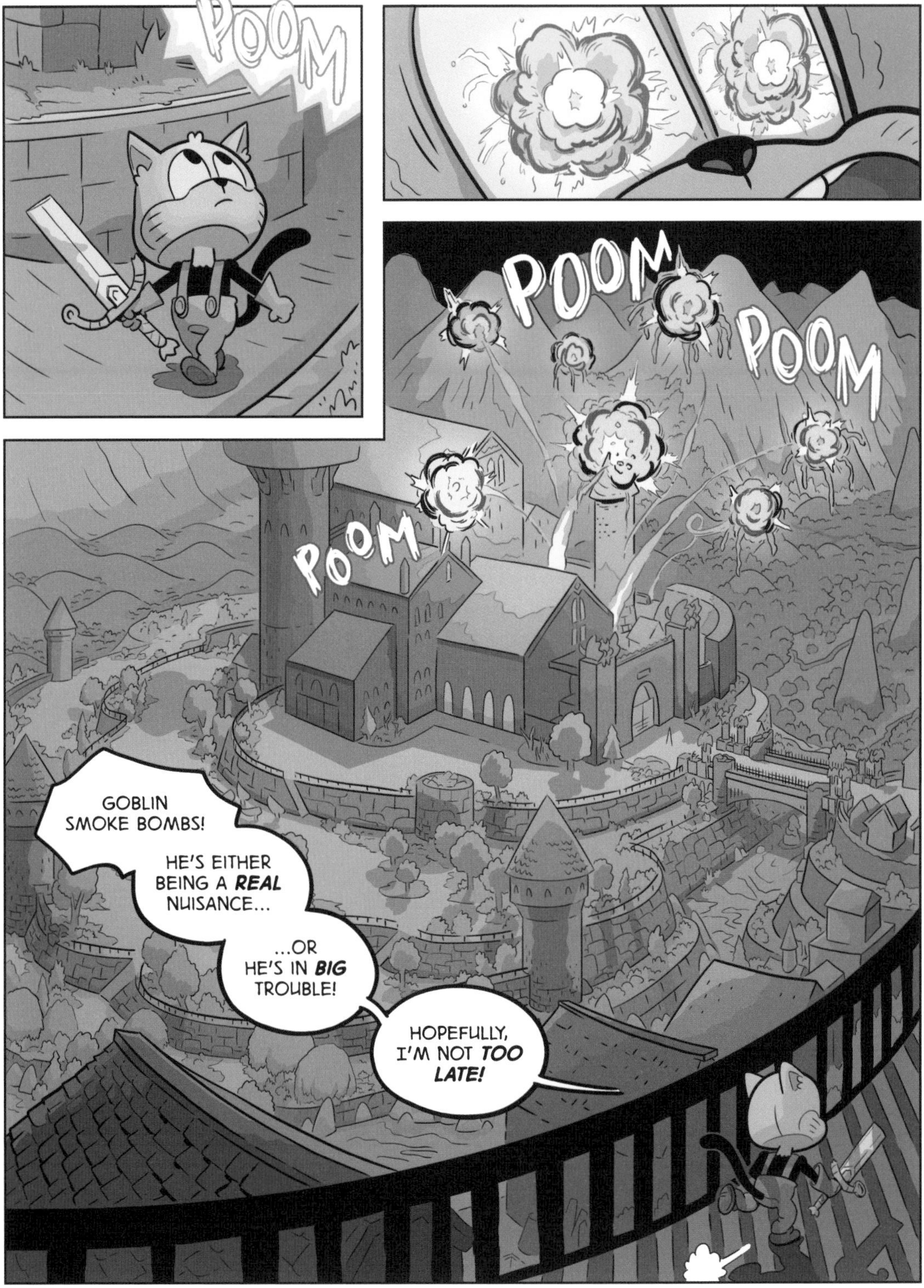
POOM
POOM
POOM
POOM
GOBLIN SMOKE BOMBS!
HE'S EITHER BEING A **REAL** NUISANCE...
...OR HE'S IN **BIG** TROUBLE!
HOPEFULLY, I'M NOT **TOO LATE!**

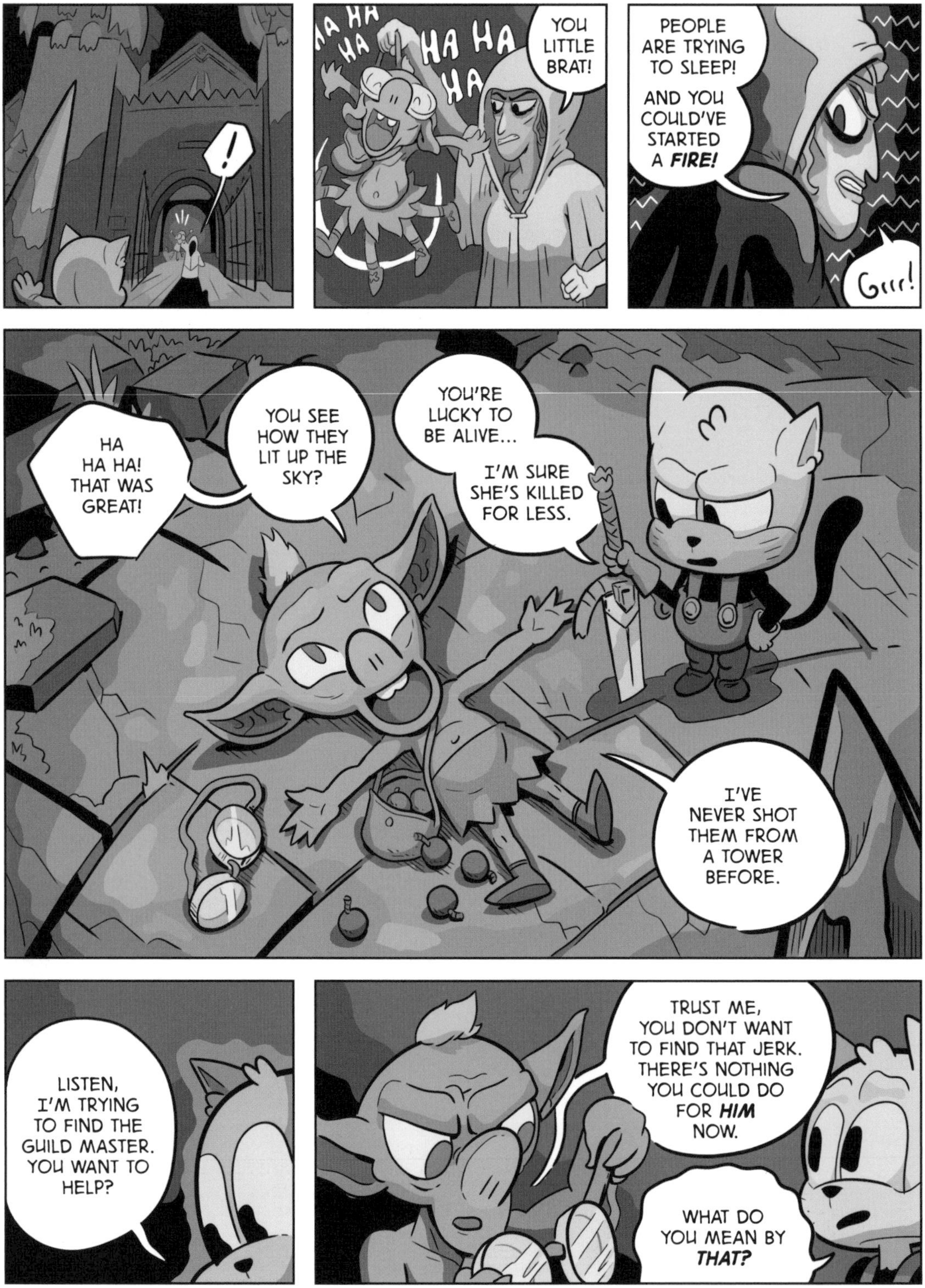
!
HA HA HA HA HA HA
YOU LITTLE BRAT!
PEOPLE ARE TRYING TO SLEEP!
AND YOU COULD'VE STARTED A **FIRE!**
Grrr!
HA HA HA! THAT WAS GREAT!
YOU SEE HOW THEY LIT UP THE SKY?
YOU'RE LUCKY TO BE ALIVE...
I'M SURE SHE'S KILLED FOR LESS.
I'VE NEVER SHOT THEM FROM A TOWER BEFORE.
LISTEN, I'M TRYING TO FIND THE GUILD MASTER. YOU WANT TO HELP?
TRUST ME, YOU DON'T WANT TO FIND THAT JERK. THERE'S NOTHING YOU COULD DO FOR **HIM** NOW.
WHAT DO YOU MEAN BY ***THAT?***

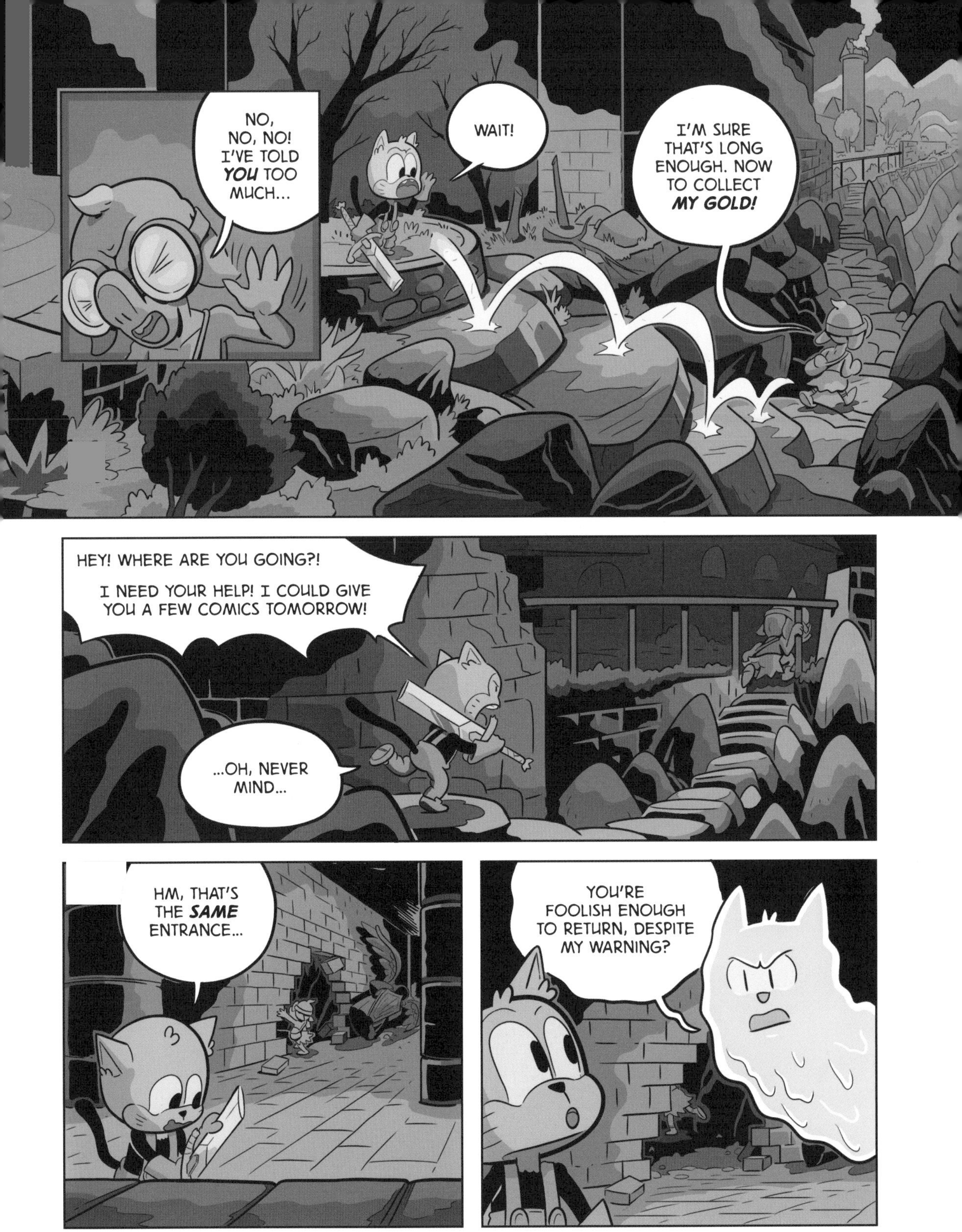
NO, NO, NO! I'VE TOLD YOU TOO MUCH...
WAIT!
I'M SURE THAT'S LONG ENOUGH. NOW TO COLLECT MY GOLD!
HEY! WHERE ARE YOU GOING?!
I NEED YOUR HELP! I COULD GIVE YOU A FEW COMICS TOMORROW!
...OH, NEVER MIND...
HM, THAT'S THE SAME ENTRANCE...
YOU'RE FOOLISH ENOUGH TO RETURN, DESPITE MY WARNING?

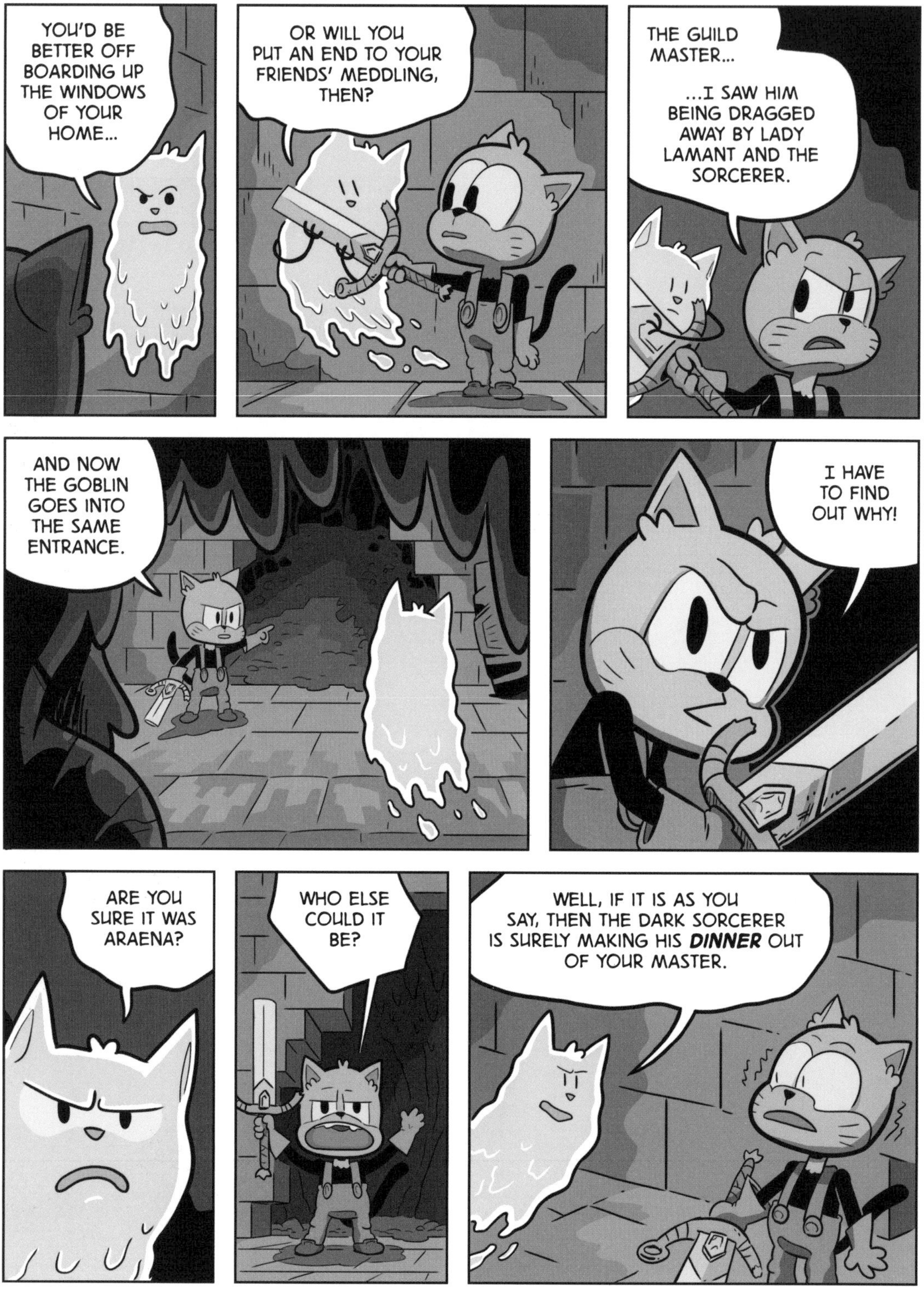
YOU'D BE BETTER OFF BOARDING UP THE WINDOWS OF YOUR HOME...
OR WILL YOU PUT AN END TO YOUR FRIENDS' MEDDLING, THEN?
THE GUILD MASTER...
...I SAW HIM BEING DRAGGED AWAY BY LADY LAMANT AND THE SORCERER.
AND NOW THE GOBLIN GOES INTO THE SAME ENTRANCE.
I HAVE TO FIND OUT WHY!
ARE YOU SURE IT WAS ARAENA?
WHO ELSE COULD IT BE?
WELL, IF IT IS AS YOU SAY, THEN THE DARK SORCERER IS SURELY MAKING HIS ***DINNER*** OUT OF YOUR MASTER.

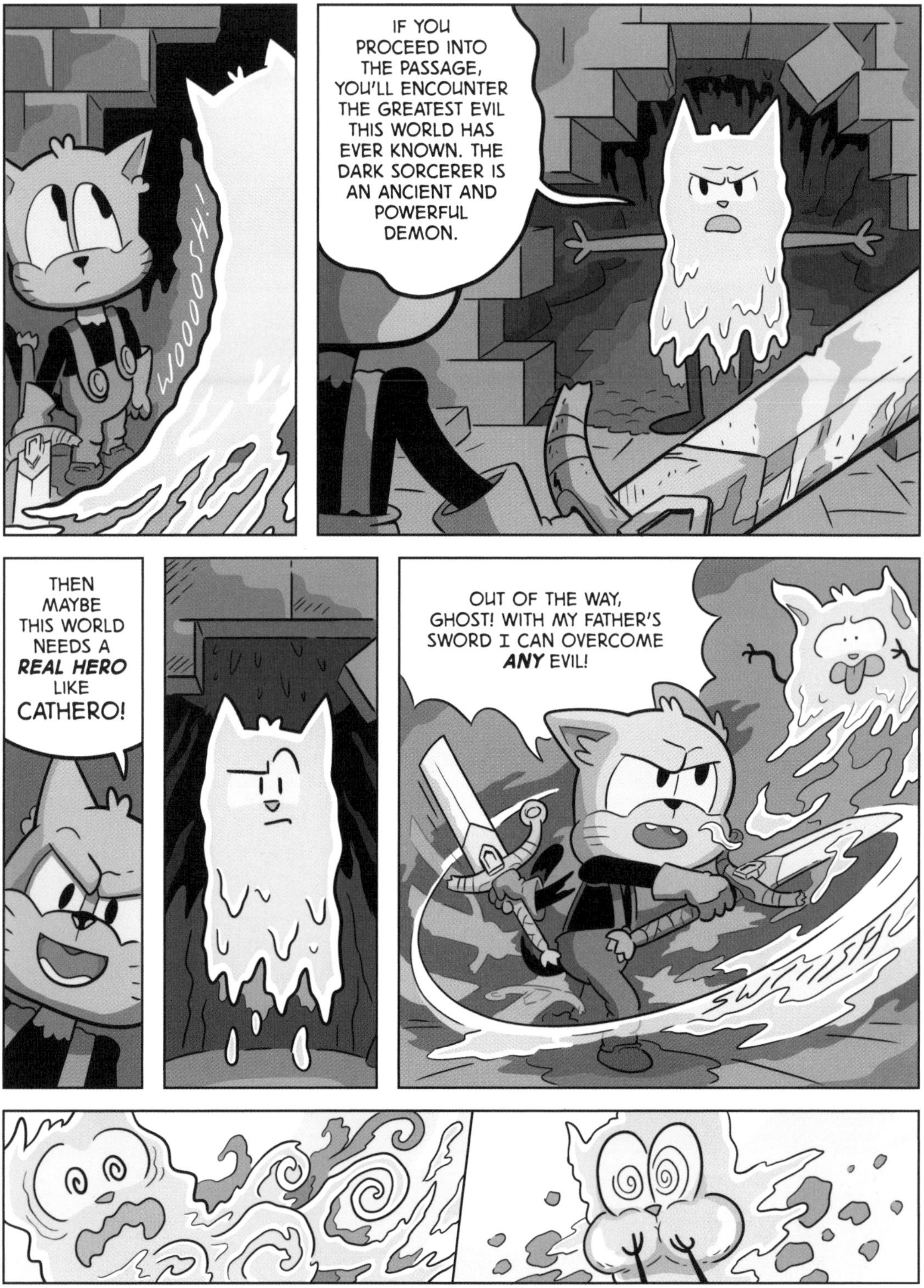
WOOOOSH!
IF YOU PROCEED INTO THE PASSAGE, YOU'LL ENCOUNTER THE GREATEST EVIL THIS WORLD HAS EVER KNOWN. THE DARK SORCERER IS AN ANCIENT AND POWERFUL DEMON.
THEN MAYBE THIS WORLD NEEDS A **REAL HERO** LIKE CATHERO!
OUT OF THE WAY, GHOST! WITH MY FATHER'S SWORD I CAN OVERCOME **ANY** EVIL!
SWISH

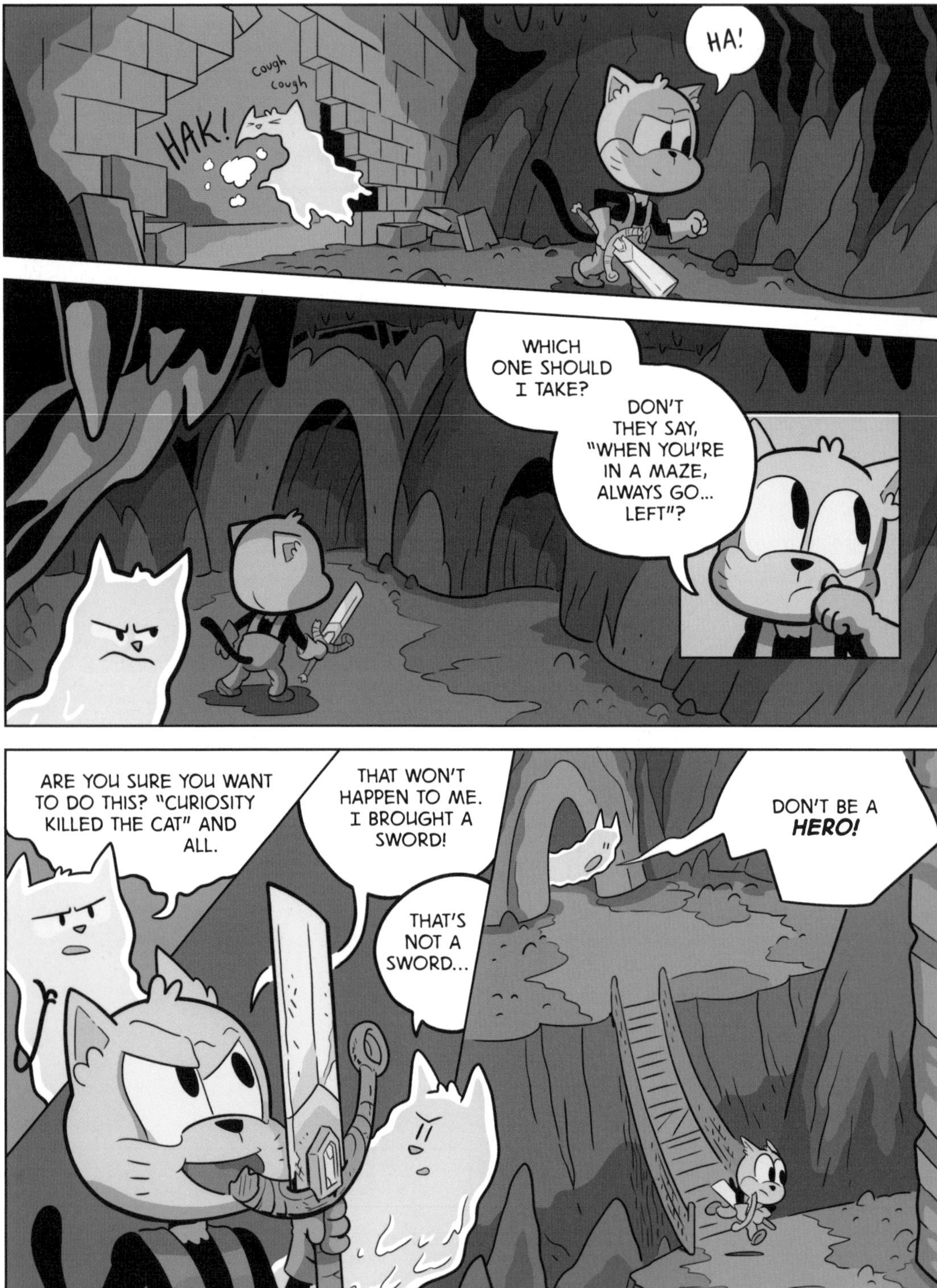
HA!
cough
cough
HAK!
WHICH ONE SHOULD I TAKE?
DON'T THEY SAY, "WHEN YOU'RE IN A MAZE, ALWAYS GO... LEFT"?
ARE YOU SURE YOU WANT TO DO THIS? "CURIOSITY KILLED THE CAT" AND ALL.
THAT WON'T HAPPEN TO ME. I BROUGHT A SWORD!
THAT'S NOT A SWORD...
DON'T BE A ***HERO!***

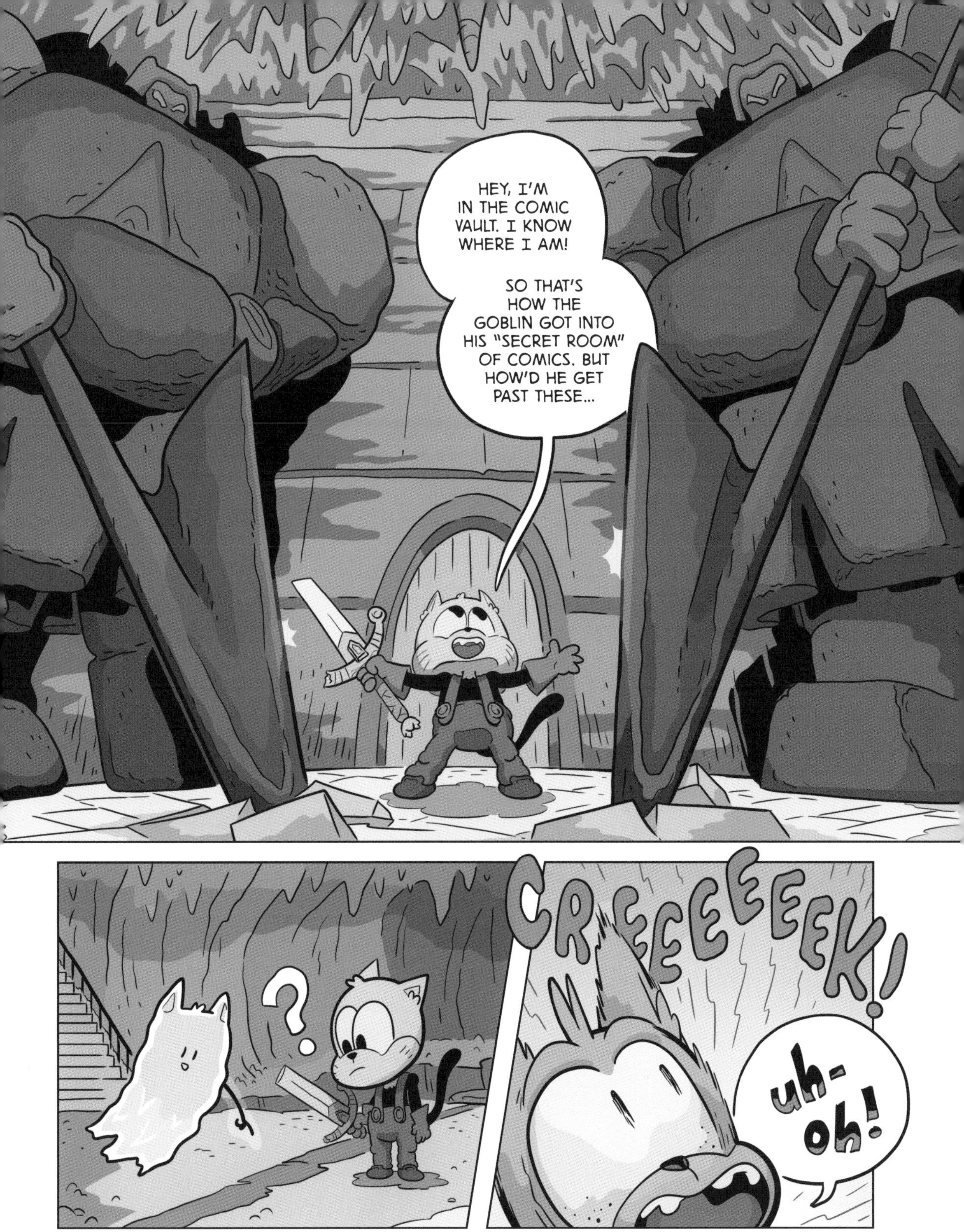
HEY, I'M IN THE COMIC VAULT. I KNOW WHERE I AM!
SO THAT'S HOW THE GOBLIN GOT INTO HIS "SECRET ROOM" OF COMICS. BUT HOW'D HE GET PAST THESE...
?
CREEEEEK!
uh-oh!

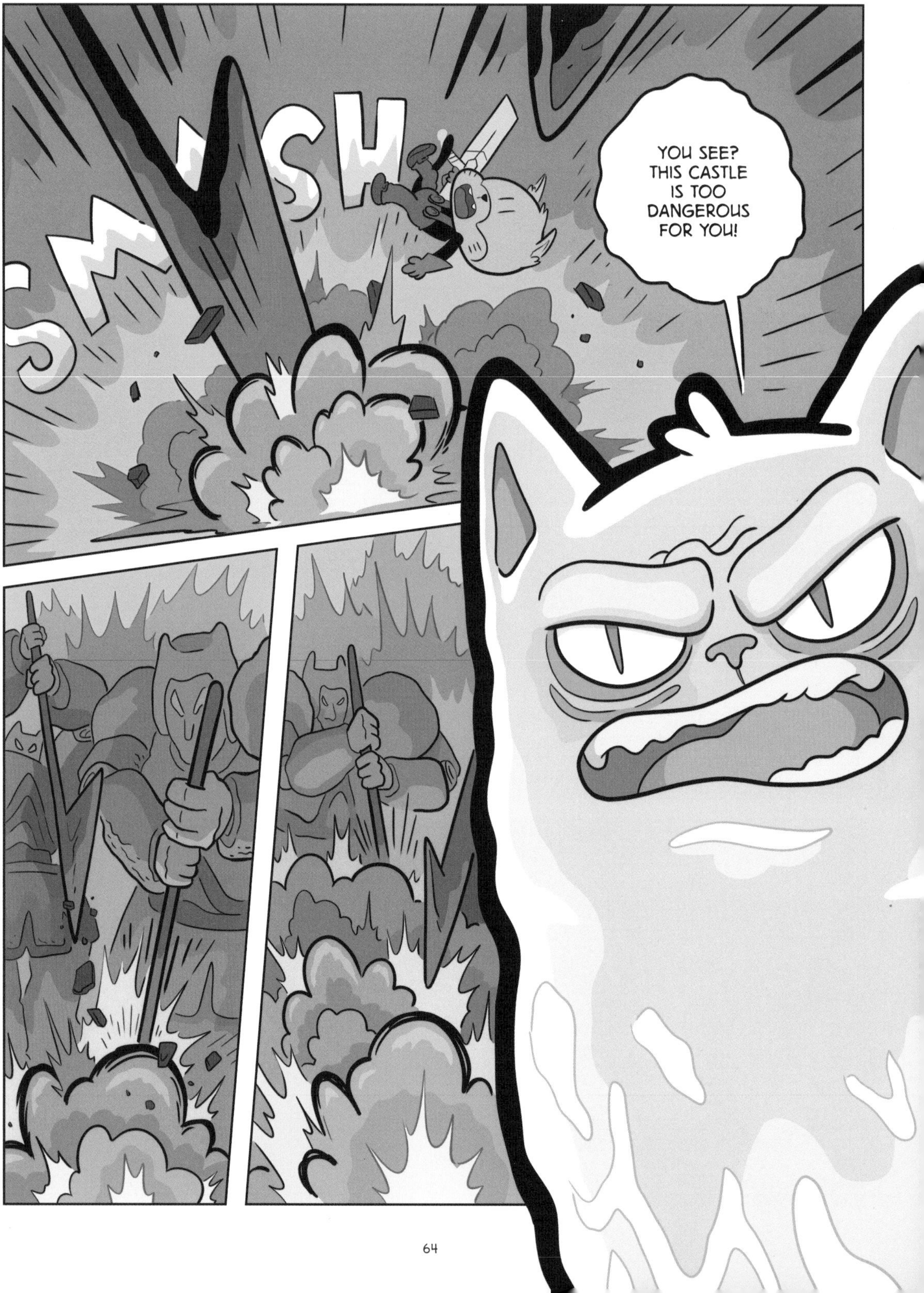
SMASH
YOU SEE? THIS CASTLE IS TOO DANGEROUS FOR YOU!

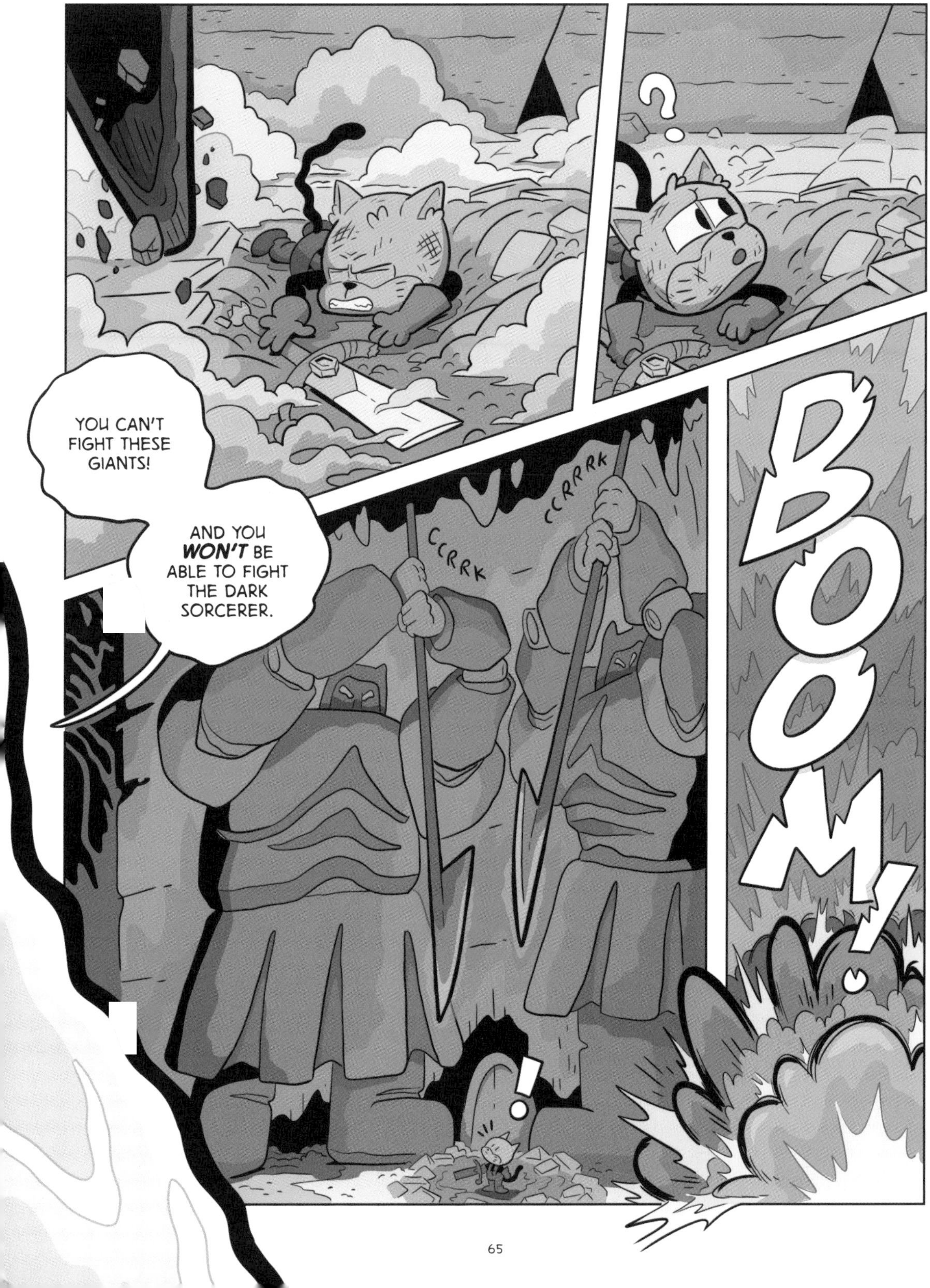
?
YOU CAN'T FIGHT THESE GIANTS!
AND YOU **WON'T** BE ABLE TO FIGHT THE DARK SORCERER.
CCRRK
CCRRRK
BOOM!
!

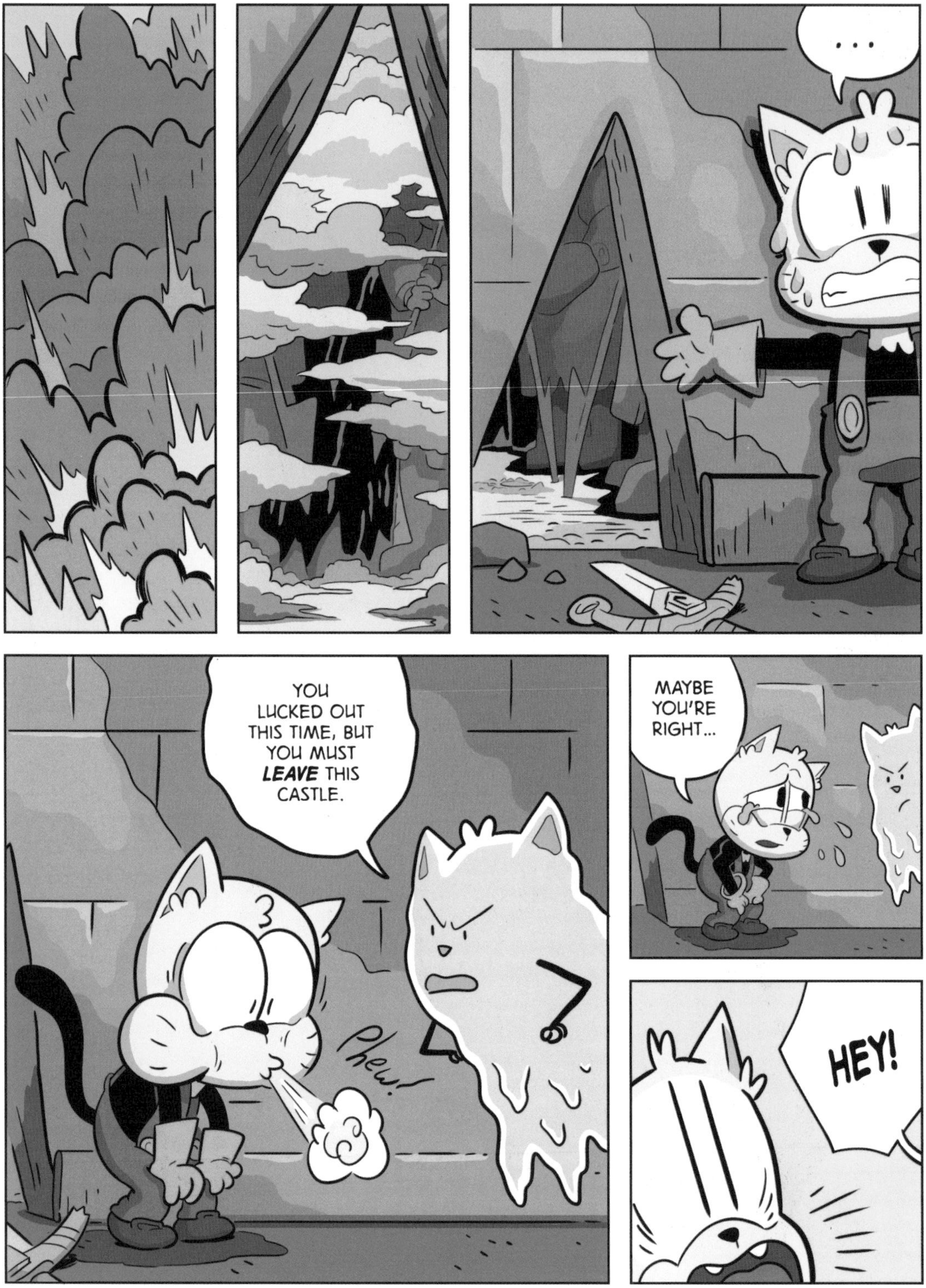
...
YOU LUCKED OUT THIS TIME, BUT YOU MUST **LEAVE** THIS CASTLE.
Phew!
MAYBE YOU'RE RIGHT...
HEY!

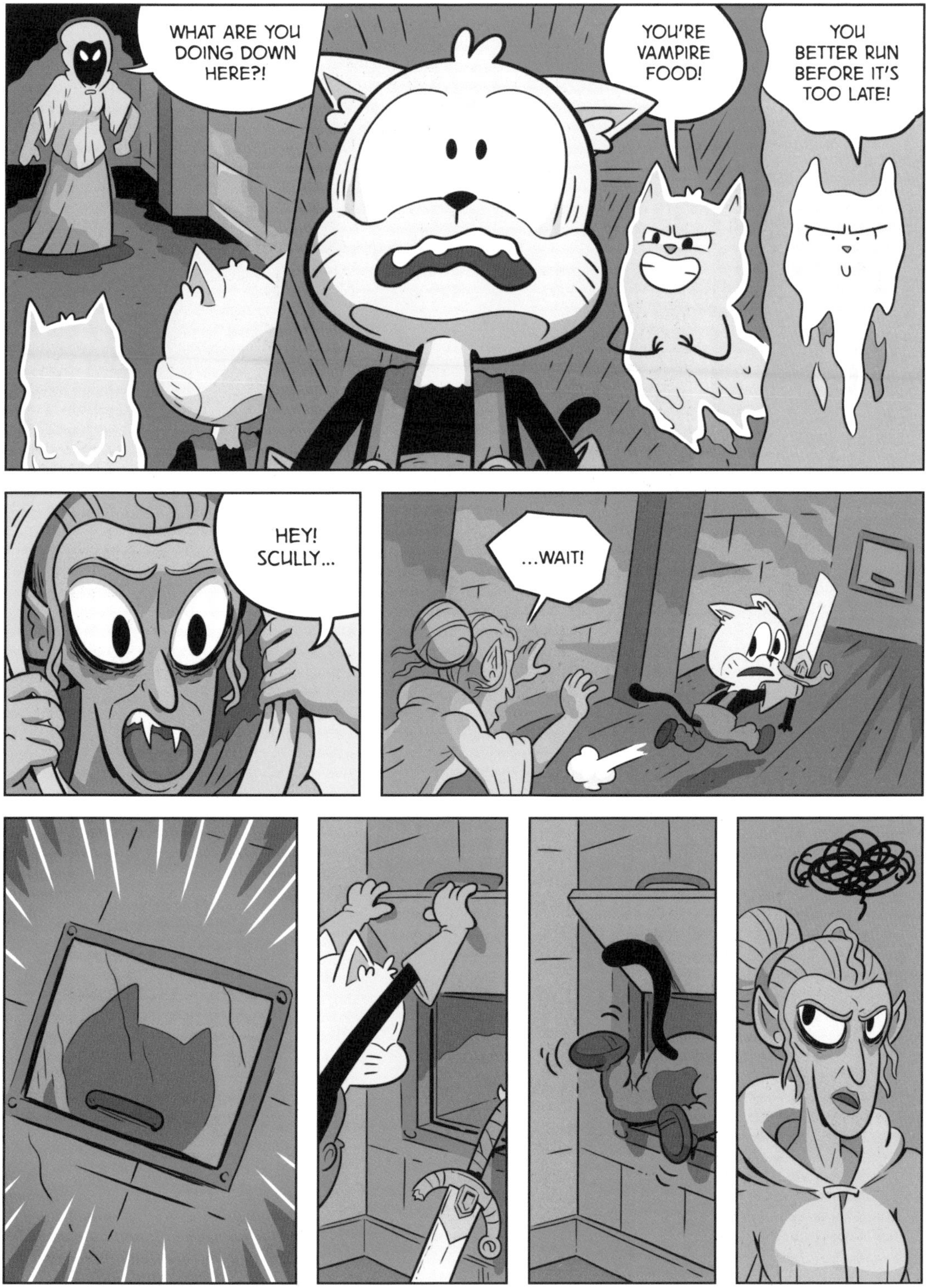
WHAT ARE YOU DOING DOWN HERE?!
YOU'RE VAMPIRE FOOD!
YOU BETTER RUN BEFORE IT'S TOO LATE!
HEY! SCULLY...
...WAIT!

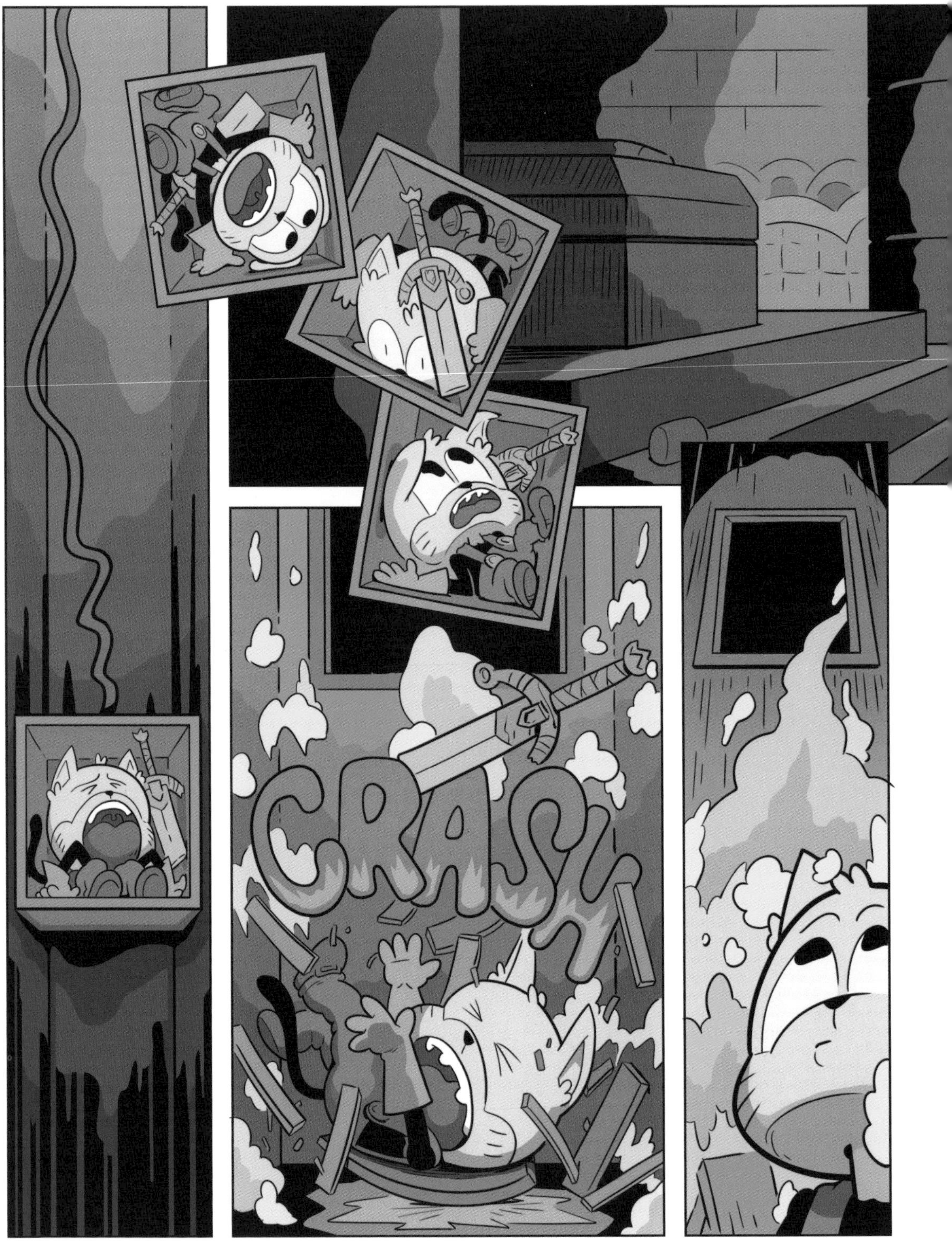
CRASH

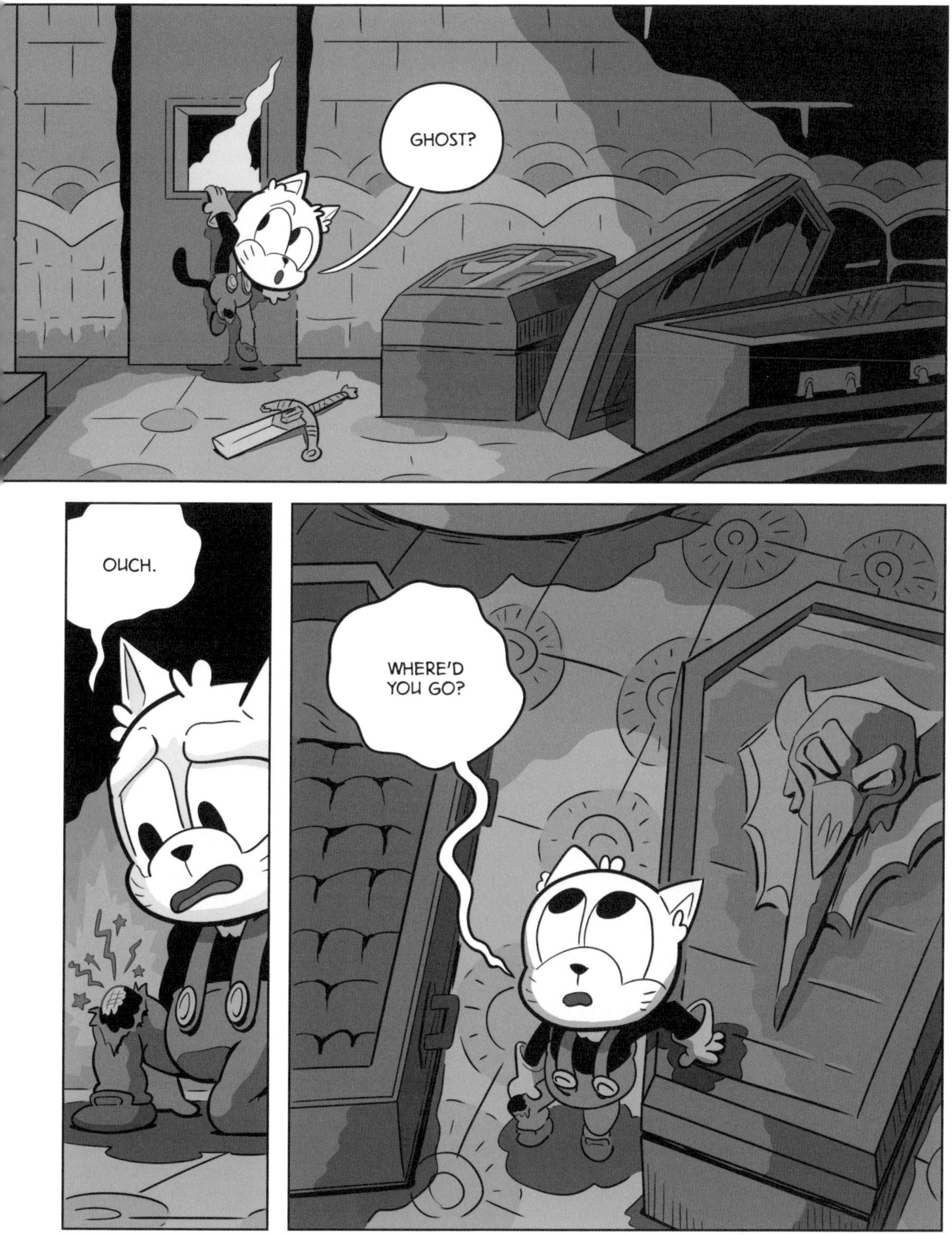
GHOST?
OUCH.
WHERE'D YOU GO?

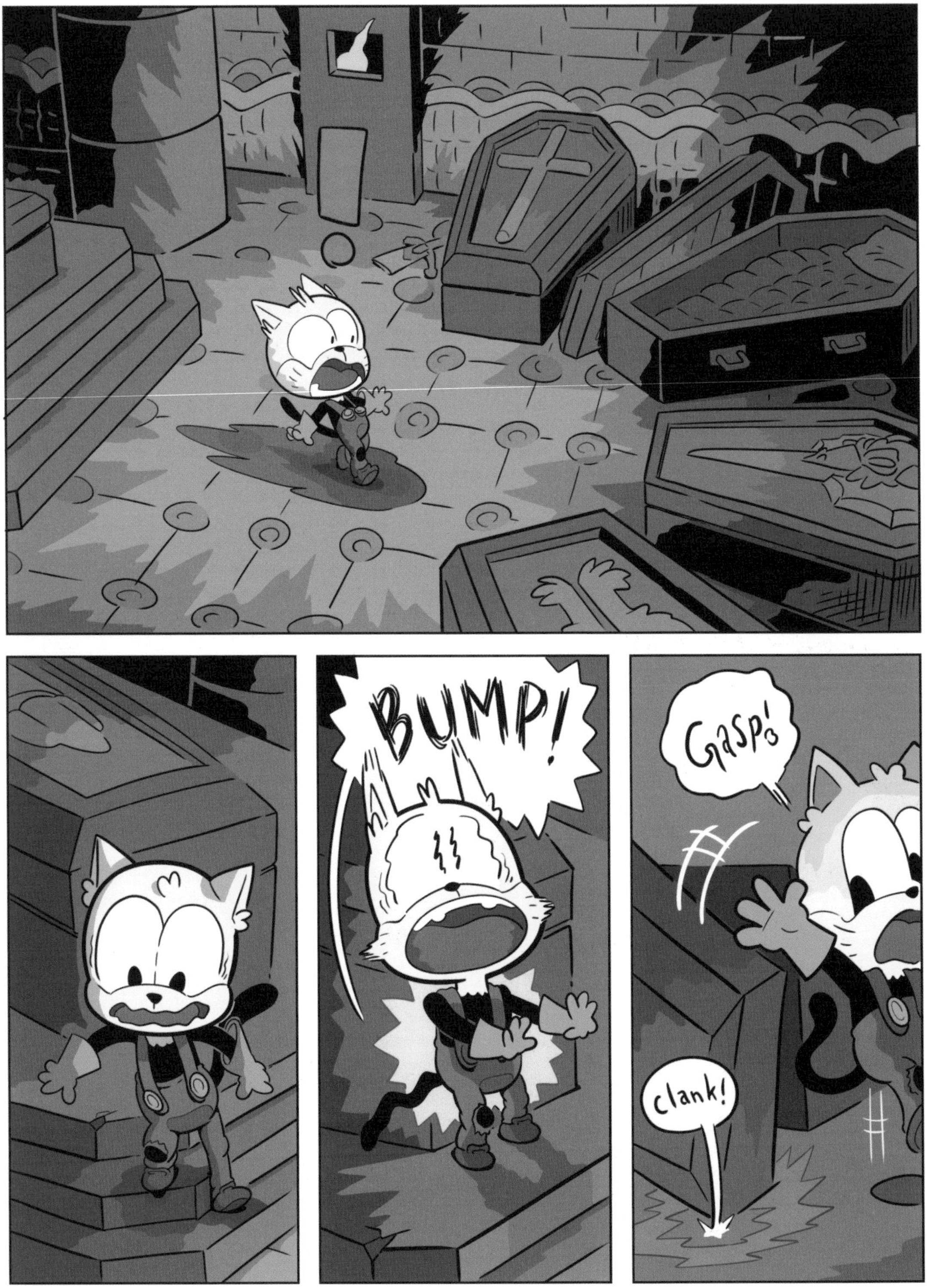
BUMP!
Gasp!
clank!

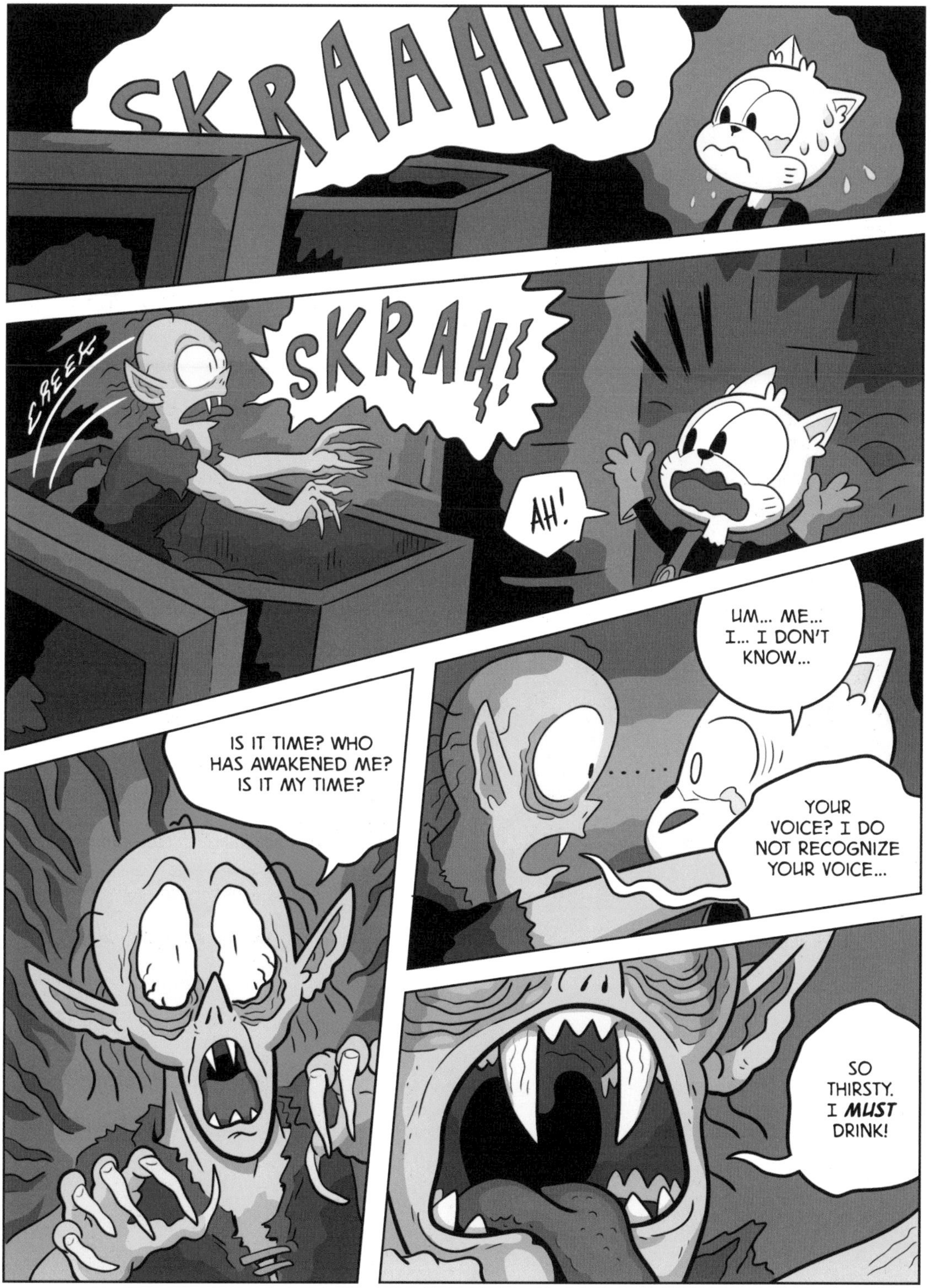
SKRAAAH!
CREEK
SKRAH!
AH!
UM... ME... I... I DON'T KNOW...
IS IT TIME? WHO HAS AWAKENED ME? IS IT MY TIME?
YOUR VOICE? I DO NOT RECOGNIZE YOUR VOICE...
SO THIRSTY. I ***MUST*** DRINK!

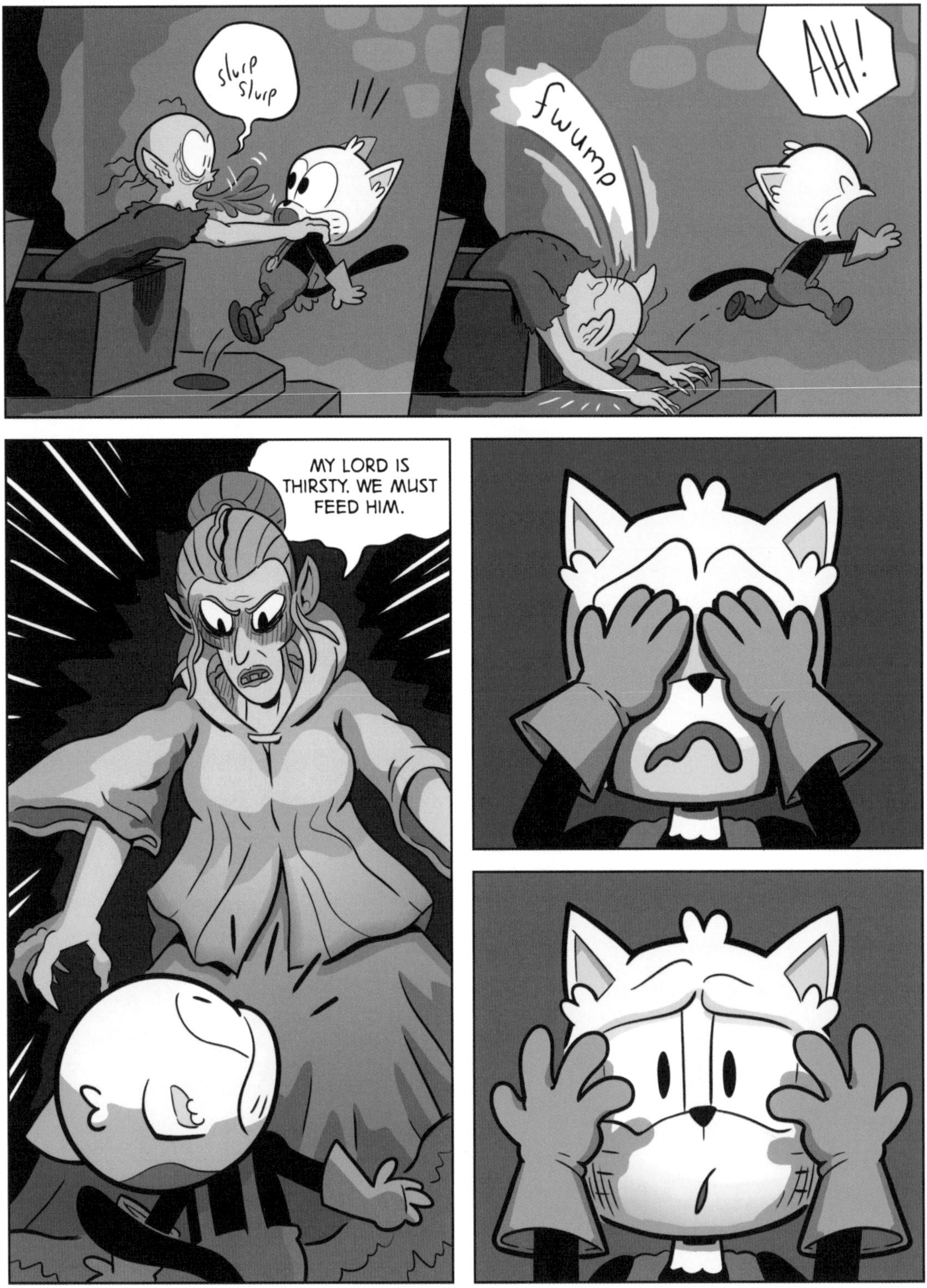
slurp slurp
fwump
AH!
MY LORD IS THIRSTY. WE MUST FEED HIM.

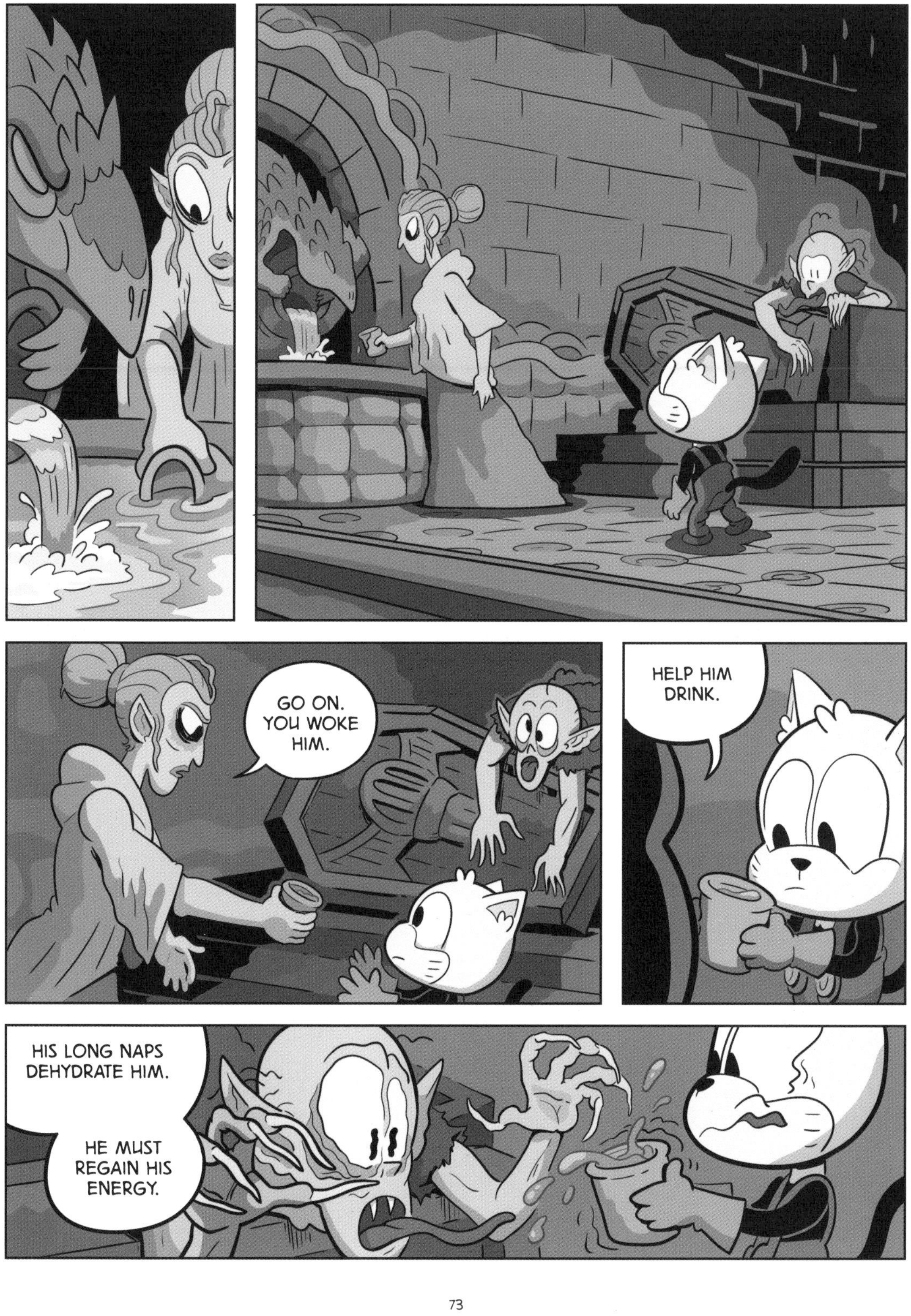
GO ON. YOU WOKE HIM.
HELP HIM DRINK.
HIS LONG NAPS DEHYDRATE HIM.
HE MUST REGAIN HIS ENERGY.

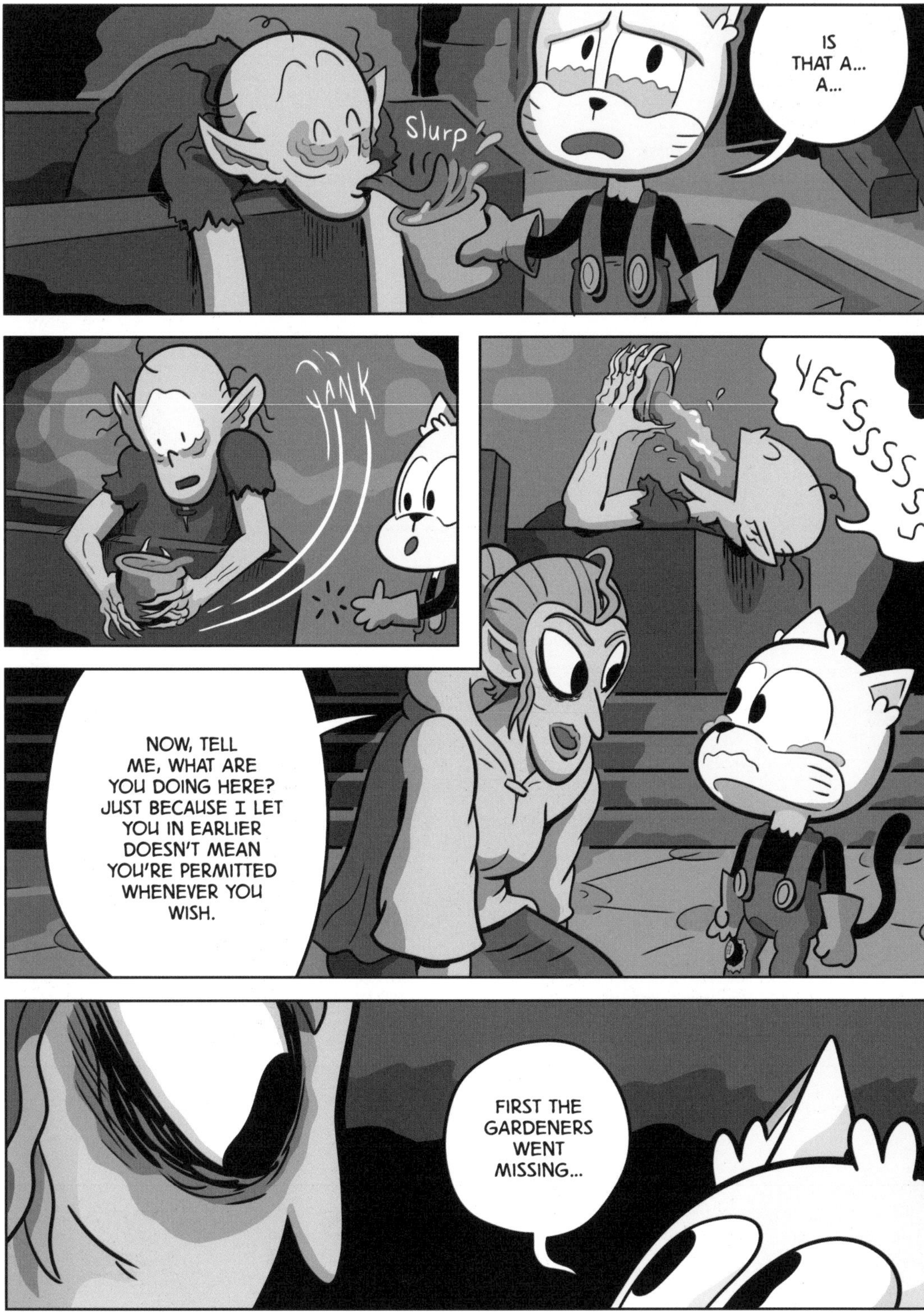
Slurp
IS THAT A... A...
YANK
YESSSSSSSS
NOW, TELL ME, WHAT ARE YOU DOING HERE? JUST BECAUSE I LET YOU IN EARLIER DOESN'T MEAN YOU'RE PERMITTED WHENEVER YOU WISH.
FIRST THE GARDENERS WENT MISSING...

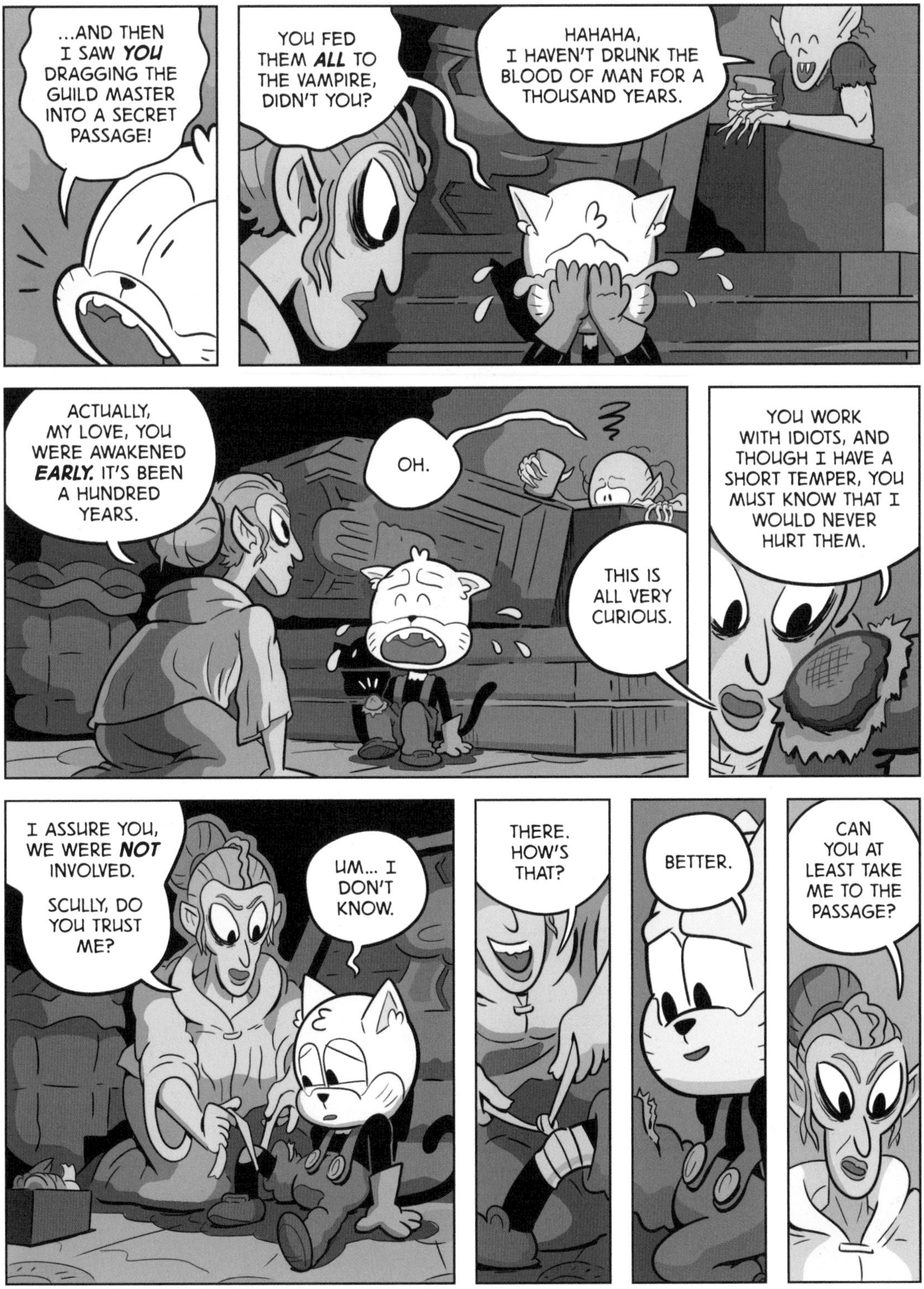

...AND THEN I SAW *YOU* DRAGGING THE GUILD MASTER INTO A SECRET PASSAGE!
YOU FED THEM *ALL* TO THE VAMPIRE, DIDN'T YOU?
HAHAHA, I HAVEN'T DRUNK THE BLOOD OF MAN FOR A THOUSAND YEARS.
ACTUALLY, MY LOVE, YOU WERE AWAKENED *EARLY.* IT'S BEEN A HUNDRED YEARS.
OH.
THIS IS ALL VERY CURIOUS.
YOU WORK WITH IDIOTS, AND THOUGH I HAVE A SHORT TEMPER, YOU MUST KNOW THAT I WOULD NEVER HURT THEM.
I ASSURE YOU, WE WERE *NOT* INVOLVED.
SCULLY, DO YOU TRUST ME?
UM... I DON'T KNOW.
THERE. HOW'S THAT?
BETTER.
CAN YOU AT LEAST TAKE ME TO THE PASSAGE?

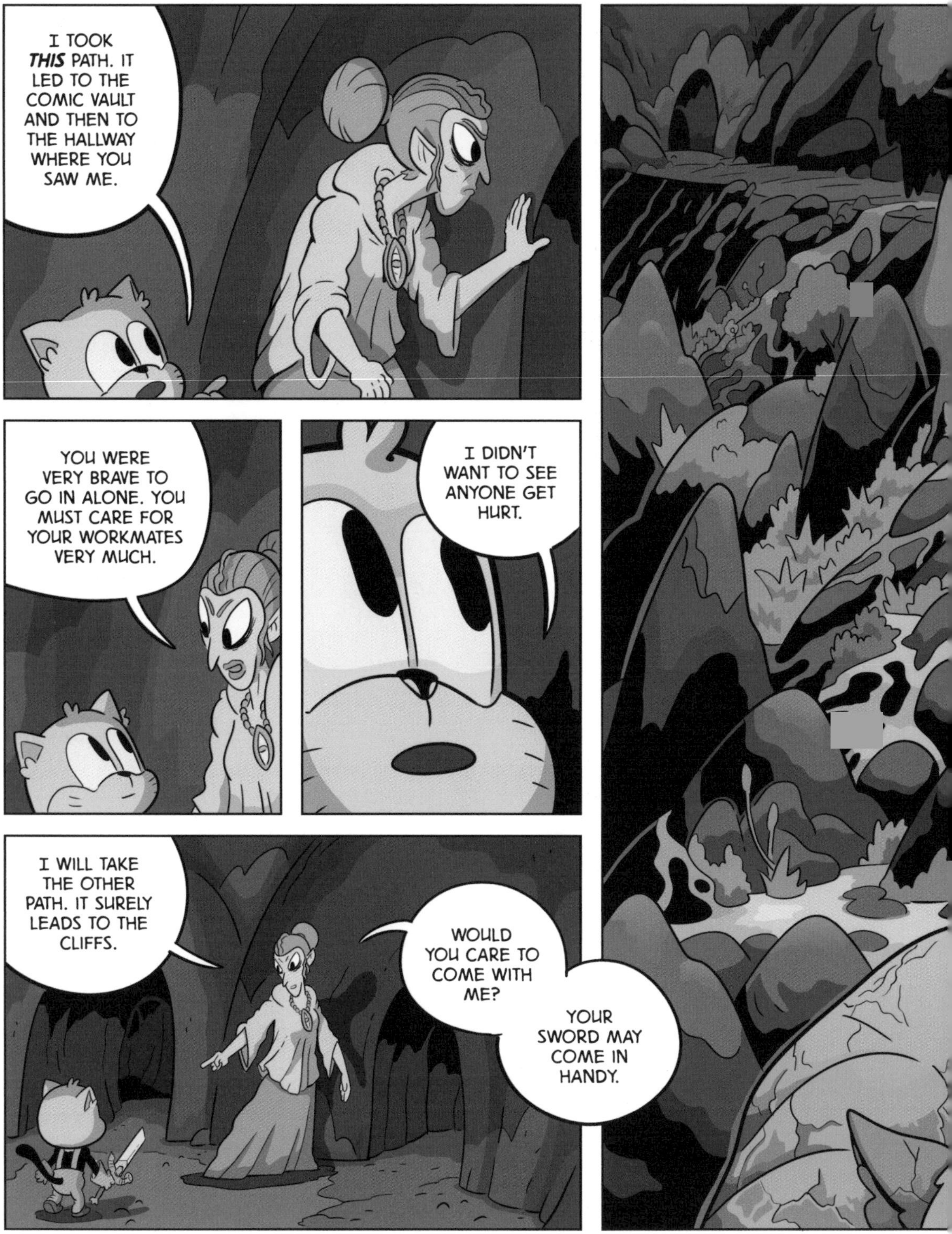
I TOOK *THIS* PATH. IT LED TO THE COMIC VAULT AND THEN TO THE HALLWAY WHERE YOU SAW ME.
YOU WERE VERY BRAVE TO GO IN ALONE. YOU MUST CARE FOR YOUR WORKMATES VERY MUCH.
I DIDN'T WANT TO SEE ANYONE GET HURT.
I WILL TAKE THE OTHER PATH. IT SURELY LEADS TO THE CLIFFS.
WOULD YOU CARE TO COME WITH ME?
YOUR SWORD MAY COME IN HANDY.

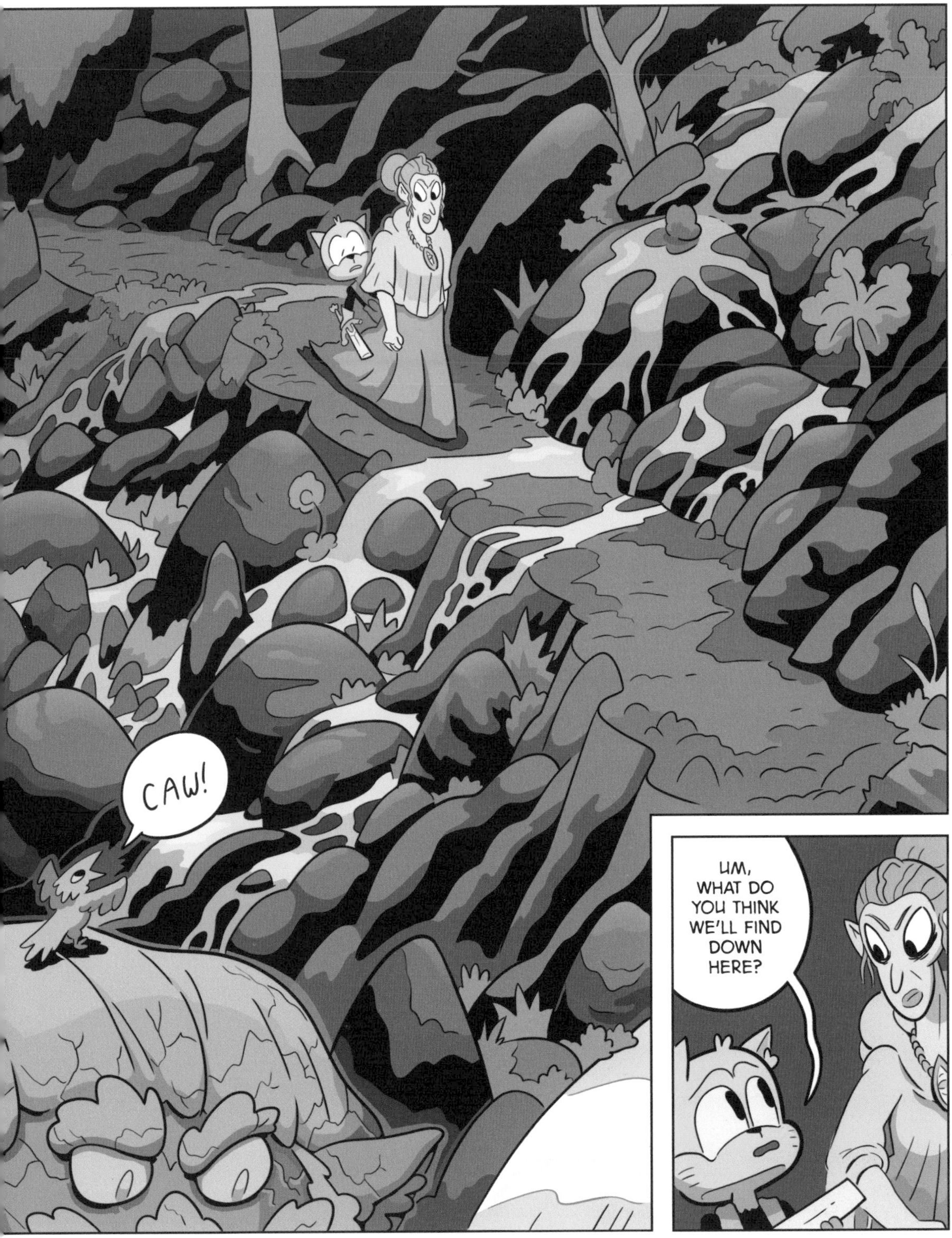
CAW!
UM, WHAT DO YOU THINK WE'LL FIND DOWN HERE?

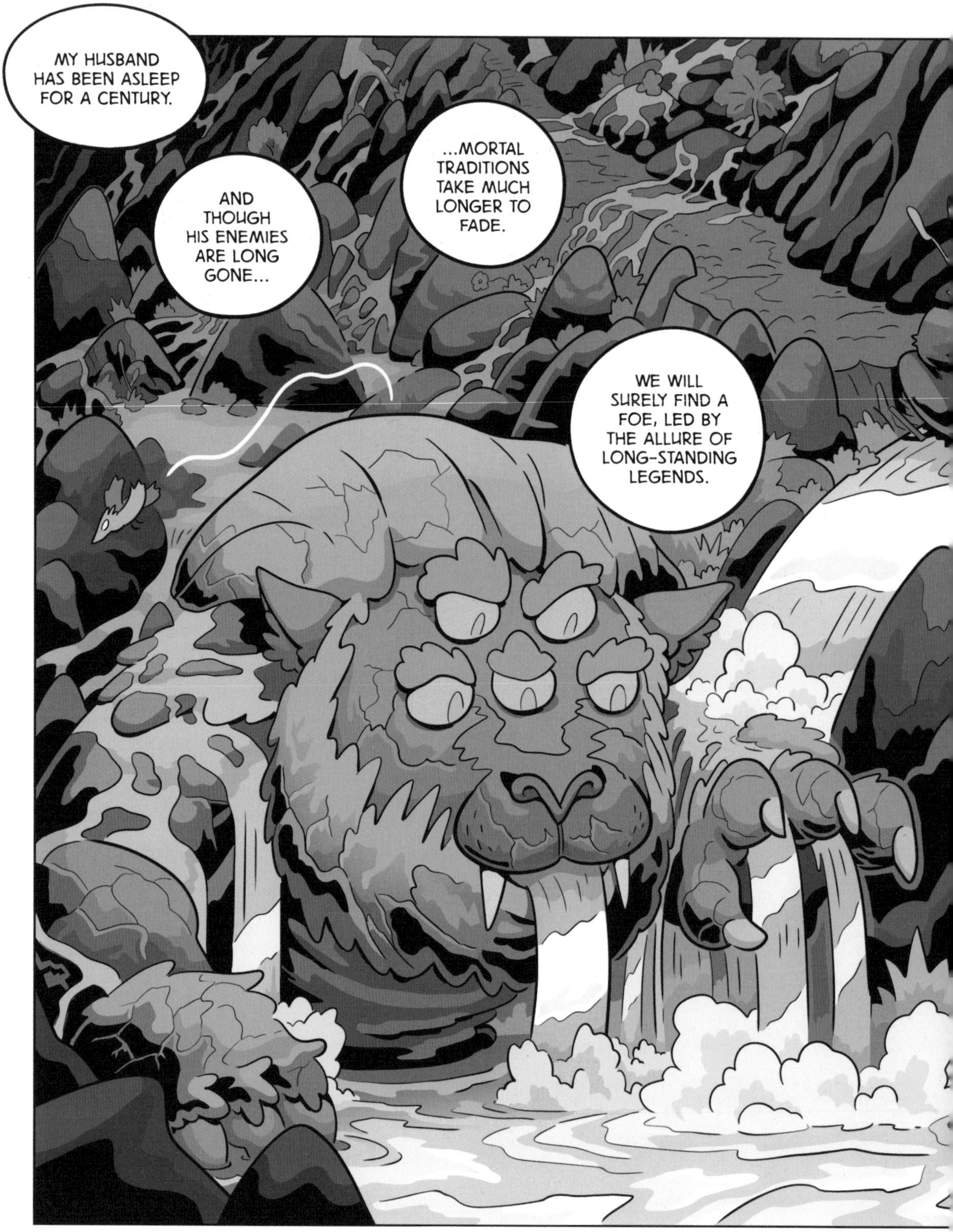
MY HUSBAND HAS BEEN ASLEEP FOR A CENTURY.
AND THOUGH HIS ENEMIES ARE LONG GONE...
...MORTAL TRADITIONS TAKE MUCH LONGER TO FADE.
WE WILL SURELY FIND A FOE, LED BY THE ALLURE OF LONG-STANDING LEGENDS.

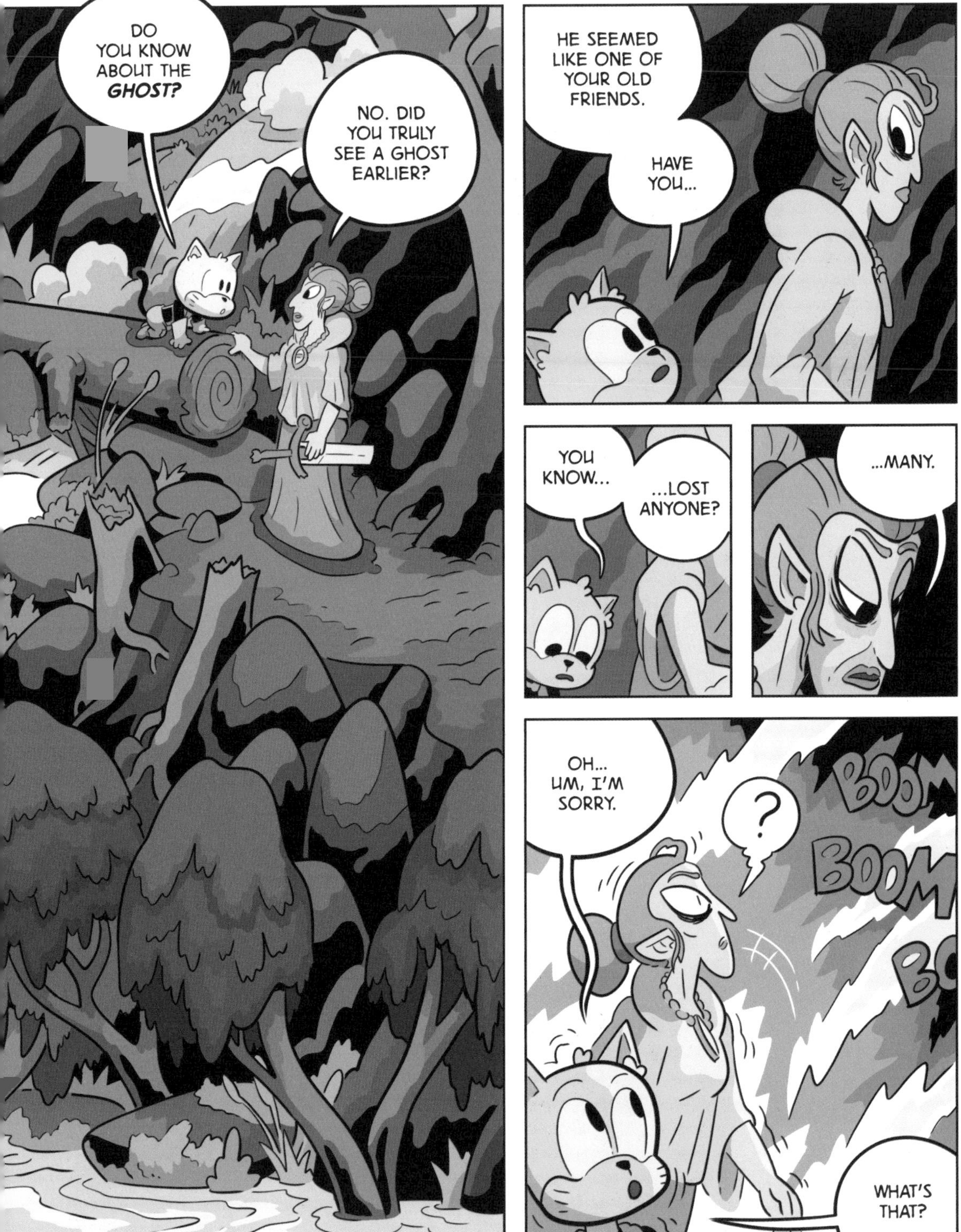
DO YOU KNOW ABOUT THE ***GHOST?***
NO. DID YOU TRULY SEE A GHOST EARLIER?
HE SEEMED LIKE ONE OF YOUR OLD FRIENDS.
HAVE YOU...
YOU KNOW...
...LOST ANYONE?
...MANY.
OH... UM, I'M SORRY.
?
BOOM
BOOM
BO
WHAT'S THAT?

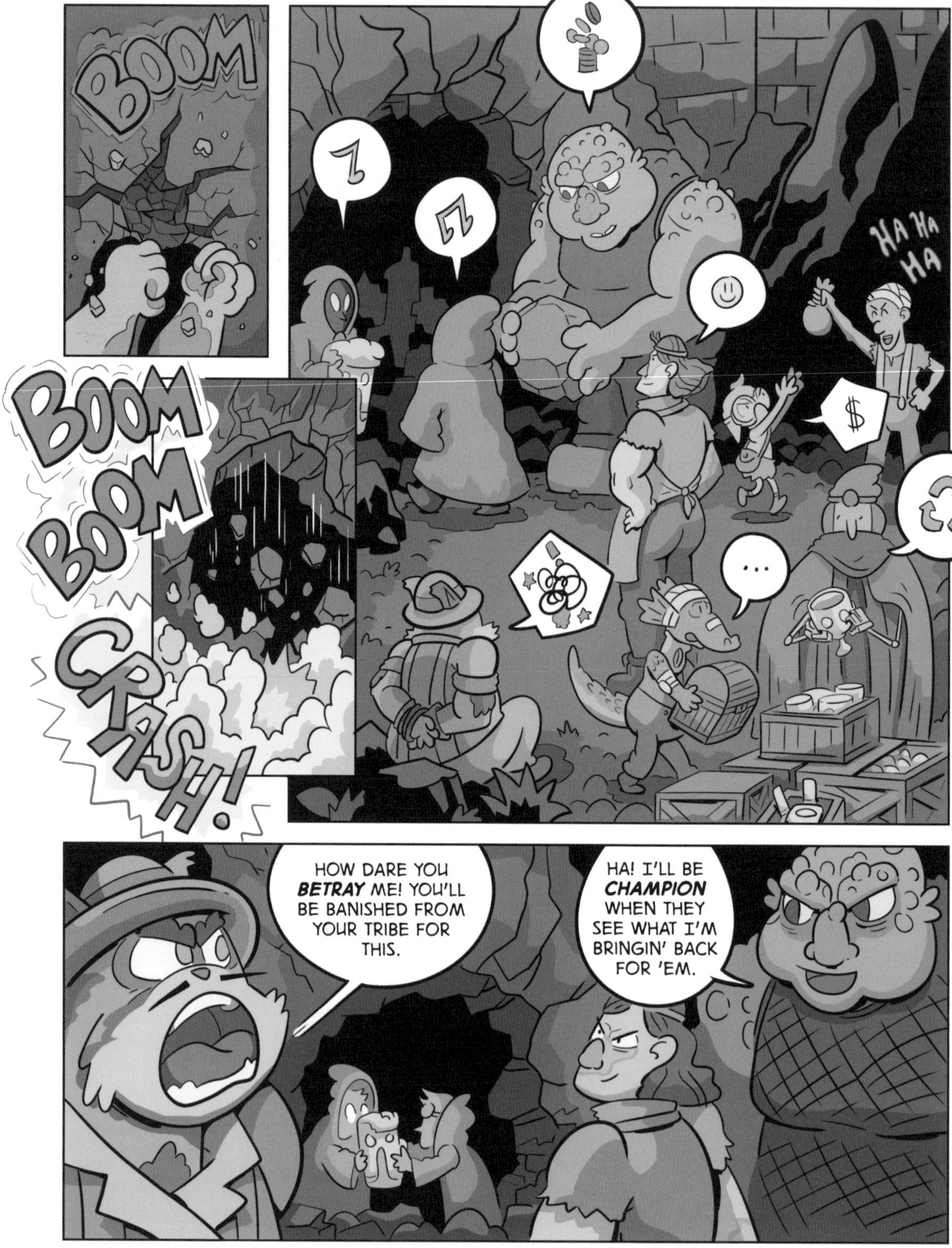
BOOM
BOOM
BOOM
CRASH!
HA HA HA
$
...
HOW DARE YOU BETRAY ME! YOU'LL BE BANISHED FROM YOUR TRIBE FOR THIS.
HA! I'LL BE CHAMPION WHEN THEY SEE WHAT I'M BRINGIN' BACK FOR 'EM.

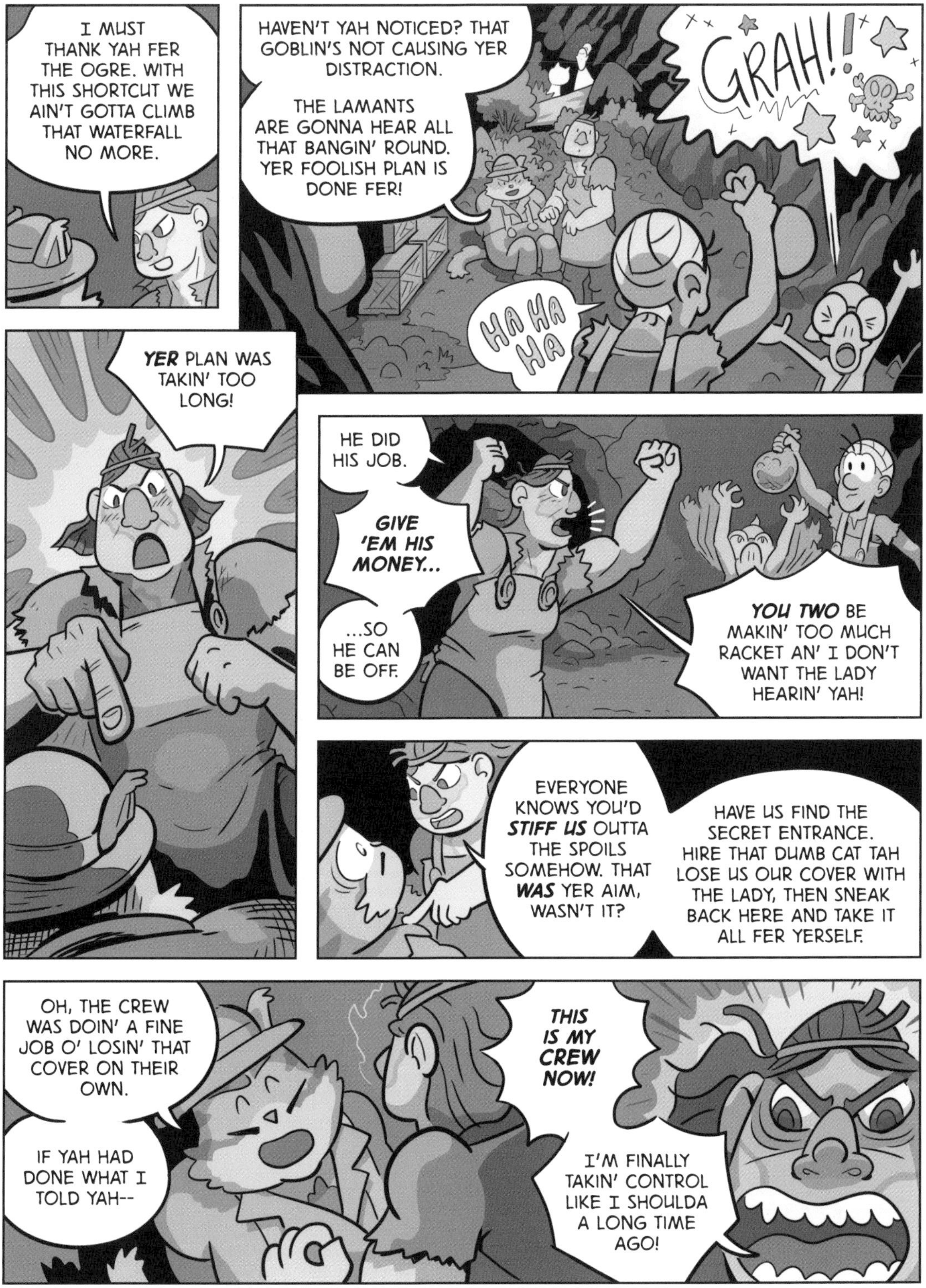

I MUST THANK YAH FER THE OGRE. WITH THIS SHORTCUT WE AIN'T GOTTA CLIMB THAT WATERFALL NO MORE.
HAVEN'T YAH NOTICED? THAT GOBLIN'S NOT CAUSING YER DISTRACTION.
THE LAMANTS ARE GONNA HEAR ALL THAT BANGIN' ROUND. YER FOOLISH PLAN IS DONE FER!
GRAH!!
HA HA HA
YER PLAN WAS TAKIN' TOO LONG!
HE DID HIS JOB.
GIVE 'EM HIS MONEY...
...SO HE CAN BE OFF.
YOU TWO BE MAKIN' TOO MUCH RACKET AN' I DON'T WANT THE LADY HEARIN' YAH!
EVERYONE KNOWS YOU'D STIFF US OUTTA THE SPOILS SOMEHOW. THAT WAS YER AIM, WASN'T IT?
HAVE US FIND THE SECRET ENTRANCE. HIRE THAT DUMB CAT TAH LOSE US OUR COVER WITH THE LADY, THEN SNEAK BACK HERE AND TAKE IT ALL FER YERSELF.
OH, THE CREW WAS DOIN' A FINE JOB O' LOSIN' THAT COVER ON THEIR OWN.
IF YAH HAD DONE WHAT I TOLD YAH--
THIS IS MY CREW NOW!
I'M FINALLY TAKIN' CONTROL LIKE I SHOULDA A LONG TIME AGO!

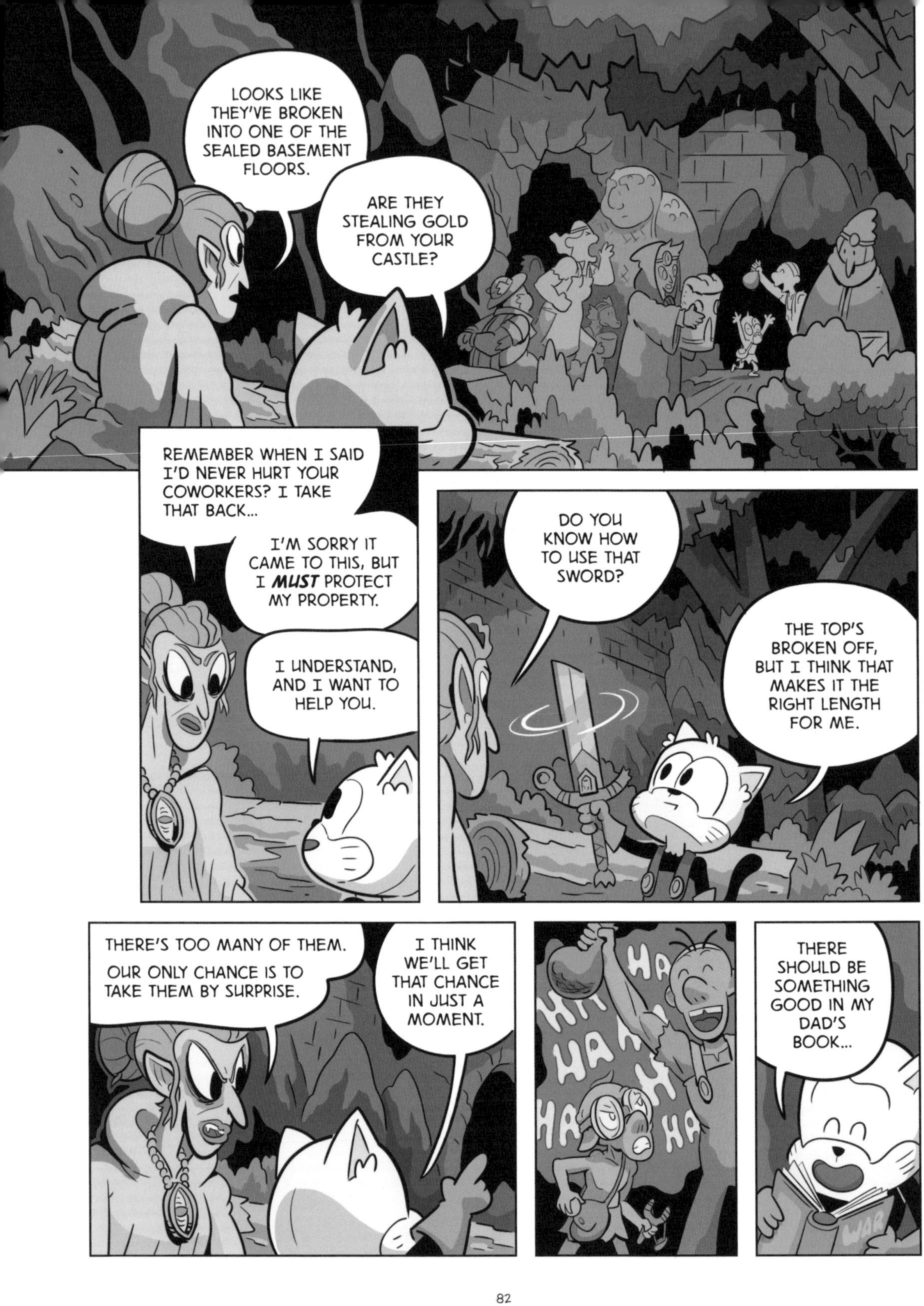
LOOKS LIKE THEY'VE BROKEN INTO ONE OF THE SEALED BASEMENT FLOORS.
ARE THEY STEALING GOLD FROM YOUR CASTLE?
REMEMBER WHEN I SAID I'D NEVER HURT YOUR COWORKERS? I TAKE THAT BACK...
I'M SORRY IT CAME TO THIS, BUT I MUST PROTECT MY PROPERTY.
I UNDERSTAND, AND I WANT TO HELP YOU.
DO YOU KNOW HOW TO USE THAT SWORD?
THE TOP'S BROKEN OFF, BUT I THINK THAT MAKES IT THE RIGHT LENGTH FOR ME.
THERE'S TOO MANY OF THEM.
OUR ONLY CHANCE IS TO TAKE THEM BY SURPRISE.
I THINK WE'LL GET THAT CHANCE IN JUST A MOMENT.
HA HA HA HA HA HA
THERE SHOULD BE SOMETHING GOOD IN MY DAD'S BOOK...
WAR

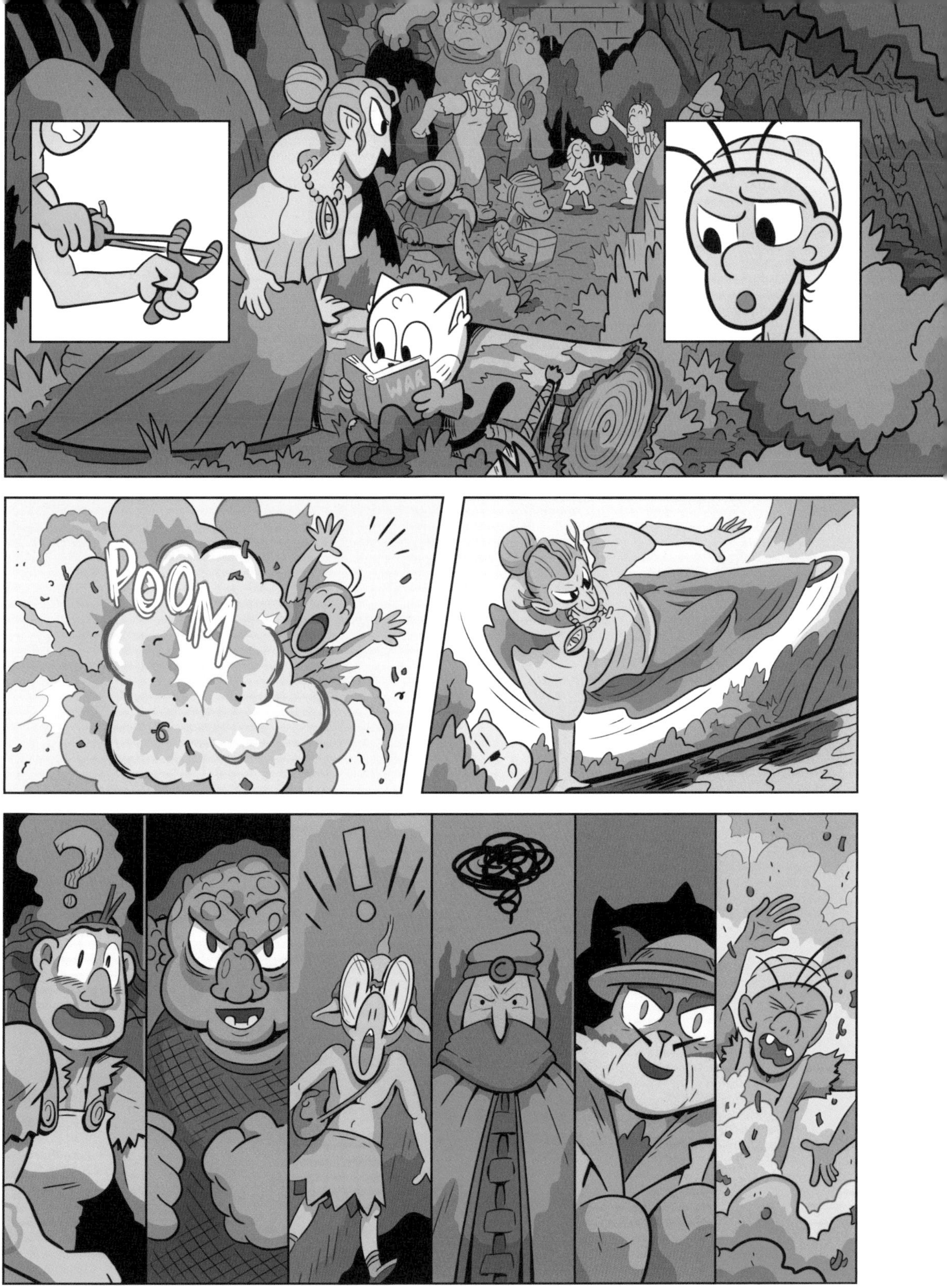
WAR
POOM
?
!

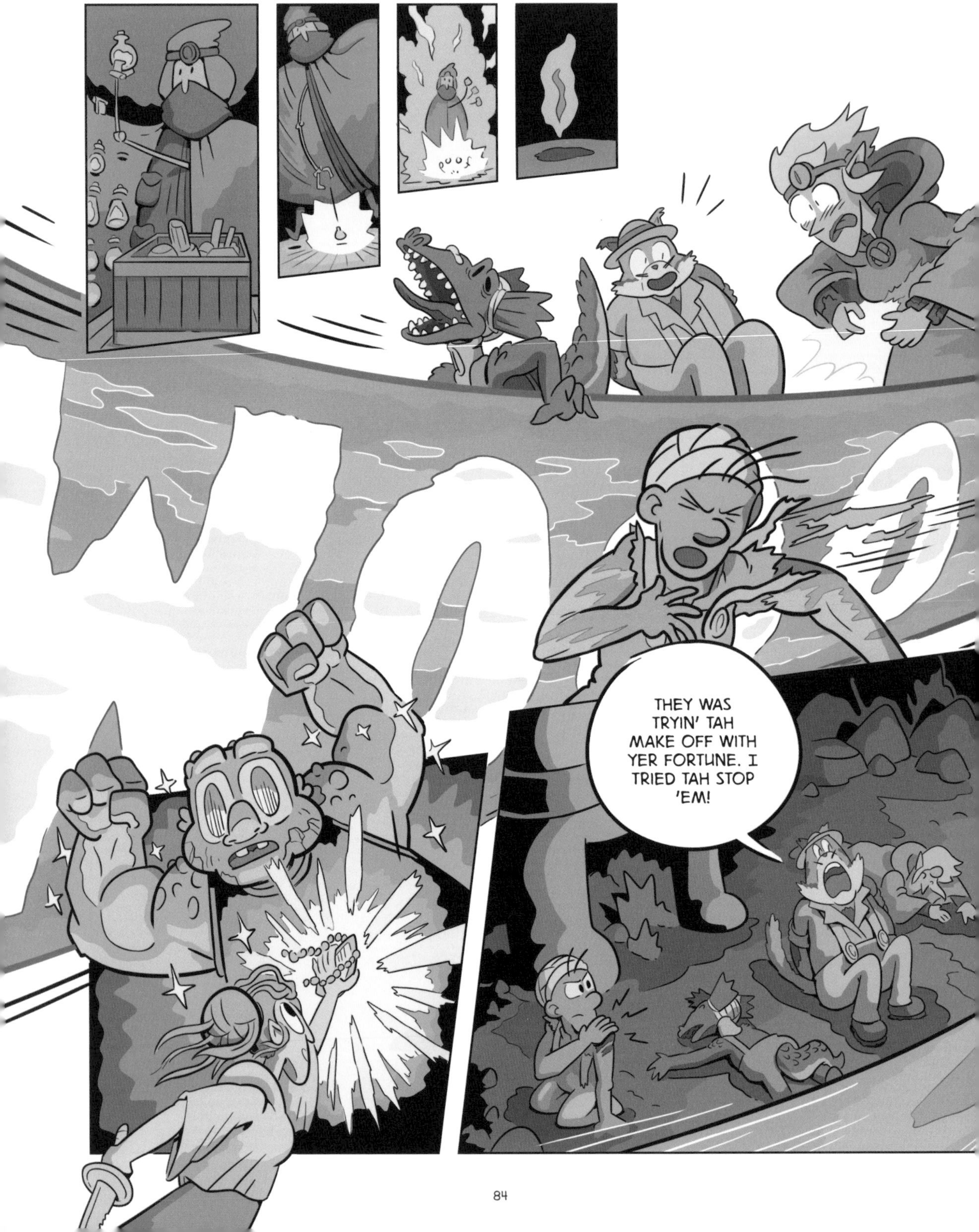

poof
WOO
THEY WAS TRYIN' TAH MAKE OFF WITH YER FORTUNE. I TRIED TAH STOP 'EM!

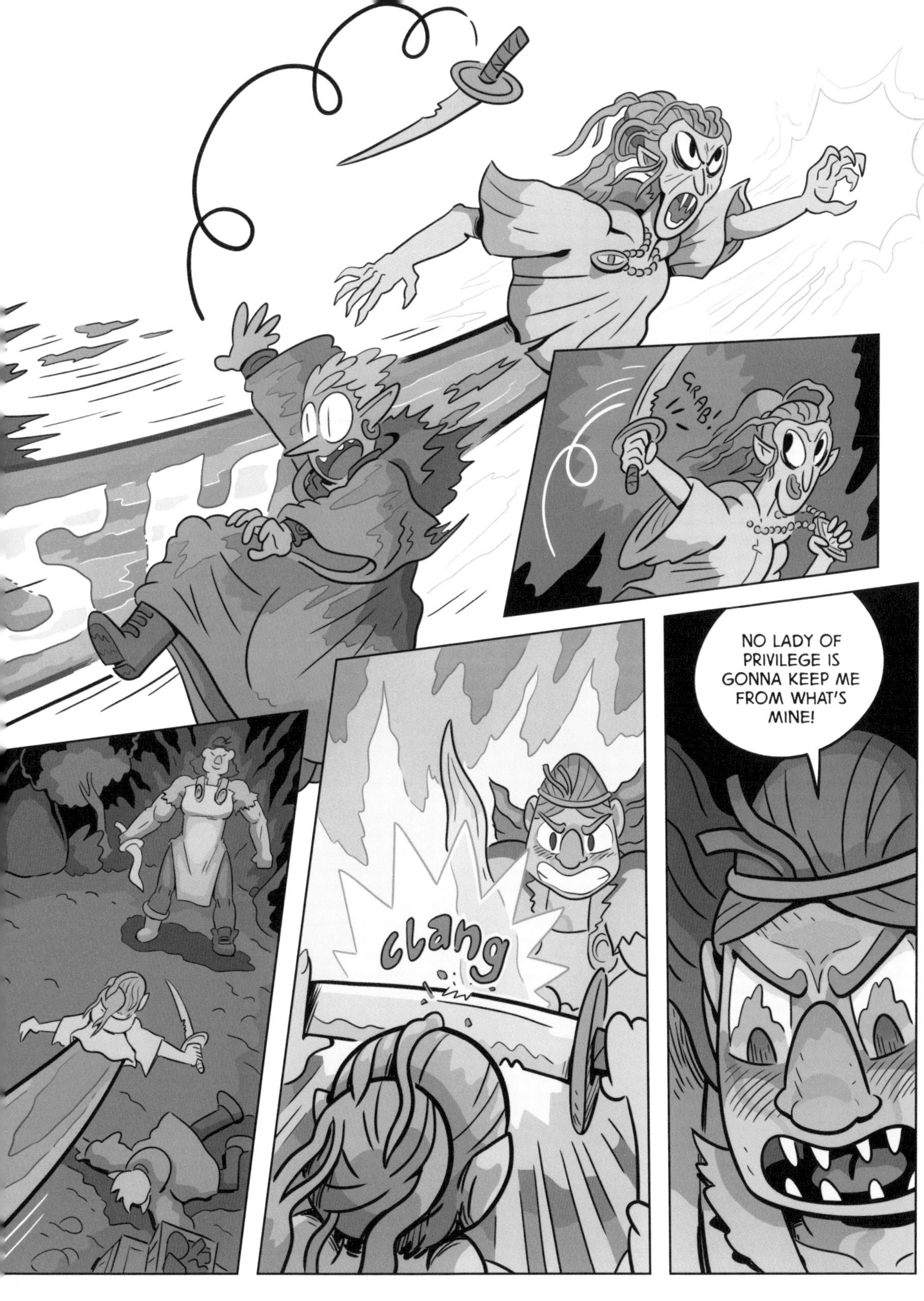
GRAB!
CLANG
NO LADY OF PRIVILEGE IS GONNA KEEP ME FROM WHAT'S MINE!

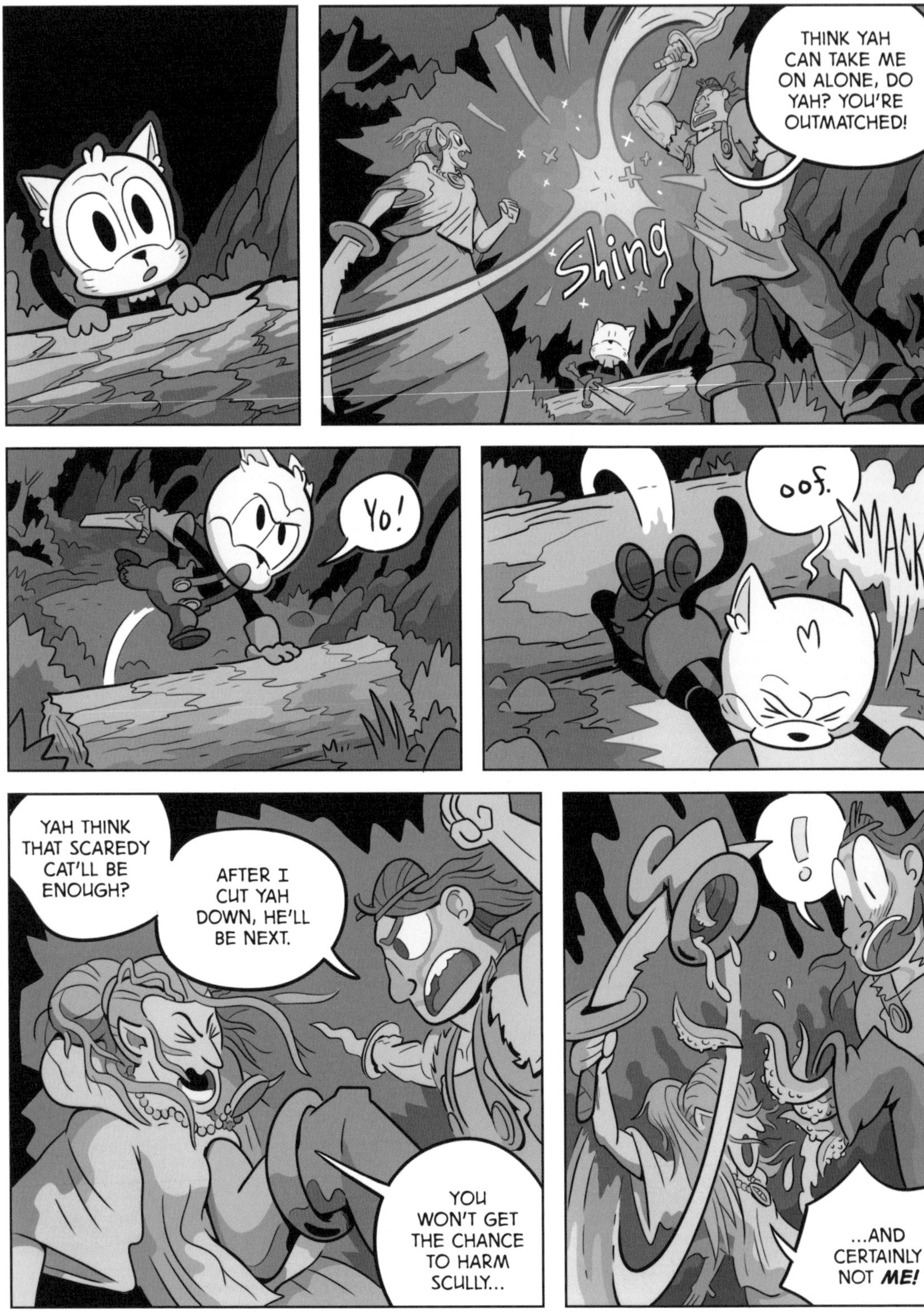
THINK YAH CAN TAKE ME ON ALONE, DO YAH? YOU'RE OUTMATCHED!
Shing
Yo!
oof.
SMACK
YAH THINK THAT SCAREDY CAT'LL BE ENOUGH?
AFTER I CUT YAH DOWN, HE'LL BE NEXT.
YOU WON'T GET THE CHANCE TO HARM SCULLY...
!
...AND CERTAINLY NOT ***ME!***

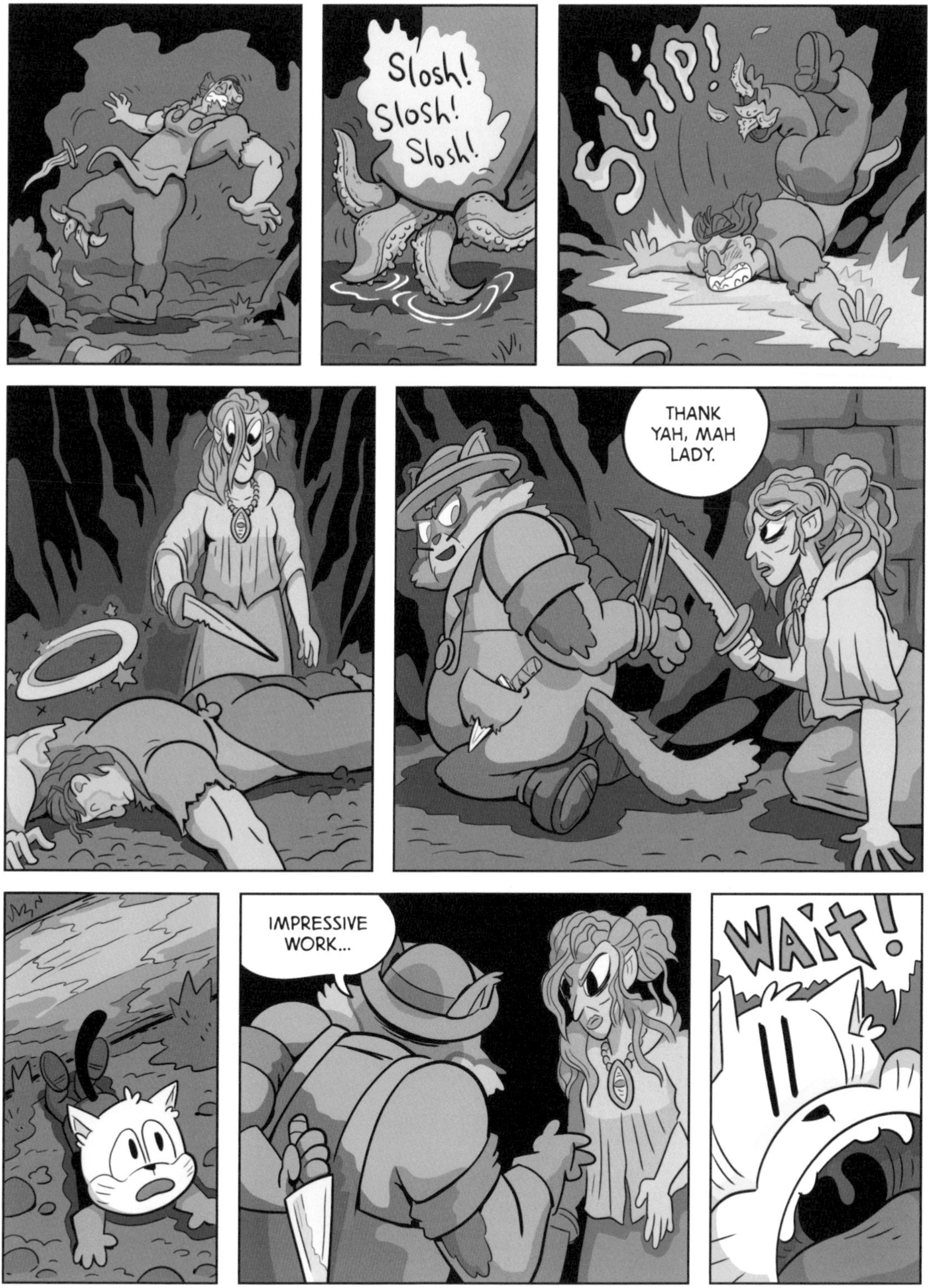
Slosh! Slosh! Slosh!
SLIP!
THANK YAH, MAH LADY.
IMPRESSIVE WORK...
WAIT!

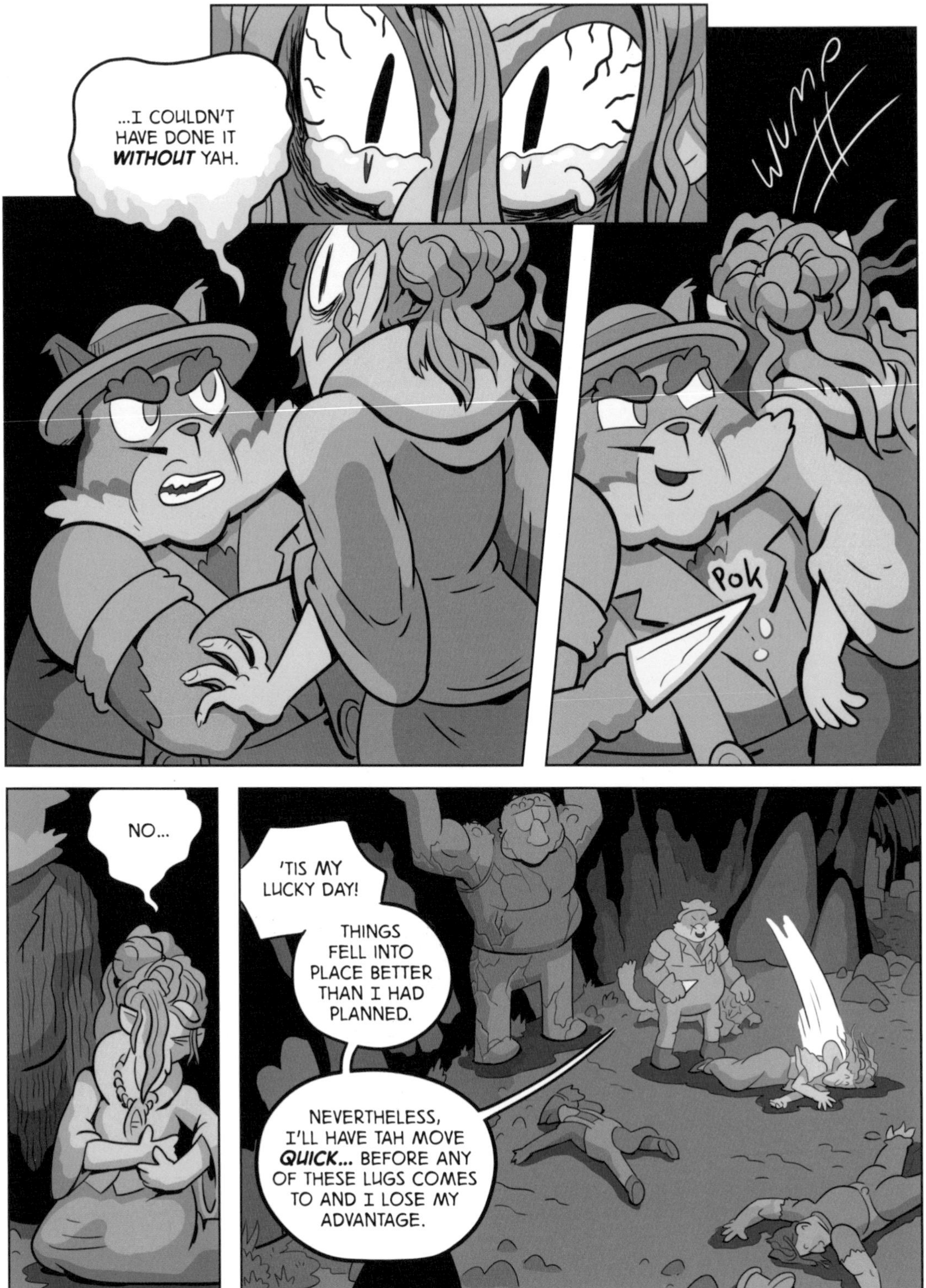

...I COULDN'T HAVE DONE IT ***WITHOUT*** YAH.
WUMP
POK
NO...
'TIS MY LUCKY DAY!
THINGS FELL INTO PLACE BETTER THAN I HAD PLANNED.
NEVERTHELESS, I'LL HAVE TAH MOVE ***QUICK...*** BEFORE ANY OF THESE LUGS COMES TO AND I LOSE MY ADVANTAGE.

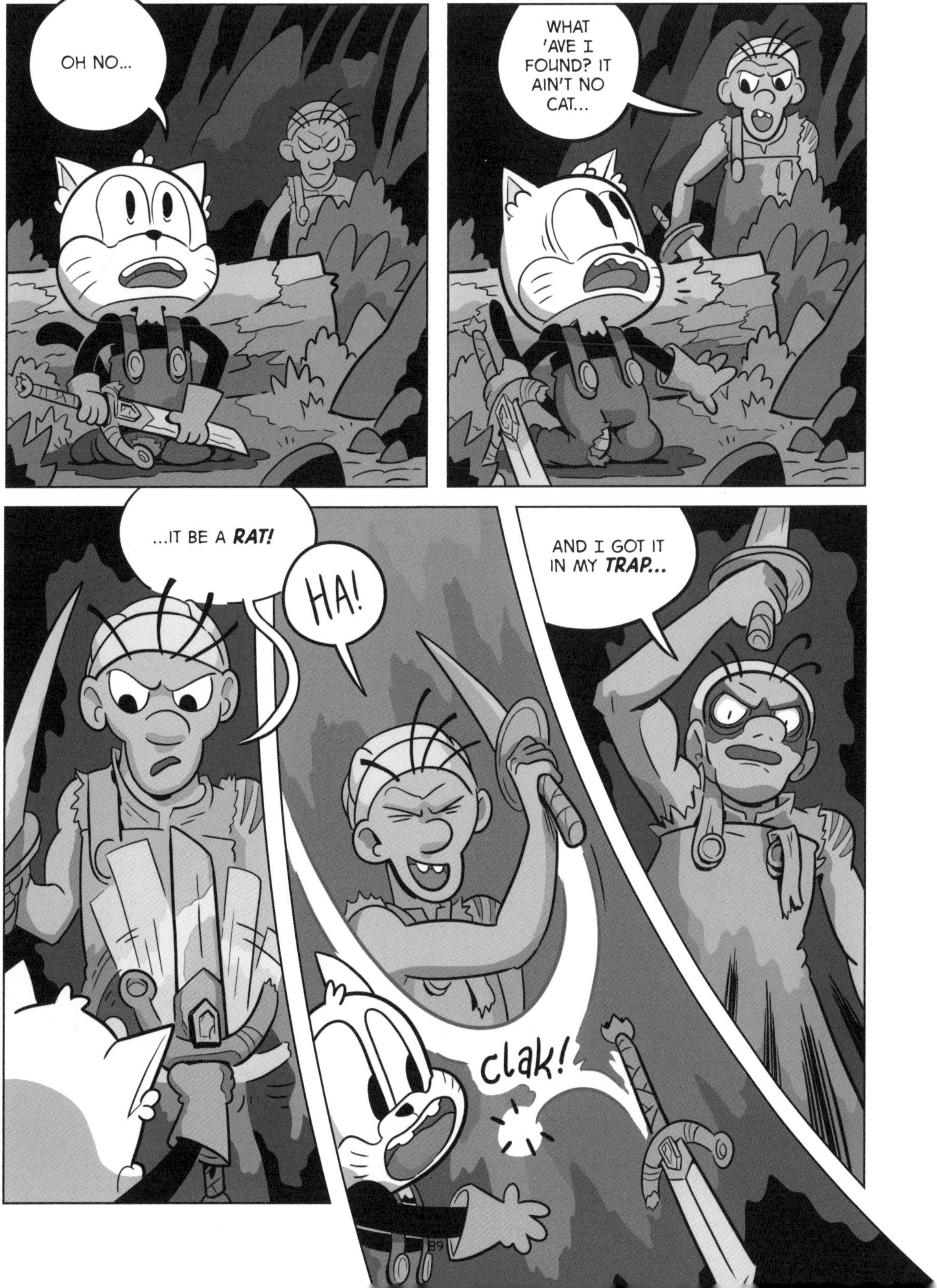
OH NO...
WHAT 'AVE I FOUND? IT AIN'T NO CAT...
...IT BE A *RAT!*
HA!
AND I GOT IT IN MY *TRAP...*
CLAK!

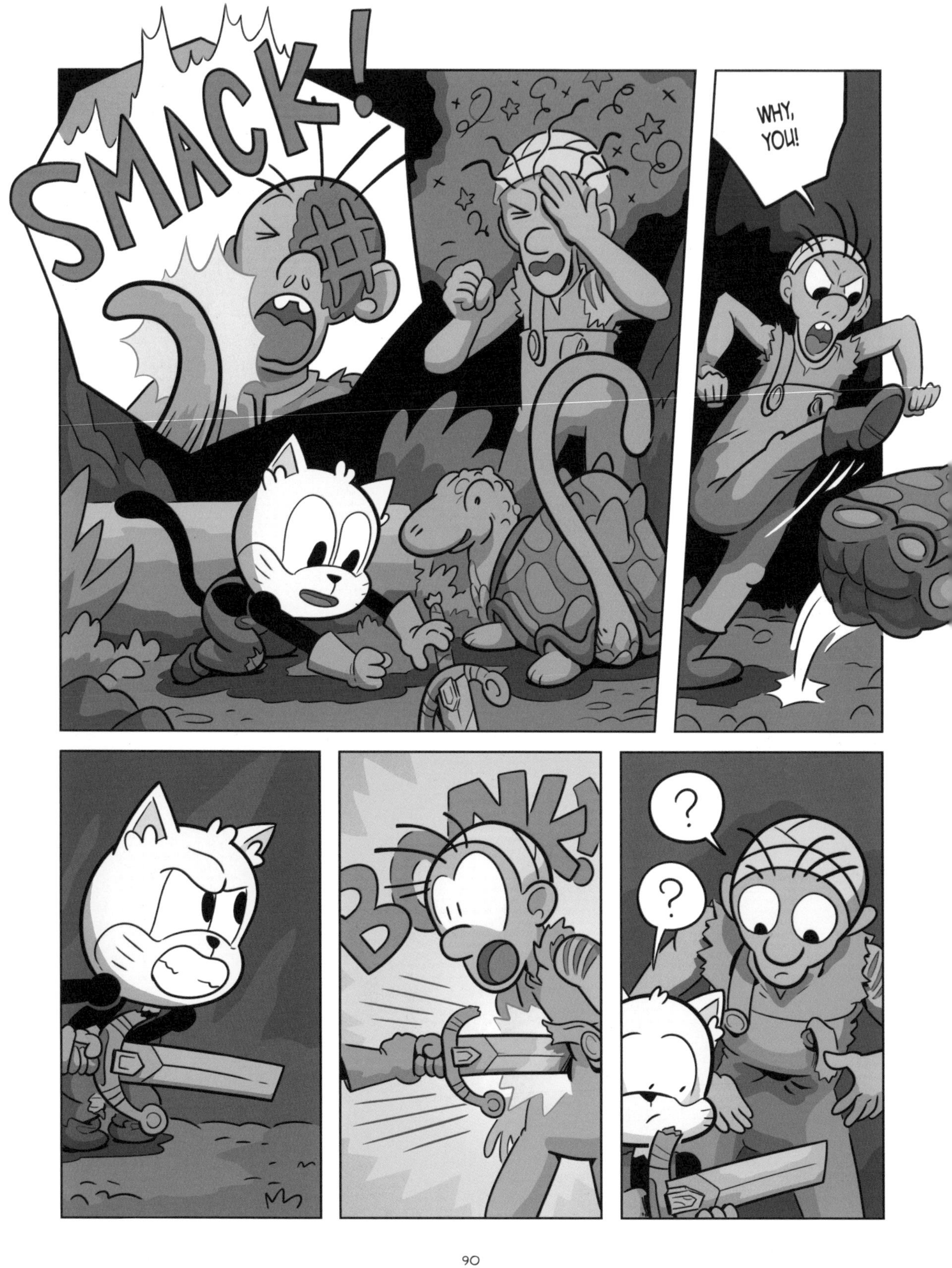
SMACK!
WHY, YOU!
?
?

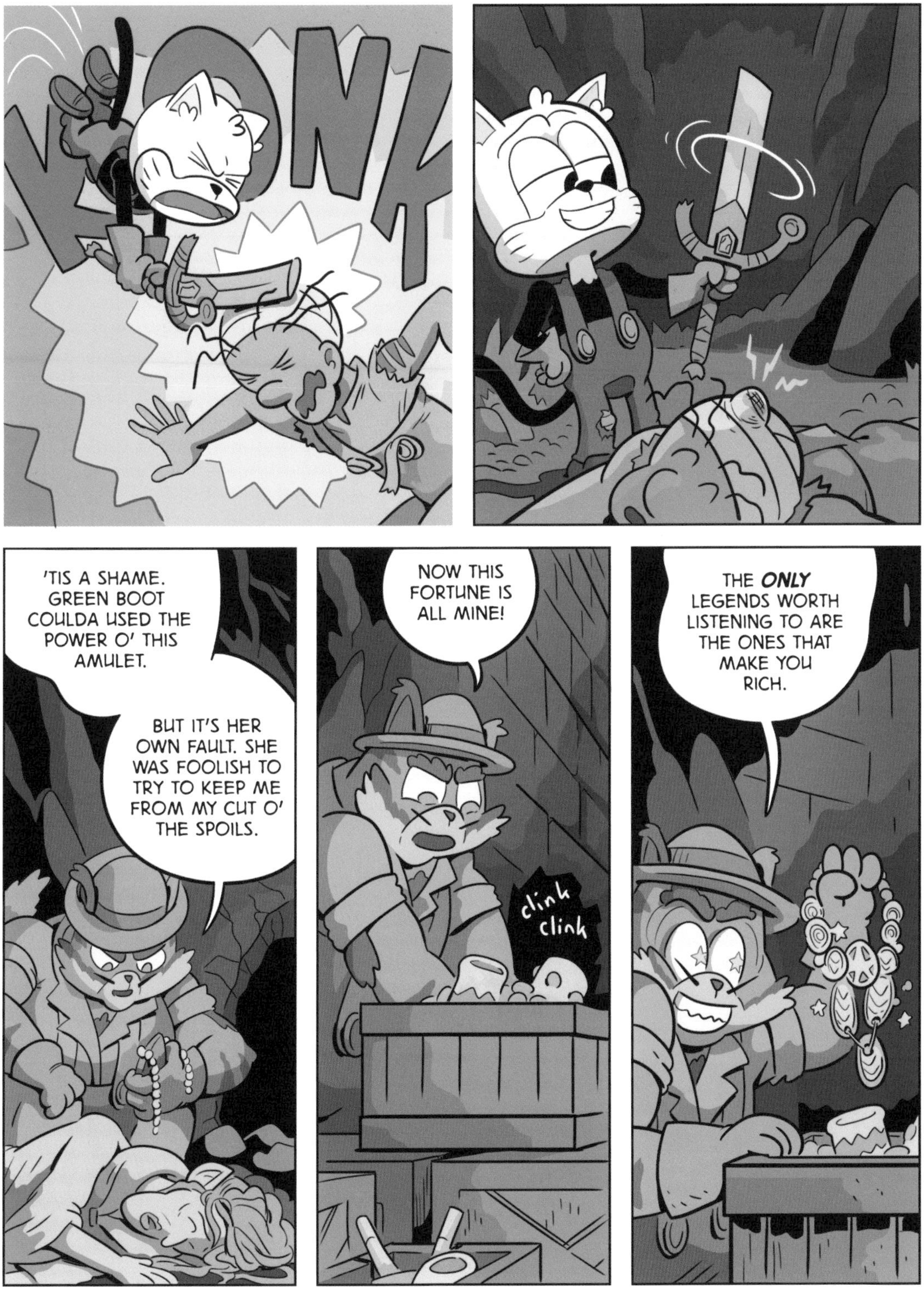
'TIS A SHAME. GREEN BOOT COULDA USED THE POWER O' THIS AMULET.
BUT IT'S HER OWN FAULT. SHE WAS FOOLISH TO TRY TO KEEP ME FROM MY CUT O' THE SPOILS.
NOW THIS FORTUNE IS ALL MINE!
clink clink
THE **ONLY** LEGENDS WORTH LISTENING TO ARE THE ONES THAT MAKE YOU RICH.

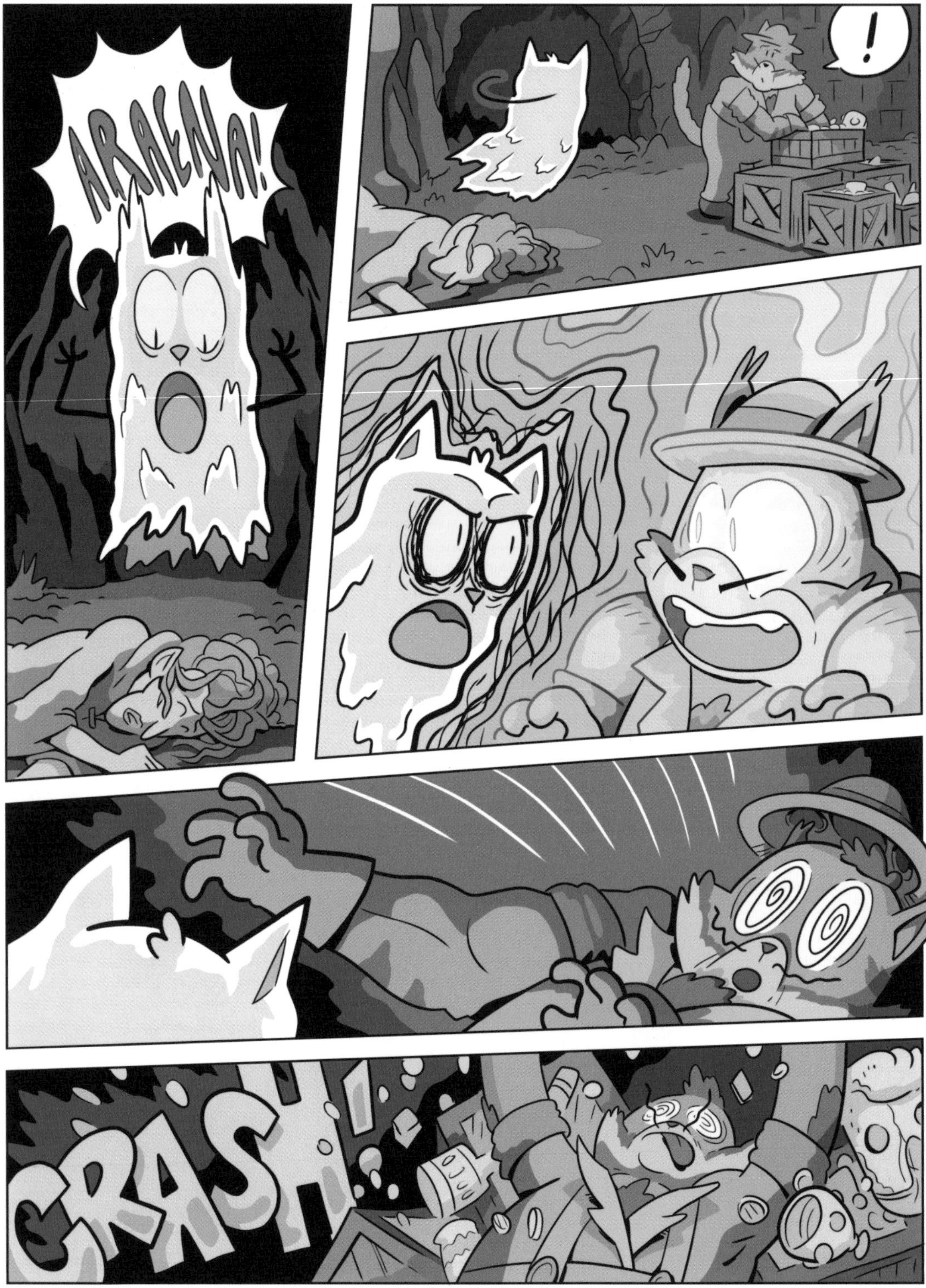
ARAENA!
!
CRASH!

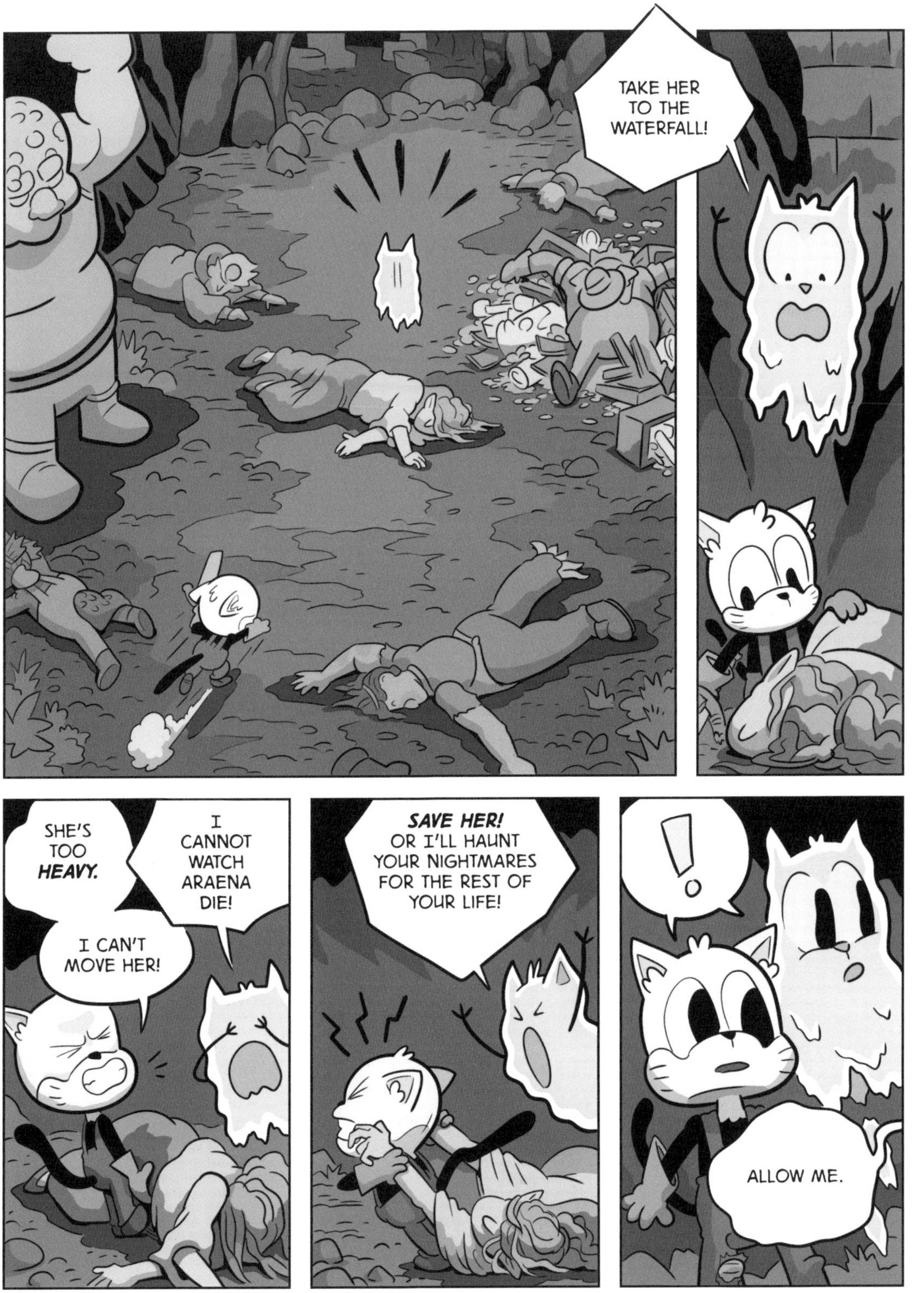
TAKE HER TO THE WATERFALL!
SHE'S TOO ***HEAVY.***
I CAN'T MOVE HER!
I CANNOT WATCH ARAENA DIE!
SAVE HER! OR I'LL HAUNT YOUR NIGHTMARES FOR THE REST OF YOUR LIFE!
!
ALLOW ME.

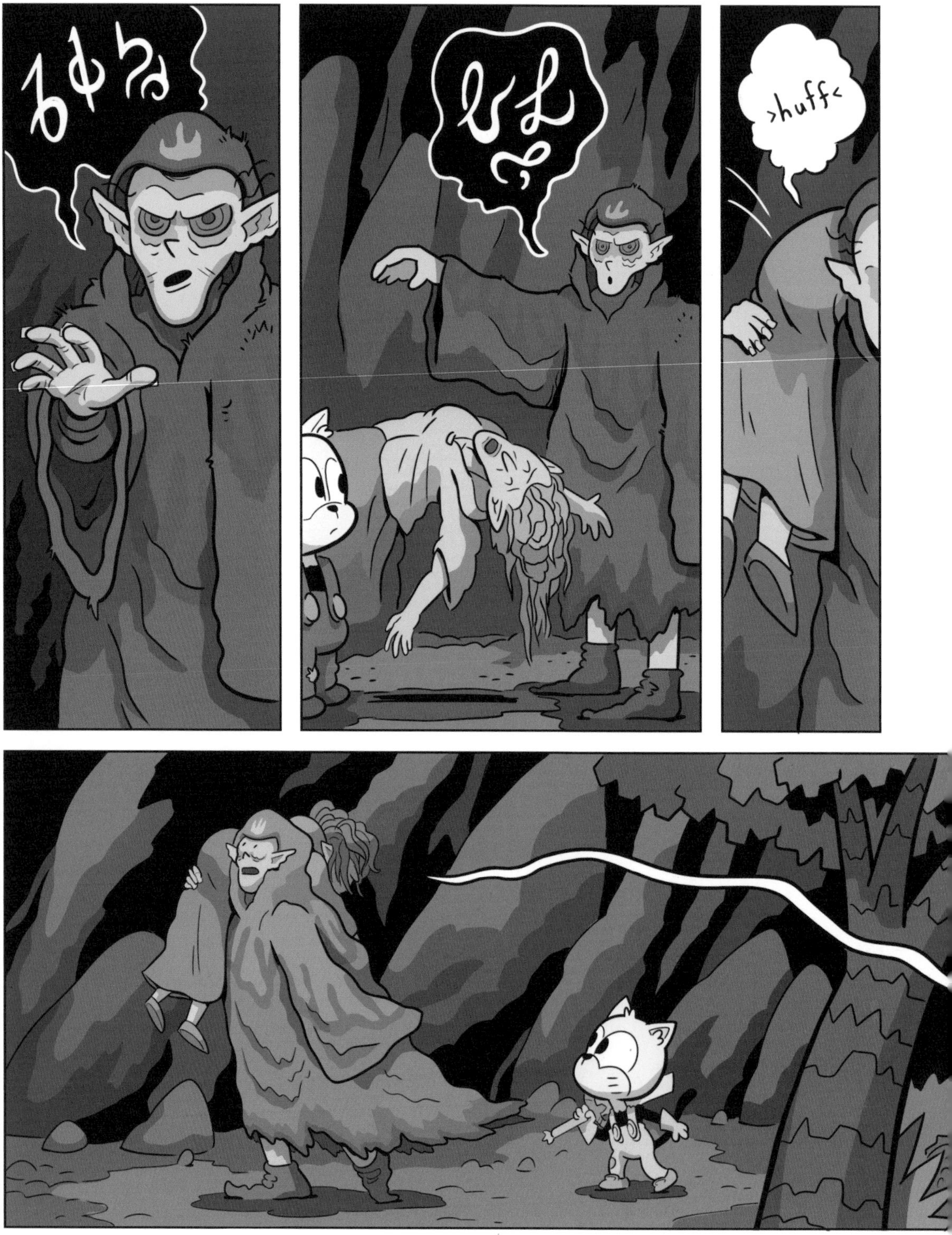

>huff<

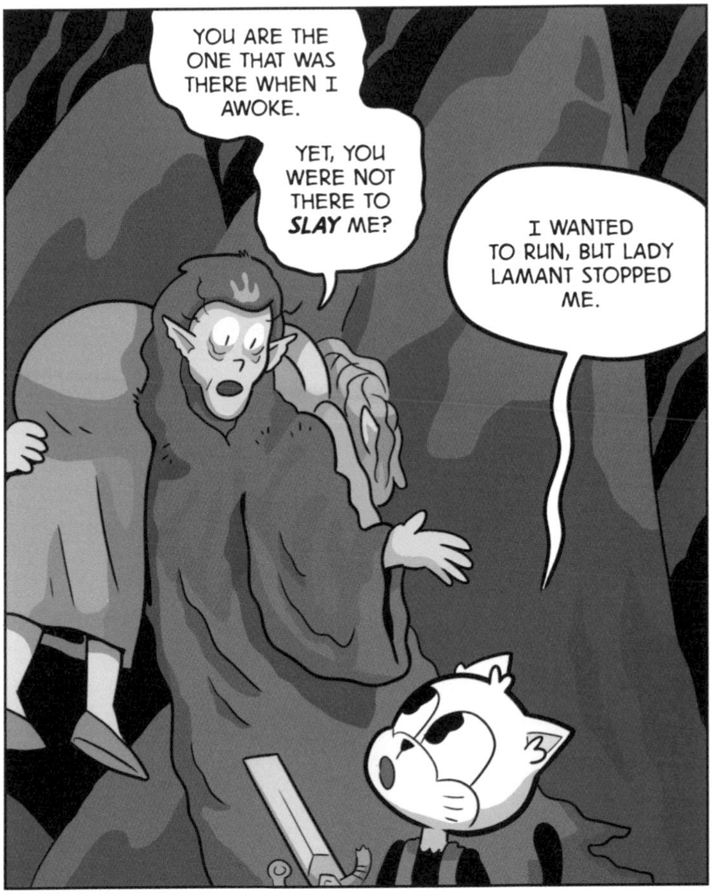
YOU ARE THE ONE THAT WAS THERE WHEN I AWOKE.
YET, YOU WERE NOT THERE TO **SLAY** ME?
I WANTED TO RUN, BUT LADY LAMANT STOPPED ME.

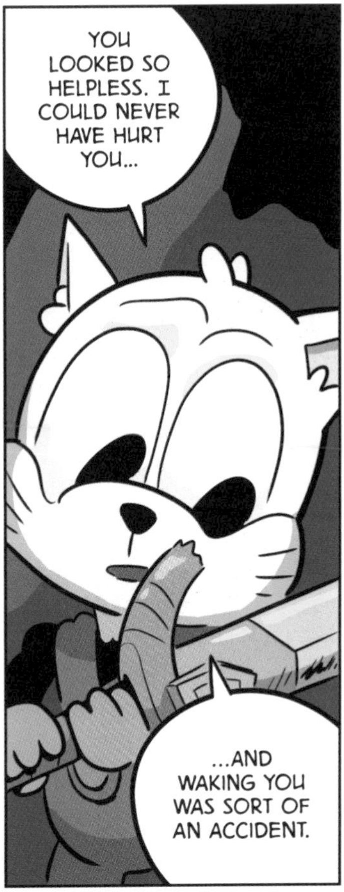
YOU LOOKED SO HELPLESS. I COULD NEVER HAVE HURT YOU...
...AND WAKING YOU WAS SORT OF AN ACCIDENT.

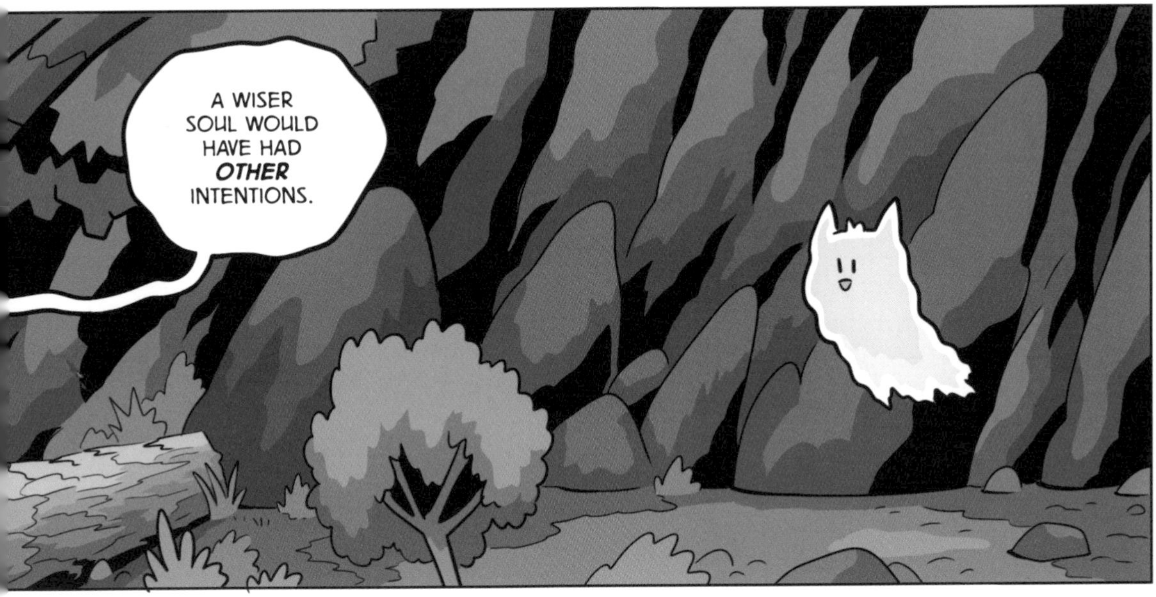
A WISER SOUL WOULD HAVE HAD **OTHER** INTENTIONS.

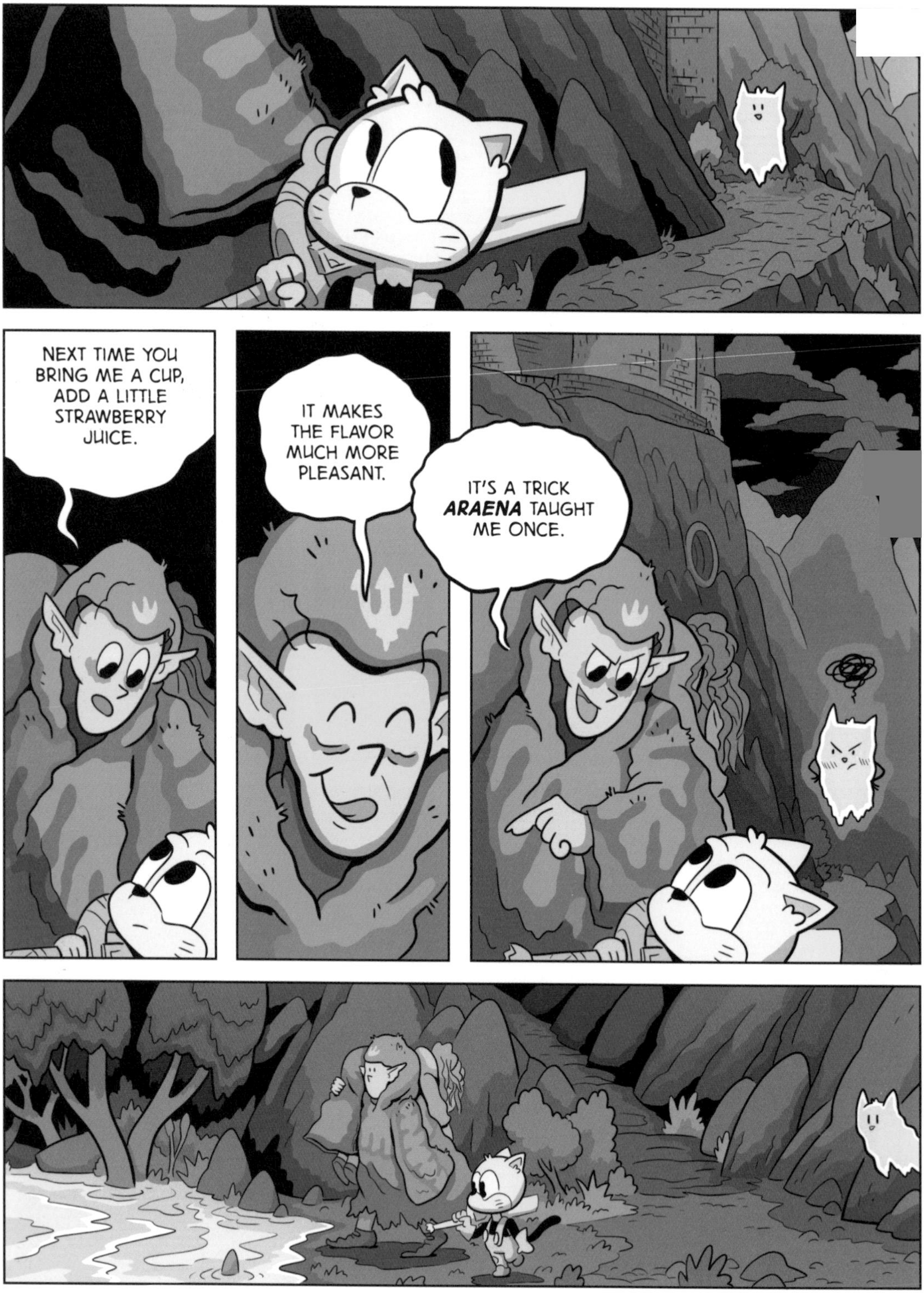
NEXT TIME YOU BRING ME A CUP, ADD A LITTLE STRAWBERRY JUICE.
IT MAKES THE FLAVOR MUCH MORE PLEASANT.
IT'S A TRICK **ARAENA** TAUGHT ME ONCE.

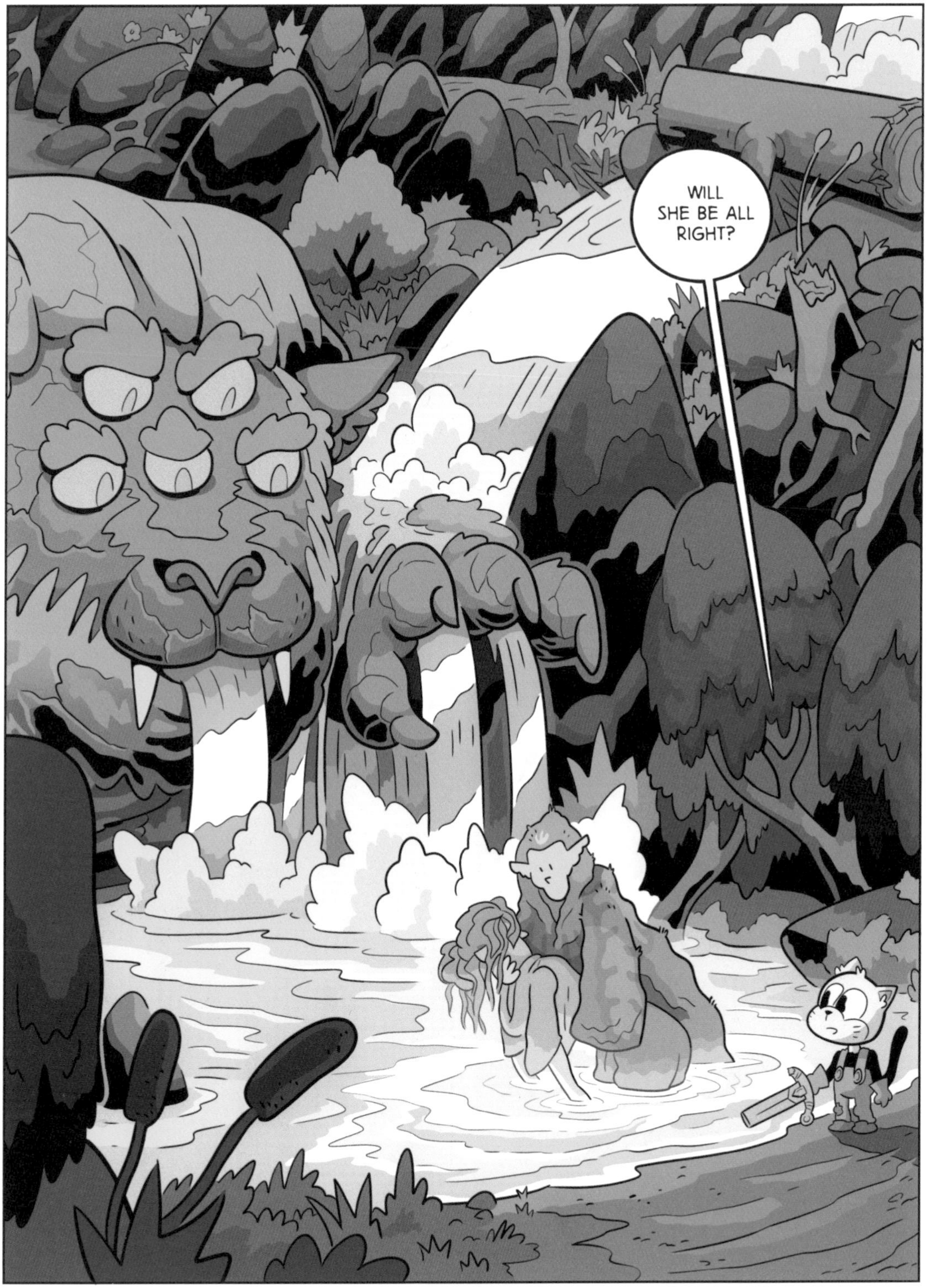
WILL SHE BE ALL RIGHT?

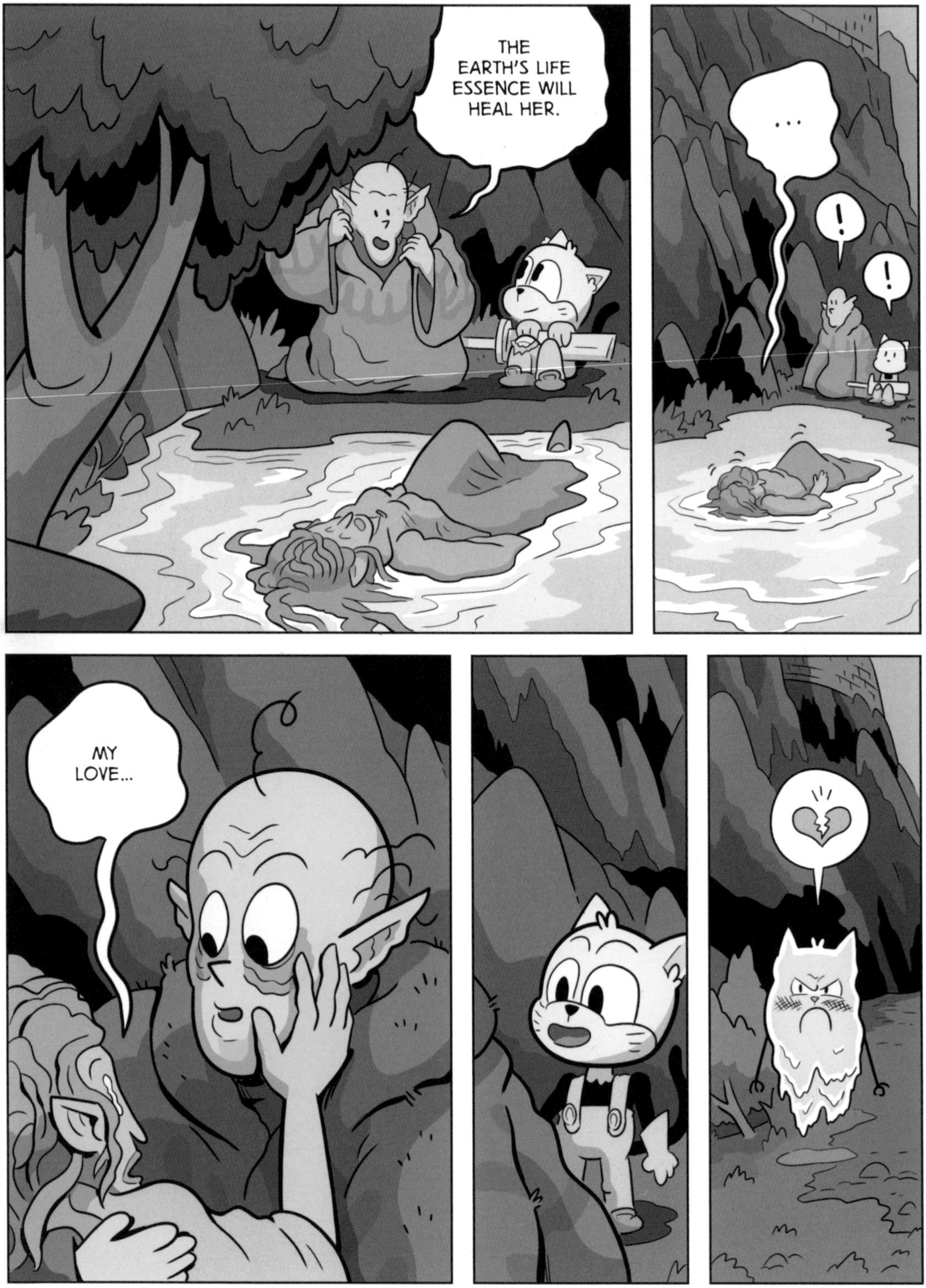
THE EARTH'S LIFE ESSENCE WILL HEAL HER.
...
!
!
MY LOVE...

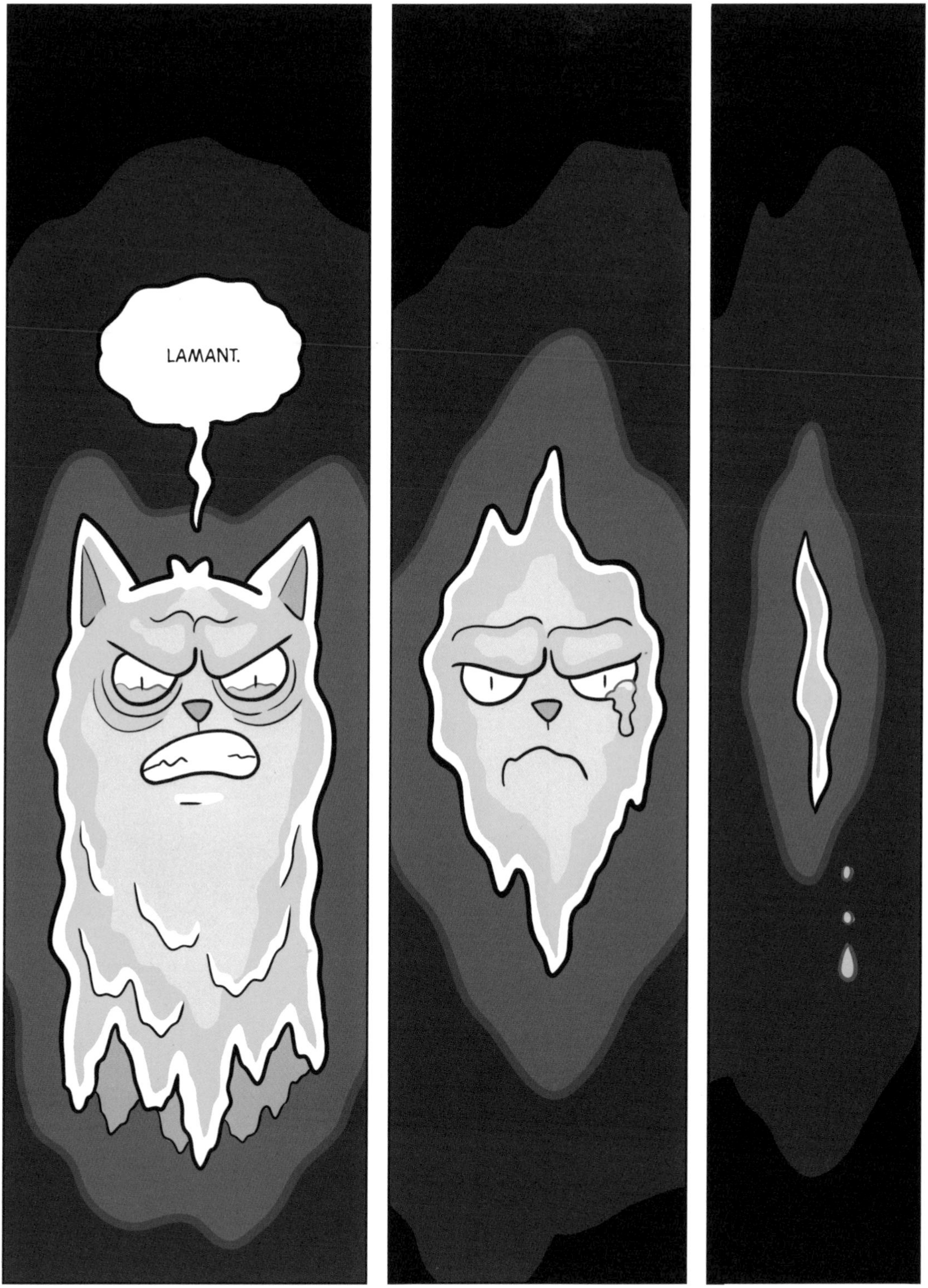
LAMANT.

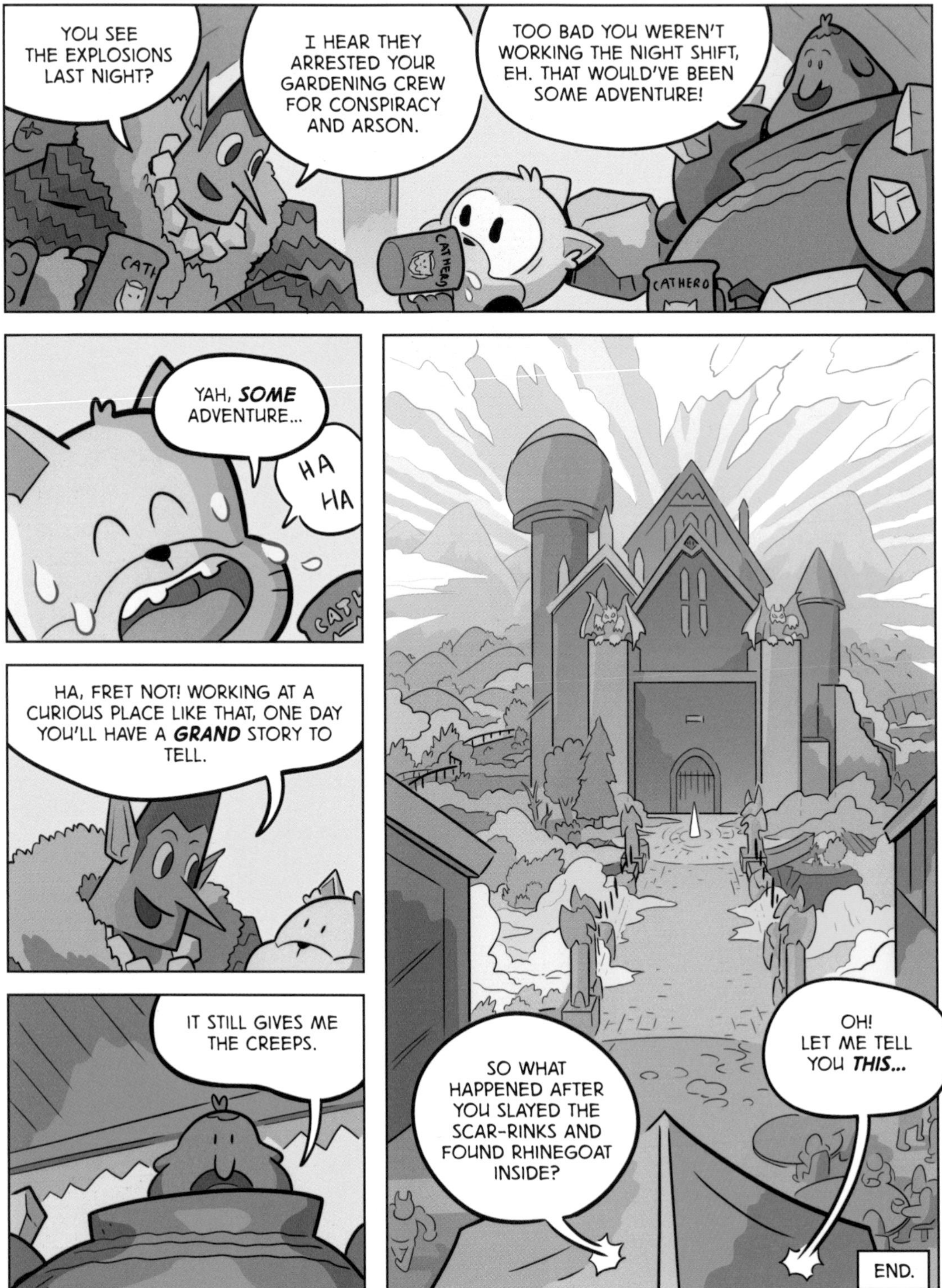

YOU SEE THE EXPLOSIONS LAST NIGHT?
I HEAR THEY ARRESTED YOUR GARDENING CREW FOR CONSPIRACY AND ARSON.
TOO BAD YOU WEREN'T WORKING THE NIGHT SHIFT, EH. THAT WOULD'VE BEEN SOME ADVENTURE!
CATHERO
CATHERO
YAH, **SOME** ADVENTURE...
HA HA
HA, FRET NOT! WORKING AT A CURIOUS PLACE LIKE THAT, ONE DAY YOU'LL HAVE A **GRAND** STORY TO TELL.
IT STILL GIVES ME THE CREEPS.
SO WHAT HAPPENED AFTER YOU SLAYED THE SCAR-RINKS AND FOUND RHINEGOAT INSIDE?
OH! LET ME TELL YOU **THIS...**
END.

—NS

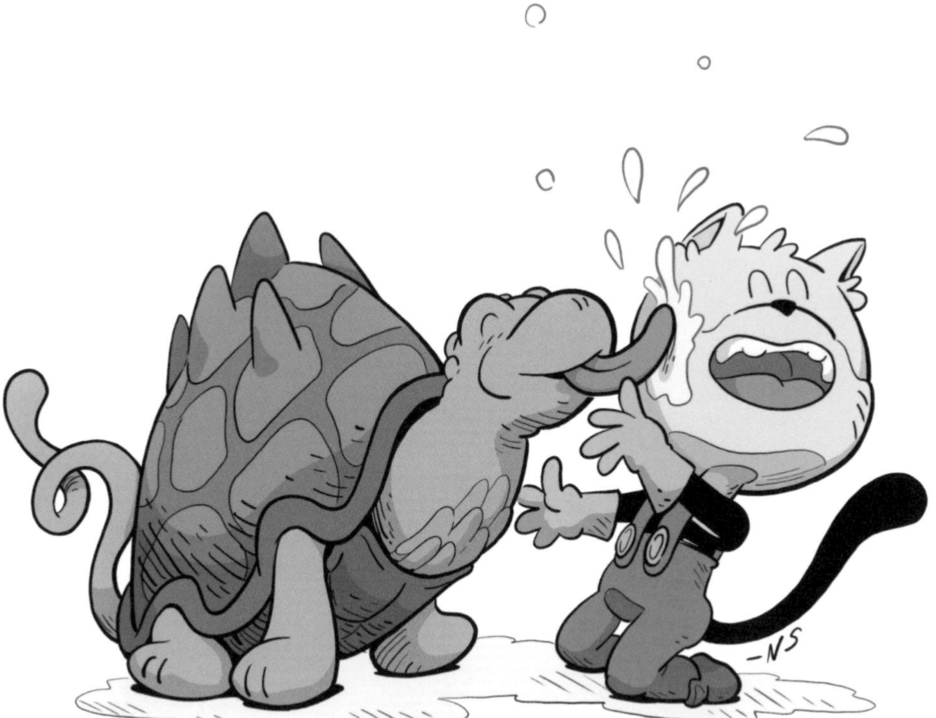
-NS

PORT LAMANT

ORIGINALLY FOUNDED AS A SEAPORT TOWN, PORT LAMANT HAS SERVED VARIOUS ROLES THROUGHOUT THE YEARS AS A TRADE PORT, A NAVAL BASE, AND A RESPITE FOR THOSE EXPELLED FROM NEIGHBORING KINGDOMS. IT HAS MANAGED TO REMAIN AN INDEPENDENT STATE REGARDLESS OF EXTERNAL TURMOIL, THOUGH ITS ALLIANCES HAVE SHIFTED NUMEROUS TIMES.

A CENTURY AGO, EARTHQUAKES LIFTED PORT LAMANT INLAND AND CREATED A NEW VALLEY BETWEEN THE CITY AND THE SEA. ITS IMPORTANCE AS A PORT HAS NOT CHANGED, HOWEVER, THANKS TO THE MAGIC OF THE CITY'S RULING FAMILY, WHICH BRINGS IMPORTS ACROSS THE MOSTLY DANGEROUS NEW VALLEY. WITH THE TRADE ROUTE MAINTAINED AND RECENT GOLD DISCOVERIES IN THE NEARBY MOUNTAIN RANGE, PORT LAMANT CURRENTLY ENJOYS ITS MOST PROSPEROUS PERIOD.

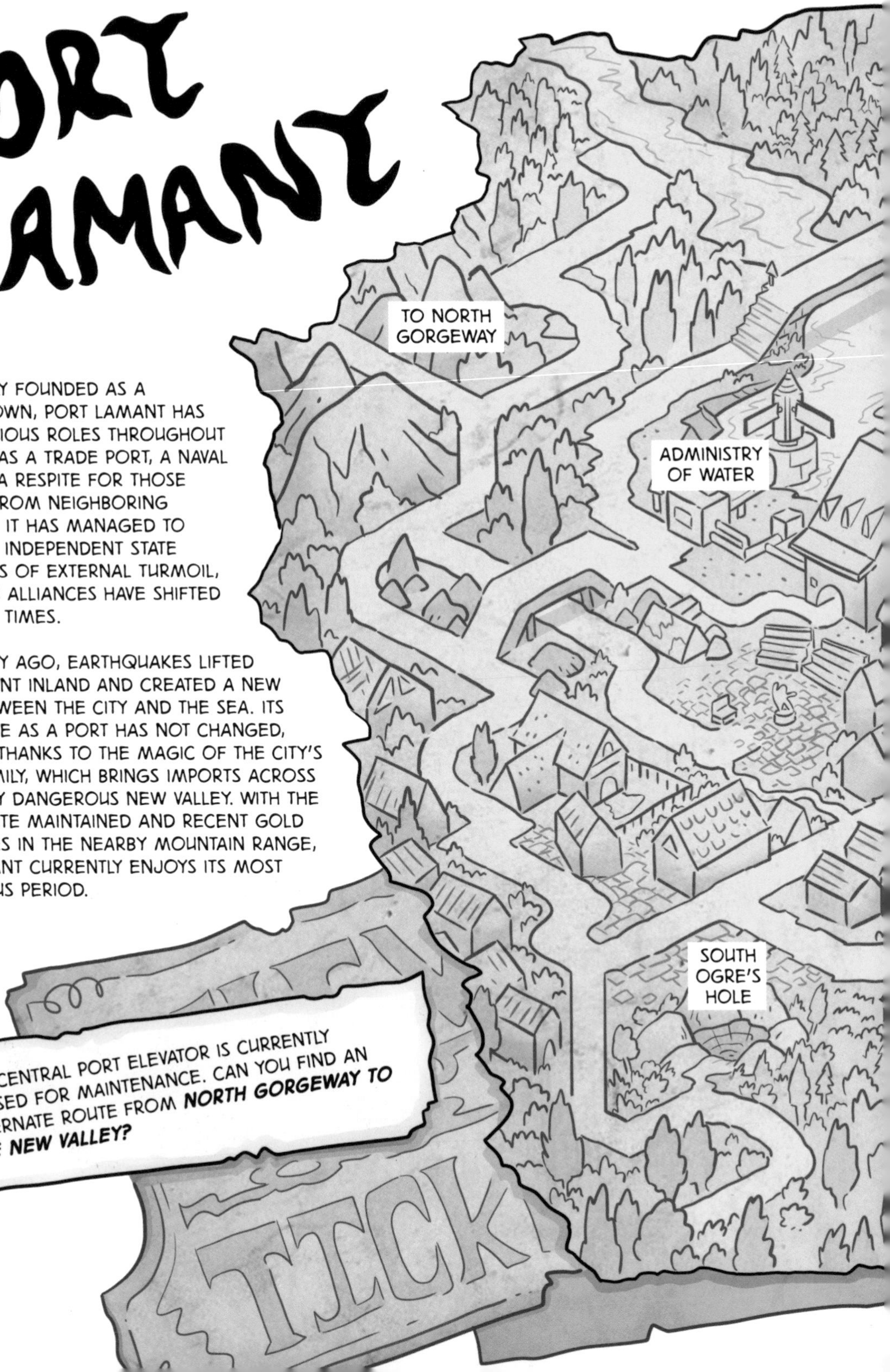

TO NORTH GORGEWAY
ADMINISTRY OF WATER
SOUTH OGRE'S HOLE
TICK

THE CENTRAL PORT ELEVATOR IS CURRENTLY CLOSED FOR MAINTENANCE. CAN YOU FIND AN ALTERNATE ROUTE FROM ***NORTH GORGEWAY TO THE NEW VALLEY?***

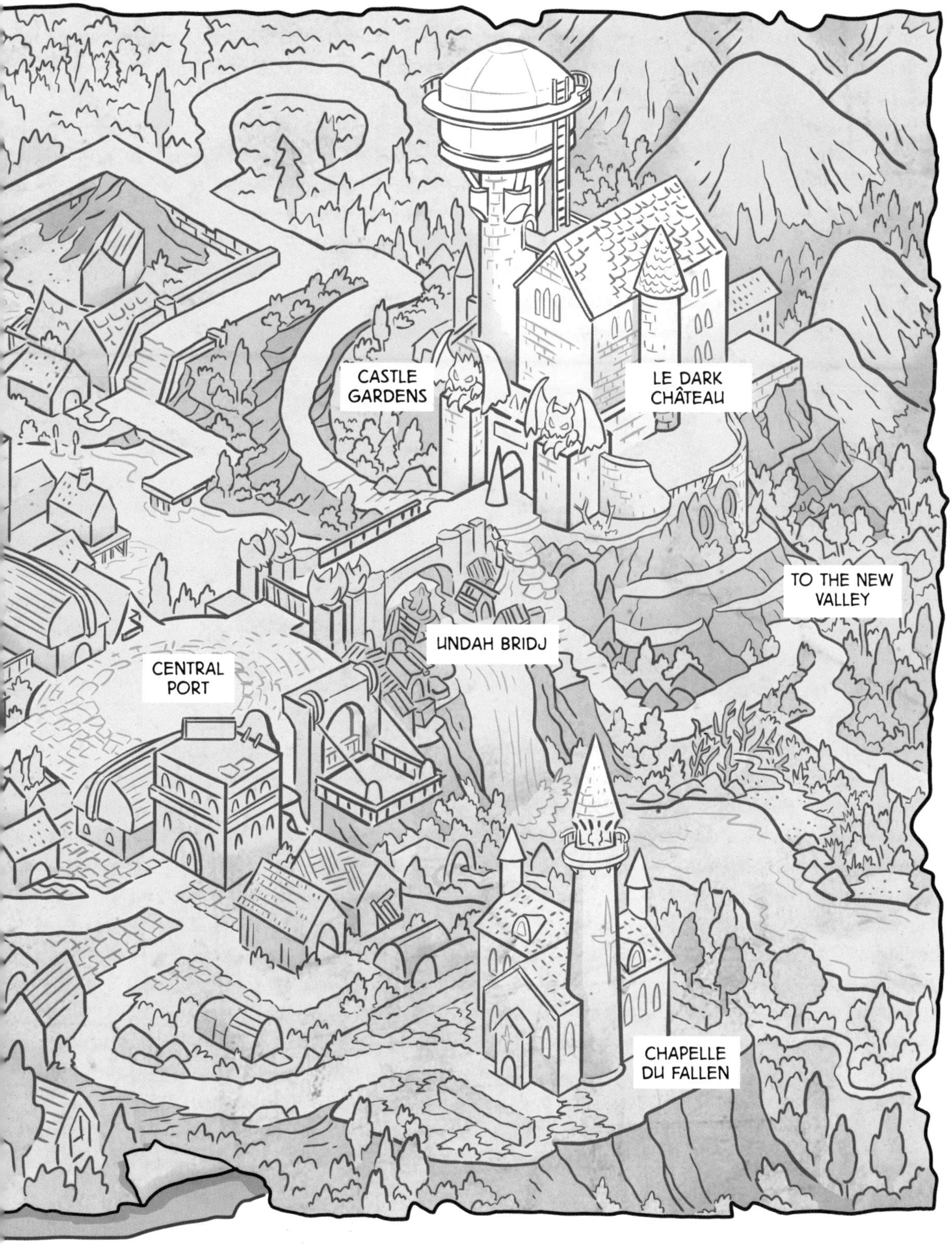
CASTLE GARDENS
LE DARK CHÂTEAU
TO THE NEW VALLEY
UNDAH BRIDJ
CENTRAL PORT
CHAPELLE DU FALLEN

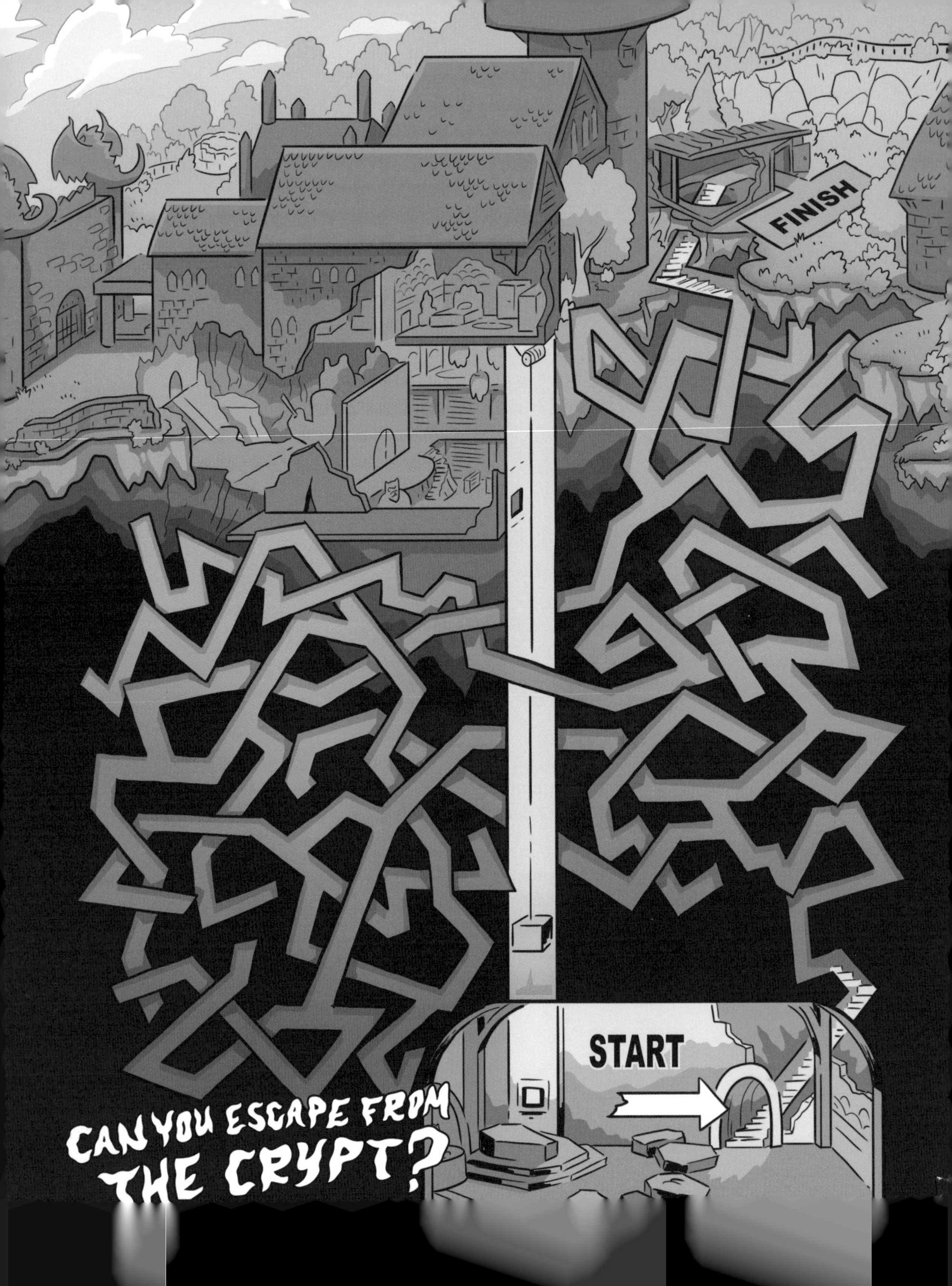
FINISH
START
CAN YOU ESCAPE FROM
THE CRYPT?

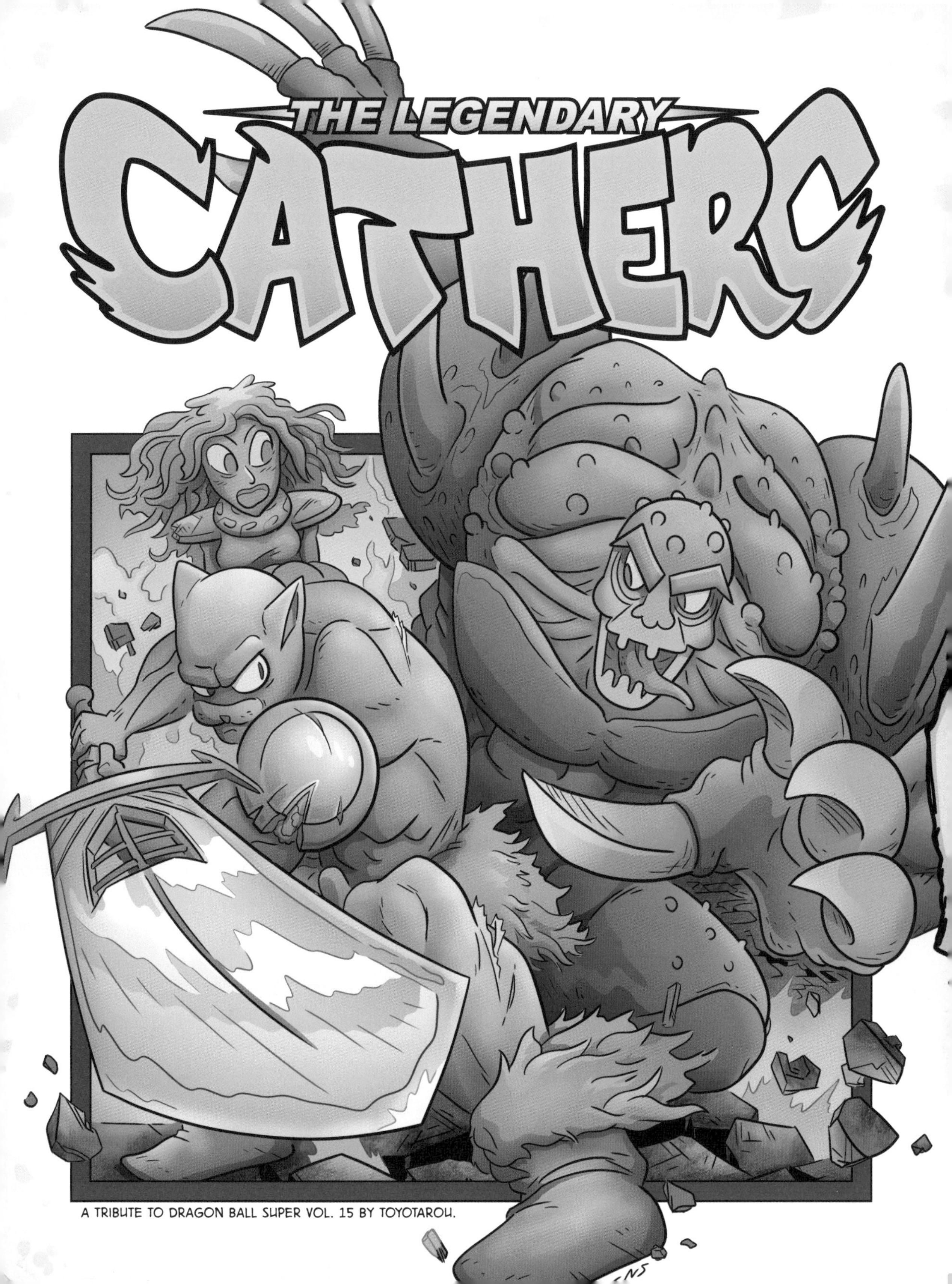
THE LEGENDARY
CATHERG
A TRIBUTE TO DRAGON BALL SUPER VOL. 15 BY TOYOTAROU.

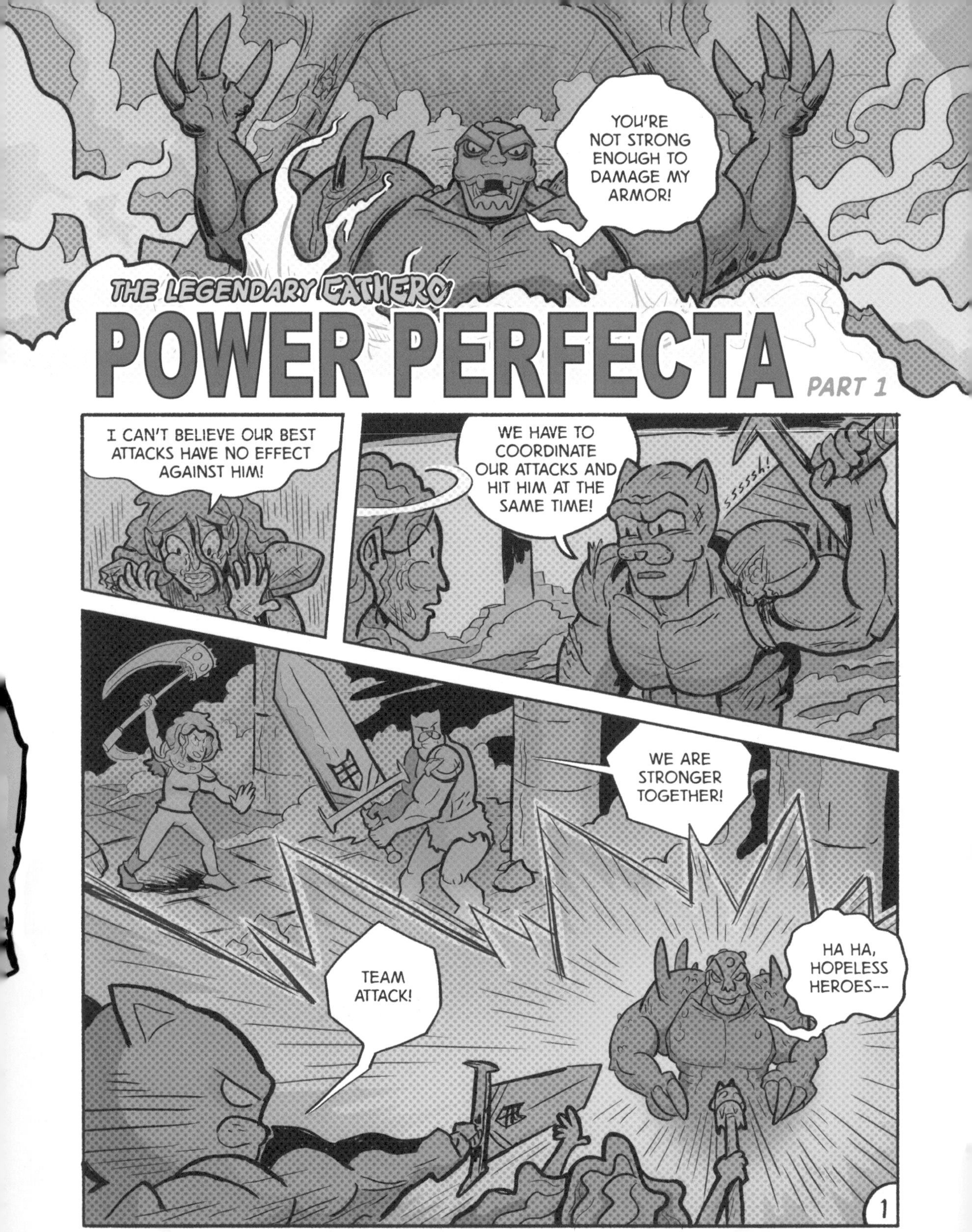
YOU'RE NOT STRONG ENOUGH TO DAMAGE MY ARMOR!
THE LEGENDARY CATHERO
POWER PERFECTA
PART 1
I CAN'T BELIEVE OUR BEST ATTACKS HAVE NO EFFECT AGAINST HIM!
WE HAVE TO COORDINATE OUR ATTACKS AND HIT HIM AT THE SAME TIME!
ssssssh!
WE ARE STRONGER TOGETHER!
HA HA, HOPELESS HEROES--
TEAM ATTACK!
1

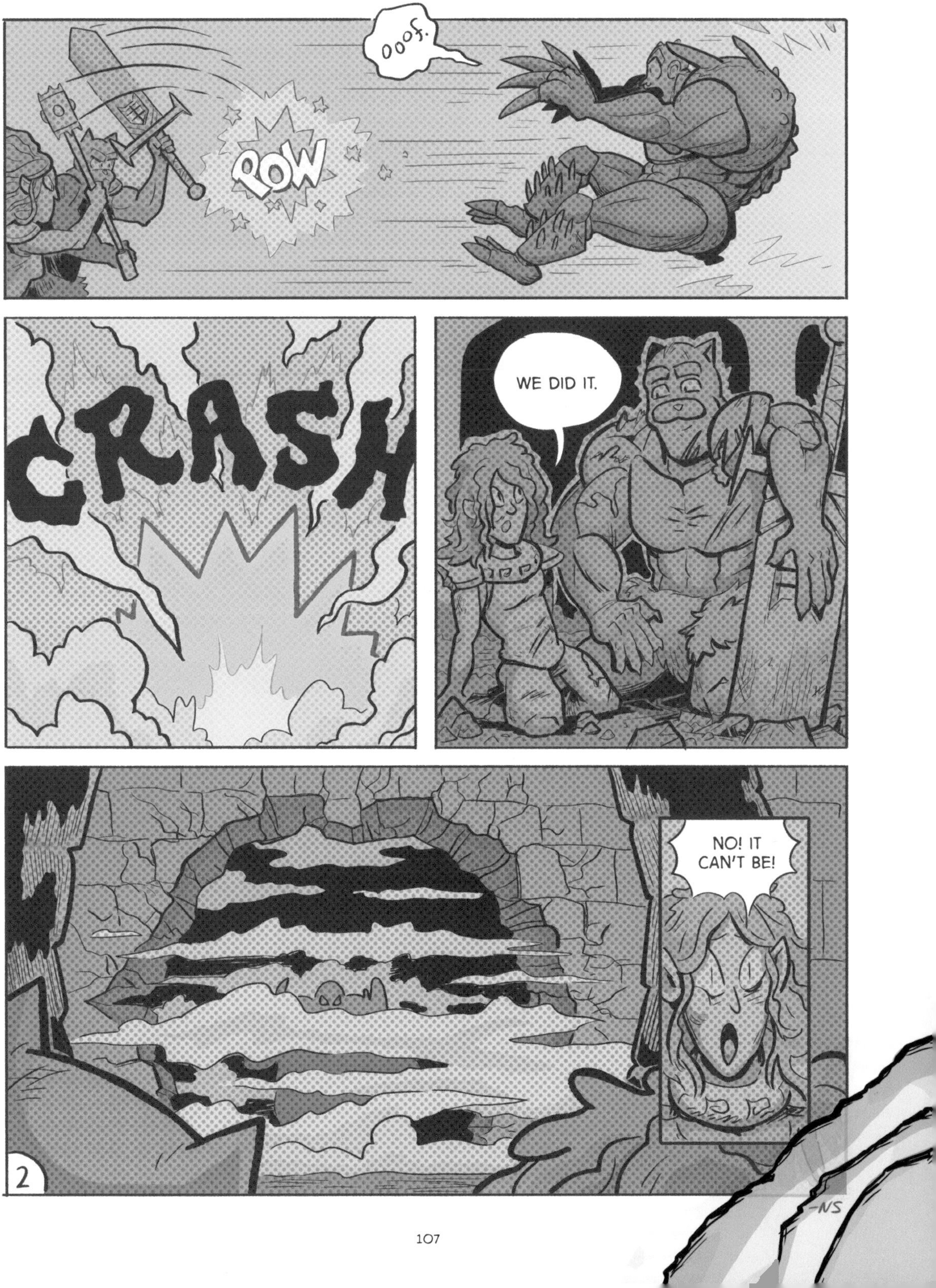

Ooof.
POW
CRASH
WE DID IT.
NO! IT CAN'T BE!
2
-NS

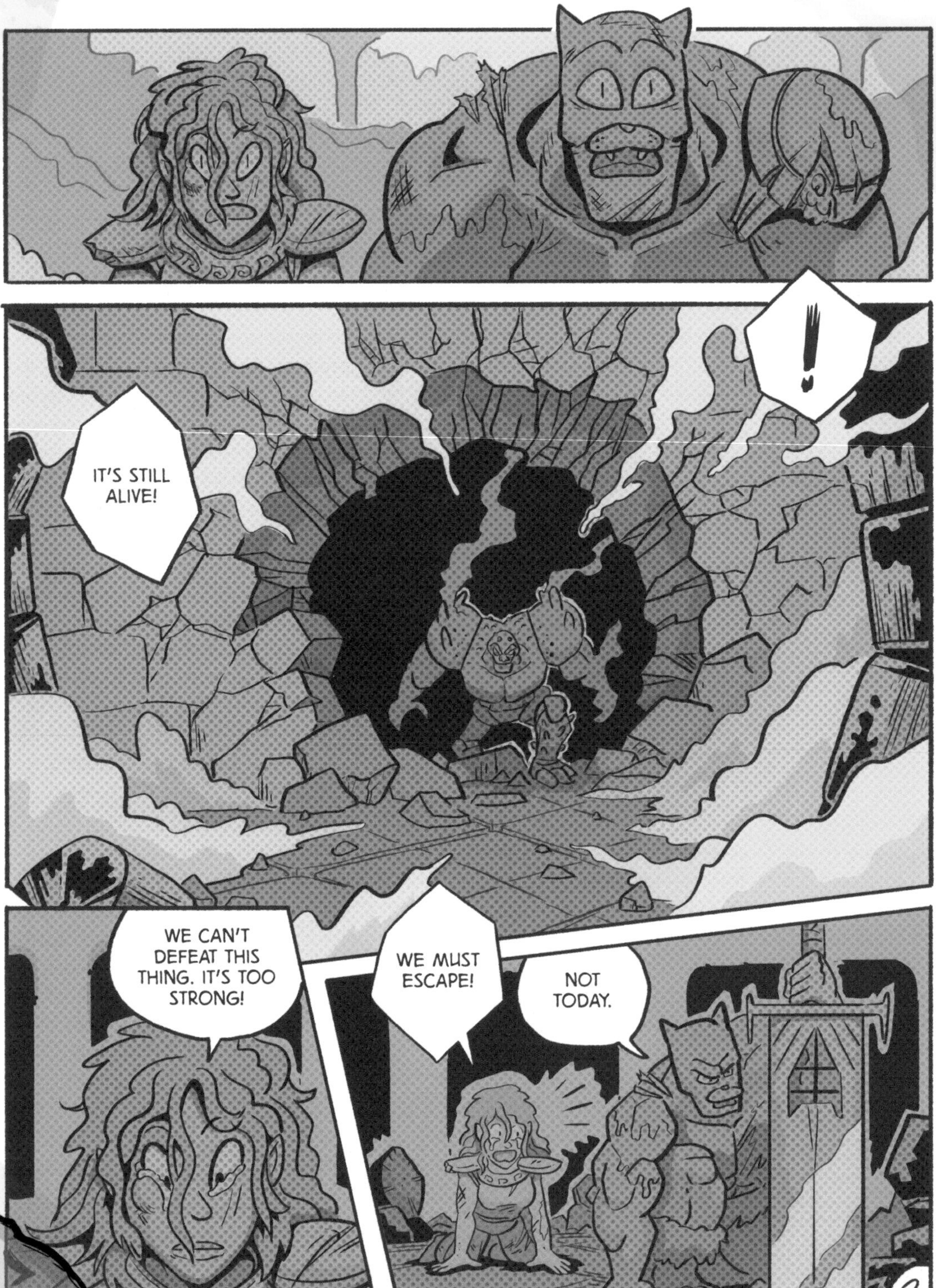
!
IT'S STILL ALIVE!
WE CAN'T DEFEAT THIS THING. IT'S TOO STRONG!
WE MUST ESCAPE!
NOT TODAY.
3

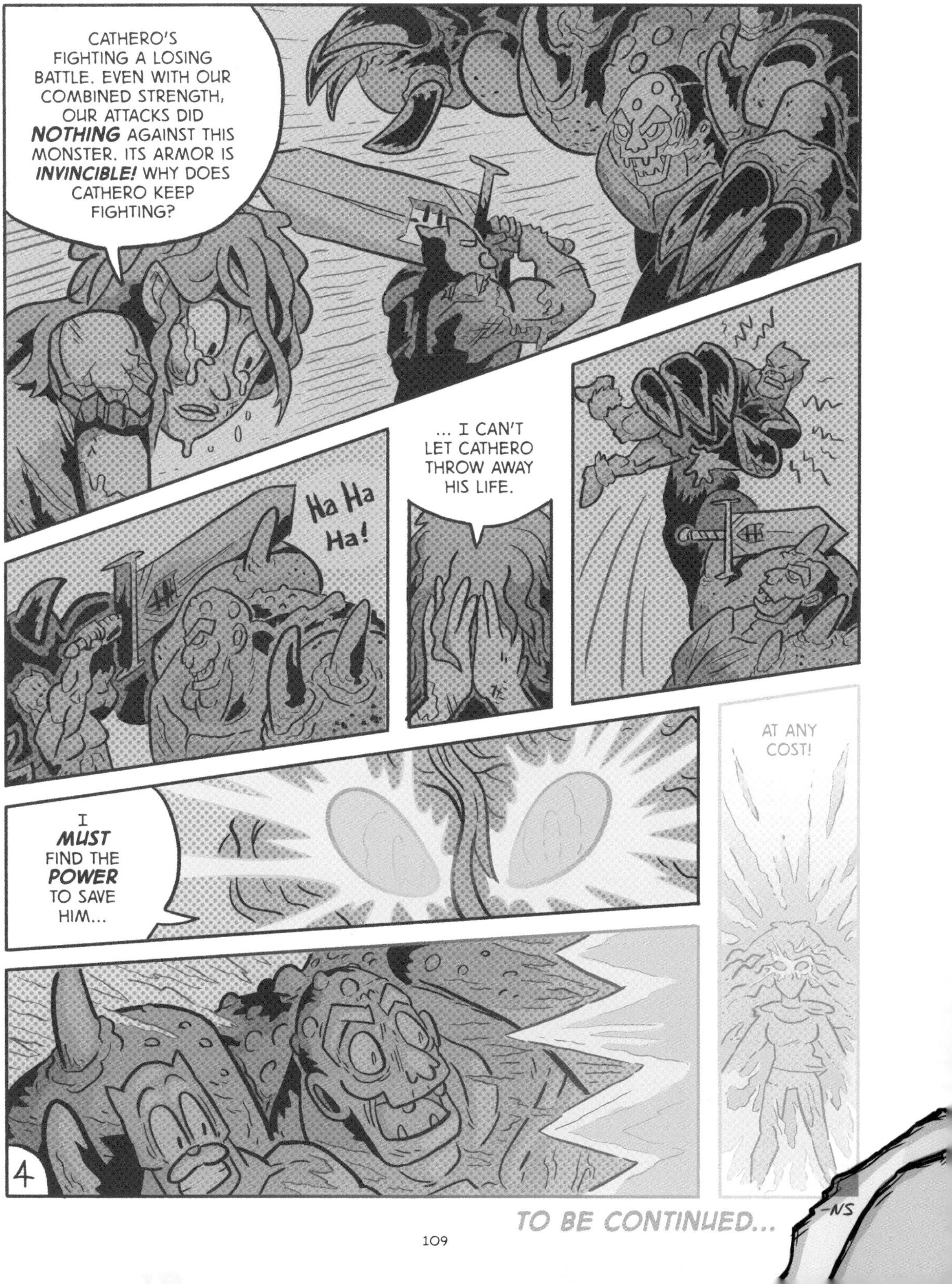
CATHERO'S FIGHTING A LOSING BATTLE. EVEN WITH OUR COMBINED STRENGTH, OUR ATTACKS DID **NOTHING** AGAINST THIS MONSTER. ITS ARMOR IS ***INVINCIBLE!*** WHY DOES CATHERO KEEP FIGHTING?
Ha Ha Ha!
... I CAN'T LET CATHERO THROW AWAY HIS LIFE.
I **MUST** FIND THE **POWER** TO SAVE HIM...
AT ANY COST!
4
-NS

TO BE CONTINUED...

CATHERO

IN "THE CHATTY THIEF"

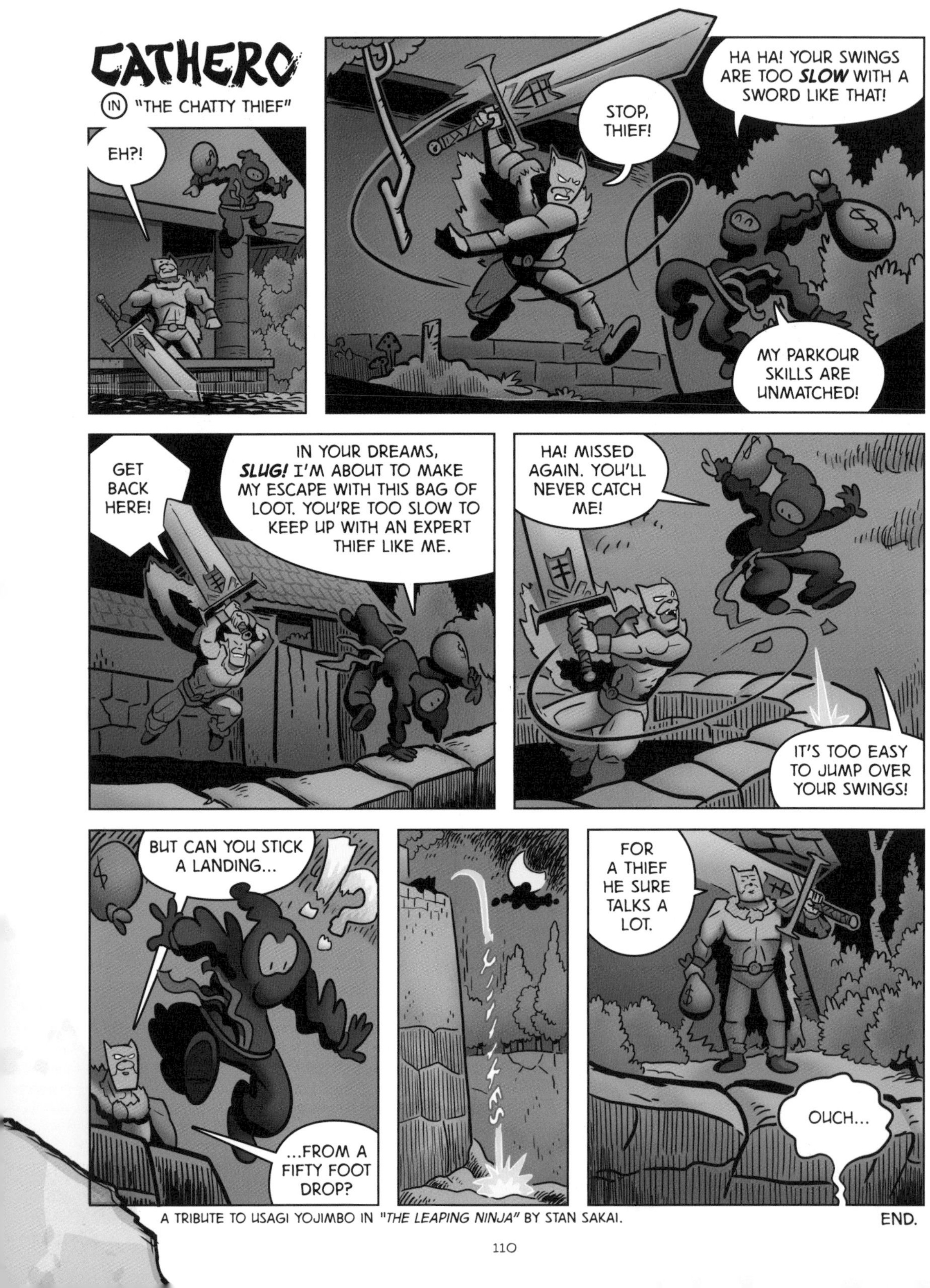
EH?!
STOP, THIEF!
HA HA! YOUR SWINGS ARE TOO **SLOW** WITH A SWORD LIKE THAT!
MY PARKOUR SKILLS ARE UNMATCHED!
GET BACK HERE!
IN YOUR DREAMS, **SLUG!** I'M ABOUT TO MAKE MY ESCAPE WITH THIS BAG OF LOOT. YOU'RE TOO SLOW TO KEEP UP WITH AN EXPERT THIEF LIKE ME.
HA! MISSED AGAIN. YOU'LL NEVER CATCH ME!
IT'S TOO EASY TO JUMP OVER YOUR SWINGS!
BUT CAN YOU STICK A LANDING...
...FROM A FIFTY FOOT DROP?
FOR A THIEF HE SURE TALKS A LOT.
OUCH...

A TRIBUTE TO USAGI YOJIMBO IN "*THE LEAPING NINJA*" BY STAN SAKAI.

END.

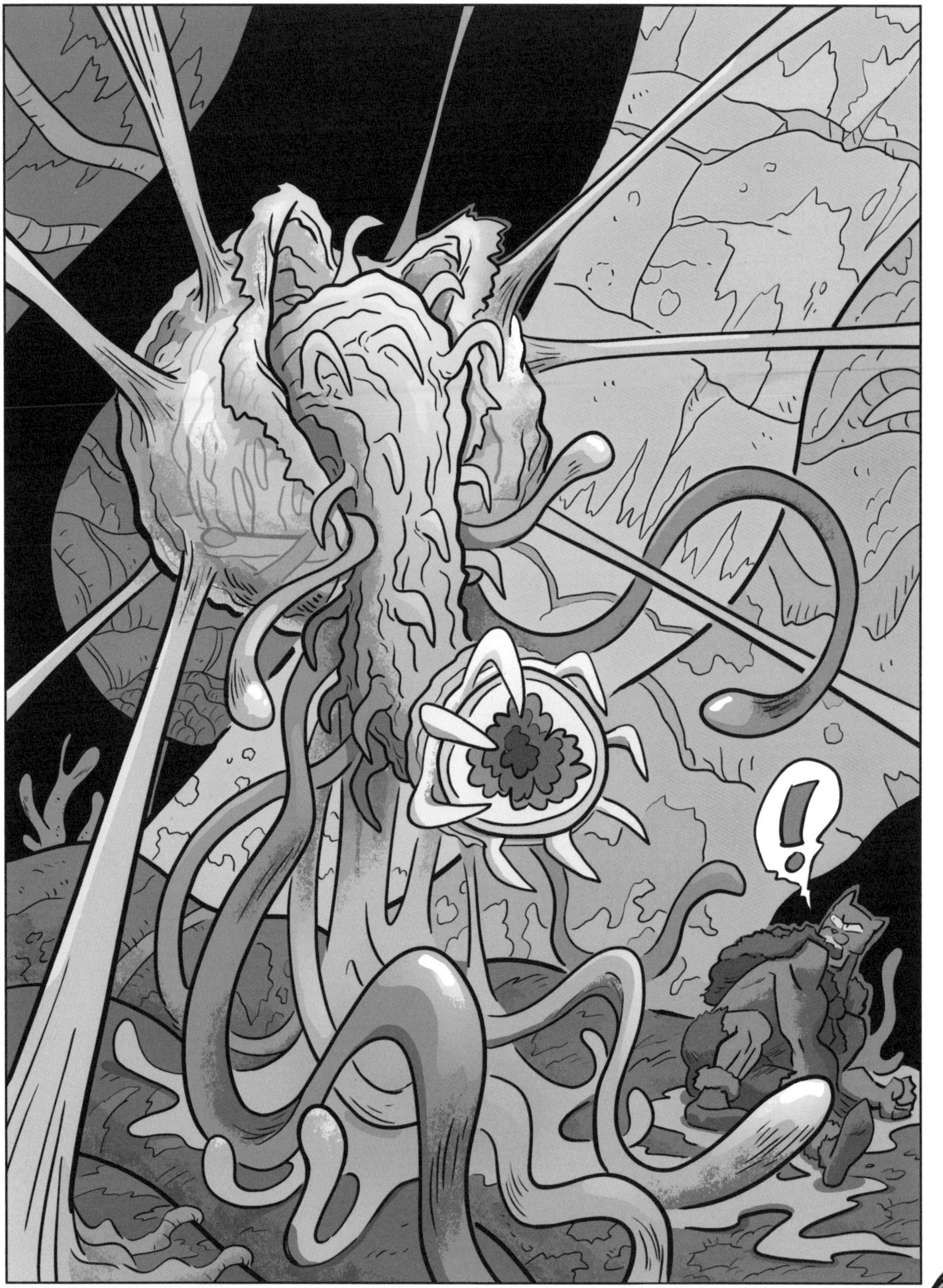
!

A TRIBUTE TO *MADMAN* BY MIKE ALLRED.

-NS

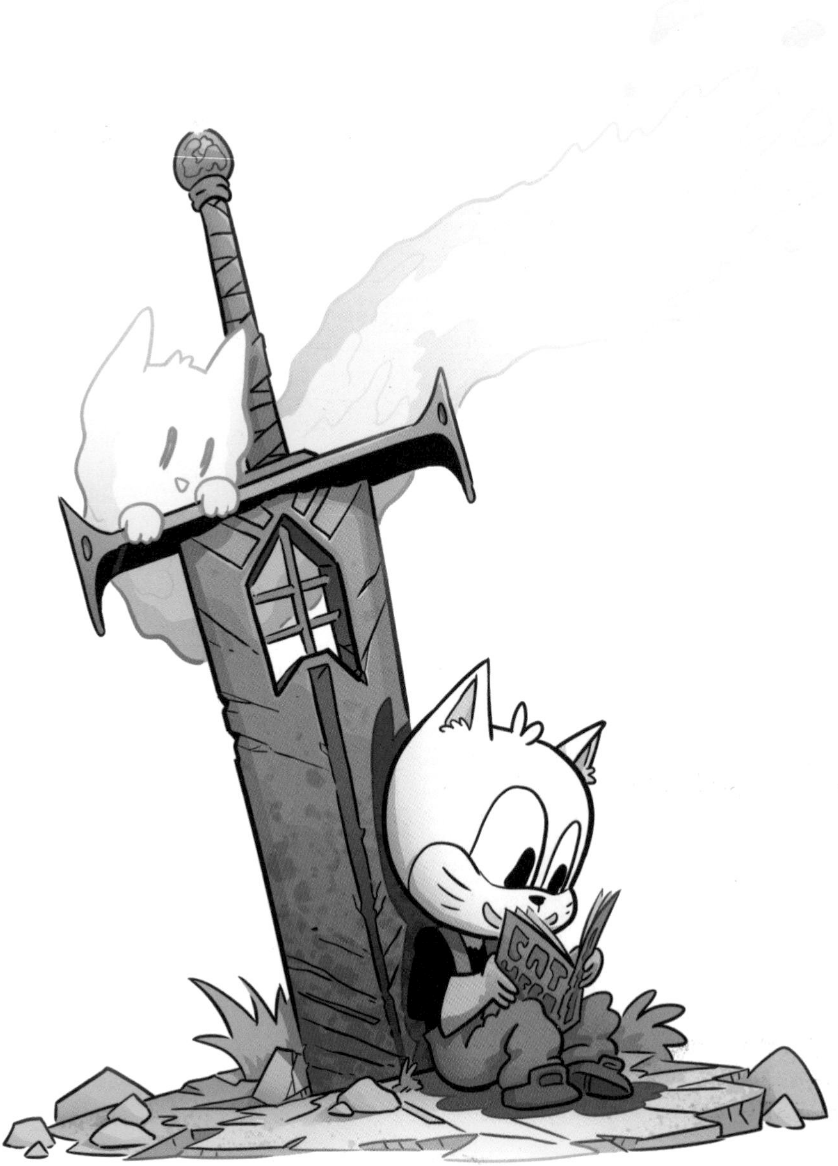
CAT